MARCH
of the
GREEN BEETLES

Title: March of the Green Beetles

Author: Lindsey D. Linden

Genre: Fiction, action-adventure

ISBN: 978-0-9863482-3-5 Trade paperback
ISBN: 978-0-9863482-4-2 Electronic epub format
ISBN: 978-0-9863482-5-9 Electronic mobi format
Format: Trade paperback and e-book
Publishing date: June 1, 2016

Description: March of the Green Beetles, the fast-paced, action-filled sequel to The Lion of Djibouti, is the tale of two cities—two worlds—linked together by the past, the present, and the future. Drugs, ivory, warlords, slavery, gang wars, rebellion, and organized crime are the threads binding the port cities of Djibouti and Newark, New Jersey, to the same fate.

Cover Design and Formatting by Damonza

Beetle by Skyscraper – Own work, CC BY 3.0

Flower by Von Zebruno – Eigenes Werk, CC BY-SA 3.0

Edited by Nicole R. Klungle

LINDSEY D. LINDEN

MARCH of the GREEN BEETLES

1

1986

LIONEL ANGLED HIS face to the sky, hoping to feel the slightest whisper of a cooling breeze. But the night air remained heavy and still, sticky with moisture. Bunching a red kerchief in his hand, he dabbed sweat from the back of his neck and sighed. Growing yams. He grunted. Another day of bending, kneeling, digging, hauling—monotonous, he thought, never ending. Sweat constant, conditions oppressive: humid, hot, and uncomfortable. Stuffing the kerchief into the side pocket of his white linen pants, he glanced wistfully toward the setting moon.

A farmer. He shrugged. Life could be worse, he knew—a lot worse. At least he and his family had food. And every now and then, when he could get some of his yams to market, he saved a few zaïres. But getting yams to market in Kongolo was proving harder then ever of late. Travel was dangerous, unrest with the government spreading, increasingly turning violent. And the soldiers—the soldiers!—they thought nothing of looting or stealing! If they wanted something, they took it—yams no exception. Zaire was not a safe country at the moment. Even here, he admitted, here on the two acres he worked at the eastern fringe of the jungle, far from a major city, he could no longer say he and his family were out of harm's way. Pulling the red kerchief back out of his pocket, he wiped the sweat beading on his forehead.

Turning to go inside the one-room, grass-covered earthen hut he shared with his wife and two children, Lionel swatted at a bug flying near his face. Jerking his head slightly back, he followed the shiny glint of green, watching it come to rest upon his leg. In the waning moonlight, he could see the shimmering glint of color was a common flower beetle. Strange for the insect to be active before sunrise, he thought. Perhaps it was the stifling humidity. The bug was confused.

Before Lionel could bend to flick the beetle from his pants, another beetle alighted next to it. A moment later, one more landed—and then another—and then two more. Perplexed, Lionel watched the bugs for a moment, wondering if he was witnessing some sort of mating ritual. When the group of green beetles arranged themselves in a single line and began crawling down his leg toward the ground, he smiled. *Surely I am witnessing something unusual,* he thought. Curious as to what might be taking place, he watched the slow-moving procession with growing interest.

As the first hint of daylight crept over the horizon, Lionel observed the beetles begin to vibrate, their shells radiating a soft, green-tinged light. Somewhat alarmed, he was about to brush the insects off his leg when the farthest beetle dropped to the ground. Two other beetles—separate from the ones clinging to the fabric of his pants—immediately joined the bug. When a second beetle dropped from his leg and two more beetles appeared next to it, Lionel looked out across his fields to see where the insects might be coming from.

"Mãe de Deus," he gasped. Trembling, he took a stutter-step backward.

"Rosa," he hoarsely whispered. "Misericórdia. Rosa. Deus, por favor. Mercy."

* * *

Ed Taylor lifted the baby boy up in his arms, a beaming smile on his face.

"Well, just look at you," he said. "Worth all the wait and fuss, weren't you? Though I hope, for your momma's sake, you break this habit of keeping everybody waitin'." He chuckled. "Look how tired she be. Why'd you want to wait until four in the morning to arrive?"

With a good-natured laugh, Ed shifted the baby so the boy faced the woman lying in the hospital bed.

"That there's your momma. Course, you know that, don't you?" He laughed. "Her name's Belinda."

"Yutanda, Dad. Yutanda."

"I thought you were asleep," Ed said, frowning.

Yutanda slipped an arm out from beneath the sheet, extending her hand toward her baby.

"How can I sleep when I know you're telling my son—"

"My grandson."

"—things he shouldn't listen to."

"Boy's not even a day old yet, Belinda. He don't know what I'm saying."

"Momma," Yutanda sighed, looking over to the woman seated in an armless, teal-blue plastic chair at the foot of her bed. "Help me, please."

"Now, Ed, it's time you stopped this Belinda nonsense. Yutanda's done given birth to her own child now. Ain't right you go carrying on with this… this… this little name game you've been playin'. Not your place to be confusing the issue of what the boy's mother's name is." Elizabeth Taylor smoothed the front of her rose-patterned brown and white dress. Giving her husband a serious look, she said, "So you just stop it, you hear? Stop it right now."

Ed looked at his wife and then at his daughter, his face crinkling. When he started to laugh, both women rolled their eyes.

"See what you have to look forward to, little one?" he said, chuckling. "Women just love to gang up on a man for the littlest of things."

Ed playfully jiggled the baby's arms, turning the boy so he could see Elizabeth.

"That's why I'm gonna teach you how to fish. So when the *noise*"— scrunching up his face, he gave Yutanda and Elizabeth a mischievous look— "gets to be too loud, you can go somewhere peaceful and quiet, remember why God put you on this earth." Turning the baby toward him, he said, "You just gonna love fishin'—a real nice way to pass the time. Real nice."

"Nice?" Yutanda teased. "Slimy, icky worms. Gooey chicken guts. Smelly fish, sharp hooks. And you wonder why I never wanted to go with you. Yuck," she told him, puckering her face. "But maybe little Menelik will take to it better than I did," she added in a weary voice. "Though I'm not sure how often we'll be getting down to Virginia."

Yutanda looked at her father's expression and shook her head. "Now don't go getting all sad on me, Dad. You just got that lost-puppy-dog look in your eyes."

"Don't like hearin' you talkin' this way is all," Ed replied. Looking to Elizabeth, he added, "Don't think your momma likes hearin' it, neither."

"Now, Dad, you know I have a job to do. I can't just put everything aside, everything I've worked for—what Menelik and I worked so hard for—and run off to Virginia. People are counting on me."

Ed's face took on a pensive look. "Thought maybe, once you held the baby in your arms, you'd change your mind." His eyes shifted uncertainly between Lizbeth and Yutanda.

"Boy has a right to breathe some fresh air and feel the grass 'tween his toes. Can't get that here. Newark—" His bushy silver eyebrows pinched together. "Just a whole bunch of dirty concrete."

Yutanda pulled her hand back beneath the sheet and closed her eyes. Ed saw wrinkles appear on her forehead.

"It's my home. It's *our* home," she said, nodding at the baby, her eyes glassy. "Where we—where Menelik and I—put so much effort into wiping away that dirt."

Sliding her arms out from under the sheet, Yutanda held them out toward her son. Ed brushed a finger over the boy's head before placing the child next to her in bed.

"Don't you worry none, Yutanda," Elizabeth interjected. "Your daddy's just runnin' off with words like he sometimes does."

Smiling, she leaned over and grasped Ed's forearm.

"I'm sure there are some good places to fish around here," she offered. "And if there are, your daddy will find 'em," she went on, addressing Yutanda. "But plenty of time to sort all that out. Ain't that right, Ed?"

Ed knew well the look in his wife's eyes.

Smiling, nodding, he said, "That's right. If there be a green space about—a place to put a line and hook in a creek or a pond—I'll find it. Little Menelik won't be missin' out. No, sir. I'll see to that. You just do what you need to do," he told Yutanda.

"Best we give you and little Menelik some rest now," Elizabeth said, standing. "Your daddy and I will go get something to eat and then get some supplies for you and the baby and take them to your apartment. Nurse said you'll probably be ready to be discharged by then. We'll be back before you know it."

Elizabeth bent and cupped her hand around her daughter's cheek. "He's a fine-lookin' boy, Yutanda. You should be proud."

Yutanda nestled her cheek into her mother's hand.

"Say goodbye to your grandson now, Grandpa," Elizabeth teased, looking at her husband. "We best be on our way. Leave these two to themselves for a time."

Ed looked at the baby. "Decided on his full name yet?"

Yutanda smiled.

"Menelik Edward Taylor-Arbagna."

"Taylor-Arbagna. Hmm, has a nice ring to it, it does. All right, then, Menelik Edward Taylor-Arbagna," Ed said, bending to his grandson. "We'll be back to fetch you and your momma real soon."

Kissing his fingertips, he placed them upon the baby's head.

"Yup, going to go get me a map of the area right now and see just where you and me can escape the *noise*."

When Elizabeth cuffed him on his shoulder, she, Yutanda, and Ed all laughed.

* * *

Claire was right. The stars are brilliant here.

So close to the earth, he felt if he reached up, he could almost touch them. Closing his eyes, he sensed the energy of the night sky radiating upon his skin.

"Etiyopiya. Look."

Teimbaka opened his eyes to find John Too standing on the other side of his brother's grave, pointing a finger to his neck. Teimbaka looked down to see his necklace of green beetles—the one John had made for him—pulsating. Tentatively, he placed his hand beneath the string of dried grasses holding the beetle carcasses together, slowly lifting it away from his chest. The metallic green shells glowed and dimmed as if breathing. Using his dula for support, Teimbaka arose from his knees to stand. A gust of cold wind swirled around his body.

"Are they alive?" John Too asked.

With a slight bow of his head, Teimbaka slipped the necklace from his neck, holding it outward.

"Perhaps John knows," John Too offered, shifting the weight of the bow and sack of arrows slung across his back. "Perhaps he knew they would do this when he made them."

Teimbaka looked to the small wooden cross Claire had placed at the head of his brother's grave, a necklace of green beetles draped across the arms.

"Your brother's do not glow," John Too remarked, as if reading Teimbaka's thoughts. "Perhaps yours carries a message from the Mother."

As John Too finished speaking, the crown of a full moon appeared on the horizon, spreading soft light over the shadowed rugged terrain below. The light imparted substance and definition to the dark shapes contained within the murky gorge on the eastern side of Ras Dashen.

When a tingling sensation enveloped his hand, Teimbaka looked to see the wings of the dead beetles unfolding, each insect separating from the tether of dried grasses to hover over his brother's grave. In a blinding flash, the insects burst into flame, the mounded earth showered with flecks of glittering ash.

"We should go back."

Teimbaka saw the boy looking toward the moon rising as a beacon to the east, where Claire and John awaited their return. Drawn back to his brother's grave, he saw the ashes of the beetles had turned cold and gray.

"Sister Lady—she's alone," John Too said. "Something feels—" He shook his head. "Something is coming."

Teimbaka shifted his gaze from John Too to the necklace of green beetles draped over the wooden cross. Pulling his shamma close about his shoulders, he shivered.

"The night grows cold," he muttered. "We'll need a fire." Offering John Too a brief smile, he added, "John will protect Sister Lady. As will the others."

John Too remained silent, his attention fixed upon the cresting moon.

"We'll leave at first light," Teimbaka reassured him. "Help me gather wood."

* * *

Lowering the pair of high-powered binoculars, Bacha Alba blinked several times, his yellow-brown eyes affixed to the caravan of trucks moving northward on the valley road. Seven, he counted. Each truck riding high on its axles, tarp-covered beds bearing no extra weight. Empty, he concluded. Hauling nothing—at least for the moment.

Guessing where the trucks were heading, he smiled. The road would abruptly end in a dozen kilometers. The bridge the vehicles would need in order to cross the gorge that lay ahead was no longer there. He and his men had blown it up two days ago. The trucks would have to come back this way. He would be ready when they did. His smile widened.

"Abdul! Hassan!" he called.

Two men outfitted in army fatigues crawled up on either side of him.

"Yes, General," they replied, bowing their heads.

"Once the government trucks travel another kilometer, go down to the road and bury two landmines where the tract narrows. There," he pointed. "Where the road curves around the large outcropping of stone."

"It shall be done, my general," they replied in unison.

"And be swift. Take Hussein and Ahmed with you. Post them several hundred meters up the road as lookouts."

"It shall be as you wish," Abdul replied, crawling backward. Abruptly halting, he asked, "Will the trucks be filled with weapons when they return, my general?"

Bacha Alba glanced back at the dark-eyed, thick-bearded man.

"I doubt the fools would send a caravan of trucks to transfer arms without a tank or several armored vehicles along for support." Pausing to check the progress of the trucks, he said, "It would seem the government has sent its soldiers to relocate more villages."

He looked at the man and smiled. "Make contact with the buyers. We will sell the women and children for whatever money they may fetch. And the men," he grunted, "they will have the choice of fighting with us—or meeting Allah."

"As you say, my general," Abdul replied, bowing his head in deference.

"Go then. The rest of us will prepare."

As Abdul and Hassan edged back several meters, Bacha Alba rolled sideways. When he was certain the boulder he was hiding behind would cover his wiry frame, he stood and wiped dust from his black and green camouflage fatigues. Shouldering an AK-47, he walked toward the forty men under his command.

"Relieve yourselves if need be and then ready your weapons," he announced to the gaunt, bearded faces watching his approach. "Allah has presented us with an opportunity to earn his blessings today. Jihad Akbar!"

"Jihad Akbar!" the men shouted.

"Allahu Akbar!"

"Allahu Akbar!"

Bacha Alba raised his AK-47 above his shoulder to the sound of cheering voices.

Yes. God is great, war is great, he thought, smiling back at his men. *Better when there is profit.*

* * *

White smoke billowed upward in cackling bursts, drippings from a roasting chicken fueling licking flames.

"Thomas! Make certain you turn it!"

Thomas looked up from the book he was reading and dutifully lifted the skewered chicken from the crescent-ended metal rods erected on either side of the fire. He offered Claire a smile before turning the bird over and placing it back on the spit. With a resigned sigh, Claire stirred a shallow tub of water—and the clothes immersed in it—with a thick staff of wood. Bending sideways, she checked beneath the metal tub to see if the small fire needed more kindling.

When the first shouts of "Bouda!" erupted, an uneasy shiver ran down her spine, giving way to quiet acceptance when the shouting of the ancient name became a chant. The children, well aware who sent Peter Gunstard to his grave, looked upon John as a hero. Closer to some sort of mystical entity, Claire observed. And the stories told about him—Bouda—had grown wilder with each re-telling of his tale.

Bouda appeared out of the wind, the children would say, pelts of dead hyenas flowing behind him like wings as he flew down from the rocks, the horn clasped within his hand aglow with the sun's fire. And when Bouda plunged the fiery horn into the devil-man's eye, the earth trembled and shook, the horn conjuring forth a great spirit bull elephant, the trumpeting of the beast so powerful, rocks and boulders split before crumbling to dust.

With every rehashing of his tale, the legend of the mystical hyena-man had grown more ostentatious. The story became embellished with undertones of the supernatural. John was now looked upon as a spiritual figure from folktales of old, the children of the camp—the score who'd drifted into Claire's care over the past weeks—embracing him in near godlike status.

Yet, the memory of what John had done to her, Claire could not erase. Even though John Too had repeatedly told her—and John—that what happened to them wasn't either of their faults, she couldn't escape the thought that it was. It *was* their fault. Would always *be* their faults. No matter how hard they might try to forget or forgive their time of enslavement to the heroin Susenyo had fed them, what they had done to each other—to themselves—was a part of who they'd become. There was no escape.

Claire turned and faced John with a taut smile.

"We must go!" he said.

Claire could see sweat glistening on his forehead.

"Teimbaka and John Too have not returned," she replied, glancing uncomfortably into his eyes. "What is it that—?"

"Trucks. Soldiers," he rushed to say. "Come to take more people away."

"I'm sure they're heading across the gorge to the villages beyond," she offered.

"The bridge is gone."

"The bridge? How is that possible?"

She recognized anger in his dark brown eyes, watched the nostrils of his slender nose flare.

"I told Teimbaka before he left," came his terse reply. "The warlord—his men—destroyed it."

"He didn't— He's been preoccupied— He didn't tell me."

"We must go!" John shouted, grabbing her wrist. "Now!"

"You're hurting me," she snapped, twisting her arm free.

"I'm sorry," he blurted, a look of sheer pain sweeping across his face. "I would never— I would— I didn't mean to."

"Thomas!" Claire abruptly shouted, looking over to the boy. "Cover your fire!" Touching John on his shoulder, she said, "God will see us through this." Seeing tears welling in John's eyes, she softly added, "Go. Gather the children."

Lips trembling, John raced off.

Using the staff of wood, Claire tipped the shallow tub of water over on its side, extinguishing the fire in a hissing rush of steam and smoke.

"Thomas!" she yelled. "Are you ready?"

She turned to see the dark brown face of the man dressed in army fatigues smiling, showing off a mouthful of yellowed teeth. Holding the stick-skewered chicken up beneath his nose, he dramatically inhaled its aroma, motioning with an imposing weapon in his hand for Claire to approach. Frantic, Claire scanned the campsite, searching for a way to escape. She became dismayed when she saw the children bunched together, guarded by four armed soldiers. The man holding the chicken yelled something to her, his tone angry. Someone grabbed her by the arm, shoving her roughly forward.

"Go!" a voice barked. "Trucks wait!"

The soldier holding the skewered chicken laughed.

* * *

"Reverend Mother."

The woman's voice echoed in the silence of the near empty chapel.

"Forgive my intrusion, Reverend Mother," she went on, lowering her voice to a soft whisper.

"What is it that is so important you disturb my time of reflection, Sister?"

Sister Sarah inched forward, bending closer to the kneeling Reverend Mother. "A man."

Reverend Mother turned her head, a look of reprimand on her face.

"A reporter, or a photographer of some kind. He brought this."

Sister Sarah extended a worn, heavily wrinkled envelope toward Reverend Mother. The older woman—with close-cropped silver hair and sagging age lines around her mouth and eyes—pushed her rounded, wire-frame glasses up the bridge of her hawk-like nose. Glancing up into the face of Sister Sarah—young, round, smooth skinned—she accepted the envelope. As she studied the correspondence, the wrinkles around her eyes, forehead, and mouth grew deeper.

"I'm afraid I don't know what this has to do with me, with us," she remarked out of hand.

"He says—the reporter—that he has another. Given to him in Africa. Djibouti—wherever that is. The first one"—she pointed to the envelope Reverend Mother held—"has a reference to the Sisters of the Holy Cross in it. He's here—the reporter—in France for a short time. He seems—" Sister Sarah raised her bushy brown eyebrows. "He seems to think the woman who wrote these letters—a Sister—is in danger, or in need of help."

Reverend Mother tugged at the rounded collar of her light blue, long-sleeved shirt. When she stood, she smoothed the material of her ankle-length navy blue skirt before genuflecting toward the small shrine erected on the altar.

"We'll talk outside."

*

Bright sunshine colored the sharply vibrant greens of the grass and foliage arranged in symmetrical patterns behind the Solitude of the Savior. Reverend Mother lowered her head, allowing her eyes to adjust to the bright sunlight and piercing blue of the sky, before speaking. Sister Sarah waited in silence two steps behind.

"I don't understand why this man brought this here. It is addressed to"—she held the envelope closer to her face—"a Mr. and Mrs. Waterman in Kennett Square, Pennsylvania."

She gave Sister Sarah a questioning look.

"In the United States. What possible reason would this man have for bringing this here?"

"I asked the same, Reverend Mother, when he first showed it to me. He says the second letter—one without an envelope—prompted him to read the one you now hold. I don't know much more than that. He said he was going—" Her pale cheeks took on a flash of pink as she looked away.

"Going? Going where, Sister? Why do you look so embarrassed?"

"Drouet Claudine, " Sarah replied, saying the name quickly.

"A bar? But it is not even mid-morning."

Reverend Mother clasped the silver cross hanging from the thin silver necklace around her neck and closed her eyes.

Sister Sarah stood obediently by, watching the lips of the older woman move in what appeared to be a silent prayer. When she saw Reverend Mother cross herself and open her eyes, she edged a half step closer.

"I don't want this," Reverend Mother told Sister Sarah, holding the envelope outward for the younger woman to take. "It does not concern us." Holding the envelope by a corner, she shook it, giving Sister Sarah a hard, unforgiving look.

"Dispose of it, or do whatever."

"But the man, he said he would be back in an hour. What am I to say?"

"Say nothing, Sister. Just hand it back to him and leave. Better yet, just leave it outside the gate. Tape it to one of the bars. I'm sure he'll find it."

Reverend Mother placed the envelope into Sister Sarah's hand and turned back toward the Solitude of the Savior. Sister Sarah looked down at the envelope, her brow furrowing.

"He says the letter asks—" Sarah hesitated, her eyes cast toward the ground. "For those whose hands may touch this—may they see and feel God's will upon the words."

Glancing quickly to Reverend Mother, she went on.

"He said it is nothing short of taking part in a holy pilgrimage. That these letters be delivered to the destination to which they were sent."

* * *

Rue Thompson hung up the phone and yawned. Transatlantic business. *Nothing but a headache,* he thought, *tiresome.* Especially when a seven-hour time difference came into play. But worth the hassle on occasion—as tonight's phone call had been. Heroin, cocaine, hash—containers of it—would be on the docks in Newark by week's end, if weather held. Checking the numbers Akmir had supplied, he grabbed the calculator on his desk and punched the keypad several times.

"Yes, indeed," he said with a sigh. "Ten million—give or take an ounce." He chuckled.

Glancing at the face of the calculator, he shifted his attention to the charts smoothed out on top of his desk. Running his fingertip across a maritime map of the Northern Hemisphere, he traced a route from the Suez Canal across the Mediterranean Sea, then further over the Atlantic Ocean to New Jersey. As he stared at the map, he knew there wasn't much he could do besides wait and hope for calm waters.

At the sound of a buzzer, he pushed away from his desk, rolling his office chair slightly right. Checking four eight-inch television monitors mounted on the desk's wooden extension shelf, he uttered, "Right on time, my man."

Feeling underneath the desktop overhang, Rue pressed a hidden button, scrutinizing the figure pulling open the back door of the warehouse. As the man traversed a long hallway, Rue followed his progress with interest, noticing how the grainy figure carried himself as he ascended a flight of stairs and moved from one closed-circuit monitor to the next. When a third monitor showed the man standing in front of Rue's office door, Rue gave a reassuring tap to the butt of the Glock handgun taped under his chair.

"Thank you for coming," he said as a tall, muscular man pushed open the door and slipped into the room.

Rue smiled. The man—wearing a waist-length, high-collar, snug-fitting brown leather jacket, his chest muscles bulging beneath a skin-tight chocolate brown T-shirt—reminded Rue of a character from an old Shaft movie.

"Pants leather too?" Rue quipped.

"Nylon," the man grunted.

With a tight, brief smile, the man adjusted his black Wayfarer sunglasses and sat down in the low-backed chair opposite Rue's desk.

"You dig?"

"You mean, do I like?" Rue asked, glancing down at his own pants. "Can't see those on me," he said, laughing.

"Why am I here?"

The man's face suddenly looked stony and cold; lips a slender line on a square-jawed face, his eyes, hidden by sunglasses, menacing nonetheless.

"Get right to it then, Mr. Cat? Is that what I'm supposed to call you? Or do you want the full El Gato Negro shit?"

Rue saw a slight wrinkle appear on the man's forehead.

"This 'bout your trouble with the feds? Losing your assembly seat crimpin' your style?"

"Just a temporary setback. Nothing for you to worry about, Mr. Cat. Oh, Jesus, man, I can't call you Mr. Cat. What am I supposed to call you? What do your other clients call you?

The man ran a hand over his clean-shaven head.

"Why am I here, Thompson—or is still Reverend?" the man asked in a bored tone of voice. "And C, call me C. That make you happy?"

"C," Rue snorted, glancing down at the desk drawer he was edging open.

When he looked back up, C had a .44 Magnum pointed at Rue's head.

"Somethin' 'bout my name you don't like?"

Clenching his jaw, Rue stared into the lenses of C's sunglasses. Slowly he reached into the drawer, removed a Polaroid photo, and tossed it across the desktop.

"That's why you're here," he said, nodding to the photo.

C twirled the Magnum once on his finger before holstering the gun beneath his left arm. He picked up the photo and studied it for a moment.

"Kill her and dump her body in the bay?"

Rue frowned. "Nothing so base, least not for the prices you charge. Could have gotten someone cheaper to do that."

C looked more closely at the picture. "Nice enough lookin' bitch. What'd she do to you?"

"Yutanda Arbagna, or Taylor-Arbagna as she currently goes by. And you don't need to know what she did."

"Find out on my own. Take but a minute. Maybe I should come back later when you want to be upfront with everything."

"Just sit yourself down," Rue ordered as C began to push out of the chair. "And all right," he hurried to say. "I'll save you the trouble. The girl's a reformer."

Rue's hand flashed with gold and diamonds as he pointed to the picture.

"She's taken—been temporarily given—the assembly seat vacated by her deceased husband."

Rue swiveled his chair from side to side as he chose his next words.

"Both were—are—a couple of goody two-shoes: urban housing projects, adult education programs, addiction counseling for troubled youths, small-business funding, rent relief—" He dismissively waved his hand through the air. "The whole nine yards."

"You want me to beat on her for doin' good?" C looked genuinely confused.

"No, no, no—nothing like that. I need someone to get close to her. Get to know her, her movements—her frame of mind. You see, her husband was killed on a government-backed trip," he said with a wink. "Just had a baby—on her own now—big bad world 'bout to squeeze in on her. See what I'm getting at? Probably lonely, in need of a friend—or more."

"You want the bitch to fall for me?" C frowned.

"I was told you could do that, amongst other things. Told you could do pretty much whatever I asked, whatever I needed. You come highly recommended." Rue validated the statement with a few definitive nods.

"Lady's been yappin' about dock and custom reform. Doesn't much care for the amount of drugs hitting the streets. Apparently has the ear of the new mayor, has a meeting set up with him and the suits who oversee the Port Authority."

C lowered his head and peered over the top rim of his sunglasses.

"While I have every confidence the new mayor will come around to our way of thinking in the near future," Rue said, "until that time, I need to be a step ahead. That's where your new friendship with Arbagna—the bitch— plays in."

Rue studied C's expressionless face. "You understand?"

"Got it." C confidently replied. "That it?" he asked, lifting his chin as if to say, "Is the meeting over?"

Rue held out a small piece of paper. "This is her address," he told him, bending forward and placing the note at the edge of the desk. "And you might want to get some other, um, conventional clothes. The girl went to Barnard. She's educated."

Rue ran a fat hand over his slicked-back hair. "She'll be a tough cookie." He seemed to drift off in thought for a moment before adding, "Just wish she wasn't so set on God's almighty path of righteousness."

"Don't worry your fat black ass none, Reverend." C stood and folded his arms across his chest. "I spent two years at Princeton before the draft board decided they wanted me in Nam more then they wanted me in class working toward a degree in political science. And even though I was pulling a three-point-seven and wore the latest Ralph Lauren, I was deemed another worthless, throwaway African-American male, best shipped out to defend our country, then get an education. The draft board neglected to address the fact I was deferred under the Selective Service Act of 1948 and subsequent articles of exemption and deferment later added. And though I had 2-S status, I wasn't extended that privilege. Suffering from being black, you see. Nineteen seventy-two: those were the times. Still are."

Rue shook his head and started to laugh. "Just as advertised," he got out between chuckles. "Need a bridge blown? Call the black cat, they told me. Throat slit? Safe cracked? Information gathered? A one-shot kill from a hundred yards away?" Rue nodded several times.

"Say you spent time in the Foreign Legion after your time in the army." Pausing for a moment, Rue took stock of the man. "Done all kinds of things, I hear. Heard you could even get a nun to jerk you off if you wanted," he said, laughing. "Or get a prostitute to swear to a life of chastity." Tilting his head back, Rue laughed up to the ceiling.

"Okay, then," he continued when he managed to get himself under control. "What's your plan?"

Rue looked across his desk to an empty room.

* * *

Lionel and his wife, Rosa, stood with their two children, Marcos and Vera, at the entrance of their hut—where they'd been standing most of the day.

Rosa had wanted to take the children and run away as soon as she saw the sea of green beetles moving through their fields. But Lionel wouldn't hear of it. They were witnessing something out of the ordinary, he had told her. Perhaps something sacred, a force beyond their comprehension. They dare not change what God had set in motion.

But it was late afternoon now. Even he—Lionel—could not believe the number of beetles that had passed in front of their hut since dawn. Millions upon millions, he guessed.

"Why do they go north, Papa?" his son, Marcos, asked.

"Marcos, Portuguese, por favor. You know your papa knows little of the languages you are learning," his momma, Rosa, said.

"Is okay, I think," Lionel offered, clasping his son on the shoulder. "I compreender."

He smiled at his wife.

"I no say, Marcos," he told his son. "No say, por que norte."

The first rumble of an approaching thunderstorm echoed across the sky. Looking eastward, Lionel saw a wall of thunderclouds rising thousands of feet into the air.

"Papa, the end!" It was Vera's voice, excited, soft—small-sounding. "I see the end!"

Lionel bent and placed one of his rough, callused hands to his daughter's cheek.

"Deus mostra misericórdia," he whispered.

As one, the family followed Vera's pointing finger toward the edge of the jungle. Marcos slid his small hand into his father's, repeating his father's words.

"God shows mercy."

2

TEIMBAKA AWOKE WITH a nudge to his shoulder. Yawning, he waited for John Too to say it was time to go. But what he received was a second, harder nudge.

"I'm awake," he said, opening his eyes.

Barely able to make out a hint of light on the eastern horizon, Teimbaka realized dawn had not yet arrived. The force of a third nudge nearly smashed his nose into the ground.

"John Too!" Twisting his body sideways, he snapped, "Why do you—?"

Quickly sliding his legs up under his waist, Teimbaka rose to a crouch, reaching for the spear he'd placed next to him before going to sleep.

A large mountain monkey squatted opposite him, glaring, upper lip flipped over its nostrils, displaying four impressive incisors. The beast studied Teimbaka's face for a moment before unleashing a chilling scream. When the piercing call was answered with similar raucous cries, Teimbaka brought the spear to his chest, ready to defend himself. Glancing quickly about, he could see dark, hairy shapes surrounding him. Even in the dim light he could sense the intensity in the beast's eyes.

The large monkey or baboon—he wasn't sure which—screamed a second time. The animal—at least fifty pounds, Teimbaka judged, over three feet in height—rose to stand on its hind legs and gestured upward with its chin. A male, Teimbaka observed. The leader, he assumed. Surveying what he could see of the beast's troop, he suddenly wondered if John Too was among them.

"John Too!" he called out.

The big male raised an arm, balling a hand into a fist. In a blur, the animal pounded the ground while pointing toward the pale band of light spreading across the horizon.

"East? The boy? East?"

The monkey stared at the approaching dawn.

"Claire," Teimbaka muttered.

Fur-covered fingers touched his chin. Startled, Teimbaka flinched at the beast's touch, confused when the monkey began pointing south.

"But the boy, he went east? I must follow him."

The great cape of fur around the animal's head and shoulders shook from side to side, the monkey animatedly thrusting his chin out, gesturing south.

"The children, Sister Lady—east," Teimbaka told him. "I go."

Light spread higher above the horizon, pale yellow creeping into a slate-gray sky. Seeing sunrise near, Teimbaka took a step toward it. The great male leaped in front of him, postured on all four appendages, tufted tail held high in the air, bare crimson chest puffed out for display. Snarling, the beast widened his jaws, showing off his massive teeth. Teimbaka raised his spear in front of him, holding it sideways against his chest.

"Let me pass," he calmly said.

The great male rose to place a hand against the wooden spear. Moving as a man, the mountain monkey walked the few steps to the grave of Teimbaka's brother. There he squatted, fingering the necklace of green beetles draped around the cross. Again, gesturing with his chin, he motioned south. Teimbaka bent to gather his bow and sack of arrows, stepping eastward as he straightened. The monkey took hold of his arm, pulling him south.

* * *

Accompanied by a colony of fifty-some mountain monkeys, Teimbaka traveled southward for the greater part of the day, staying to ridge tops and plateaus where possible. Hastening through valleys and gorges when forced to cross. Steering clear of villages and dwellings, he and the animals moved with determined purpose, a concerted journey southward with a slight veer to the west.

At times, Teimbaka struggled to keep pace with the thick-furred creatures, for the baboon-looking monkeys were strong and swift, able to traverse the rough, rocky terrain with ease. Where they came upon open ground, the animals ran unfettered, but Teimbaka labored, having to sprint to keep up. The beasts were faster than a man, their stamina impressive. Toward late afternoon, a sharp cry from the lead male brought the troop to a halt. Leaning on his spear, catching his breath, Teimbaka gazed out over the edge of the plateau they'd been navigating, studying the broken, downward-sloping landscape. The highlands, he saw, were coming to an end.

A kilometer or so further to the west, Teimbaka could see a cloud of moving dust. Curious, he took a step forward, but a tug to the bottom of the bow strapped across his back coaxed his attention behind him.

"What's out there? Why have you—?"

A baby spirit elephant, eyes filled with fear, stared up at Teimbaka, tears sliding down its cheeks. Teimbaka dropped to a knee.

"Why do you cry?" he softly asked.

The baby spirit elephant looked past him toward the moving cloud of dust.

An angry scream from the male monkey jolted Teimbaka to his feet, the animal leaping upon him, grasping his spear with both hands while kicking outward with his legs. Teimbaka stumbled backward, the great male pushing him along until the land beneath Teimbaka's feet gave way to empty space.

As he tumbled downward, a chorus of screams raced after him. Teimbaka rolled to an abrupt stop against the unforgiving rounded face of a boulder. He turned to find the troop of mountain monkeys gathered at the edge of the plateau. And then, quite suddenly, the beasts fell quiet. In the silence, Teimbaka could hear the whine of a motor and the *thump, thump, thump, thump, thump* of helicopter blades. And then he heard a rifle shot.

* * *

The elephant lay motionless, blood flowing from a fist-sized hole just behind its eye. As the elephant gasped for air, red foam bubbled from the corners of its mouth. Past the dying beast, the droning of the helicopter alternately receded and intensified, a dozen or more elephants moving in panicked circles below the flying machine. Teimbaka sprinted toward them, spear gripped tightly in his hand. As he drew near, the helicopter swerved, pushing waves of dirt and small stones into his body and face. Crouching low, he scurried back, glimpsing the barrel of a rifle emerge from the cockpit.

Sliding his bow from his shoulder, he slipped an arrow from the satchel, nocking it to string as a man leaned out, foot braced against the runner, and took aim at the animals below. Teimbaka let the arrow fly.

A flash, a sharp resounding boom, the rifle jerked sharply skyward before falling to the ground. Teimbaka's arrow was embedded in the man's shoulder. The man stared down at him, a grimace of pain etched upon his face. In a gust of swirling dust, the helicopter banked away.

* * *

Teimbaka waited with the wounded elephant until it died. Hand placed gently upon the beast's neck, he murmured soft words of the Mother's compassion to the animal until the beast's spirit passed from flesh to essence in a final, shuddering exhale. Silent, stoic—like human mourners at a wake—the group of surviving elephants stood off at a distance before filing by the dead one by one—heads bent, trunks dragging atop the soil—before moving off, wandering aimlessly toward a dimming sun. With a look back to the highlands, Teimbaka glimpsed what he thought to be the baby spirit elephant—a shimmering flash of white-hued gold—standing on the edge of the plateau. But in the next moment, the phantasm was gone, a silhouette of a bird in its place, its call forlorn and hollow as it unfurled its wings and took flight into the sky. With the eye of the dead elephant staring lifelessly up at him, Teimbaka pulled his shamma close about his neck.

Hissing static, the crunch of dried grass, the sound of footsteps—careless and hurried—intruded upon the somber moment. Teimbaka listened to the sounds, muscles tensing, the hissing static conjuring forth images of the bulky black boxes soldiers would talk into when he'd been forced to pass through government checkpoints. Suddenly a voice—small, metallic, crackling—erupted.

"Kill him! Fan out and surround him! If he gets away…." The voice broke apart in an explosion of garbled electricity.

Gathering his weapons—bow, sack of arrows, steel-tipped spear—Teimbaka took stock of his surroundings. Hearing footsteps to the right of him, others directly ahead, he moved left before coming to an abrupt stop. Holding his breath, he heard the unmistakable click of a rifle bolt as footsteps hurried to block his path.

Staying low, Teimbaka raced forward, breaking into a squatted run in an attempt to keep ahead of the person trying to outflank him. Using clumps of tall grass and thorn bushes for cover, he made his way toward a small grove of trees. When he heard footsteps closing in on him, he pressed his body to the ground, shimmying under a thorn bush for cover. Fists clenched, he held his breath and waited. For a few seconds he heard nothing, and then footsteps moved past, heading back in the direction he'd just vacated.

"A mile out!" the distant, garbled, static-filled voice screamed. "Cut and go! Cut and go! Make sure—" A burst of crackling electricity, a pop and a hiss, and the voice abruptly stopped, footsteps—loud, running—filling the interlude, heading in the direction of the dead elephant. Suddenly, a sputtering motor came to life. Confused, Teimbaka stood.

One of the three men standing near the fallen elephant held a smoke-spitting, whining, unwieldy tool, blade spinning in a blurring circle, puffs of petrol-laced smoke spuming into the air. Teimbaka remembered seeing a similar tool once before when he'd passed a logging camp. Chainsaw, he had come to learn the tool was called. Used to cut trees for lumber.

When the man put the spinning blade into the elephant's face—behind the jowls near the base of the tusk—Teimbaka became enraged. Nocking an arrow to his bow, he aimed and shot, pulling a second arrow from his sack as soon as the first left the string. The loosed arrow struck the man with the chainsaw in his shoulder. The man dropped the tool to the ground, staggering back. His two companions—armed with automatic weapons—turned to fire. Teimbaka swung his bow toward the man nearest him, letting the second arrow fly, then dove right as bullets shredded a bush left of where he'd been standing. Edging backward on elbow and knees, he rolled toward a clump of thorn bushes. Using the foliage for cover, he rose to a crouch, putting another arrow to his bow. But when he drew his string back and rose to take aim, he saw the men had disappeared. He listened. Nothing. He waited. Still nothing. And then the sky exploded.

A helicopter zoomed past three to four meters above him, filling his head with the thump of blades and the grinding whine of the engine. In a wave of dust and debris, Teimbaka covered his ears while he watched the helicopter set down near the dead elephant. Immediately, the three men he'd been listening for rose up behind the dead carcass, one man draping his arms across the shoulders of the other two, an arrow sticking out of his thigh. The two uninjured men dragged the other man to the helicopter, then pushed him into the open seat of the cockpit. Stepping upon the helicopter's runners, they grabbed hold of the cockpit's frame. The helicopter lifted off, banking hard to the north.

No sooner had the sound of the helicopter faded away than the sound of a revving engine and a strained suspension system took its place. Teimbaka turned to see a jeep come to a jolting stop some twenty meters away.

"You there!" a uniformed man riding in the back of the vehicle shouted. "Stay where you are!"

Teimbaka saw a rifle swing toward him.

"Anti-poaching rangers! You are under arrest!"

Teimbaka took the arrow off his bowstring and placed it into the satchel strapped across his back. As three uniformed rangers began to get out of the jeep, Teimbaka turned and sprinted for the grove of trees.

* * *

Peter Benjamin sipped an espresso, his thoughts immersed in the aperitif of anisette poised between his fingertips. While he preferred Sambuca—the taste was smoother—he wasn't going to complain. Especially since the proprietor of the small bistro had been good enough to serve him a drink while everyone else was ordering morning croissants and *café*. Anisette would suffice—for now.

His attention drawn to the slender peel of lemon floating on the surface of the espresso, he compared the darkened edges of the fruit rind to the state of his life. Stained, bitter, foul, the lone piece of lemon skin proffering the reflective question *Why am I here*? Peter stared at the darkened shred of yellow husk, wondering what his answer would be. Deciding to confer with the fluted glass of anisette, he took a sip of the licorice-imbued spirit, passing the question to his alter ego, Dirk Savage. Grunting, he assessed the man: Dirk Savage, globe-trotting photojournalist.

Dirk Savage was Peter Benjamin's byline name. Peter choosing the fictitious persona fresh out of journalism school some eighteen years earlier. Thinking the sound of the name, the look, was just the sort of moniker a world-traveling photojournalist should have. Eighteen years—he twisted the number around in his thoughts. What had once been a promising and somewhat lucrative career had grown stale. Brown around the edges, like the lemon twist in his espresso. Taking another sip of anisette, he lost himself in thought.

*

"Why do you want me to have these?"

Dirk stared up into the face of the big black ape, as he called him, wondering what the ploy was. No one from the Consortium, as they were known—whether he was a part of the inner circle or just an underling doing odd jobs—did anyone any favors unless there was an ulterior motive. Glancing at the wrinkled letter and the old envelope Bin'ka set in front of him, he wondered what that motive could be. And, therefore, wondered how it would affect his life—literally.

"For the article and photographs in *La Nation*. For reporting the story of the fire at the warehouse on the dock just as it was relayed to you. Our way of saying thanks."

Bin'ka rolled his massive shoulders at the statement while surveying the clientele of the brothel where they were meeting.

"Akmir feels the woman's parents"—he nodded to the envelope and letter on the table—"might be inclined to reward the person who could bring word of their daughter to them." He shrugged. "He thought, maybe, a little extra money might be of use to you."

Smiling, Bin'ka fanned a massive black hand in front of his face in an attempt to push the billowing hookah smoke away. "But there are others who might be interested in the story if you're not."

Before Bin'ka could take back the pieces of paper, Dirk grabbed them and placed them inside his shirt.

*

"*Excusez-moi.*"

Peter stirred from his reverie to find the proprietor standing in front of his small table.

"*Encore une plus anisette pour le monsieur?*"

"How long have I been here?" Peter asked, wondering if the stately looking woman was indeed Claudine, the namesake of the small bistro he'd stumbled upon.

"How?" The woman furrowed her brow for a moment, the nuanced beginnings of crow's-feet coming to life around her rich, brown eyes. "Ah, *le temps*—time, yes?"

"Yes, time," he told her, smiling, running a hand across the black stubble on his chin.

As the woman turned to look at the old wooden cuckoo clock hanging on the wall above the case of pastries and bread, Dirk took the moment to admire the way her tight-fitting white blouse accentuated her breasts.

"*Une heure,*" she told him, smiling.

"An hour?"

"*Oui.*"

"How much do I owe you?"

"*Revenez plus tard,*" she said with a wink. "Later, come, yes?" She seductively laughed, sliding a finger down his cheek as she walked away.

Peter nodded, latching on to how she said, "Later, come." Downing the last of the anisette, he made eye contact with Claudine before stepping outside.

* * *

Dirk Savage crossed Avenue Yzeux as he made his way down Rue des Hirondelles. A pretty enough street, he thought, far different than the streets in Djibouti. How he had ended up in that forsaken city remained a mystery he himself could not quite fathom.

It—Djibouti—had been a photojournalist's dream for a while, when relief aid was pouring in from all parts of the Western world and the story of the great famine in Ethiopia captured the front page of every leading newspaper and magazine around the globe. The world press had clamored for stories and photographs of the event, television crews flying into the region on a daily basis. Dirk sold photographs to *Life*, *Newsweek*, and *Time* when the story was hot, the crown jewel of his work coming when he helped write and document a featured article on the famine and relief effort for *National Geographic*.

How quickly that lucrative time had come to a screeching halt, he thought. Fucking warlords, flies, disease, civil war—the emergence of a few radical Islamic cells spreading south from North Africa—hadn't helped. Nor the plethora of corrupt local, regional, and national governments anyone coming to the area had to deal with. Yeah, all those factors had ruined the whole money-for-exclusive-photographs market. Newspaper, magazine, and TV crews suddenly gone—overnight, it seemed. The story coming to an abrupt end, no one but the truly dedicated staying on after the story had become passé. After the pictures of skeletal bodies and starving children had become too morbid, too routine. The constant horror of famine and drought numbed the viewing public's interest, he supposed, a handful of dedicated relief workers the only foreigners deciding to stick around to try to help. But they—volunteers from various NGOs—had already been in Djibouti for god knows how long anyway.

But those dedicated souls—the aid workers—they weren't the story the world—he grunted—the fucking noble, compassionate world—wanted to hear about. No, none of those selfless, self-sacrificing people were glitzy enough or rock-starry enough to be of any interest to the world community. No, no one gave a shit about any of the relief workers or the doctors or nurses who'd stuck around—poor fucking do-gooders, as he liked to refer to them. They might just as well be dead too, he observed, just like the hundreds of thousands of other nameless souls who'd perished from starvation, disease, and civil war.

Forgotten nobodies. That's what they were, he'd concluded. Not worth a second thought, or—God forbid—a passing mention on the evening news. The noble fucking world—he grunted again. Like the whole tragic mess—the famine and the botched relief effort—was just some frightening nightmare out of the Old Testament. A passage to be recalled from time to time, read from crinkled, yellowed pages from a dusty, leather-bound book, referencing the power of an all-seeing, all-powerful, all-forgiving god. A passage to remind the feeble-conscience human race a swift and merciless judgment was a whim away. That whatever god they believed in should be forever feared and held in reverence because famine, death, disease, and misery could be instantly decreed by the unquestioning wisdom of some all-knowing supreme being. Chortling, Dirk turned his head and spit on the ground.

When he arrived at a fork in Rue des Hirondelles, Dirk went left, following Rue de la Solitude to his destination, the Solitude of the Savior. Taking a deep breath, popping a breath mint in his mouth, he tried to calm himself. It wouldn't be smart to hold a conversation with a nun—a Reverend Mother, he reminded himself—in the agitated state he was working himself into. Reaching inside his jacket, he felt for the second letter Bin'ka had given him. The woman who had written it—Claire, Sister Claire—was or had been in Ethiopia. Either smack-dab in the middle of the famine when she'd penned the letter, he'd deduced, or somewhere damn near close to the center. War, warlords all over the fucking area she was in—if she was still alive. He shook his head; why would anyone—anyone—want to be there? And how did she get there? Who knowingly would send anyone there? He thought again of the conversation he had had with the big gorilla, Bin'ka, and grunted.

*

"But there are others who might be interested in the story if you're not. He thought, maybe, a little extra money might be of use to you."

Big ape; he sure knew how to play me, didn't he? Like I had a choice in the matter.

Why *was* he here, he sarcastically asked himself again. Envisioning the lemon peel in the bottom of his espresso cup—limp, lying in dirt-colored foam, bits of black grounds scattered beneath it—he realized, *That's why— because I'm the fucking dregs of the world.*

* * *

Sitting on the front steps of the Solitude of the Savior, Sister Sarah waited for the mysterious man—as she imagined him to be—to return. He'd said he'd be back in an hour, she reminded herself, but it had been longer than an hour. An hour and twenty minutes had already passed. An hour and twenty-one minutes, actually, but she continued to wait just the same. Glancing at the front gate at the entrance to the Solitude of the Savior for the dozenth time, seeing no one standing there—again—she returned to the book of poetry she was reading. When the buzzer from the street sounded a few minutes later, she dog-eared the page she was skimming and got up.

*

By only allowing herself a few furtive glances toward the man standing on the opposite side of the gate, Sarah hoped to suppress the stirrings of physical arousal. Her body reacting similarly earlier in the morning, when she'd first set eyes on the man. And when their hands had touched when he had given her the envelope— No, she told herself, she wouldn't think of that moment, admonishing herself for entertaining such sinful, lustful thoughts. She would need to kneel on cement for the remainder of the day, begging the Virgin Mary's forgiveness for having been so weak as to fall prey to such bodily yearnings.

"I'm sorry if I'm a little late," the man said in such a way Sister Sarah was immediately inclined to forgive him.

Looking into his sparkling blue eyes, Sarah felt her body go weak. And when he smiled at her, she quickly turned her face toward the ground so he wouldn't see her blushing.

"It was such a long trip from Djibouti," he added. "I've lost track of time on a number of occasions the past few days."

She watched him lift a sun-bronzed hand to his tanned, angular face.

"Not sure how much sleep I've gotten either," he told her, running his fingers through his longish black hair.

She looked at his face; it did look weary, she thought. But there was something else—something more—a sadness of some kind. Or was she just imagining it, to make him seem more mysterious?

"Passing the time in prayer?"

Glancing up into his eyes, she saw he was looking at the book in her hand.

"Poetry," she rushed to say. "Robert Frost. I'm originally from New England. I, I've— I've been drawn to his poems since I was little."

"Ah, Frost, yes. One of my favorites too."

He shifted the weight of his tall, muscular-looking frame to his other foot. Sarah noticed his worn boots. The soles chipped away in places, laces different colors; one, sand hued, the other, dark brown.

"I read him extensively one semester in a creative writing course my junior year at UVA."

Sister Sarah stared into his eyes, an unnerving warmth spreading from her groin to her thighs.

"Which one?"

"Which one?" she repeated, slightly flustered.

"Poem. Which poem were you reading?"

"Oh," she said. "The Road Not Taken."

She lifted the book up as if she was going to hand it to him.

"It's one of my favorites," she added, glancing at the book as if to reaffirm her statement. "He was very—very insightful."

"None more so," he agreed.

Sarah nodded, her thoughts drifting elsewhere. The road not taken, the road she couldn't find, closing when she was just about to enter. Hidden behind a wall of deceit. Whispered about but never unveiled. Those who might have helped her find the road preoccupied with covering it up. Twisting simple words—her words—into meaningless interpretations of what she really *meant* to say.

Closing her eyes, she tried not to think about that girl—her—and the road she couldn't find—the way out, the way to sanity. Thank God for the Holy Mother! The Virgin Mary visiting her in a dream, changing everything, giving her hope there was a place in the world where she could feel safe. And for the past three years, the road she had chosen, the road that had opened for her—the Virgin Mary's road—had led to safety. She was a second-year Novitiate; the commitment to her vows lay just ahead. Determined to keep her life within the community of the Marianites of the Holy Cross, she'd allow nothing—nothing—to prevent her from attaining that life.

"Sister? Sister, did you hear me?"

Opening her eyes, Sarah realized she would need to pray extra long and hard. Yes, extra long and extra hard. Impure thoughts—the warm wetness between her loins—needed to be expunged. Penance administered.

"Oh, oh my. I'm sorry. I— I—"

"No need to apologize," the man graciously told her. "I'm sure you've been up for hours yourself."

She looked at him, not certain what to say, distracted and a little annoyed with herself for feeling physically aroused.

"So will she see me? Did she say she would help?"

"Who?" Sister Sarah asked with complete innocence.

"The Reverend Mother. Did you speak with her?"

Sister Sarah pulled at the sleeve of her light blue blouse. Clearing her throat, she said, "Yes. She's waiting for you now."

* * *

John Too smelled rotting flesh before he saw the overturned truck at the bottom of the embankment, front end charred and riddled with bullet holes. Sidestepping a crater in the middle of the road, he stood perfectly still. Were there others, he wondered? Landmines. He was becoming all too familiar with them. Normally, more than one would be placed in an area, he knew. Especially on packed-dirt roads like the one he was traveling on now. Searching the stretch of road around him, he saw a patch of freshly disturbed earth five yards ahead and a foot or so nearer the road's shoulder. The truck must have passed over it and then ran right over the top of the other one—the one that had blown half the front chassis away. Slowly, scrutinizing every inch of compacted soil, he stepped off the road and scrambled down the steep embankment where the truck had come to rest.

Not far off he could hear the cackling rants of hyenas. The scavengers would be coming soon, he knew; the stench of rotting flesh traveled fast. Looking up, he was surprised there were no vultures yet. Perhaps the hilly terrain and deep ravines had something to do with the birds not being able to locate the kill, he thought. Leaving his attention focused to the sky, he searched for a thin column of smoke, perhaps two. Sister Lady said she would wait. He gauged he was no more than a kilometer away from where they had parted the day before last. Smoke would lead him back to camp. But the sky was empty. He grew uneasy.

Moving past the truck, he saw blood on the door, a puddle of it on the foot runner and the ground beneath. Though he was tempted to bend and touch the blood to gauge its freshness, the call of a hyena spurred him to keep moving. Passing the covered back bed of the truck, he looked inside. Empty—save for dark splotches on the metal floor. Turning, he broke into a jog before coming to an abrupt stop. The buzzing of a thousand frenzied flies filled his head. And then he saw the bodies. He shut his eyes.

There were eight in all, stripped of clothing from their necks to their waists. Stomachs slashed open, guts spewed out, each man's hands bound behind his back, most missing the back portion of their heads. Yet one man—lighter of skin than the others—had not been shot or mutilated, meeting death in a more brutal fashion: a large spike driven into his forehead. Judging by the crack in his skull and the amount of blood splattered in every direction, the spike had been hammered into his skull with several strokes. Dangling from the sides of the man's frozen, twisted mouth John Too saw a glint of silver. Bending closer, he could see links of a thin silver chain. Taking an arrow from the sack strapped across his back, he slipped the arrowhead beneath the links, and lifted the necklace toward him. A small silver cross—like the one Sister Lady wore—came up from the man's throat. John Too stared at the forged piece of bloodstained metal, his eyes blurring. Would the men who did this treat Sister Lady in the same manner? Would they pound a spike into her head and stuff her cross down her throat? Overcome with a moment of rage, he stood and screamed.

A tormented, guttural wail answered.

* * *

"Do not go back there." John rolled the horn of the impala around in his hand, the razor sharp tip pricking the soft flesh on the underside of his arm. When he looked at John Too, his dark eyes flamed from slanted rays of sun. John Too took a step closer to the mouth of the shallow cave where John was seated.

"Where are Sister Lady and the others?" he asked.

John stared at him, grinding his jaw. "Gone," came his terse reply.

"Where?"

"She's gone!" John screamed. "Gone!"

John Too let his eyes drift to the surrounding terrain, seeing nothing but rocks and formations of stone. Not a single weed, bush, or plant growing amongst them.

"Why didn't she wait?" he asked. "And the others, John—the children, like us—where are they?"

"I am not a child! Not like the others!" He glared at John Too. "Not like you!" John wrapped the hides of hyenas around his shoulders and stared at the ground.

"Why do you wear those again?" John Too asked, nodding to the hyena pelts. "That was what you were—not what you are."

"I am bouda!" he shouted. "It *is* me!"

John Too stepped closer.

"They took her!" John screamed, brandishing the impala horn in front of him. "She wouldn't go! Wouldn't go when I told her! Said I was hurting her!"

John Too saw the veins in John's neck throbbing.

"They took her!" he wailed, slumping to his knees, tears trickling down his face. "And pulled everyone from the trucks—pushed them in a circle."

John's sorrowful expression changed into a scowl. "Separated the soldiers from the women and children." Pausing, he added, "Then butchered the men like sheep. And when they found— when they found—"

John placed a hand to his neck, rubbing his thumb against his index finger.

"Like Claire's—they pinned him to the ground and pounded a spike into his skull." Glancing over his shoulder, John peered into the darkness of the cave. "He screamed," he went on, his voice devoid of emotion. "And Sister Lady—Claire—fell to her knees. Sobbing—until they dragged her away."

"Where, John? Where did they take her? And who? Who did this?"

"They threw her into one of the trucks—forced everyone into them and drove away. There were too many," he told him, his voice dropping to a whisper. "Forty or fifty men. I could do nothing." Pausing, he started to tremble, tears running freely down his cheeks. "She said I was hurting her."

"Where John?" John Too pressed. "Who were the men?"

John stared past him, blinking. "The warlord; Bacha Alba," he muttered.

"Where, John? Where? Do you know where he took Sister Lady and the others?"

John ran the back of a hand across his eyes and nodded.

"Show me, then. Take me to Sister Lady."

* * *

The horde of green beetles stopped at the edge of the rain-swollen Lualaba River, hesitating at the sound of rushing water and the daunting sight of white-capped wavelets churning in their path. Without fanfare or a noticeable means of communication, the phalanx of green beetles turned north.

3

THERE WAS A chill to the wind Yutanda hadn't anticipated. Gathering the front of her knee-length wool coat close about her neck, she shuffled her booted feet, trying to stay warm. Her eyes drifted from the murky, choppy waters of Newark Bay to the mammoth container ship moored twenty yards in front of her.

The ship was bigger, longer, and taller than what she thought a container ship would be—massive. *So much for pictures in magazines*, she thought. Peering up at the vessel, she felt like an ant standing in front of a hundred-foot oak tree.

Checking her wristwatch, she glanced back to her parked car. The mayor-elect and the officials from the New Jersey–New York Port Authority were due to arrive in twenty minutes. She wondered if she had enough time to find a pay phone and call her parents—to see how little Menelik was doing—but she immediately decided against it, aware that if she wasn't around when the new mayor and the powers overseeing the docks arrived, she'd appear incompetent. And she couldn't afford to seem inept. The city was counting on her. Besides, she thought, Menelik was in good hands, wasn't he? Thank goodness for grandparents!

Opening her briefcase, Yutanda took out a notebook and pen, sifting through spiral-bound sheets of paper until she found one blank. Doing a slow turn, she absorbed the activity going on around her.

Somewhat mesmerized, she watched palettes of cargo offloaded from freighters by giant cranes. Vehicles of all shapes and sizes swerved in and out of the row upon row of stacked shipping containers. Men in hard hats scurried toward giant fishing nets laden with crates; forklifts fed open bays of waiting trucks with merchandise; entire stacked palettes were hoisted onto empty flatbed railroad cars. She shook her head. The scene reminded her of a city, one no outsider understood. What were the rules, she wondered? Who's pulling the strings? Who decided which containers or which ships would be inspected?

The task of pinpointing how illegal drugs were entering the port was going to be more difficult than she thought, the seaport huge, sprawling, confusing. One would need an army to try to check every container, she realized. How were they—how was she—going to stem the flow of drugs funneling through it? Close to fifty thousand pounds of illegal narcotics smuggled into port every year, law enforcement officials had told her, the payload growing larger by the week. Demand on the street at an epidemic level, fueled by the creative, deep-pocketed, well-oiled machine of organized crime. Yutanda placed the tip of her pen at the corner of her lips and sighed.

What was it Menelik had said to her on occasion? "The ravagers of the world know no boundaries"? Well, he was certainly right about the boundary aspect, she observed. The drug trade had gone global; Europe, parts of Africa, Southeast Asia, Mexico, Peru, China—all fighting for a piece of the business.

"How do you fight a world?" she had asked him once.

"You must meet them on every street corner until they yield," he had told her.

She could still hear the conviction in his voice.

Thinking of him reminded her how much she missed him—there was an emptiness inside her that hadn't gone away, or wouldn't. The fact that the Ethiopian government had never found his body in the wreckage made his death even harder for her to accept and fed the small, futile hope she'd been clinging to that he was still, somehow, alive. She'd prayed he was—alive—every night. Prayed he'd just show up one day, and everything would go back to the way it was. Only better—because now they had a son.

Down the pier from where she stood, one of the massive bridge-like cranes set down a small cargo net filled with wooden crates. As soon as the netting touched pavement and the crane's coupling device released, four white panel vans pulled up, two men climbing out of each cab. Immediately they began loading crates into the back of the vehicles. *Odd*, she thought.

They—the men—didn't look like longshoremen. They weren't dressed like longshoremen—wearing jeans and black T-shirts—no hard hats, gold chains draped around their necks. Who were these guys? she wondered. Clicking the ballpoint pen, she noted the crane number—74—while moving a few steps closer so she could see the name of the ship. Foreign, she guessed, writing down J-a-m—.

"Hey, lady, whatcha think you're doin'?"

Yutanda jerked her hand to her chest with a start. Turning, she felt a tinge of panic run through her.

"Assemblywoman Yutanda Arbagna," she said to the three young black males standing behind her in a semi-circle. Extending her hand, she added, "I'm here to meet the new mayor of Newark and some of the officials of the port."

She searched the faces of the three young men dressed in black leather vests with red bandanas tied around their heads, hoping her position—assemblywoman—would garner some sort of respect, but the sunglasses the three young men were wearing made it hard to discern much about them. Their faces emotionless, mouths rigid. She let her hand fall back to her side.

"And you are?" she asked, glancing at her notebook, placing the pen to paper.

In a blur, the one directly across from her, the middle one, thrust his hand forward and slapped the notebook from her hand.

"I asked you a question, bitch."

Yutanda glanced quickly to her car, hoping—praying—to see the mayor-elect and his entourage arriving. But there were no other cars parked near hers.

"Ain't nobody here gonna help you, lady," one of the others said, lunging at her.

Startled, Yutanda stumbled backward. As she struggled to keep from falling to the ground, she heard the three men laughing.

"Did you hear what I said?" she admonished them, regaining her balance. "I'm an assemblywoman of the twenty-ninth district of Newark. A public official, part of the government of New Jersey."

She glimpsed the man to her right flick his wrist, barely hearing the click before a steel blade flashed.

"You wouldn't dare," she scoffed. "Not with all these witnesses."

"Ain't no witnesses here, bitch," the one in the middle mocked. "See for yourself," he told her, chin jutting forward.

Hesitantly, Yutanda took a quick look around, her breathing becoming labored when she couldn't see a single person on the pier.

"That your car, bitch?"

It was the one with the knife who asked. She glared at him.

"Keys," he stated, holding his free hand out toward her. "Give 'em up."

Reflexively, Yutanda felt for the ring of keys in the side pocket of her coat.

"Yeah, we need a car," the one on the left said, laughing as he reached out and grabbed her by the collar.

In one swift, powerful move, he spun Yutanda around, wrenching the coat from her body. Her briefcase and the small shoulder purse she was carrying fell to the cement. Then one of the men pushed her—hard—sending her falling sideways. A sharp pain shot through her hip and shoulder.

"And we need gas, bitch," one of them taunted. "You best have cash in this purse."

"Help!" she yelled. "Help me!"

The kick to her stomach was jolting. For a moment she couldn't breathe.

"What kinda panties you got on lady?"

She felt her skirt lifted off her thighs.

"Looky here, boys. Bitch be wearin' grandma undies."

She heard the three of them burst into laughter. And then she felt hands on her legs. Clenching her muscles, she tried to get up, but a slap to her face left her numb.

"Yo, take her keys and bring the car," she heard one of them say. "We gonna need to take her someplace else."

Blinking tears from her eyes, she squinted up to see her ring of keys tossed to an open hand. A hollow, sinking feeling grew in her stomach as she heard footsteps running toward her car.

"Need to be taught a lesson, miss assemblywoman bitch."

The knife appeared in front of her face, twisting in the man's hand.

"That right," a different one added. "This pier don't need nobody snoopin'."

"That right," the one holding the knife agreed. "We fine just the way things be," he added, placing the point of the knife on the tip of her nose.

The blade lifted away when a puttering noise drew the man's attention.

"What the fuck this dude think he doin'?" the man with the knife complained.

Still dazed from the slap to her face, Yutanda caught a glimpse of a motorcycle heading toward them. Hearing the engine rev, she watched the bike speed up. The other man—the one not armed—drew a knife from the pocket of his jeans.

"Dude don't know the rules here," he said, flicking the knife open.

Yutanda slid her legs beneath her to rise. One of the men kicked the arm she was using as support.

"Stay down, bitch," the bigger of the two men warned.

She fell flat to the cement as the motorcycle came to a stop ten yards away. The engine went quiet. The rider pulled off his shiny black helmet and swung his leg over the seat.

"Maybe you boys can help me," the rider said.

Yutanda stared at him open-mouthed. The two men flashed their blades by their sides.

"I'm trying to find the information center."

Yutanda watched him run a hand over his smooth-shaven head.

"My brother's supposed to be pulling into port sometime today on a freighter." Looking down at the woman on the ground, he asked, "Lady, you okay? Need some help?"

"Get on your fuckin' hog and take a hike, man," one of her two assailants hissed. "Lest you find yourself gettin' cut."

"Ma'am," the motorcycle man went on. "Can I help you to your feet?"

Yutanda felt her head nodding up and down. The motorcycle rider placed his helmet on the seat of his bike, taking a step toward her. Her two assailants stepped in front of him, swinging their knives. Yutanda tried to scream but no sound came out of her throat. In a state of shock, she watched the rider kick out his leg while swinging an arm upward. In unison her assailants cried out, one falling to the ground, clutching his knee, the other dropping his blade, holding his arm. And when the one who was on the ground tried to slash the leg of the rider, the man bent and grasped the man's wrist. She could hear the bone snap as he twisted it backward.

As the motorcycle rider approached her, offering his hand, the sound of screeching tires made her gasp. Taking hold of the motorcycle rider's arm, she rose to her feet while her two assailants hobbled over to her car.

"My—my car!" she exclaimed to the sound of screeching rubber. "My wallet—ID—the key to my apartment!"

She clutched the motorcycle man's arm.

"They're in my purse! They have them! They have them!"

"Lady, calm down. Don't worry." The motorcycle rider turned his head and watched the speeding Camry drive through the gate to the service road beyond. "They won't get far."

His eyes were soft, brown, calming. She blinked, exhaling, her head coming to rest on his chest. She felt his hand brush over the back of her shoulder.

"You hurt anywhere?" he gently asked.

Lifting her head, she took a step back.

"I'm— I— Thank you," she stammered. "I don't even know who you are."

"I'm—"

She saw him look over her shoulder. Turning, she saw five black Town Cars driving through the gate at the far end of the pier.

"The mayor," Yutanda muttered. "Finally."

The motorcycle roared to a start. Before she could motion for him to stop, the rider donned his helmet and the bike sped away.

* * *

"Sweet Jesus, Yutanda, you alright? Did you get yourself to the hospital?"

Elizabeth rushed over to her daughter, wrapping her arms around her as soon as she stepped through the door of the apartment. Ed was right behind her, baby Menelik in his arms.

"Noah told us all about those punks robbing and assaulting you," Ed blurted out. "Why'd you go down to the docks alone, girl? You coulda got yourself killed," he scolded. "You got a son now; don't that mean anything to you?"

"Ed!"

Elizabeth lifted her face off her daughter's shoulder.

"Girl needs compassion right now, not scolding."

"Sorry, sorry—ain't thinkin' straight."

Reaching his hand out to touch his daughter, he drew it back when the baby started to cry.

"You just sit yourself down and I'll get you something to drink," he offered, shooting Elizabeth a concerned look. "Hush now, little Menelik," he told the baby as Menelik continued to cry. "Your momma's home now."

"Baby needs his mother," Elizabeth interjected, taking a step back to peer into Yutanda's face. "You ready to hold your son?"

"Who's Noah?" Yutanda asked, confused, taking the baby from her father's arms.

"Come sit on the couch, dear," her mother told her. "Ed, why don't you get our daughter a glass of wine, and in the meantime"—she ushered Yutanda over to the three-cushioned beige couch situated along the wall and sat down next to her—"I'll tell her about how your car was returned"—she smiled at her daughter—"as well as your keys and your purse and everything in it." A big smile breaking out on her face, Elizabeth gushed, "His name's Noah. The man who helped you today."

Clasping one of the baby's hands with both of hers, she went on.

"Noah Kunda's his full name." Nodding as though she was quite pleased, she added, "Seems like one heck of a nice man."

* * *

Claire wondered where she was and what was going to happen. It had been a week since she'd been abducted—*they'd* been abducted. And since the first day—after they had found the cross about her neck—she'd been separated from everyone. What were these men—these soldiers? What were they going to do with her? And what had they done with the children? She fingered the bracelet of green beetle carcasses around her wrist. Even though the tent they had placed her in was murky, the shells of the dead insects emitted a soft green light. She stared at them, knowing they had saved her life.

Shifting her weight to relieve the pressure on her lower back, she couldn't help but wonder how much longer she was going to be tied up. It was painful to be hunched over her knees for so long a time, hands tied to her ankles. She thought about calling out and asking to be untied, but she knew no one would care. None of the men—the soldiers—would speak to her after they'd witnessed the bracelet glow. And their leader—Bacha Alba he called himself—wasn't inclined to help her. Not after their last conversation.

*

"So you are an infidel," he had casually remarked when the men holding her yanked the collar of her tunic down to reveal the silver cross hanging around her neck. "A believer of the false god."

The men holding her shouted at her, spitting on her feet.

"I am a Sister of the Holy Cross," she defiantly told him. "I worship the teachings of Jesus Christ and those of the Father and the Holy Spirit."

"A sister, you say? Meaning nun?"

He stepped a bit closer.

"Are there others with you?"

When he grabbed her by the chin, she saw traces of lunacy in his yellow-brown eyes.

"Are you worth something, perhaps? Will someone pay to get you back?"

His breath was foul; she tried to edge away.

"Or are you a worthless whore whose only use is to do my men's bidding."

He laughed. And somehow, she'd wrenched her hand free from one of the men holding her to slap him across the face.

"*Sharmuta!*" the soldier screamed into her face.

And when one pulled a heavy knife from a sheath strapped to his leg and tried to stab her with it, she had raised her arm to block the blow. That's when the bracelet of green beetles had started to glow. The soldier's arm froze, the knife shaking in his hand.

"*Sihr,*" the man had whispered, quivering.

And then all around her she heard the same word muttered in fear.

"*Sihr.*"

But where his men seemed to be afraid of her, Bacha Alba had showed no such emotion. After briefly massaging the cheek where she'd struck him, he'd slapped her across the face with an open palm and laughed.

*

Claire awkwardly rubbed her cheek across her knee, remembering the slap, worried about the children. Every time she thought of them—what was happening to them—she couldn't block the image of the eight executed soldiers from her mind. The savagery, the mindless brutality—she'd never imagined such barbaric behavior still existed. Realizing her naïveté when she had been forced to watch each man sliced open, his head blown away. The sick atrocities human beings were capable of still lurked inside of us, she'd concluded. Satan's dark evil sin still a blemish upon man's soul, God allowing the devil's immorality to remain within the human spirit as a test of His teachings. *Perhaps, in the end,* she thought, *God will judge us by the atrocities that we've committed against one another since the beginning of our existence. Or judge us on our efforts to cleanse ourselves, rid ourselves of the Devil's influence. If that's how we are to be judged,* she observed, *judgment day will be swift and damning.*

The flap to her tent opened. A child, a girl she did not know, took a tentative step toward her, holding a plate of food in her outstretched hands. Claire watched her eyes focus upon the bracelet of green beetles, fear on her face.

"There, child, you have nothing to be afraid of," Claire gently told her.

The girl lowered her eyes and stopped. Claire could see her trembling.

Behind the girl, Bacha Alba appeared, dressed in black and green camouflage fatigues. His deep brown face appeared black in the darkness of the tent, his yellow eyes flaming when he struck a match to light the lantern he carried. Setting the lantern on the ground, he gathered the flowing ends of his green and white keffiyeh, arranging the cloth over his shoulder. Smiling, he stepped to Claire, untying the ropes about her wrists. As she was about to speak, he drew a large flat-bladed knife from his boot and placed the tip to her lips.

"*Idda-yiddi,*" he barked, motioning the little girl forward with the knife.

Staring wide-eyed at the knife, the girl approached, holding the food out in front of her: a round of injera with a small dollop of paste in the middle.

"Bless you child," Claire said to her.

When Claire touched the little girl's hand in an effort to convey her gratitude, the girl slapped Claire's fingers and ran out of the tent.

"You are *sihr sharmuta* to her," Bacha Alba laughed. "Evil slut," he explained with a wide grin. "She is shamed to have been made to serve you."

"Where are the children who were with me?" Claire tersely asked, breaking off a piece of bread. "What have you done with them?"

"Eat," Bacha told her as he scratched at his scraggly beard. "They no longer need concern you. Most have already been moved."

Claire stopped chewing.

"The rest leave in the morning."

"Leave? Where?" she asked him, her voice rising. "What have you done with them?"

Bacha studied the tip of his knife, tilting it one way and then the other, watching the reflection of the lantern's flame on the steel blade.

"Who can say where? Sudan, Uganda, Somalia—perhaps somewhere closer," he told her, shrugging. "Wherever the traders have buyers waiting."

"Thomas!" she gasped, her eyes going wide. "Dear God, what have you done?"

She threw her food it at him, but the man turned his head to the side, the bread and paste flying harmlessly by. He laughed.

"You should not waste what has been given," he lectured. "You can always be forced to eat," he went on, his voice becoming harsh. "There are ways to coerce you to do many things. As, perhaps, your new owner will make you aware of."

He sat down opposite her, crossing his legs.

"But, if I find that you are worth more to someone who may be searching for you, you will not need to be coerced to eat or drink—or perform acts of… kindness." He chuckled. "You understand, yes? Perhaps it best you spend your time praying that someone is searching for you—your order, perhaps? Parents?"

The anger she felt turned into a painful melancholy at the mention of her family. So many years had passed since she'd seen or heard from them. Were they still alive? Had any of the letters she had written found the way to their mailbox? Had the order, the Sisters of the Holy Cross—had they ever contacted her parents to tell them she'd gone missing? Was someone searching for her? She'd never considered the possibility, her life intertwining with Teimbaka's almost from the moment she'd arrived in Africa. The drought, the famine, the misery of the world in which they—she and Teimbaka—walked was consuming, the two of them embracing the sufferings of the Ethiopian children as their own. *They* were her family now—the children—her parents forgotten. All the things flowing into her head—all the things Bacha Alba was saying—numbed her, leaving her feeling strangely empty. She stared at the bracelet around her wrist, wondering why God had placed her here.

"So I would pray if I were you," she heard him say.

"Pray," she muttered with a shake of her head. "What would you know about prayer? You and the butchers you lead."

She glared at him.

"Killing in the name of your god. It's blasphemy."

"Silence, whore! Do not speak of Allah in a tone of insolence!"

When he reached out to grasp her, the beetles began pulsating, the soft green glow radiating to a ring of blinding light. Bacha Alba withdrew his hand.

"You would be dead by now, if not for that trinket," he told her, nodding to the bracelet. "I would have shot you myself if it weren't for the simple-minded beliefs of my men. They see you as some ancient symbol that should be feared."

He ran the tip of his finger along the sharp edge of his knife, a drop of blood trickling down its shiny face.

"So I play along to keep them happy. Just as I do when it comes to the more radical beliefs they embrace."

With a puzzled look, Claire asked, "Are you saying you are not a believer in Allah?" She shook her head, her face awash with confusion. "Then why do you kill in his name?"

"Do not misunderstand what I tell you. Allahu Akbar!" he abruptly shouted. "Jihad Akbar!" he yelled.

Outside the tent, Claire could hear the answering shouts of his men. She shied away when he leaned nearer.

"I am a believer and a follower of Allah, the Blessed One," he said in a soft voice. "But the extreme doctrine that some of my men wish to follow"—he turned his head to the flaps of the tent and remained silent for a moment—"I do not consider them to be the teachings of the Prophet."

His mouth twisted as though he had placed something distasteful in it.

"But to survive, to grow an army, to become"—he paused—"profitable, I must pretend"—he shrugged, running the dull edge of the knife along her ankle—"to see things as they do."

Claire pulled her bound feet toward her body.

"Surely you know that you will burn in hell for what you have done. Your soul—if you have one—is drenched in the blood of Satan. Even your Allah would recognize this. And for what? What end is it you hope to reach with your slaughtering?"

Claire watched his strange, odd-colored eyes study her from head to toe. Looking down at her sandaled feet, she pulled the edges of her calf-length blue skirt closer to her ankles, twisting the frayed ends of her tunic's brown cuff before tightening the plain white scarf tied about her head.

"You were once considered pretty?" he asked. "Perhaps when you were young? I can see this, yes."

He bent forward and grabbed her forearms. When she tried to jerk away, he slapped her. Stunned, she didn't think to react when he retied the ropes around her wrists.

"You see," he said. "Your trinket cannot really protect you. It is only a belief that makes it seem as though it can. Like religion, yes?" he asked, shoving her arms down toward the ground. "When many believe, it is strong, can move mountains—so we are led to believe."

He smiled.

"But if a few believers begin to doubt, the belief—the religion—weakens. And weakness here," he went on, motioning to what lay outside the flaps of the tent, "is quickly devoured." Rising slowly to his feet, he looked down at her and said, "So all the things you say are 'awash with the blood of the Devil,' I see as a means to strengthen a belief that is needed to keep control in my hands. Once I have grown an army, when I have bought the weapons I need, I will take as much land and wealth as I can claim. Drugs, ivory, women, children—whatever money is needed to accomplish this— this is the ending that will be, the ending that leads to a beginning."

Taking a step to leave, he stopped and turned.

"So pray", he told her again. "And eat," he laughed. "Because if I need to sell you, you will not fetch the price that one should pay for a woman with white skin. But perhaps, perhaps if I receive some word"—he nodded to himself—"soon, for your sake, that someone is willing to pay for your return, then we will need to come to some understanding, you and I. For if you are worth more money than a common whore, you will be with us for some time yet, I would think." Winking at her as he pushed the flap of the tent back, he added, "I do not much care for women as skinny as you."

She could see his yellow eyes looking her over.

"Yes, you need fattening up," he said laughing. "*Sihr sharmuta*—we will speak again."

* * *

Sarah welcomed the burning shards of pain shooting up through her knees. The rough, unfinished cement of the utility room floor was hard and unforgiving—the very reason she had chosen it. The more pain she could inflict upon her body, the more her body would be cleansed.

She had been praying in the lightless box of a room of unfinished cinder block walls in the basement of the Solitude of the Savior for three nights, ever since Dirk Savage had met with Reverend Mother. Pain and prayer her focus—pain and prayer—for whenever her thoughts strayed from those two manifestations and wandered to the image of Dirk Savage, a warm wetness materialized in her loins. And she couldn't have that, wouldn't allow it. She was too close, she knew, too close to undertaking her final vows. Sexual yearnings at this point in attaining Perpetual Commitment to the order were unwanted and unwelcomed. So she prayed for clarity, her sexual urgings troublesome and confusing. Her sex drive had been dormant since her sophomore year in high school when—no, she told herself, she wouldn't remember. But nonetheless, the existence of any impure thoughts at this juncture of attaining sisterhood was something she would need to rid herself of. No matter how the presence of the man affected her. She wasn't an animal, she told herself. She could control how she felt, control her yearnings, control her body's wants and desires.

Penance—prayer and pain—these were the paths to purity, to the safe embrace, the love and teachings of the Blessed Mother. She would adhere to her penance and conquer the adolescent surges of lust welling inside her. She would not allow them to take control, because sexual desire only led to sin.

But still, as the pain in her knees reached the point where tears formed in her eyes, she could not keep herself from thinking about the morning that lay just ahead. At ten o'clock, Dirk Savage was set to return to the Solitude of the Savior and learn what Reverend Mother had found out about Sister Claire.

Squeezing her thighs tightly together, she pushed in on them until every muscle in her lower body trembled. But try as she might, the warm wetness between her legs remained. Making a fist, she savagely punched herself in the groin. Bursting into tears, she crumpled to the cold, harsh cement.

* * *

"*Qu'est-ce que vous faites?*"

Dirk turned his head and whispered, "To the toilet. Go back to sleep."

Claudine made a soft groaning sound and pushed her head further into her pillow. "Oh," he thought he heard her moan, but he wasn't sure.

Rolling out of the queen-size bed, he pulled the sheet and blanket back up over the woman's smooth bare buttocks. Stepping across the wooden floor to the small en suite bathroom, he quietly pulled the door close behind him. With a sigh, he shuffled over to the sink and twisted both faucets on, adjusting the flow of hot and cold.

Using the small amount of light coming through the bathroom's circular window, he grabbed a washcloth from the towel rack and placed it beneath the warm running water. When the cloth was soaked all the way through, he wrung most of the excess water out and applied the cloth to his penis, giving the skin of his shaft a good cleansing before running the washcloth through his pubic hair. Not quite satisfied, he rinsed the washcloth out, repeating the whole procedure over. After he was done, he felt the skin of his flaccid penis with the fingers of his free hand. Satisfied, he nodded.

"Now we're ready for the morning fuck," he whispered, smiling down at his manhood.

Stretching his arms up over his shoulders, he gave a contented sigh and peered out the window. It had been a good—no, it had been a great three days, he thought to himself. Claudine was everything he'd hoped she would be—eager, adventuresome, hungry; the sex was great, especially for a woman her age. *Surely she's in her late thirties*, he told himself. *Who says the younger the better?* Claudine proved that notion a big lie. Except for her hairy underarms, Dirk thought she was almost perfect. *God, did she know how to do some wonderfully nasty things.*

But it was time to go.

Whatever Reverend Mother would reveal this morning about the woman who'd written the letters Bin'ka had given him, it was time to move on. He was broke, in debt, his gear—cameras, typewriters, clothes, boxes of photographs, and what little worldly possessions he still owned—back in Djibouti. Held as collateral with Akmir and the Consortium.

The Consortium—dear God, how'd he end up involved with them? They had him by the balls and were pulling the leash tethered around his testicles, demanding he return. The not-so-veiled warning in Akmir's voice on the phone the day before had made the point abundantly clear. The Consortium—Akmir—wanted answers. What was it about this Claire woman they were so interested in? He still couldn't quite grasp the reasons. Perhaps the whole scenario would become clearer after the morning's meeting with Reverend Mother. At least he hoped the reasons would be clearer. Thinking back to the phone call with Akmir, he was afraid of what would happen to him if Reverend Mother didn't have something of interest for him to report.

*

"What has this holy woman told you about the girl who wrote the letters?" Akmir had barked over the phone.

"She's not a holy woman," Peter had scoffed. "She's a just nun—a dried-up old prune. She just goes by Reverend Mother."

"Why must you always be so argumentative? You quibble over non-sense. Tell me what you have learned."

Akmir had sounded agitated.

"Well, first off, there really isn't a nunnery here, if that's what you call it. They use this place as a retreat. It was fortunate that this Reverend Mother lady was even here. It's just her and some novice nun she brought along with her. They're on a pilgrimage or whatever, paying homage to their patron, or founder, or something along those lines. Some priest or saint or something. There's a shrine to him here. Father Moreau, I think his name is."

"You're running off at the mouth," Akmir had curtly interrupted. "Stick to the woman."

"She was—the reverend lady—reluctant at first. Very suspicious. Can't say I blame her. Strange man shows up out of the blue and inquires about some nun she knows nothing about. A mysterious nun at that, who's written some letters from a country they don't even have a mission in, or a clinic or a school for that matter."

The silence on the other end of the telephone line had made him squirm.

"But I used my boyish charm—"

"Do you wish me to tell the warlord Abdi of your improprieties with one of his wives?"

"Okay, okay, okay—Jesus, Akmir. I'm getting to it."

"Then proceed!"

"She made a few phone calls while I was there. It took a little doing—evening vespers or whatever—but she finally got through to one of the orders in the U.S. Apparently there was a Claire Waterman who began her discernment at their Kensington, Maryland, location—that's one of the states in the United States by the way—some twenty years ago. But most of the nuns who were there back then are gone, and the one who was the

Reverend Mother at that time has passed away. So they didn't have all the facts on the girls who've been indoctrinated there right at their fingertips. They said it would take a day or so to research their files."

"I am writing the note of your infidelity as we speak."

"But they're calling back with all the information they have on the girl early tomorrow morning!" he rushed to say. "I have a meeting with Reverend Mother scheduled for ten in the morning! So I'll have the information then!"

"Which wife was it? Ah, yes, I remember. Nebet, the Egyptian girl."

"Akmir, Akmir! Hey, are you there?" Dirk had yelled into the phone.

He could hear Akmir laughing through the receiver.

"Come on. I'll call you by noon Paris time, okay? Are you going to be there—in your office? I'll have to call you collect since I don't have a phone at my disposal. But I'll know everything there is to know about this Waterman woman by then. One way or another, I guess."

There had been a long silence.

"Akmir—you there? Are you listening to me? Noontime tomorrow, okay—okay?"

After a long pause, Akmir had replied with one word. And it was uttered coldly.

"Noon."

And then the line had gone dead. He'd set the phone down and sighed. Noon. Fuck.

*

Cupping running water into his hands, Dirk splashed some on his face. Turning off the faucets, he grabbed a hand towel. He still didn't get it—the urgency to know about this Claire woman. And he was normally pretty sharp about what motivated people. But he couldn't quite see the angle Akmir was playing. He wondered if—and what—Adiam knew about all of this nun crap, and wondered if it didn't have something to do with the power struggle he'd heard was taking place between Akmir and Adiam. A few hours from now, they'd all know, he guessed. And then *he* would know if there was something in all this nun business for *him*, something he could use for his own purposes.

"*Coq?*"

Claudine's voice seemed far away through the closed door.

"*J'ai besoin de toi.*"

Looking down at his already stiffening penis, he whispered, "She needs us."

Vive la France, he thought. *Vive la France!*

* * *

The sound of millions upon millions of beetle wings opening and closing produced a continuous buzz, like that of a dozen electrical transformers bristling with current. Having traveled upriver—northward—the beetles reached a point where they could see and sense the opposite bank. But the current ran swift at the narrowing, the water choppy, swirling, rising and falling as it gushed through a shallow gorge. To cross, the insects would need to fly—there was no other way.

One by one the beetles opened their elytra, stretching out their thin back wings. One beetle near the front of the swarm—somewhat larger, but indistinguishable from the rest of the beetles in every other aspect—rose into the air and flew forward. Keeping low, the beetle was halfway across the river when the currents of air swirling above the rushing water pushed its body upward before pulling it sharply down. The beetle crashed into the gurgling river and was instantly swept away. Undeterred, two more beetles lifted off and flew forward only to meet the same fate as the first. The buzzing from the impatient insects waiting to cross the river rose to a crescendo, shimmering torsos shifting from side to side, several lifting off the ground, hovering before setting back down.

Sensors located in the beetles' feet and abdomen detected tremors in the ground long before the elephant appeared. When they saw the massive form heading toward them, they—as a single entity—moved back from the edge of the riverbank. Spellbound, sensors searching for stimuli, the beetles watched the lumbering beast struggle to balance a fifteen-foot sapling lodged between its tusks and trunk. Approaching the riverbank, the elephant tossed the sapling up and outward. The beetles' roaring buzz subsided as each end of the slender tree came to rest on solid ground on opposite sides of the river. Grunting, shaking bits of bark and soil from its trunk, the elephant turned to leave, beetles swarming across the tree bridge as soon as the beast took a step away.

4

"WHY'D THE MOTHERFUCKER have to break my fuckin' wrist, man?"

"Maybe 'cause you swung your blade out at him, fool."

"Well, I was pissed. That kick to my knee hurt like shit. Fuckin' kung fu shit."

Rue laughed, brushing aside the thick black bangs hanging over his eyebrows.

"Twister's right," Rue told the young man seated across from him, the one sporting a brand new white plaster cast on his left arm. "The deal was to scare the bitch and then get out of there."

"Always gotta be the tough guy, right, Bongo?" Twister gibed, taking a swig of beer from the bottle of Bud in front of him. "Maybe you'll just stick to the plan next time." Bongo's mouth twisted into a sneer.

"Guess you won't be usin' that arm for a while," the third young man seated at the table sarcastically added.

"Fuck you, Griper," Bongo spit. "Fuck all yous."

"How'd you three end up together?" Rue asked, shaking his head. "Must have been some crazy-ass alignment in the universe the day you all met."

A very large body appeared behind Rue's shoulder, setting a tray of beers and shots down in the middle of the table where the four men were seated.

"Four Crowns with beer chasers," the very large man announced. "Add it to your tab, Mr. Super Freak?" The man looked down at the three younger men seated at the table and chuckled. "Or you want I should shake the cash out of these boys?"

Rue turned his head and smiled up at the six-foot-seven, three-hundred-and-twenty-pound mass of girth and muscle.

"Yeah, Goliath, my tab, if you would," Rue replied, flicking the long black hair of his wig back over his shoulders. "They've had a rough day."

Goliath studied the three young men in matching red bandanas, black leather vests, and dark sunglasses, and smirked.

"Put your empties on the tray," he ordered. "Be back to clear when I get time." Giving Twister, Bongo, and Griper a dismissive look, he shook his head. "Always a pleasure, Mr. Super Freak," he said to Rue.

When Goliath left, Rue lifted a tumbler of Crown Royal from the tray and raised it in the air.

"To a job well done," he toasted. "Drink up."

* * *

Yutanda was just about finished warming up Menelik's baby formula when her phone rang.

"Already?" she complained, looking at the bright blue clock mounted on the wall above the breakfast nook in her small kitchen. "Who's calling at six in the morning?"

Setting the bottle back in the pot of hot water, she moved the pot from the stove to the countertop. She shifted Menelik to her right arm and lifted the receiver on the fourth ring.

"Hello?" she said.

"I'm sorry for calling this early."

She wasn't sure she recognized the voice. Was it the guy on the motorcycle? What did her mother say his name was? Noah?

"Did I wake you?"

"No," she replied. "I—um—I never—um—"

"I just wanted to make sure you were all right. I hope you don't mind me calling. Your mother gave me your number when your parents invited me in yesterday."

She listened to him talk, uncertain what to say.

"So are you—okay? You know, after a fall, sometimes the next day you hurt where you didn't the night before."

Yutanda found herself staring at the wall, shaking her head.

"I guess I should introduce myself," she heard him go on. "My name's

Noah, Noah Kunda. I'm the guy who was on the motorcycle yesterday—at the docks. Do you remember? Do you even remember being at the docks yesterday? Have you seen a doctor?"

Menelik started to squirm and whine.

"Look, Noah, it's really nice of you to call," she found herself saying. "But I really can't talk right now. I'm feeding my son. I feel awful for not being able to thank you for—for saving me. I'm still in a bit of shock over it all."

"I understand, Yutanda."

"You know my name?"

"Well, sure, I sort of had to look through your belongings to be able to return your keys and such."

His voice was smooth and easy to listen to, she noticed.

"Oh, of course, how stupid—"

"Hey, it's all right. I know yesterday couldn't have been—wasn't a pleasant experience. I just wanted to make sure you were safe. I wasn't able to catch those three gang members. They ran off when I cornered them at a dead-end street. Not sure if they were Five Percenters or Bloods. I don't know too much about the gangs down there anymore."

"Gangs?"

"Yeah, some gangs have a pretty strong influence on the docks. Before my younger brother got his act together, he was almost pulled into one. He says they're still around. He sees them whenever he ships out on a freighter at the seaport."

Yutanda's mind started to whir. Gangs, crime, crack cocaine, heroin; a piece of the puzzle she was trying to patch together started to fall into place.

"Noah, look, you really don't know me, but I would very much like to—"

She had to cut herself off as Menelik started to wail.

"Look, I have to go," she almost yelled into the phone as she shifted Menelik into her other arm. "Can we meet?"

Menelik started squirming to the point where she needed both hands to hold him. She barely got the receiver balanced between her shoulder and her ear.

"Noah," she hurried to say. "I'm scheduled to be at a photo op at the

Metropolitan Museum, at the new African art exhibit that's opening. Could you meet me there at noon today? I realize it's a—"

Menelik screamed so loud into her free ear that Yutanda let the phone fall to the floor. Just before it landed with a loud crack, she heard Noah's voice say, "Sure."

* * *

Teimbaka didn't like people eating elephant meat. Knowing spirit elephants existed made the thought of killing an elephant for food disheartening. But these three men—they'd called themselves rangers—he supposed he couldn't hold it against them. Better the murdered animal was utilized for something good, he reasoned. Better than letting it rot. But as he watched the three men cooking the meat, he still didn't much like what they were doing. But he was curious about them—about these rangers. What were they going to do with the tusks they'd harvested from the animal? Where were they taking them? He'd watched them from the grove of trees after they climbed out of their vehicle. Confused as to why they hadn't made a real attempt to follow him. Maybe it was the weapons, he supposed, or the lack of powerful ones. How did these three men stop poachers from harvesting ivory when all they were armed with was an old jeep and three rifles? When the poachers—at least the ones he had seen—had a helicopter and automatic weapons and who knows what else?

Careful not to make any sudden movements that might cause the dried grass to snap, he slithered beneath the frame of the ranger's vehicle, pulling the folds of his shamma above his head. When he sensed he was safe, he took a furtive peek at what lay in front of him.

The campsite fire was large. He could feel the heat radiating on his face. At least these rangers knew they needed a large fire. Teimbaka gave them credit for that. Out in the middle of the bush, hyenas, lions, jackals—even packs of wild dogs—hunted and scavenged for food; the night was filled with danger. And the aroma of roasting elephant meat was a strong lure. Predators and scavengers would certainly have picked up the scent long before he had. Anticipating the men cooking the meat they'd butchered from the dead animal, he'd taken the precaution of rolling in dirt and elephant feces. His scent putrid, he knew he'd be safe. Good Claire wasn't with him, he thought. She would not be pleased by his odor.

He thought of her then, Claire: where she was, what she was doing—if she was safe. John Too had been worried. And where was *he*, he wondered? Why hadn't he awakened him before he left? He hoped the boy was with Claire now, keeping her safe.

"Do you think they'll follow?"

Teimbaka emptied his mind as a man spoke, the voice sounding uncertain, afraid. Teimbaka studied the profile of the ranger he could see in the fire's half-light. The man's features—smooth skin, no stubble or beard—conveyed youth.

"Hard to say what they will do, Kamua. But I don't think they will. Retrieving two tusks is not worth their time. They could have ten elephants down by the time it would take them to track us and—"

Teimbaka saw the man nearest him, the one with his back to the jeep, shrug his shoulders. It must be he talking, he reasoned. Teimbaka wondered what the man meant: What would happen if the poachers did track the three rangers and find them? Would the poachers kill them over two elephant tusks?

"Not *could*, Selam," another voice interjected.

Teimbaka couldn't see the man speaking. He must be sitting opposite the one named Selam, he observed.

"You mean, *would*. It is as Selam says, Kamua, they won't bother with us. There are too many elephants to kill and too much ivory to be had. We would bring them nothing but a price on their heads."

"Not that that would deter them," he heard the one named Selam say.

There was silence then, filled by the crackle of wood. Sparks rose into the darkness. Someone must have placed another log on the fire, Teimbaka reasoned.

"Is the meat ready?"

"Soon," Selam replied. "Soon."

"I'm so hungry," the younger sounding of the three said. "The smell of it is making me crazy."

"I am sure the smell of our food has attracted others who feel the same as you do, Kamua. Best keep our rifles close tonight," Selam advised.

"And best keep it with you, boy, when you go to take a piss. And god help you if you need to squat for a shit."

Teimbaka struggled to keep from chuckling as the three men burst out laughing.

"Good advice, Tengene," Selam managed to say. "Nothing worse than being in the midst of passing a load when a lion happens upon you!" he exclaimed in jest.

"Make you wish you had remained in Kenya if that happens, Kamua."

It was the man he couldn't see—Tengene—who spoke. And as soon as the words left his mouth, the joyfulness of the moment abruptly ended.

"I am sorry, Kamua. I— I was stupid."

Teimbaka lowered his head to the ground as the youngest of the three stood and looked into the darkness. In the wavering light, he recognized the expression on the young man's face. It was one he had seen many times before: the look of one who is still alive remembering those who've been taken. Out of the corner of his eye, as he studied the young man's face, he saw the figure of the man he had not yet seen stand and take a step toward Kamua.

"It's alright, Tengene," Kamua told him, stretching an arm out behind him as though keeping something away. "I am not a boy any longer. The memory does not render me useless as it used to."

"I didn't mean—" Tengene started to say.

"It is why I left there," Kamua told him as he turned to face him. "I will not go back until I have found the butchers who— I will avenge the slaughter of my village."

Teimbaka saw the face of Kamua harden, the expression reminding him of John when the boy had returned from his travel in Mek'ele.

"Maybe some of the poachers we were chasing today are part of those who did the killing," Kamua coldly offered.

No one spoke for a time, Teimbaka thinking there were no words to ease the pain Kamua seemed to be feeling.

"It could be, yes, Selam?"

As Kamua turned to look at the man seated some ten yards in front of where Teimbaka was hiding, Teimbaka felt the boy's eyes pass over him.

"It's already dangerous work we do, Kamua. You know this. We are outnumbered a hundred to one and ill equipped to take on the poachers we happen to catch. Our rifles," he said, grabbing hold of a carbine and shaking it, "are no match for automatic weapons and helicopters and grenade launchers. It would be suicide to seek out the encampments of warlords and mercenaries."

"I am not afraid to die," Kamua bravely stated.

"An easy statement to make when you are young," Tengene responded. "When you feel indestructible. But what good would your death do? Think, Kamua. Who would remain to carry on the fight, remember those who were killed if you are gone?"

Teimbaka watched the younger man's chin drop to his chest, the ghosts of the children from the camp of Sister Lady suddenly wailing inside his head. Reminding him they were still part of him, waiting to be avenged.

"Sit, Kamua," Selam said. "The meat is ready. Tomorrow promises to be another long and dangerous day."

"And I am starving," Tengene added with a clap of his hands as he squatted back down close to the fire.

But Kamua didn't move to join them, turning his face to peer into the darkness.

"I know where you look."

It was Selam who spoke. Teimbaka shifted his eyes to the man's back.

"Last reported by headquarters, the poachers move their camp across the border of Sudan whenever they wish, depending on the movement of the elephants. Scores of carcasses spotted the last time the observation plane flew over the area. But that was a month ago, before its engine locked up."

Kamua remained staring into the night, saying nothing.

"We'll head that way tomorrow."

Kamua turned with a smile.

"But only to observe. We can't do too much else."

"Still," Kamua said.

"Remember why you were brought on, Kamua," Tengene interjected. "Our purpose is to protect elephants, not engage a small army of poachers."

"Are they not the same?" Kamua shot back.

"No, they are not," Selam firmly told him. "Perhaps one day—when our numbers are greater and we are equally outfitted with weapons—perhaps then we will be able to put an end to the killing."

Teimbaka saw Kamua's head tilt downward. He could sense the young man's frustration.

"Sit. Eat. Tomorrow we go westward, closer to the Sudanese border.

Perhaps we will get lucky," Tengene continued. "Perhaps we will stumble upon a few and make a few arrests as we almost did today."

"That would be our only hope, Kamua," Selam concurred. "To take them a few at a time."

Teimbaka watched Kamua's head nod. When he heard the clink of steel on steel, he looked back at Selam.

"Now—are you ready to eat?" Selam asked Kamua as the blade of his drawn knife glittered with the light of the fire.

Smacking the dull side of the knife against the barrel of his rifle, he produced the clinking noise once more.

"So sit while you are able."

Teimbaka watched his back begin to shake when he started to laugh.

"Because after we eat—you have first watch."

As he listened to the good-natured laughter passing between the men, Teimbaka focused on what Selam had said. Scores of elephants killed, a small army of poachers with an encampment near the Sudanese border. Looking westward from his hiding place, he found the ethereal form of the baby spirit elephant standing alone in the darkness some twenty paces from where he lay. Quietly, as swiftly as the dried grass would allow, he crawled backward. When he reached the area where he had left his weapons, he gathered them and moved off to join the young spirit beast.

* * *

John Too watched the last of the trucks pulling out of the warlord's camp, his stomach churning. Some of the children he'd watched loaded into the trucks he knew, others he did not. But he could tell each child was scared. Could see fear on their faces. Hear it in their crying. He wanted to follow the trucks, to help the children. At one point, scrambling out from the cover of the rock formation he was hiding behind before John grabbed hold of him and pulled him back. But now, as his eyes lingered on the last departing truck, he felt empty, the numbing, hollow feeling growing stronger as he listened to the sound of the vehicle's engine slowly fade to nothing.

"Look," John whispered.

John Too followed John's gaze to the camp below. A small figure was making its way across the open compound, carrying what looked to be a cup and a plate.

"A girl," John Too said in a soft voice. "She came from over there," he told John, pointing a finger at one of the larger tents erected around the perimeter of the camp. "It must be where food is stored."

John grunted.

As the girl slowly made her way toward one of the smaller tents located on the far side of camp, John Too surveyed the surrounding terrain.

East, the edge of a valley stretched back to the highlands, the ground between the ridgelines fertile, much of it sectioned into cultivated rectangles of browns and greens. North, following the tract the trucks had taken, a curving snake of a dirt road twisted through an array of hills and rocky gorges. To the south lay a level stretch of open land with groupings of trees bordered by an east-running ridge, an elevated line of green grass with outcroppings of striking gray stones. To the west, a steep cliff arose against the base of a solitary mountain, the hint of a winding trail—silver in color from John Too's vantage point—originating at the base. A tent, equipped with a communication antenna, sat just right of the trail's mouth.

Letting his gaze drift up the face of the cliff, John Too wondered if the trail didn't mask hiding places where marksman had been posted to stand watch. If there were marksmen, he reasoned, it would mean the camp was guarded on all sides. For north, south, and east, sandbagged bunkers had been erected, each containing a mounted, long-barreled machine gun, two soldiers stationed with each weapon. John Too glanced at his bow and then looked at John's impala horn. He shook his head.

"How many do you think?" John whispered.

John Too looked at him and shrugged. "Too many," he replied. "Four went with each of the three trucks." He peeked over the boulder. "At least thirty or more left in camp."

John turned the impala horn over in his hand and frowned.

"Look," John Too said.

A man dressed in dark camouflage fatigues stepped out of a tent, holding open the flap for the girl carrying the cup and plate. When the girl entered, the man followed. A moment later, John Too saw the flap lifted upward, the man backing out the entrance holding the end of a rope. When the girl who'd brought the plate and cup reemerged right after, the man handed her the rope and stepped away.

"Claire!" John hissed.

John Too studied the hunched-over woman led from the tent, wrists bound by the rope the girl held. The woman moved stiffly, her steps slow, her hands placed to her brow, shading her eyes.

"We must go to her."

As John moved to rise, John Too reached over, placing a hand on his shoulder.

"We must wait until dark," John Too told him, pressing down on John's shoulder to keep him in place. "I have thought of a way."

John raised his face to the sky and howled like a wounded hyena.

* * *

Dirk tried to remember every detail of his conversation with Reverend Mother as the driver of the truck he was sitting in droned on. It had been a long, roundabout way to get to the regional airport outside of Le Mans. But the ride was free—sort of—the scenery beautiful. Squinting, he glimpsed swaths of vibrant greens fields and woodlands while pretending to be asleep. He would have preferred sitting upright to admire the countryside between Le Mans and Orléans with open eyes, but Claudine's friend couldn't keep quiet. Pointing out every detail of the passing terrain or relating worthless bits of information about villages and towns they drove by. So after a few pleasantries were exchanged at the trip's outset—Dirk using his best attempt at speaking French—Dirk pretended to fall asleep. But the man—Jean was his name—kept rambling on. Trying to concentrate on the conversation he'd had with Reverend Mother was difficult. But he was giving it his best shot. He had to. His future depended on it.

*

"It seems as though, when her parents did not receive word from her after several months had passed, the father became so distraught he suffered a stroke. He died from a successive aneurysm two days later. The mother, apparently, went through—and is still suffering from—some type of shock and has been in seclusion ever since."

"Excuse me, Reverend Mother, but isn't that—doesn't that seem like a long time to you, to be in shock? I mean it's been what, fifteen years?"

Reverend Mother slipped her rounded, wire-framed glasses down her nose with an audible sigh.

"It's not my place to make a judgment of that nature, Mr. Savage," she told him.

"Please, call me Dirk."

"Dirk, then," she replied, clearing her throat. "I'm only relaying to you what was said to me. Shall I continue? Or do you wish to pick apart every detail as I give it to you?"

"My apologies, Reverend Mother," he had been quick to say. "Please continue."

Before Reverend Mother went on, Dirk glanced over his shoulder to see Sister Sarah staring at him. *Hasn't she ever seen a man before?* he remembered wondering. *God, she must be a sheltered one*, he thought. He supposed they all were.

"As I was saying, the mother has been a virtual recluse since her husband's death. But she still makes contact with the sisters in Maryland through an attorney in Philadelphia. From what I was told, the attorney has been trying to locate Sister Claire—Claire Waterman—since her father's passing—to no avail up to this point. There is a matter of a trust fund her father set up for her right after she was accepted into her time of Novitiate."

"I'm sorry, Reverend Mother, novitiate or novice? Are they the same thing? I'm not certain what that term means in this context."

"Novitiate is a very important time in the process of giving oneself over to a life with God, the final step in attaining a life devoted to chastity, poverty, and obedience, Mr. Savage. It is when the congregation learns— and the novice comes to understand—if she is ready to live a contemplative, apostolic lifestyle and follow the essential elements set forth in the order's constitution."

"So, it's just not as simple as saying you want to become a nun, then. A girl, a woman, has to go through some sort of process?"

Sister Sarah snickered behind him. Reverend Mother gave the girl a withering look.

"No, it is not as simple as just saying you want to become a nun, Mr., um, Dirk," Reverend Mother had replied with a slight shake of her head and a clear note of disdain in her voice. Before she continued, Dirk noticed her eyebrows twitch.

"It is actually a series of steps, a time of learning and reflection that can last, for some," she pointedly remarked with a glance toward Sister Sarah, "as long as ten or twelve years, until the time of Perpetual Commitment is bestowed. But we are straying from the point, are we not?"

They had been standing in the middle of a walkway running through the center of the manicured grounds behind the Solitude, as Reverend Mother referred to the compound. The sun had come out from behind a cloud. Dirk remembered squinting to keep the woman's face in focus. He remembered gesturing to her with an open palm to continue.

"She was nineteen at the time, as far as the records of the Kensington order state. And her father—a man of some prominent wealth—wanted to make certain Sister Claire—his daughter—was well provided for in case of unforeseen changes to the family's state of health or the possibility of her devotion to the order, shall we say, faltering when the time of her Perpetual Commitment arrived."

Dirk remembered reminding himself to keep his mouth closed as the Reverend Mother looked at him before continuing.

"From what the Kensington order has told me, the trust is awaiting her signature for the funds to be released to her. As the sum is substantial— over several million dollars now, with accrued interest—the attorney handling the transaction is requiring the signature of Claire Waterman to be given in his presence. Therefore, Sister Claire must return to America before the trust will be released to her. As to what she will do with the funds after her signature is applied to the required documents, that is not the attorney's concern."

"Several million dollars? That's quite a sum."

Dirk looked around for a moment, losing himself in the pristine lawns and hedges of the Solitude's gardens while trying to process everything flowing through his mind.

"And what if she can't be found?" he'd asked. "Or what if she has met some terrible ending?"

The Reverend Mother had taken a moment to scrutinize him then. He could see her eyes trying to discern just who he was and what he really wanted.

"If Sister Claire—from what was relayed to me—has been taken into the Lord's kingdom, the trust reverts back to her mother. If she can't be found, or won't return to America, the trust will remain as is, in a state of limbo, until such time Claire Waterman is decreed deceased and her mother also declared as such. If that were to be the case, the father has willed the trust to some sort of foxhunt association."

She had shaken her head at that and frowned.

"I will tell you, Mr. Savage—"

"Dirk—please."

"I will tell you, Mr. Savage."

Was she telling him to shut up? he thought. He watched her face flush with a tinge of red before she continued.

"The Order would very much like to see her return. And if you could facilitate that in any way, they would be deeply indebted to you for providing them with the means that would so greatly help those in need—both in America and throughout the world."

"I don't understand. Providing them with the means?"

Reverend Mother had taken off her glasses at that point and took a deep breath. She closed her eyes for a moment. When she opened them again, they were focused, clear as the next words she spoke.

"Sister Claire, if she is found to still be in good standing with the order, has committed herself to a life of service and poverty. If this indeed is still what she wishes for her life to be, then the order will be supportive of her signing the documents that will release the funds. It would only go to follow, Mr. Savage, that she in turn, in the good faith and commitment to her order, would refuse the funds for personal wealth and bestow upon the order the gift of the funds to benefit the poor and needy of our world."

She had paused then, perhaps giving him time to absorb what she was saying.

"It would only go to follow, wouldn't you agree, Mr. Savage? From the two letters you have provided me with, it would appear Sister Claire has indeed embraced the doctrine of her order in the purest sense. The funds the trust could provide would well serve the children she herself has written about."

She had taken a handkerchief from the pocket of her skirt and wiped off her glasses. When she was done, she placed her glasses back on the bridge of her nose and locked her gaze onto his.

"So as I was saying, if you can facilitate the return of Sister Claire to America, you would be providing countless needful souls with a means to a better life. That is why you have come here, isn't it? You said yourself: you felt Sister Claire was in some sort of danger. So it only stands to reason you have arrived here by God's hand to help her in her plight. And in doing so, helping thousands more."

He had smiled as best he could manage and nodded while his thoughts raced with all the possibilities that had just been placed before him.

"You mentioned in our previous meeting there is another letter describing where she can be found? Is that letter in your possession?" she'd asked.

*

"*Aéroport Le Mans-Arnage.*"

Dirk opened his eyes and pretended to stretch. As the truck pulled up to the small regional airport, he grabbed hold of his travel bag and said a quick "*Merci.*" Without looking back at Jean, he climbed out of the cab, swung the door shut behind him, and walked to the airport office.

* * *

Chris Mason ran a pencil-thin beam of light one final time over the array of colored wires and fuses before closing the metal door and securing the padlock. Dressed in a red bandana, black leather vest, and sunglasses, he looked just like the three young men Rue had hired to scare Yutanda Taylor-Arbagna.

That was his hope, anyway—if a cop or one of Rue's flunkies saw him fooling around the back of the building housing Rue's office—that he fit the description of one of the three punks who had assaulted the assembly-woman on the docks. Nothing to make the cops think—or Rue Thompson think—he was anything but a troublemaking loser up to no good, just another young strung-out nigger hanging around an alley looking for a score.

Chris flicked off his flashlight and grunted. *Troublemaking nigger,* how many times had he heard that phrase used? But when he pictured the three idiots he'd scuffled with on the dock, he nodded. *Apt description,* he thought, *three brainless punks in over their heads.* Why the one had tried to slash him, he didn't understand. *Stupid,* he thought. Nobody was supposed to get hurt. That was the plan. But maybe the broken wrist would smarten the boy up a little. Fat chance of that happening, he knew. Boy as reckless as that had little hope of getting smarter anytime soon. Idiot would be dead in a year or two, he figured. But that was the boy's problem, not his. His problem was Yutanda Taylor-Arbagna—and subsequently, Rue Thompson.

As Chris saw it, Rue Thompson was no different from the warlords, corporate spies, crime lords, and various governments he had worked for since walking away from his stint in the Foreign Legion. Having spent a few years in one of the Legion's elite squadrons based in Africa, Chris had come to understand the complexities involved in reaching clear objectives. Oft times, what appeared a simple operation turned out to be anything but. Certainly, in this case involving Yutanda Taylor-Arbagna, there was more going on than Rue Thompson was letting on. Wanting information on her movements? Chris scoffed. That could easily be accomplished by planting a bug in her phone. Why risk hiring him to "befriend" the woman, as Rue put it? People left trails. Fingerprints, license plate number, address, make of car, height, weight, color of eyes, a misspoken word about who they were pretending to be. Hiring him to do a job a wiretap could accomplish was a recipe for disaster, as far as he was concerned. And he planned on being one step ahead of any unforeseen disaster—two if he could manage. With that thought in mind, he diligently wiped down the padlock and telephone box for any fingerprints he might have left.

"Why you disrespectin' our colors, man?"

The voice was young, full of bravado.

"We don't wear no fucking leather vests," a different voice spit.

Chris wondered how many men were standing behind him.

"And sunglasses? Sheeeeit—ain't none of us wear those, 'specially at night. You blind or somethin', fool?"

Okay, there were at least three. He wondered what weapons they were carrying.

"Nothin' to say?"

It was the first voice again, directly behind him—the leader of the group? He'd know soon enough.

"Maybe the man just sayin' his last prayers, is all. Maybe he tryin' not to shit himself."

There was laughter then—from five, maybe six men, he guessed.

"Ain't no reason in the world you all need to stop to hassle me," Chris said, purposely keeping his back to the group. "You might just want to be cool, continue on what you're doing—let me do the same."

He spoke in a calm, level voice. He wasn't out to antagonize anybody. He didn't need any trouble. He hoped they might take his advice.

"Fuck you, man."

So much for hope, he thought.

"Turn around, bitch boy," a different voice barked.

"Fuckin' wearin' the colors on your head. But you ain't no Blood. Got some sissy-ass vest on. You tryin' to make the brotherhood look like fags?"

Chris heard the distinct click of a switchblade before another voice snapped, "You need yourself a lesson in protocol, nigger."

Chris whirled, pouncing on the man holding the knife. Grabbing the man's wrist, he twisted, thrusting sideways, the blade plunging into the man's opposite forearm. Gripping the hilt of the knife, he pulled it from the man's bleeding arm. A slash left and then back to the right left two more gang members grabbing their shoulders, crying out in pain. Crouching, coiling his body, he launched himself into the air, delivering a crushing heel-to-cheekbone kick, sending a fourth gang member flying backward, the man's body landing with a thud, skull cracking against cement. A flicker of movement out of the corner of his eye brought him tumbling forward. After rolling twice to his right, he rose up off the pavement and threw the switchblade, the knife finding the gunman's hand, the tip of the blade protruding from the man's palm as the gun dropped to the ground. Before any of the wounded gang members moved, Chris leaped to the gun, one hand reaching for the weapon while his other grabbed the ankle of the gang member who had drawn the gun, jerking him hard off his feet. The back of the man's head collided with the asphalt, the jolt knocking him unconscious.

Ejecting the magazine clip from the Glock, Chris removed the weapon's slide, calmly eyeing the gang members. Placing the magazine clip into his vest's outer pocket, he tossed the slide bar away.

"Like I said: no need to stop and hassle me. Just here trying to make a livin'."

The three wounded gang members started toward him. Countering, Chris leaned over and pulled the switchblade out of the unconscious man's hand.

"No need to take this further," he warned. "Don't feel like killin' no one tonight."

The three hesitated, exchanging hurried glances.

"Man, who the hell you think you are?" It was the leader talking. "You be on Blood turf, wearin' Blood colors, disrespectin' us like we ain't nothin'. You know what we can do to you? You know how many brothers gonna come lookin' for your black ass?"

They started toward him again. But before they could take two steps, the switchblade flashed through the air, embedding in the leader's leg just above his knee. The man crumpled to the ground, curse words spewing from his mouth.

"Get the motherfucker!" he screamed. "Fuckin' kill the nigger!"

When Chris reached behind his back and drew out an eight-inch Bowie knife, the two remaining Bloods looked at each other and froze.

"Take a good look at me boys," he told them. "You know me? Take a hard look. Tell me if you do."

"We don't know who the fuck you are, man!" the leader barked as he pulled the switchblade out of his leg. "But I'll tell you what, asshole, I sure as—"

Before he could say another word, Chris leaped next to him, stomping a heavy black combat boot down on the man's leg directly on the knife wound. As the man opened his mouth to scream, Chris delivered a swift karate chop to his throat, leaving him gagging, gasping for air.

"Now, you know me?" he snarled at the two Bloods still standing.

"Naw," one instantly said. "We don't know you, man. Ain't never seen you before."

Chris nodded.

"Let's keep it that way," he casually advised, twisting the big Bowie knife out in front of him. "And if you ever see me around here again, just remember what you said: you don't know who the fuck I am. And even if you think you might," he said, looking at the Bowie knife and then around at the three Bloods on the ground, "remind yourself it ain't none of your concern."

With a final kick to the wounded man's leg, Chris turned and walked to the far end of the alley. There were still things he needed to do tonight. And he had an early date tomorrow.

"Coffee and croissants in the morning?" Yutanda had asked him as they had left the Metropolitan Museum.

"Perfect," he'd replied.

5

EDEN ROCKED BACK and forth, her arms wrapped around her body in an effort to stay warm. The men, the soldiers—*ebob caca*, she thought of them as—didn't want her near them. Because she was taking care of the *sihr*, as they called the woman—the witch—the one tied up in the tent, the one with the magic bracelet. So the soldiers—the snake shit—were keeping her in an unlit, drafty tent. Far from the fires they lit at night to keep themselves warm and keep predators away. Wanting nothing to do with either the girl—her—or the prisoner—the *tabib*.

Tabib; Eden rolled the word around her head. Her mother—when she had had a mother, before the soldiers had taken and sold her—had warned her of witches. From the time Eden was able to understand what her mother was saying, she would tell Eden about tabibs, how they waited for unsuspecting children who wandered alone at night, snatching them to use their body parts to cast spells. Eden had listened to the stories of tabibs wide-eyed and never wandered off on her own at night again after hearing such horrible, scary tales. *Yet, look at me now*, she thought, *far from everyone else in camp, alone, easy prey for the tabib kept a few hundred paces away.*

Ebob caca! Why did they choose me to feed the tabib and make me go with the woman when she needs to pee? Why? Why? The woman might very well materialize at any moment and cut out my heart. Ebob caca! Even you are scared of her!

She stared at the front of the tent for a moment, her mind whirring with all sorts of scary thoughts.

They're going to sacrifice me to the tabib! That is why they keep me here! She will appear while I am sleeping and cut out my innards. Ebob caca! I hate you! I hate you!

Yet, there was a small voice inside of Eden that kept trying to tell her the tabib, the woman, was not evil. *How could she be?* the tiny, silent voice inside of her asked. How can she be evil when she wears a bracelet that glows? One made out of green beetles. How did she come by them? she wondered. And what magic do the beetles hold? *And the woman's face, her eyes, her voice, they are not harsh and cruel, as evil is,* the little voice inside of her would say each time she was taken to the tabib's tent. *Just the opposite,* her voice would murmur. *See the kindness, feel the warmth, hear the softness. It is not evil that resides in this woman,* her voice told her. *Look closer, do not be afraid, open your heart.*

Shivering, Eden hugged herself as tightly as she could. Perhaps the *ebob caca* would bring her a blanket.

* * *

John used the razor-sharp tip of the impala horn to puncture the tent. Once the horn was inserted, he tilted it downward, slicing an opening in the canvas just large enough for a small boy to climb through. No sooner had the opening been made than John Too twisted his body through.

"*Ay zosh,*" John Too told the trembling girl staring up at him. "Don't be afraid."

The girl started to whimper.

"*Ay zosh. Seh-lahm nesh way?* Be at peace. *Tinagerialesh Ingleezigna?*" John Too asked.

The girl nodded and mumbled, "*Awo*—yes."

"Good," he told her, crouching next to her. "I am called John Too. And he," motioning toward John as he struggled to get his body through the narrow opening. "He is called John."

The little girl cowered away at the sight of John, her face gripped with fear as she looked upon the hyena hides tied around his shoulders and the impala horn held within his hand. Seeing she was about to scream, John Too moved quickly to her side, cupping a hand over her mouth.

"*Ishy, ishy,*" he whispered. "Quiet. He is *gwadegna*—friend. *We ne de me, wundim*: my brother."

"Bouda," she gasped when John Too removed his hand from her mouth. "He is bouda."

John Too giggled, glancing quickly at John.

"Smells like bouda, yes?" he remarked, laughing softly. "The hyena skins are old. The flies," he went on, looking back at her with a wide smile, "they are his friends now. Follow him everywhere," he told her, pinching his nostrils closed.

When the little girl smiled and began to giggle, John Too nodded.

"Good sound, good words," he told her, lightly touching her hand. "Good man he is," he reassured her as John knelt down beside them. "He watches over us."

"A good bouda?" she asked, her eyes fixated on John.

And as her eyes drifted down and across John's imposing form, she saw the bracelet of green beetles on his wrist.

"Like the tabib's," she whispered in awe. "Like the witch," she repeated, looking at John Too. "But his does not glow."

"Yes—Sister Lady," John Too said with a nod. "But she is not a witch. She is a daughter of the moon and the sun. It is why we are here."

John Too saw the girl's face scrunch up with confusion.

"What are you called?" he asked her.

"Eden," she told him, wiping her eyes. "Eden."

* * *

Lord, I ask that You place Your hand upon me and replace my fear with love and hope and peace. Let me not be afraid of what I do not see, and allow me to place my trust in You. Lift the fear from my shoulders and move away the mountains that arise to block my path. Protect me with Your shield of strength. And may the power of the Holy Spirit guide me so I may forever praise You and Your loving care. I ask this through Christ our Lord, amen.

Claire pressed her lips to her silver cross, letting them linger, taking solace in the words she silently recited, hoping the power of the Father would bolster her faith. Her back ached; her wrists and ankles stung where rough fibers of rope rubbed her skin raw. Tired, near exhaustion, hungry and thirsty, she wondered when they—her captors—would get around to bringing her food and water. It was past the normal time. Perhaps they had forgotten, she thought. Perhaps they had meant to forget. Perhaps it was a new form of punishment. She closed her eyes.

Is this God's ending for me? She tried to push the thought out of her mind. What had she just asked of Him? Were the words she had spoken so frail? *I am a hypocrite,* she admonished herself, *to ask for His love and strength and hope—and then question Him.* She shook her head, wiping her eyes across her knees. *If I could only stretch! If I could only walk!* Her thoughts rushed back upon her with fury. *People have been slaughtered and kidnapped and sold into slavery—and I sit here and whine about an aching back.* She couldn't help but wonder if her faith was slipping away. *Where is Teimbaka? Why hasn't he come? Surely he must know we've been taken!* She wanted to scream, wanted to lift her face to the sky and scream *Where are you, Teimbaka? Teimbaka!*

In the midst of her thoughts, the flap of her tent opened. Anticipating Bacha Alba entering, she tried to calm her emotions. But it wasn't Bacha Alba holding the lantern when it passed through the entrance of the tent; it was the little girl—the one who had been taking care of her, the one Alba said viewed her as an evil slut. *Is this girl able to see into my past? Is that why the warlord chose her to see to my needs?* she wondered. *Is the little girl a seer?*

"Salaam," Claire greeted the little girl. "Thank you for bringing me food," she told her, seeing what the girl held in her other hand. "Did you bring water as well?" she asked when the girl set the lantern down and turned to face her. "And I need—I need to use the bathroom again," she apologized. "*Bet—shinta?* Do you understand?"

Claire saw the little girl smile mischievously.

Bacha Alba stepped into the tent, one hand holding a tin cup, the other holding the big knife normally strapped to his leg. Without saying a word, he thrust the cup outward for the little girl to take, spilling some of its contents. With a dismissive grunt, he stepped over to Claire, his blade swift, rising and falling as he bent. The bindings around her wrists fell to the ground. As the warlord stood, the little girl spoke.

"*Shinta,*" she said, glancing at Bacha Alba while motioning with the tin cup toward Claire. "*Shinta,*" she repeated. "*Caca?*" she added, shrugging her shoulders.

"Why didn't you speak of this before, before I unbound her hands?"

The anger in his voice made the little girl start to tremble.

"And you," he spat, turning to look down at Claire. "Why do you have to piss so much?"

"Why do I have to—? Ugh! What would you rather me do, soil myself?" Taking a deep breath, she softened her expression and added, "Perhaps you would rather I soil myself in your presence."

Before the warlord could reply, a tortured howling—like that of a wounded beast—suddenly swept down through the camp from the mountain. Claire noticed the expression of concern on the warlord's face. She too had heard the call of the tortured beast—whatever it was—earlier in the day, and wondered what strange animal could make such a haunting, tormented call. And why the beast lingered so close the warlord's camp.

"Will you untie my ankles now?" Claire pressed the man, a note of frustration in her voice. "And please," she added, addressing the little girl, "please—the water."

Claire saw the girl glance toward the warlord, who merely grunted. Claire reached for the tin cup as the little girl stepped near. Taking the cup from the girl's hand, she put it to her lips and drank.

"Bless you, child," she said, sighing after she swallowed. "Bless you."

The strange tortured howling sounded again. But this time closer. And when the echo of the call subsided, a chorus of other voices answered. Hyenas, Claire recognized them as, well remembering the beasts' cackling rants.

"Still need to piss?" the warlord asked her with a sardonic smile. "The beasts are out this night. One may be lurking behind the rock where you have been—"

"Yes," she hurried to say.

"The *sharmuta* is so brave," he mocked. "You sure you are not afraid?"

Claire thrust her ankles out toward him, trying her best to keep her expression unreadable.

"If you are not, perhaps you should be," he told her as he bent to cut the rope binding her legs together. "Because your bracelet seems to be—" Jerking her arm upward, he said, "You see? It has stopped glowing."

The warlord thrust her arm down and laughed. But his laughter was short-lived, for the howling of the hyenas seemed nearer, the tormented, haunted cry of the strange beast louder than them all. Claire could see the look of worry on the warlord's face, and maybe something more, she thought, maybe a touch of fear. Maybe Bacha Alba shared more of his men's superstitions than he would like to admit, she observed.

"Go!" he shouted. "Go relieve yourself! And be quick! For if you are not," he said, placing the point of his knife to the cheek of the little girl, "your little slave will be the one who pays for your insolence."

To her surprise, the warlord laughed, seemingly happy about something as he drifted into a moment of thought.

"We have things to discuss, you see, *sihr sharmuta*." Pausing to chuckle, he added, "But perhaps I should start calling you by your name, yes?"

With a wink, he grabbed her by her hands and jerked her to her feet.

"Sister Claire Waterman."

"How? How is it—how is it you know my name?" she stuttered, pulling her wrists free of his grasp. "I—I have never told you."

She looked at him, confused.

"*Abeed*," he barked to the little girl. "Take her to the bushes! Be quick!"

The little girl rushed to place the food she was holding down on a blanket in the corner of the tent and hurried back to Claire. Seeing the girl shaking, Claire reached out, taking her hand. As they made their way out of the tent, Claire felt the little girl press something into her palm.

"We will talk of many things, Sister Claire," Bacha Alba said with a laugh. "Yes, many things. So hurry. Go!"

Claire stepped out of the tent, glancing downward to see what the girl placed in her hand. The girl tugged on her shirtsleeve and shook her head. Claire nodded in return, enclosing the carcass of the green beetle within her fingers, clutching it to her chest. As the two neared the bushes surrounding the big rock Claire used for privacy, the machine gun stationed at the far end of camp erupted.

* * *

John was scared. The eyes of the hyenas surrounding him glassy orange, set to flame by the fires burning in the warlord's camp. Why had the animals come? Why so many? he wondered. Did they want him to howl again? Or were they simply waiting for the right moment to attack, to rip him apart to avenge the deaths of the hyenas whose pelts he wore? As the pack began inching closer, he raised his face to the sky and howled.

The walls of the narrow ravine where John had chosen to keep watch over the camp were steep, his howl—and those of the hyenas who answered—flowing outward and up, echoing off the opposite ridge line, swirling back upon the soldiers below. The clamor the calls produced—fear-filled voices of the soldiers calling out to one another, panicked shouts to gather weapons—elicited a smile. Edged on by a growing sense of power, John lifted his face to the sky and howled once more. With his scream booming between the opposing ridges, John began his descent, keeping to a crouch, using boulders and darkness as a shield. Halfway down the seventy-meter drop from his hiding place, he felt the presence of the hyenas mirroring his movements. When he reached the base of the steep ridge, he paused to catch his breath.

Closing his eyes, John lost himself to the hyenas' panting, inhaling their energy, absorbing their strength. Opening his mouth, he breathed deeply, ribs expanding and contracting, his breath flowing in a rhythm with the beasts around him. The hyenas bunched close; John felt the heat of the their bodies, their thick fur prickling against his skin. Bodies tense, paws raking the ground, the animals paced from side to side. John mimicked the pack, gouging the earth with the tip of his horn, shifting his weight from one foot to the other. His adrenaline building, John felt the low-pitched rumble deep in his stomach swell to a guttural roar. Looking skyward, he unleashed a tormented howl, the hyenas answering with a chorus of haunting calls, the night shattered into echoes of frenzied power.

With a leap forward, the animals surged behind him, running, sprinting, charging toward the fires filling their eyes. John felt the churning of a hundred pounding paws through the soil beneath his feet, lungs straining for air, blood pumping, fevered energy pushing the pack forward, forward, forward. Moving as one, the pack swept closer to the camp of the warlord with wildness in their eyes, the primal urge of the hunt flowing through their senses. Rushing, running blindly ahead, reason lost to instinct, John and the hyenas raced forward, ignoring the shouting men.

A burst of thunder, the sound of a hundred hammers striking metal, squealing wails of pain, and two hyenas jerked sideways, crumpling to the ground. *Two of us!* John thought. *Two of our own hit by bullets, ripping our flesh, sending pain into our bodies, cutting into our muscles, blood seeping from our wounds—our blood!* Anger. Fury. Enraged, he stood and faced the two men firing the long-barreled weapon, wishing he were close enough that he could plunge the impala horn into their necks.

Raising the horn over his head, he wailed, jaws opened wide, eyes filled with the flames of the fires. As the two soldiers swiveled the gun toward him, the bracelet of beetles began to glow. The light emanating from the carcasses of the insects bathing John in an eerie green hue; the dark forms of the swift-moving hyenas at his waist turned ghoulish—a horde of haunted creatures with radiant eyes and snapping jaws. The soldiers fell to their knees, calling out to Allah. John glared at them in screaming fits of laughter and rage. The soldiers near to him threw down their weapons and covered their eyes. Beckoned by the pack to follow, John sprinted into the darkness.

* * *

As soon as the big gun began to fire, Eden quickened her walk, pulling the woman—the tabib—behind her. The voice of the warlord—angry, shouting orders—receded as they moved further away. Eden hurried the woman along, grabbing her by the arm to keep her from falling. But Eden didn't stop to let the woman get her balance. She couldn't; there was too little time. *Gwa chi cho!* her head screamed. *These people—the bouda and the tabib—are scary—scary monsters!* What was she doing? her thoughts yelled. *Gwa chi cho!*

*

John Too raised the bow to his shoulder at the sound of approaching footsteps. Aiming chest high, hand steady, arrow nocked to string, ready to fire. He hoped the people drawing near were Eden and Sister Lady, but he couldn't be sure. And he wasn't going to be taken prisoner if they weren't. He had seen firsthand what Bacha Alba's men had done. Slaughtering captives, selling children and women into slavery: these were not men, he said to himself, they were evil—worse than a wild beast driven to madness by the sickness that eats away at the mind. No wonder the boy had been so despondent the last time he had spoken with him. No wonder the Son of the Father felt so alone. Evil seemed everywhere, unquenchable. The boy having told him as much when Gunstard had been killed; evil would remain, he'd said. Then how was it ever to be defeated? John Too wondered. Could it be defeated? The string of the bow quivered between his fingers as a small, dark hand pushed a branch aside. Wide-eyed, Eden stared at him, her gaze flicking nervously between his face and the arrow. When a larger figure appeared behind Eden, he whispered, "Sister Lady."

*

Claire bent, drawing John Too into her arms. Squeezing him tightly, she felt her body begin to shake, emotion draining into the boy's shoulder. Relieved, exhausted, scared, overjoyed; her lips quivered as she spoke.

"John Too."

After kissing his cheek, she drew her face away to look into his, for the briefest moment glimpsing the glitter of ivory and gold within his eyes.

"Where is Teimbaka?" she abruptly asked, glancing over the boy's shoulder. "Is he waiting somewhere?"

"The elephants," he told her. "They have called him."

"Then who were they shooting at—the warlord's men?"

"Come, Sister Lady, hurry. John is waiting on the other side of the ridge."

*

As the boy took hold of the tabib's hand and began to run, Eden hesitated, wondering if she should follow. But angry shouts from the camp behind her and the thought of returning without the woman—to face the wrath of the warlord's knife—made her decision easy. Running toward the ridge—with the woman and the boy just ahead of her—she couldn't stop her mind from screaming, *Gwa chi cho! Tabibs! Boudas! What am I getting myself into? What am I doing! What have I done?*

* * *

Teimbaka felt as though he was in a dream—part of an ancient, mystical tale where the world of the dead and the living intertwined. All around him, spirit elephants drifted inches above ground in cloud-like forms, shimmering layers of gold and white contained within wispy outlines, edges of ethereal bodies shaped and re-shaped by a breeze he could not feel. As far as he could see, in every direction, the spirit beasts moved within a pale, ghostly mist. Walking in their midst, he felt the lifeblood of the entities seeping into his soul.

Holding tight to the drooping ear of the baby spirit elephant walking beside him, Teimbaka gazed around in awe. Hundreds of ghost beasts surrounded him—no, thousands—thousands, he guessed. Young and old, and those aged in between—breathtakingly strong with tusks curled toward the sky—their number multiplying as he looked on.

Twisting and curling, the mist enveloping the spirit elephants began to swirl, luminous vapor converging and expanding, flaring into needlepoints of shimmering white light. Where the substance touched his body, Teimbaka felt his skin tingle and go numb, ice crystals briefly forming, clinging to his skin before melting and sliding to the ground. Sensing heaviness in the essence—lingering and powerful—Teimbaka bowed his head and continued on, his every step layered in shrouds of sparkling white frost and veils of crystalline moisture.

Subtly, lambent upon the fog's ceiling, a ribbon of golden light shown, creeping slowly into his awareness, enticing his focus upward. Sunrise? he wondered. Or did the diffused aura represent something else, something only existent in the spirit world, something the elephants were leading him toward, wanting him to see? Next to him, the baby spirit elephant stopped.

The eyes of the young spirit beast had always been a mixture of color, glowing shades of pink, red, and white. But now, as the ethereal beast looked up at him, Teimbaka gazed into orbs of translucent milk-like vapor with round black centers. The pupils resembled dark, hollow tunnels, hinting at a vast emptiness contained within. An endless darkness, he imagined, leading to a place he did not wish to go. The beast's eyes made him shudder.

When a trumpeting call swept over the spirit herd, Teimbaka jerked his head around, a sense of panic surging through him. For the eyes of every spirit elephant he looked upon were hollow black, the sense of hopelessness traumatizing. It was as though the beasts' empty stares were portals to an eternal void of lost souls.

Emotions rushed outward from the vacant blackness of the spirit elephants' eyes, coiling around his chest, constricting and suffocating. Struggling to breathe, face awash with confusion, Teimbaka frantically reached for the baby spirit elephant. But the ethereal form was in a state of flux, its body ebbing and flowing. Grasping a handful of fog, his fingers went numb.

Suddenly, the glittering vapor lifted toward the sky, drifting upward until it reached a point above the tallest spirit elephant. There it hovered—slowly spinning—before its motion abruptly ceased. Teimbaka felt the trunk of the young spirit beast take his hand, moving him several paces forward. Beneath him, he could feel a tremor run through the earth, soil swelling, breaking open. Disfigured forms of elephants ascended from the chasms, faces sheared away, lower jaws missing, some without heads. In unison, the morbid entities moved toward him.

As he turned to run, the baby spirit elephant gripped his arm, keeping him in place. Looking down, Teimbaka saw the eyes of the young ghost beast had changed again, milky-white vapor given way to empty black.

"You there!" he heard someone shout. "What are you doing here?"

Looking up, Teimbaka peered ahead, searching for the dome of sparkling mist, trying to make sense of what he was seeing. Some fifty meters from where he was standing, he saw several mounds of ivory tusks. Beside these, two men stood guard, each staring at him, armed with automatic rifles. Beyond the guards stood a dozen tents. In a clearing past the tents sat the helicopter he'd seen the day before.

Taking a step back, Teimbaka reached out for the baby spirit elephant. But the ethereal beast wasn't there. Vanished—as was the rest of the herd.

* * *

"Christian Aid has an office in Assad—that's a seaport in the Eritrea province of Ethiopia. That will be your jumping-off point, so to speak, after flying into Djibouti and reacquainting yourself with Mr. Savage. Sister Sarah—are you listening to me? Did you hear any of what I just said? You look as though you're in a trance."

"I—I'm—um, I'm just trying to—"

Sarah couldn't finish what she was trying to say, her head spinning. What Reverend Mother had been telling her since she had joined the matriarch for evening vespers was overwhelming—and not in a pleasant way.

"If you don't think you're up for this, Sister, just say so. Though the order would have to find another to go in your place—and that would waste valuable time—you would not be judged for your decision. What they— what the order is asking of you, although unorthodox, is no more than what we would ask of any in the congregation."

Sarah continued to stare at Reverend Mother, waiting for her to say more, waiting for the confusion she was experiencing to be dispelled.

"So what should I tell them? Sister? Sarah, what should I say when they call back? Sarah? Sister Sarah."

Sarah could sense Reverend Mother's growing irritation, could hear it in her voice. She had been around the woman for some time now. Long enough to know that, on occasion, the woman was given to moments of short temper. Sarah chalked it up to the woman's age—late sixties or early seventies, the overriding reason for having made the pilgrimage to the Solitude of the Savior. And why she, Sarah, had been chosen by the congregation to accompany the aging matriarch on what many believed would be her final trip overseas. She knew it was a test of sorts when the offer from the congregation to travel with Reverend Mother had been presented to her. And knew it was a proposition she couldn't very well turn down. Traveling with Reverend Mother on her pilgrimage would bring her that much closer to her Perpetual Commitment, she understood. So there was no acceptable excuse for not traveling with the "old bird," as some of the novices called her. And now this, this new and final—she hoped—test of her commitment to the order. To travel to the Horn of Africa and find this Sister Claire— the one with the seven-million-dollar trust fund—so the woman could be brought back to America. How could she say no? But Africa—especially the area they were asking her to go? It had never dawned on her that she would be asked to travel to Ethiopia. Such a famine-stricken, troubled land she had heard it to be. Filled with civil conflicts, drought, and poverty. The Sisters of the Holy Cross didn't even have a mission there. And Dirk Savage; what did he have to do with all of this? And how was she supposed to find him? And why would he want to help her find this Sister Claire? She had noticed the change in the man's expression when the subject of money was broached. Departing hastily after the sum was revealed: anyone could see the man was interested in finding Sister Claire as a means of gaining access to the money.

"The order made several phone inquiries overnight. Through various sources they—we—have pieced together a fairly good picture of the man."

"Man?" Sarah repeated, confused.

"Mr. Savage," Reverend Mother said, sighing and shaking her head. "They doubt he showed up here on a whim. After thinking over his sudden appearance, they thought it best to gather what information they could on him."

Reverend Mother tapped her fingertips on the back of the pew in front of them, staring at the stained-glass windows above the altar.

"A very good journalist, apparently—photographer as well. Very well respected for a number of years. Quite a number of feature articles picked up by the international press. But then something happened. No one knows what. Only that he returned from an assignment in Somalia changed—bitter, self-destructive. Took to alcohol and gambling and—"

The Reverend Mother paused, as if she wasn't quite certain she wanted to continue.

"Drug use—the addictive type, needles—and prostitutes—some no older than eleven or twelve, I was told—disgusting, sinful."

Sarah saw Reverend Mother's mouth twist, the word *sinful* spoken as a condemnation, the expression dredging up an image she did not want to see. Shutting her eyes, she refused to let the memory surface.

"The order does not believe he wants to find Sister Claire out of the goodness of his heart. No," she said with a definitive shake of her head. "No, they don't believe he wants to find her on that premise at all. That is why they have decided to send someone from the congregation to locate her on our behalf. Someone young enough to handle the task, someone who will represent the order in the manner that exemplifies our constitution."

The Reverend Mother gave her an expectant look.

"Christian Aid," Sarah heard herself saying. "I don't understand. There won't be any representative from the order there to meet me? How am I to get to this place—Assad?"

"Dear Lord, child." Reverend Mother sighed, exasperated. "I've already been over that." She crossed herself and said, "Give me strength."

"Please forgive me, Reverend Mother," Sarah hurried to say. "This has just come as such a—such a—"

"Very well, very well, Sister. I suppose it does sound a trifle daunting." Taking hold of Sarah's hand, she went on to say, "No harm in explaining it again."

Sarah sensed the smile Reverend Mother gave her was forced, regardless of the woman's kind tone of voice.

"Through a contact made by one of our fellow Brothers stationed with the congregation of the Holy Cross in Uganda, a Father from the Eritrean Orthodox—Tewahdo, I believe it is called—Church in Asmara will be on hand to meet you in Djibouti. His name is Father Gebre. I have been assured he is a most sincere and kind-hearted man, a true and devoted servant of the Lord Jesus Christ. Through him, you will be able to locate Mr. Savage and either accompany him on his travels to find Sister Claire or learn of her whereabouts. In either case, Father Gebre has apparently offered to assist you in any way possible. But the first order of business will be to locate Mr. Savage—which shouldn't be hard, from what I have been told—and then get you to Assad, where Christian Aid has an office."

She paused for a moment, giving Sarah's hand a squeeze.

"Apparently they can reach many areas where there really is no formal government structure in place. And they have many contacts in the city Sister Claire mentioned in her first letter—Mek'ele."

"Mek'ele," Sarah halfheartedly mumbled. "But that letter, Sister Claire's letter—" Her fingers found the silver cross hanging from the necklace around her neck. She twisted it back and forth. "That was in 1972, wasn't it? That's nearly fifteen years ago. She could be anywhere by now."

She hadn't meant for her voice to sound so disrespectful, but she could see by the Reverend Mother's astonished expression that her manner of speech had been interpreted that way.

"What I mean to say is—"

"I know very well what you mean, Sister. And your elevated opinion of your intellect simply means you have not embraced the humility one would expect of someone who has been immersed in the steps of incorporation as long as you."

Sarah felt her face go flush. She could see Reverend Mother's jaw grinding, her head slightly bobbing.

"I beg your forgiveness, Reverend Mother," she blurted out, awkwardly posturing herself face forward on the bench pew where they were seated. "Please, I beg of you," she implored. "I will do whatever the order asks of me." Tears welling in her eyes, she looked up at the woman and whispered, "Please forgive me."

The stern, unforgiving look on the Reverend Mother's face was deflating. Sarah winced. But in the next instant, the older woman gently rested her palm atop Sarah's head.

"Great as the sea was her sorrow—but great as the sea is her compassion," she said with a pat to Sarah's head.

"And her hope for the Resurrection," Sarah replied, wiping away her tears.

"Doubt clouds the path laid before us, Sister. The Lord Jesus Christ is with you. Trust in Him. Let Him guide your way."

Sarah pushed up from the pew, smoothing her blouse and skirt.

"I am ready, Reverend Mother. When do I leave?"

Reverend Mother nodded and smiled before saying, "The plane departs at midnight. Come, Sister, we have much to do."

* * *

The bird—brown hooded with a red beak and teal-blue wing and tail feathers—eyed the procession passing below him with hungry interest. Perched on a branch in a pocket of dense woodland, he'd heard the approaching horde of insects long before the first appeared. But he hadn't expected to see such a gathering of beetles like the one he was witnessing. Nor was he expecting to see these particular types of beetles. But what did it matter? Food was food. One couldn't afford to be picky. And it wasn't like he was the only one who had taken notice of the slow-moving feast. Branches all around him, both low and high, filled with shrikes, bee-eaters, sunbirds, and other kingfishers like him, all eager to gorge on the insects marching on the forest floor.

*

The beetle leading the mass of insects was a vibrant, metallic green female, *Taurhina longiceps,* marked with an unusual spot of purple in the shape of a circle on her right elytron. The splash of purple an anomaly, making her easy to pick out. And though she herself couldn't see the lush spot of color decorating her body, which was otherwise indistinguishable from others of her kind, she had often wondered why birds seemed more attracted to her, and why males of her species showed such keen interest in her—even when the urgings of mating season had come and gone.

Vibrations stirring air, clusters of ultraviolet light darting from place to place, and the overwhelming smell of feathers supplied her sensors with enough information for the female beetle to understand that an attack from birds was forthcoming. But the instinct to stop and hide was not relayed, the urge to keep moving too strong, overriding what would have been the normal behavior for each and every beetle behind her.

As she came upon a slight depression in the forest floor, she paused a millisecond, rubbing the claws of her back legs together. Slightly altering her course, she crawled atop a slender-stemmed fern extending out over a long, shallow dip, the turquoise tint of the foliage a stark contrast to her metallic green body. Moving with purpose, she scuttled to the tip of the plant's far-thest-reaching leaf, where a lone shaft of sunlight shown through a hole in the canopy of leaves above, bathing the curled tendril in a golden glow. Once inside the beam of sunlight, the flower beetle positioned her body so the purple spot on her elytron could absorb the energy from the sun.

*

The brown-hooded kingfisher was the first to move, eyes set on the lone beetle crawling on a raised branch of a plant. Pushing off his perch, wings propelling him forward with short double thrusts, he dove toward the bee-tle. Around him, he sensed hundreds of shapes taking flight, wings held close against bodies to attain maximum speed.

Adjust, adjust, adjust—folded wings extended—push, push, push—air-speed slowed, leg uncurled, foot extending, head angled to the side. The beetle neared his grasp. When the bird was inches from the shimmering morsel of food, the forest exploded in a blinding flash of booming thunder, waves of expanding energy repelling him upward and back.

Spinning, tumbling, disoriented, struggling with balance and speed, shrill cries of hundreds of startled birds clouding his mind, the brown-hooded kingfisher regained control. Dazed but unharmed, he hovered above the horde of green beetles for a moment before flying off toward the waters of Lake Tanganyika.

*

As the flock of attacking birds scattered in every direction, the metallic green flower beetle with the spot of purple on her outer shell calmly unfolded her elytra, stretching out her transparent inner wings. With a slight whirring sound, she lifted off the tip of the airy blue-green fern, flying to the front of the ever-moving mass of determined insects.

6

BONGO REMOVED THE long pink and white plastic straw from his drink and slurped the icy liquid dripping from the end. After sliding the straw out of his mouth, he slipped it underneath the edge of the cast encasing his wrist, using it to scratch two areas he couldn't reach with his fingers. Sighing, he pulled the straw back out from beneath the cast and put it back in his drink. He took a sip and smacked his lips. Adjusting his sunglasses, he tapped the bottom of his cup against the steering wheel. He reached for the radio knob, but pulled his hand back when he remembered the instruction he'd been given. Tilting his head back he sighed, a sour expression on his face.

Sitting in an old Pontiac Firebird on a warm June evening by Newark Bay, Bongo was doing his best to ignore the disagreeable smells wafting in off the murky brown water. Though not as putrid as it could be during the hot, humid months of July and August—when anyone who worked by the bay would pray for a thunderstorm to breathe some freshness In the air— the water stank like hell just the same. Already bothered with the task he'd been given, he didn't appreciate the stench adding to his angst. He didn't like surveillance work—never had—but he especially didn't like it when he felt like it was just a big waste of his time. Like it was now. Like it had been for the past three plus hours.

What the fuck am I supposed to be looking for anyway? he wondered for the umpteenth time. "Suspicious shit," Super Freak had told him. Well, what the hell did that mean down here? Down here where everyone had something to hide or went around with their faces in a bag so they wouldn't be a witness to anything. What the fuck did suspicious mean? He shook his head. *Goddamned Super Freak dude is wacked. Probably smokin' too much PCP*, Bongo thought. Watch for anyone who looked like an undercover cop, the Freak had told him. Well, shit—that could be anyone. He probably looked like one himself.

Bongo repositioned his body in the bucket seat of the dented, beat-up old 1968 Firebird, placing his Slurpee on the center console. Bending forward, he began pounding out a beat on the lower rim of the steering wheel.

"Oh—what the fuck—uh huh, uh huh—am I doin' here?" he half sang, half rasped, his fingers tapping out a funk-based beat. "When I should be in my crib—uh huh, uh huh— drinkin' beer. Ooh—what the fuck—boom boom shacka lacka—am I doin' here? I could be high—I should be high— watchin' all the fine ladies passin' by."

He chuckled.

"Dig it, bro. That's the shit."

Bobbing his head to the beat he was feeling, he repeated the last line. "I could be high, should be high, watchin' all the fine ladies passin' by. Doot doot doot, bop bop bop," he went on, continuing to beat on the steering wheel with the index fingers of both hands, "watchin' all those fine ladies passin' by."

"What the fuck you doin', idiot?"

Startled, Bongo jerked in his seat, banging the top of his head against the roof of the car.

"Yow—shit, man. What you sneakin' up on me for? Stupid black-ass motherfucker," he hissed, rubbing the top of his head. "Ain't you supposed to be at the other end of the terminal?" Bongo looked out his window, an accusatory expression on his face.

"And ain't y'all supposed to be watchin' what's going on out there?" Twister sarcastically countered, nodding toward the shipping dock. "'Stead of sittin' and singin' shit-ass crap and poundin' on the car wheel? Sounds like you're fuckin' chokin' on a canary or somethin'."

Bongo broke out into a smile and started to weave and bob his head up, sideways, and down.

"Tight. Did you dig it?" he asked, continuing to sit-dance to the beat of the funk rhythm flowing through his body. "I could be high, should be high, watchin' all the fine fuckin' ladies passin' by," he rasped in a halfhearted attempt at singing. With a final drum roll to the lower rung of the steering wheel, he smiled up at Twister and exclaimed, "Shit yeah!"

The expression of condescending disbelief on Twister's face unraveled as he broke out in laughter. Slapping the vinyl roof of the chocolate-brown Pontiac, he bent at the waist, looked through the driver's side window at Bongo, and managed to say, "You're one fucked-up dude, man." Reaching in through the open window of the car, he smacked Bongo on the back of his neck. "Yeah, one fucked-up dude," he told him, shaking his head.

"Whatever, man," Bongo shot back, rubbing the spot on his neck where Twister had smacked him. "Just need some dude with a recordin' studio to lay a track down for me, and I could be a motha-fuckin' star."

"You trippin'. Ain't nobody gonna pay to hear some fool talkin' rhymes. That ain't music," he scoffed.

"Be tight if you lay it down with a funky beat," Bongo said, tapping out a rhythm on the steering wheel. "Just ahead of my time, is all. You'll see. Just need a break, is all."

"Whatever, man. Stop talkin' shit. Grippity man wants to know if you've seen anything"—Twister paused and slid his Wayfarer sunglasses up and down on his nose so Bongo could see his wiggling eyebrows—"you know, suspicious."

Bongo took off his sunglasses and frowned.

"Where is Mister Super Freak's mouthpiece, anyway, man? Maybe he could explain to me just what the fuck *suspicious* supposed to look like down here?" He pinched the bridge of his wide, flat nose. "Only thing I's seen so far look out of place is two fag-lookin' dudes making out behind a stack of container cars. Ain't nothin' out of the ordinary about that in this day and age, is it?" He wiped his eyes with the back of his hand before putting his sunglasses back on. "Especially when it looked like two Euro dudes who've been out at sea for too long." He laughed.

"What you bitchin' 'bout? Least you gotta a car to sit in. Shit, I've been standin' next to an old rusty crate with my thumb up my ass." Looking past Bongo into the interior of the car, he asked, "Hey, where'd you get that Slurpee?"

"Took a little detour after I dropped you off. Went back out to Corbin and found myself a little 7-Eleven." Smiling, he nodded his head. "Had myself a dog, too—with mustard and kraut," he went on in a self-satisfied tone.

Grabbing the Slurpee from the car console, he gave Twister a shit-eating grin and took a long, noisy sip.

"Ah," he sighed. "Raspberry-cola swirl."

"Fuck you, man," Twister said. "You can take that Slurpee and shove—"

"Hey—look," Bongo interrupted, nodding toward the ship moored at the end of the Elizabeth Channel dock.

Twister and Bongo were out past the end of East Fleet Street on the Maher Terminal. Bongo had parked where he could see most of the way down the longer bayside frontage of the pier—north to south—with a partial view of the shorter channel side—east to west—where Port Newark Terminal shared the slender waterway of the Elizabeth Channel.

"Does that look like—?"

"Shut up, fool," Twister told him, slipping into the passenger seat after rounding the car from the back.

"That's the motherfucker who broke my arm."

"Shut up and watch."

Bongo removed his sunglasses so he could get a better focus on the sleek black and chrome motorcycle coming into view, the chopper moving at a slow, steady pace, approaching from the west, where the entrance to the terminal off Corbin Street was located. From Bongo's vantage point some fifty yards away, the bike's engine sounded like the puttering of an old lawn mower idling inside a neighbor's garage with the door pulled down—muffled, almost surreal. Scrutinizing the man atop the motorcycle, he knew it was the same dude who'd broken his arm. Same muscular build, same height, same mahogany-brown skin.

Yet, as certain as Bongo was he was looking at the same guy who broke his arm, he still had a tiny, gnawing doubt. Mostly because the rider was wearing sunglasses with a red bandana wrapped around his head—a do-rag with long, flowing tails fluttering in the backdraft—a red T-shirt, dark pants, and black, high-topped Converse sneakers.

"Isn't that the guy?" Bongo asked.

They watched in silence as the man got off the motorcycle and started rummaging through the saddlebag attached to the side of the bike.

"What guy?" Twister replied, peeking over the tops of his Wayfarers.

"The dude that took us down, man," Bongo hissed. "The one Super Freak hired to play that scam on that dumb assemblywoman bitch."

"Don't know," Twister said, sounding distracted.

Bongo glanced over and saw Twister pulling at his own do-rag—the same bright red bandana Bongo was wearing. Same as the motorcycle guy was wearing.

"What he pull out of that saddlebag?" Twister muttered.

Bongo looked out the windshield to see the biker dude holding what looked like a foot-long Italian sub rolled up in brown butcher paper. Before Bongo could answer Twister's question, the man lay down on the tarmac next to a pallet of shipping crates and placed whatever he had in his hand underneath.

"What's he doin' now?" Twister mumbled.

"Looks like he's hidin' a hoagie," Bongo snickered, a big smile on his face.

Twister looked over at him, his mouth twisted into a frown.

When they heard the motorcycle engine rev, they snapped their attention back to the pallet of shipping containers. The man in the flowing red do-rag and red T-shirt was already on the move, steering the chopper away from the stack of containers, heading right toward the massive ship docked in front of him. Before Bongo and Twister understood what was happening, they heard the quick bang-bang-bang of a handgun and saw everyone who was within earshot of the gunshots crouch or drop to the ground. To Bongo's utter confusion, the motorcycle dude waved a gun in the air and screamed "Eee ya!" like he was some drunk bull-riding cowboy. Then Bongo heard the chopper's engine rev and watched the motorcycle jump forward, popping a wheelie before speeding away as though it had been shot out of a cannon. And when the motorcycle took a surprise turn and veered toward Bongo's car, Twister hunched down into his seat and leaned sideways, pinning Bongo against the driver's-side door.

"Man—what you doin'?" Bongo complained, trying to push Twister away.

The motorcycle zoomed by, bombarding the interior of the car with a deafening roar. Dumbfounded, Bongo looked out over the huddled body of Twister to watch the chopper zipping past, the rider flipping the peace sign. Bongo swiveled his head to see where the biker was going, but the motorcycle took a quick right turn, disappearing into a maze of stacked containers.

"What the fuck was that all about?" Bongo complained, pushing Twister off of him. "Brother must be doin' some heavy shit to be shootin' off a piece down here."

"Start the car and get us the fuck out of here," Twister urgently blurted out.

"Why?" Bongo shot back. "We ain't do nothin'."

"Start the car!" Twister shouted, pulling off his red bandana. "And put your foot on it," he yelled, reaching over to pull the red bandana off of Bongo's head. "Move, move, move!"

No sooner had Bongo started the car and peeled away than a booming explosion sounded, Bongo catching the flash of a fireball shooting upward in the rearview mirror. Left turns onto Okinawa and Egypt streets, a shortcut across a mostly empty container storage area, a bumpy crossing over the freight railroad tracks, a final left on McLester Street, and Bongo had the car speeding out of the Maher Terminal complex onto the confusing convergence of cloverleafs where I-95 merged over North Avenue. Coming to a screeching stop, Bongo idled the car for a moment, deciding which ramp to take. Off in the distance, he could hear sirens. Police, fire engines—both, he thought—approaching the terminal, using Corbin. Decision made, he hit the gas pedal, turning the car in the opposite direction. In less than thirty seconds, the car was on I-95. A minute later, it was at Newark International Airport; soon after, the vehicle abandoned in one of the vast airport parking lots.

* * *

Yutanda thrust Menelik into Elizabeth's arms.

"Thanks for coming on such short notice," she said in a rush, a set of keys jingling in her hand. "And sorry to call you over here at dinner time again. Do I need a coat?"

Yutanda could see her dad's look of disapproval, but she didn't have time to soothe his feelings. Well, that wasn't true. She had time, but she wanted to get going. From the preliminary report she'd received from her contact at the police department, the explosion and shots fired at the port might present her with an opportunity to gather vital evidence on the drug-smuggling operation. So she wanted to get down to the seaport as quickly as she could. Tired of getting her information secondhand from reports sometimes days old. Now she could be on the scene in real time, seeing for herself how the investigation was handled, how the entire operation would be plotted out—get a feel for the agency taking charge. Knowing she couldn't get any of that type of information from report placed on her desk twenty-four to forty-eight hours later, she wanted answers while the crime scene was fresh.

"Don't you even have time to sit for a few minutes to say hello?"

Hearing the tinge of hurt in her dad's voice pulled at her emotions. But the responsibility of her job, in her mind, wouldn't allow her feel sorry for herself—or her dad.

"I can't, Dad," she said, stepping by him to the door. "There's been an incident down at the seaport. I need to get going."

"Whoa—hold on there, girl," Ed told her, grabbing hold of her arm. "Why you gotta go down there 'gain? It ain't safe."

"Yutanda."

It was Elizabeth—her mom—talking now.

"Your daddy's right," she concurred, smiling down into Menelik's face. Gently placing a fingertip to the baby's nose, glancing back up at her daughter, she said, "Tell me someone's going with you. You're not going alone, are you?"

"Mom, Dad, it's okay. I'm a big girl, in case you hadn't noticed. I'll be fine." She glanced quickly at each of their faces. "Besides, there's going to be police and firemen all over the place. There's probably no safer spot in Newark right now than down at the seaport. So stop worrying," she told them, grabbing the doorknob. "I'll be home as soon as I can."

She watched her dad's face go long and his eyes drop to the floor. In a rush of guilt, she stepped over to him, wrapped her arms around him, and kissed him on his cheek. Stepping away, she paused in front of her mother.

"Watch over little Menelik like I know you always do," she said in a soft voice. Placing her hands on Elizabeth's forearms, she gave them a squeeze. "And thanks for being here".

And then she was gone, leaving Ed and Elizabeth looking at each other, shaking their heads.

* * *

By the time Yutanda fought her way across town through rush-hour traffic, units from the DEA, New Jersey State Police, Newark Police, Elizabeth Police, and Port Authority Police were crawling all over the crime scene.

Also present were local fire and rescue units and a bomb and canine unit dispatched from the New Jersey Transit Police. U.S. Customs officials were on hand as well, but Yutanda had to guess who these individuals might be because they didn't wear any type of uniform. Like Yutanda, they had ID badges hanging around their necks or clipped to their shirt pocket. And you had to get pretty close to one of the laminated squares before you could read what name was on the tag and what department the bearer was from.

After flashing her own credentials at the security checkpoint to get into the Maher Terminal, Yutanda had no trouble locating where the bomb had detonated. And although the far end of the dock had been temporarily cordoned off, she took note that the rest of the terminal seemed to be operating in normal fashion—a constant bevy of activity. It was impossible to keep track of the merchandise coming and going. Mainstream America just footsteps away by rail or truck, with an airport a few miles away. The entire scene she was looking at made her head spin. No wonder Newark—and the rest of the continental U.S.—was experiencing a drug problem. How could anyone keep track of all the containers offloading?

"One step at a time," Menelik used to tell her when they faced similar, seemingly insurmountable problems trying to get legislation passed through the state assembly after he'd won the election. She supposed he'd tell her the same now about the seaport.

Nearing the bomb area, Yutanda spotted her contact within the Newark Police Department. The woman, Corporal Stilton—a six-foot-tall Amazon type, big boned, muscular, chiseled, with short-cropped brownish-red hair and hawk-like features—cast an imposing figure. Yutanda had been a trifle intimidated by the woman when she'd first run into her while they were on opposing sides of a rally protesting the forced closing of a drug rehab house. Yutanda knew the policewoman's first name was Layla, but Corporal Stilton liked to be called Corporal Stilton. And Yutanda didn't see the sense in trying to call her anything else.

"Corporal Stilton," Yutanda said with a nod.

"Assemblywoman," the female officer responded.

"Thanks for the call."

The taller woman distractedly nodded her head, gazing up the metal gangway leading to the deck of the monstrous ship docked in front of them.

"What do we have?" Yutanda asked, trying to sound professional.

"From the prelims, it looks like some kind of gang retaliation."

"Gangs? Using bombs?"

Corporal Stilton shrugged her wide shoulders.

"Got plenty of eyewitnesses describing some clown on a motorcycle firing off a couple of shots. Red bandana, red T-shirt—typical Blood attire. Couple longshoremen say they saw the suspect place something beneath the pallet of containers where the bomb went off. And two crew members who had a good vantage point from up on the deck," she continued with a nod upward, "say they saw two other similarly dressed men in a car parked over there," she said, glancing over to what looked to Yutanda to be a storage area for container cars. "Said the car had been parked there a few hours."

Corporal Stilton gave Yutanda a knowing look.

"That's why they noticed it. Said the driver rested his head on the steering wheel a few times." Nodding, she added, "Wearing a red bandana. Just like the one the bomb suspect had on. Car peeled out just before the bomb exploded. Said the clown on the motorcycle drove right by the suspects in the car before the bomb blew, and flashed the occupants the V."

"The V?"

"The V," Corporal Stilton repeated, somewhat condescendingly. "The peace sign," she said, raising a hand and holding her index and middle fingers up before spreading them wide. "Or victory—however you want to interpret it."

"Oh, right. Got it, Corporal."

"Now, if you'll excuse me, I have other witnesses to interview."

"Just one thing before you go," Yutanda pressed, lightly touching Corporal Stilton's shoulder.

By the look the female officer gave her, Yutanda couldn't tell if Corporal Stilton was about to hit her for touching her shoulder, or construed the motion as some kind of come-on. Yutanda pulled her hand back as quickly as she could.

"Why a bomb? And who—I mean—what gang has claim to this part of the dock, to a pallet of containers?"

"If we had the answers to those questions, assemblywoman, then we'd be done here, wouldn't we?"

Yutanda gave the woman a perplexed look.

"I don't understand, Corporal. Did I say something to offend you?"

Placing her hands on her hips, Corporal Stilton squared her body to Yutanda.

"I'm just trying to get to—"

"The bottom of this? Is that what you were going to say?"

Yutanda couldn't help but feel a little intimidated when the woman stepped close to her and placed her six-foot frame directly in her face. Her nose parallel to the bottom of Corporal Stilton's neck, Yutanda was left with no choice but to look up to carry on the conversation.

"Look, Corporal, I was—"

"Yutanda," Corporal Stilton said, looking down into Yutanda's eyes. "I hope you don't mind me calling you by your first name."

Yutanda heard her voice soften. The woman's eyes, as well, lost their hard edge.

"There's not a person down here that doesn't appreciate what you're trying to do. What you and your late husband started in this community. Takes a lot of courage and effort and love to want to help those who got nothin'. This city's been left to rot. Everybody down here knows it," she said, nodding to encompass the law enforcement officials working around her. "We're all too well aware of that fact. So we're appreciative of everything you've been trying to do."

"I just want to—"

"But you don't belong down here. This isn't a place for a politician."

"Look, Corporal," Yutanda began with an air of authority. "I need facts. If I'm ever going to have the slightest chance of bringing about changes to the way this port runs its business, I need to know what's happening down here. And I can't get that from my office. So you don't need to lecture me on just where I belong and where I don't."

Yutanda found herself trembling.

"Too many kids, people, just wasting away because of the drugs flowing through these docks. It's gotta stop. Don't you see that? So I need to know just how the drugs are smuggled in and what—"

"You carry a gun?"

"What?" Yutanda asked, not understanding the question. "What do you mean, do I carry a gun?"

"How you getting home?"

"Well—I—I drove," she stammered. "My car's parked outside the gate."

"Be dark in a half hour. You gonna be gone by then?"

"Well, no, I don't think so. I mean, I want to talk to the investigators about the bomb and whether they found any drugs and then talk to Customs and see where this ship disembarked and what stops it made along the way before docking here."

Yutanda took a step back to give Corporal Stilton a questioning look.

"Are you trying to scare me? Because if you are, I don't appreciate it all that much."

Corporal Stilton's expression seemed to grow angry. Yutanda could see she was about to say something, but then the woman's face softened.

"Everything you just said: getting info from the bomb squad, drugs found on the crime scene, port of entries for ship and cargo—these are all facts that you can get from reading our report from the safety of your office. You don't need to be down here showing your face and putting yourself in—well, let's just say a potentially threatening situation."

"Threatening?"

"Threatening, as in you're putting yourself in danger and possibly the lives of the people you care about, too." Looking at Yutanda with a stern expression, she remarked, "That clear enough for you?"

"I don't understand your tone, Corporal."

"This is all new to you, isn't it assemblywoman? You think trying to change things down here—down here where you say cocaine and heroin are smuggled in—you think it's as easy as just understanding how the whole operation works."

"We'll that's where you have to start before—"

"Shit, Yutanda—don't you think we know how it works? How it's been working? And who the players are?"

"Well, if that's the case, then—"

"This isn't a TV show. These guys play for real. And I mean real—like don't-get-in-my-way-or-you're-dead real." Corporal Stilton raised her pencil-thin eyebrows and opened her eyes wide. "Like put-a-bullet-in-your-head dead, or cut your throat or torch your car while you're still in it. Yeah—you're right about there being some huge amounts of drugs coming through this port," she went on, her eyes looking at the charred shipping containers the bomb squad was going over. "Millions of dollars worth, every month. It's been a known fact for longer than I would care to admit."

"Then why—?"

"Because it runs like the well-oiled machine it is. And it's not just one player who's controlling all of it. And you can't just open every container that comes off one of these freighters unless you have a court order. And that takes probable cause. And that means going in front of a judge with probable cause to get a court order. And that means having specific intel on a specific ship with a specific manifest to point out to the judge what specific containers you believe contain drugs."

"What about customs?"

"Not our jurisdiction," she said, her expression unforgiving. "You'd have to ask them."

"That's why—"

"Look, assemblywoman—Yutanda." Corporal Stilton sighed. "You've got gangs—the Bloods, the Crips, the Ñetas, the Five Percenters—and god knows how many others. You have Italian Mafia, Israelis, Russians, Colombians, Dominicans, Jamaicans, Filipinos and even some homegrown talent—the Family—that either have a foothold on these docks or are trying to take a piece of it. There's huge money flowing in and out of this port. And not one of those groups I just mentioned is going to give up what they have invested here."

Yutanda waited for the woman to keep talking, but it was clear after a moment that Corporal Stilton thought she had explained everything.

"So what you're saying, then, is—"

"Do you carry a gun? That's what I'm saying. Because at some point, madam assemblywoman, if you're going to be putting your face out down here for everyone to see and they get wind that you're the one trying to make some changes to what they got going here and how things are done, then you're going to find yourself on the wrong side of a dark alley some night."

"You can't be serious."

"There were one hundred and seventeen murders in Newark last year, Yutanda. And that doesn't include beatings or people just up and disappearing. Think about it. A hundred and seventeen."

Yutanda took a look around the dock, suddenly feeling exposed.

"And how many do you think were drug related?"

"I—I'd have to look that up."

"That's right; look it up. As in, read it in a report. You don't need to be in every ditch where a body's been dumped and smell the rotting corpse or see the gore of what's left of someone's face that's been bashed in, do you? You can just read it in a report, right?"

Yutanda nodded. "Well, yeah, sure. I mean—"

"That's what I mean by do you carry a gun."

* * *

Chris nibbled on a slice of cornbread while he waited for his takeout order: short ribs, collards, mac 'n' cheese, and of course a tin of the best scratch-made corn bread you were going to find in Newark. The Taylors were in for a treat tonight. Having listened to Ed go on and on about what a good cook Lizbeth was, Chris knew the man and his wife would appreciate a good down-home meal. And Jim's Place had been serving up the best soul food in Newark for the past thirty years. Whenever business brought Chris down this way, he'd make a point of stopping in Jim's to grab a bite. Sitting at the counter and soaking up the atmosphere while the good folks back in the kitchen cooked up his food was what he liked most about coming to Jim's. Though the biscuits with chicken giblet gravy and the lima bean and corn succotash Jim's wife ran as a special during the summer months ran a close second. And listening to the jukebox playing the old 45s was a kick. Always brought a smile to his face hearing some of the old Motown tunes and joining in on occasion when some of the old timers in the place started singing along.

"Set me free, why don't ya babe? Get out of my life, why don't ya babe?" Yeah, that was a line Chris always found himself singing along to. And more often than not, one of the firm-bodied young waitresses Jim's always hired would start grindin' to an old James Brown song probably recorded before the girl was even born. That would normally get the whole place movin'— even the kitchen help would come out from the back of the house to show off their moves. And nobody minded if the food took a little longer getting out to the tables when the bumpin' and grindin' started. The music, the jive, just the whole scene made up for the food arriving a little later than some might like. Everything about Jim's Place was real. Like the place screamed, it had soul.

As Chris waited for his takeout order to be wrapped and put in a travel box, he let the day's events meld into the music, the smells, and the atmosphere of the little soul food restaurant. Planting the bomb, shooting up the terminal, framing the two idiot punks dissipated into the aroma of slow-roasting pork, barbequed baked beans, and the kitchen staff juking to the Temptations, "Papa Was a Rollin' Stone." As for what was to come—driving over to Mercer Street to Yutanda's apartment and visiting with her parents until Yutanda came home—he wasn't worried too much about that—what he was going to say to them or what he shouldn't say. The food he was bringing would keep Ed busy for a while, he knew. And Elizabeth—Lizbeth, as Ed called her—well, he knew she'd taken a liking to him. And he'd been playing off her fondness for him and would continue to use her affection up to a point, as long as she didn't try to pry too deep into his past or try to meddle in his relationship with Yutanda. Confident his portrayal as a freelance security advisor to the corporate world would hold up, he didn't see Ed and Elizabeth as a cause for concern. And he was pretty sure he'd have all the information Rue wanted on Yutanda in another week or two. From everything he had gathered from the wiretap he'd placed on Yutanda's phone the night he'd returned her car keys and purse, it seemed the woman was determined, well organized, and very, very bright, but also in over her head—and more than a little naïve when it came to dealing with organized crime. Better if she had stuck to getting funding for halfway houses or pushing for low-interest rates on student loans or passing legislation for free needle exchange programs for addicts than take on the drug operation at the Seaport, he thought. You don't threaten the livelihood of the Mafia, drug cartels, and gangs without expecting to suffer for it. And man, they could make you suffer. He'd seen plenty examples—too many. And he knew there'd be more to come. He just hoped Yutanda wasn't going to end up being one of them. She was an assemblywoman, for Christ's sake, not a prosecutor or judge. Just what the hell was she thinking?

"Chris, honey, you want a little more lemonade while you're waitin'?"

Chris looked at the pretty young face gazing into his and tried to remember what the seventeen-year-old waitress's name was. Whatever it was, she sure was smokin', he thought, as she rubbed one of her beautiful firm breasts across his upper arm.

"Tanya, stop botherin' the man and pick up your order for table five."

Chris tried to hide his chuckle, giving the girl a wink as she reluctantly walked past him on her way to the pick-up window behind the counter.

"Still not cuttin' nobody no slack, I see," Chris teased the silver-haired, wiry man delivering his takeout order. "Girl was just takin' care of one of your customers."

"Nah, nah, nah, nah, nah, my man. Don't feed me none of that bull. You and I both know what she was doin'."

The sixty-some-year-old put a brown cardboard box with tinfoil wrapping down on the countertop. His wrinkled face crinkling into a smile, he bent close to Chris and said in a low voice, "She'd have your balls in a vice if I didn't move her along. And you wouldn't even know she'd be turnin' the handle till her daddy come runnin' to see why you be screamin' so loud."

He laughed, slapping the counter.

"And her daddy be a Marine," he said, putting on a straight face. "One of those big mean staff sergeants runs the crap out of snot-nosed kids till they cry."

He gave Chris a knowing wink.

"So you best be happy I moved her along."

"Sounds to me like maybe you should have passed on hiring her. Seems like she could be more trouble than she's worth," Chris bantered with a shake of his head and an easygoing smile.

Tanya walked by the two just then, carrying a couple platters of pork shoulder, cabbage, and grits. Both Chris and Jim watched her saunter over to table five, their eyes glued to the teenager's rounded buttocks and the way her hips did a slow, seductive sashay.

"Hope her daddy's close by," Chris remarked. "'Cause he's got a lot of running to do till that girl's safely married."

"God help the boy he catches her with," Jim agreed. "Though, if I knew my time was near, I certainly would consider it a most wonderful way to leave this earth." Closing his eyes, he shook his head and smiled. "Surely, a most wonderful way to die."

A loud ding, ding, ding, ding from the little bell on the pick-up ledge in front of the kitchen was quickly followed by a gruff female voice hollering, "You gonna talk all night, old man? Food sittin' in the window getting' cold! Move your ass!"

Everyone within earshot—and that was most everyone in the restaurant—burst out laughing, Jim chortling himself as he gave Chris a friendly slap on the shoulder.

"Best be going before the old lady whacks me up the side of the head with a spud."

Chris took out a wad of bills and put two fifty-dollar bills on the counter. "Catch you next time," he told Jim as he grabbed the box from the counter.

"You take care, brother. And remember there be plenty of mean staff sergeants out in the world," he said, laughing. "So be good!"

Chris smiled as he walked toward the exit, giving Tanya one last lingering glance as he pushed the door open with his shoulder.

*　*　*

"I watched it all from the other terminal. Went according to plan. The bomb gave customs and the DEA probable cause. So they impounded the ship. And just like you said, they found fifty kilos of coke and fifty of heroin with the sniff dogs."

Rue listened to the voice on the other end of the phone and laughed.

"I'm sure you're right. Lot of pissed-off caballeros in Medellín tonight. No doubt they'll want to strike back, and strike back hard."

Rue glanced at the security monitors to the right of his desk while twisting his swivel chair from side to side.

"Yup. It's on the police report. Attributed to gang activity with all evidence pointing to the Bloods."

Rue nodded, wrapping the phone cord around one of his fat index fingers.

"Yeah, she was down there too. Came as soon as she got the call. Stayed around for a while and got in everybody's way. I'm sure anyone who was watching saw her." Rue leaned forward in his chair. "Look, I don't think we need to worry about her as much as we first thought. My man tells me that she's in over her head. Besides, the new mayor's come around to seeing things our way. I don't think she'll get anywhere with any new legislation."

Rue smoothed back his hair and looked at the ceiling for a moment.

"No, he's still on it. And I'll keep him on her as long as there's a need. Yeah, I agree," he said with a chuckle. "Those lunatics might take her out tomorrow if they think she had a hand in them losing that shipment."

Rue looked at the security monitors again and then checked his watch.

"Without a hitch. We could have unloaded a dozen shipments the way they sent everybody hustling over to Maher. Smooth as silk, half on its way to Philly, the other half to New York, all within a half hour. By the time anyone from Customs came back over to the Newark terminal, the containers were either gone or sealed and back in place."

Rue checked his watch again and shook his head. He frowned.

"Look, Akmir. I'm good on this end. Stop worrying. Everything's covered. If she stirs it up, the groundwork has already been laid. She'll just be another casualty of a senseless crime," he said, smirking. "Now, when's the next shipment due to sail?"

Rue broke out into a smile.

"Good. Better than I thought."

He looked at his watch again.

"Okay, look, it's late. I've— What? Kensington, Maryland? I don't know," he said, his face scrunching up with a perplexed look. "Couple of hours, I guess. Why?"

Rue checked the security monitors again, leaning in toward the screen displaying the area around the back entrance. He nodded when he saw a tall, hooded figure standing at the back door. Cradling the phone between his neck and shoulder, he reached under the desktop overhang and pushed a button while trying to make sense of Akmir saying something about a nun.

"Look, Akmir, can you tell me about this the next time we talk? I've got someone coming up to my office. Yeah, yeah—I'm sure I'll find it interesting. Okay, then. Catch you later."

As Rue was about to hang up, he heard Akmir say something more.

"What was that?" he asked, putting the phone back to his ear. "Oh, right," he said with a touch of exasperation. "As-salaam alaikum to you too."

Just as he put down the phone, the door to his office swung open. A tall, hooded figure stepped through.

"Ah, Layla—so nice of you to come."

* * *

The edge of the queen of hearts cut through the mound of white powder in short, even strokes, every dicing motion methodically grinding coarse cocaine into smooth micro-granules. Following a practiced routine, the queen of hearts then divided the powdered cocaine into three equal portions before elongating each of the subdivided parts into lines roughly two inches in length by a sixteenth of an inch wide. Finally, the queen of hearts turned her face up to the man controlling her, smiling as Griper ran his thumb and forefinger along the long, thin edge of her body and placed the cocaine residue into his mouth. Massaging the granules into his gums, he removed his fingers, pursed his lips, and softly exclaimed, "Fuckin' primo!"

Looking at the long, hostile faces of Twister and Bongo, Griper picked up the frameless square mirror he'd been using as a chopping board and offered the lines of cocaine spread out atop the reflective glass.

"You two did all the work today. Hit it first," he told them, nodding to the lines.

"And took all the fuckin' chances," Twister complained. "Still don't get why the hell he wanted us there."

"We could have been busted," Bongo grumbled. "While you and fuckin' Super Freak be somewhere jerkin' each other off."

"Be cool, my brothers," Griper responded. "It's all cool. Everything went down the way it was s'posed to. The man's happy how it played. That's why he cut us this half ounce of pure." Griper's round, fleshy face took on an expression of delight. "Partake and ride the white horse with compliments from the Freak."

"Don't be playin' us," Twister spat. "Where's the paper? The blow's icin', but you can't put it in the bank."

"Yeah, man, where's our cut?" Bongo chimed in.

Griper put the square section of mirror down, twisted his Yankees hat around so the brim faced backward, and folded his arms across his chest.

"You ever know me to do my brothers wrong?" he challenged. "Here I am offering you some pure paradise, and you don't even show me the respect of doin' a line before we get down to business. Shit—" Stuffing a hand into the side pocket of his pants, he pulled out a wad of bills. Spreading the money out into the shape of a fan, he held the display out toward Bongo and Twister.

"Benjamins," he told them. "Fifteen crisp Bennies. Five for my brother Twister," he said, counting five out of his hand and placing them on the table next to the mirror. "And five for my brother Bongo," he added, going through the same routine. "And that leaves five for me."

Heads nodding in unison as if they were thinking the same thought or hearing the same song in their heads, Twister and Bongo reached for their money with the slightest nuance of smiles on their faces. While Twister folded his five hundred-dollar bills in half and stuffed them in the front pocket of his denim pants, Bongo counted out his money one bill at a time, and when he was done, went through the same process again before slipping the cash into the top band of his underwear.

"Now—what say you we celebrate," Griper said as he rolled one of his hundred-dollar bills into a tight, hollow tube and held it out for one of them to take. "Or do you two have somethin' else you wanna bitch about?" he asked, seeing that Twister and Bongo still didn't look completely satisfied.

"Man, Bloods ain't nothin' to fuck with, bro," Twister said. "I don't wanna get in the middle of no gang shit."

"Yeah, those boys don't play, Gripe. Ain't no five pieces of paper and a little blow gonna help me if they decide to take us down."

Griper shook his head, leaned over the coffee table they were seated around, put the rolled-up bill up to his nostril, bent and snorted one of the three lines of coke up into his nose.

"We done with that," Griper told them, sniffing cocaine farther up into his nasal cavity. "Today was for looks."

He glanced at Twister and Bongo with widening eyes and a contented smile.

"We back in the shadows now. Freak's got it planned out. So be cool, be cool. And take a ride on the charger here," he offered, holding the tube-shaped bill out toward Bongo. "Trust your brother."

7

"WE'VE LOST EVERYTHING." Claire mumbled the words, her voice barely a whisper.

John Too looked over to her as she gazed out upon the waterfall tumbling from a plateau into a deep gorge.

"If we had only stayed where they couldn't find us."

John Too took a step toward her, stopping when Eden stepped in front of him.

"Mother said there is no such place," the girl told her, placing a hand on Claire's shoulder.

Claire reached up and took hold of Eden's hand.

"*Zār* can find you wherever you go," Eden went on. "You cannot hide from it, she would always say."

"Zār?" Claire asked, perplexed. "Is that a person?"

"It can take the form of one," John Too interjected, stepping closer. "Zār is evil. A demon. Something that possesses you."

"Evil—yes," Claire dazedly repeated. "So much of it. It seems—" Claire looked at each of them as though she had just awakened to find them standing over her. "It's frightening."

"Frightening?" Eden questioned. "Why would *you* be afraid?"

"I don't know anyone who is not frightened by evil," Claire said, squeezing the girl's hand.

"But you are tabib! Even the warlord was afraid of you."

To Eden's surprise, John Too started to laugh.

"And you have him!" Eden exclaimed, pointing a finger at John Too. "Zār will not dare come here!"

Claire furrowed her brow and tilted her face. Looking first at Eden and then at John Too, she said in a sad voice, "Zār has already come—and continues to. The children—Thomas and the others—they're gone." She gave Eden a quizzical look.

"Do you understand, Eden? When men—when people—kill and steal and sell those they capture into slavery, it is evil that consumes them. Call it whatever name you wish, but it is evil, and it is here, and will continue, it seems."

Claire looked away, casting her gaze to the wide, majestic waterfall of the Tekezé River and the highlands beyond.

"Look," Eden whispered, pointing to a flock of large white birds flying into view. "The sacred birds," she said, as a dozen wide-winged, white-feathered birds glided across the face of the waterfall.

"It is as he has said to me." John Too approached Claire as he spoke. "The Father and the Mother offer what is pure."

The sun-drenched mist billowing up from the bottom of the waterfall suddenly glittered with a dozen miniature rainbows.

"And we are left to choose." John Too placed a hand gently upon Claire's arm. "Paradise for those who would embrace it." The flock of white birds sailed out of sight. "Emptiness for those who won't."

Claire remained silent, staring off into space. John Too moved his hand from her arm to her far shoulder, hugging her against his body.

"You are not alone, Sister Lady. The Father and the Mother are here. Zār cannot defeat hope."

"I wish it was so," Claire replied, staring blankly ahead. "Everything," she said, shrugging her shoulders and shaking her head, "since I've come here—everything's gone, taken. I—I don't understand."

"What is wrong with her?" Eden interrupted, her tone incredulous, her attention fixed to John Too. "She is tabib. She has powers."

Bending forward, she looked straight into Claire's face.

"You have the glowing bracelet of sacred beetles. You have bouda," she told her in a stern manner. "And you have him!" she animatedly said, pointing a finger at John Too. Pulling at the purple material covering her head, she exclaimed, "Yet you say everything is gone! How can you not see? *Min fadlik!*" she exclaimed, raising her face to the sky. "Please—you have everything! Friends who would rescue you!"

Covering her face with her hands, she shook her head.

"That you would be me," she went on, her voice growing calmer. "Alone—with strangers—*gwa chi cho*—" She whirled, glaring at John Too when he chuckled. "*Then* you can say you are alone."

Her dark brown eyes softened as she looked longingly into Claire's face. "Then you will know what it is to lose all."

"I'm—I'm sorry child."

Claire stood, extending her arms. Eden stepped away.

"It was wrong of me," Claire confessed. Letting her arms fall to her sides, she added, "I was—feeling sorry for myself."

Claire closed her eyes.

"Every man shall give as he is able, according to the blessings of the Lord," she said, bowing her head and clutching the silver cross about her neck. "And bear one another's burdens, to fulfill the law of Jesus Christ." Giving Eden a sheepish glance, she offered, "Sometimes I lose my way. And zār, as you call it, seems always to be waiting when I do."

"Can't you make her feel better?" Eden pointedly asked John Too, a touch of sarcasm in her voice. "Does she not know who you are?"

"Who *he* is?" Claire confusedly asked. "What do you mean, Eden? He is John Too. A child, like you."

"Ha, no! Not like me," Eden emphatically stated, pointing a finger at her chest. "I am not *abdar*," she explained, shaking her head. "No—not *abdar*."

"*Abdar*?" Claire questioned. "What is she saying, John Too?"

"She speaks of the old ways," John Too replied, looking at the waterfall as he spoke. "Before the time of the boy. Before the Father sent him to live among his people."

"John Too," Claire lightly reprimanded.

"He—the boy—he is *abdar* now," John Too explained as he turned to look at her. "As *abdar* is in those he wishes it to be."

The close-sounding snarl of an animal took them all by surprise. John Too the first to react, darting over to where he had left his bow and satchel of arrows. But even as he bent to grab them, the foliage of the bushes near to them parted, the black muzzle of a hyena appearing.

"*Koom!*" a voice shouted from behind the animal as the hyena stepped out of the underbrush. "*Dähna hun.*"

The beast—a large male with a barrel chest and square muzzle—stopped. When John followed the beast out from the bush, the hyena moved to him, placing his head near his hand.

"*Melkam guzo yehunelih,*" John said, scratching behind the animal's ear. "Safe journey back."

With a suspicious glance toward Eden, Claire, and John Too, the hyena walked back into the thicket and disappeared. John lifted two modest-sized grouse hanging about his neck as he watched the animal depart.

"We eat," he said, holding the birds up.

* * *

Eden proved very adept at cleaning and roasting the birds, explaining as she removed the skewered grouse from atop the fire she'd constructed that she had learned the ways of caring for family at a very early age. Her mother—being Tigrinya and following the traditional ways—had schooled her in farming, fire building, water sourcing, cooking, and mending by the time she was able to walk behind an ox. Her father—a university professor from the city of Juba in southern Sudan—had taught her to read and speak in both Arabic and English. As Eden babbled on while cutting up the cooked birds, Claire began to see the girl in a new light. Eden, she realized, was not an ordinary rural farm girl who knew nothing of the world outside her own village.

"And where is he now, your father?" Claire asked as the girl served John half a grouse.

With a slight bow of her head to John, she replied, "It is hard to say. He went back to Sudan a year or more ago with one of his brothers. To join the fight for independence, he told us."

Shrugging her shoulders, she thrust the knife John Too had lent her into the second of the two birds.

"Mother told me they have been fighting there forever. No different than here," she observed, slicing through the breastbone of the second bird, splitting it in two. "Dead, captured, missing." She paused to think. "How will we ever know? Especially now."

"Now?" Claire asked as Eden served John Too.

"Now that Mother is gone," she replied matter-of-factly. "I will never see her again." She shrugged. "I know this."

"Won't you try to find her? We could help."

Eden gave Claire a surly look, but then laughed, her face changing to one of mischief.

"Oh, Tabib—you tease me. Here, eat," she told Claire, handing her half of a cooked bird.

"I would never tease you, Eden. Why would you think that? If I could be of *any* help in finding your mother, surely I would hope, in the name of the Lord, you would know I speak the truth."

"Tabib."

"Stop calling me that. My name is Claire, Sister Claire."

Eden looked first at John and then at John Too.

"What name does she go by?" she whispered as though Claire could not hear her speaking.

John Too giggled, while John nearly choked on a mouthful of food.

"She is Sister Lady," John Too said, laughing, his face alight with joy. "As she will always be."

Eden scrunched up her face, placing a finger against her cheek. After tapping her jawbone a few times, she looked squarely at John and said, "The bouda calls her something different, yes? What name do you see when you look at her?"

John looked over at Claire, his expression unreadable. Claire hesitantly met his gaze before looking down at her food.

"Sister Lady," he said after a moment had passed. "As Teimbaka first said it to be."

"Who?" Eden asked. "And what can he do?"

"He is—" Claire stopped, her face suddenly filled with concern. "Where is he, John Too? Do you know? Did the elephants say where he was needed?"

"Elephants?" Eden laughed. "Does he talk to elephants?" she mocked.

"Be silent!" John barked, jaw rigid, eyes brooding.

"Teimbaka is chosen," John Too calmly told the girl. "He hears the voice of the Mother and walks with the spirits of her children. He is a protector. The spirit elephants are bound to him—as he is to them."

Eden lowered her head, squatting down on the ground. Pulling a strip of grouse from the half of bird she had saved for herself, she placed the morsel in her mouth and began to chew. Glancing up, she eyed John Too with suspicion.

"Would you deceive me, Abdar?" she asked. "For mother once told me a tale—from the days of old as you call them—of a man who will one day appear as if out of nowhere with mountainous spirit elephants by his side. The tale says this man will put an end to the killing, that he will bring peace to this land. And to every other land that we cannot see."

She plucked another strip off the cooked grouse and stuck it in her mouth.

"Is this he? Is this Teimbaka—as you call him—is he the man of the tale?"

"Eden," Claire cautioned, "Teimbaka is just a man."

No sooner had the words left her mouth than Claire fell silent, her expression thoughtful.

"The tale my mother told me spoke of this as well. I do not know what it means—and still don't. You see, Sister Lady," she went on, talking with her mouth full of food, "the tale says the man, when he appears, will be but an ordinary man—but that he isn't ordinary at all. It makes no sense to me," she added before anyone else had a chance to speak. "No," she said with a shake of her head, "makes no sense at all."

From some distance away, a hyena called. John was quick to turn his head and listen. When the beast repeated the laughing rant, John looked to the others.

"We must move," he told them. "The warlord is tracking us. Cover the fire."

"How is it you—?" Claire fell silent, nodding.

"But where?" John Too asked.

"Where we told Teimbaka we would be waiting," Claire immediately answered.

"We can't," John told her. "There is nothing there but death—and war."

"Then we need to find *him*," Claire said with a note of urgency. "As Eden needs to find her mother. As we need to find Thomas—and all the other children."

To Claire's astonishment, Eden laughed.

"Where?" the girl asked her. "Where would you look, Sister Claire?" She grunted. "Did you not see the trucks drive off in every direction? They could be anywhere." When Eden paused, Claire saw sadness pulling at the girl's face. "And nowhere where you would want to find them."

"But surely we must try," Claire gently countered.

John Too stood, shouldering his bow and arrows.

"It is as Sister Lady says; we must try."

Eden shrugged, stuffing a large piece of food into her mouth.

"And where will Abdar do this?" she inquired, smacking her lips. "Where will we *try*?"

Claire got up from where she had been sitting and moved to stand next to John Too.

"What is it you see?" she asked him, resting a hand on his shoulder. "Where will we find Teimbaka and the others?"

"I do not know, Sister Lady," he said in earnest. "But the mountain monkeys, the baboons, kept watch to the west while Teimbaka slept. As if they were waiting for someone."

"West? But that would take us toward Sudan. Far from our home."

"All the Mother is our home," he softly replied. "Would Teimbaka not say the same?"

"There is a vast herd of elephants there," Eden said to no one in particular. "My father told me of them when he was forced to leave Juba. He said they roam a good ways north of Kenya, near the western border of Ethiopia."

"How far away is that?" Claire asked.

"Several days," Eden answered.

The calls of the hyenas drew closer, their voices swelling.

"Take them, John Too," John ordered, clasping the horn of the impala. Gazing east, where the hyenas cried, he said, "I will lead them north for a day or more. I will find you."

"John!" Claire called. "Wait!"

But John was gone, disappearing into the forest as Claire shouted his name.

Not long after, Eden, Claire, and John Too began the journey toward the border of Sudan. A sense of urgency quickened what was already a hurried pace when the haunting scream of some tormented beast rose above the laughing rants of hyenas.

* * *

Kamua squeezed the stock of his ranger-issued Lee-Enfield bolt-action rifle as the old Land Rover neared the mass of swirling vultures they had been driving toward for the past hour. Tengene had first spotted the aberration—resembling something like a giant storm cloud spinning in the sky—and directed Selam to change direction so they might study the odd formation.

Only after they had traveled a few kilometers did they realize the dark, whirling form in the sky above them were the winged bodies of hundreds of scavenger birds.

"Have you seen any of them drop down or fly lower?" he asked from the back seat of the Land Rover.

"Now that you mention it, I haven't. A little strange," Tengene added, turning his head to look back at Kamua.

"The predators must still be at the kill—and in great numbers," Selam commented as he maneuvered the Land Rover across a dry creek bed. "Make certain your weapons are ready in case we need use of them."

"But vultures are not normally afraid to land near a kill, even if a lion or leopard is still guarding the carcass. I have seen the birds hopping between an entire *pride* feeding on several wildebeests before."

"I wouldn't think we will be finding any wildebeests this far north," Tengene remarked. "You're speaking of your time in Kenya, yes?"

"What is this?" Selam uttered as he brought the Land Rover to an abrupt stop. "Am I dreaming?"

Kamua vaulted out of the back seat, moving toward the front of the Land Rover until he was parallel to the driver's-side door. He looked over at Selam and then looked ahead.

A mammoth bull elephant stood thirty paces in front of them, its massive ears casually flapping back and forth, its gaze focused squarely on the three rangers and their vehicle. From the size of the beast—somewhere between four and five meters tall, Kamua guessed—and the length of the animal's tusks, the bull was aged, perhaps all of seventy years or more. When he heard the sound of a rifle bolt sliding back, he looked questioningly at Selam. The man raised his rifle to his shoulder, aiming—it seemed to Kamua—right at the elephant.

"No!" Kamua protested. "What are you doing? Don't shoot him. He is magnificent."

"Not the elephant," Selam muttered. Refusing to take his eyes away from his rifle sight, he jutted his chin forward. "There."

The male lion was so large the size of the animal took Kamua's breath away. How could he have missed seeing such an impressive specimen standing next to the elephant? Slowly, he began raising his rifle up to his right shoulder.

"No," Selam whispered. "No movement. Tengene has his sight on him too."

Kamua did as instructed.

"What are they doing here? And why are they together?" Kamua whispered.

"Why don't you ask them?" Selam half-joked.

Kamua sighed, shifting his weight from one foot to the other, embarrassed for having sounded so stupid.

"Yes, go ahead," Tengene prodded him with a soft laugh. "I'd like to hear their answer."

Kamua edged a half step forward.

"What language do you think they understand?" he said, deciding to play along. "Arabic? Amharic? Afar? English, perhaps?"

"Try English," Tengene teased. "By the looks of them, I am certain they have been here since the British first laid claim to the land."

The three of them laughed. But when the elephant and the lion each took a step toward them, they stopped.

"Why are you here?" Kamua abruptly shouted, glancing over at Selam and Tengene with a mischievous smile. "And—and why are you together?"

The roar of the lion and the trumpeting wail of the elephant were so overwhelming, Kamua dropped his rifle and covered his ears. To his utter shock, the bull elephant charged, tusks raking soil. In a moment of terror, Kamua watched the mammoth animal rip up a huge slab of earth and propel it up and over the Land Rover. Kamua bent in the blinding rain of debris, frantically feeling for his weapon. With the sound of his heart pounding in his ears, he located the rifle, hugging it to his chest. Blinking away dust, spitting particles of dirt from his mouth, he braced himself for what he guessed would be a lion attack.

"Gone," Selam whispered. "Nothing."

As Selam spoke, Kamua listened, hearing no sounds. Even the squawking cries of the vultures had ceased.

"Look—there."

It was Tengene who spoke. Kamua following the man's pointing finger to see a figure tied face-first to a tree some fifty paces ahead, dark lines crisscrossing the person's exposed back.

"A man," Tengene mumbled.

"Come," Selam said, exiting the vehicle. "Bring the first-aid kit. Help me cut the poor bastard down."

* * *

Kamua listened to the roar of the lion and smiled. Motioning with his hand as though conducting an orchestra, he made a concise downstroke with his outstretched finger just as the blaring call of the elephant sounded.

"Good for another hour now," he said, chuckling.

"I hope they stretch it to every two hours soon," Tengene remarked, sitting on the opposite side of the fire. "Three would be even better. That way we could all get some sleep before we each take watch."

"Perhaps you could suggest it to them, Kamua," Selam joked. "Seeing how well you communicated with them before."

"Was that not the strangest thing?" Kamua replied. "And now they linger somewhere close—though I couldn't find a trace of either of the beasts when I searched. But still—still they are here," he observed, his slender face moving in a slow circle as he peered into the darkness. "Strange."

He shook his head.

"Have you ever heard or seen such a thing like this before?"

Tengene and Selam said nothing in response, remaining silent, their thoughts lost in the flames of the fire.

Kamua studied them, watching Tengene rub his fleshy cheeks up and down with his large, plump hands as if trying to adjust the fit of his face to his skull. Selam, his thin, bony features half covered in shadows, was preoccupied with something along the edges of the bright orange flames flickering in front of him. Perhaps he was revisiting a memory, Kamua thought, the man remembering a stolen kiss taken by candlelight when his wiry, bent body was lean and strong. Or, Kamua conjectured, perhaps the man was recalling an image, one he himself was seeing within the flames: torches carried by mercenaries marching upon his village, butchering all those who dared stand in their way, setting fire to dwellings, crops, and equipment.

Not wanting to revisit the memory, Kamua shifted his attention to the man they'd found, wondering—as he had been since they had come upon him—just who the man was and why he had been tied to a tree. And why he'd been whipped, and by whom, and why the man wasn't dead. Even more perplexing than who the man was, was this lion and this elephant, he thought. Ever since the two beasts had vanished in the cloud of dust, they wouldn't leave. Beginning their hourly roaring and wailing soon after Selam and Tengene cut the man from the tree. And now, even after a dozen hours had passed, they continued, blaring their cries as if keeping time with a clock. What was it the elephant and lion wanted?

Gazing at the bandages they'd applied to the man's wounds, Kamua realized it was time for them to be changed, the open gashes hidden beneath the gauze needing more honey salve applied. The lash of the whip had torn deep into the man's flesh. Infection—if it set in—would surely be the end of him, Kamua knew. But as Kamua started to reach for the first-aid kit, he thought better of it, deciding to let the man sleep. Rest, or any moment of peace the man could find, would do him good. For the poor bastard—as Selam persisted in calling him—was nearly dead when they had carried him to the Land Rover. And when they had turned him on his side to tend to his wounds and discovered the jagged scars raked across his chest and the smaller, fresher ones streaking his face, they all shook their heads, muttering what prayers they could remember. The man's body was a battlefield, Kamua observed, the multitude of scars leaving Kamua to wonder what hell the man had already been through—and why he was being made to suffer once again.

"Can you take the first watch, Kamua?" Selam asked.

Kamua nodded, saying, "Yes. I am good. You two rest while the beasts offer us some quiet," he joked.

"Yes, please Kamua, if you happen to see your two friends, tell them to knock it off for the night so we can sleep," Tengene said, chuckling, though the weariness in his voice made Kamua believe he wouldn't find it so amusing to be kept up all night.

"And tell the bigger one not to throw any more dirt," Selam added with a laugh, "I am still picking bits from my hair."

Kamua chuckled at the banter, but slid his rifle onto his lap as Tengene and Selam laid themselves down on the ground with their backs to the fire.

Once Selam and Tengene were settled, Kamua got up and walked the few paces to the pile of wood they'd gathered before sunset. Shouldering his rifle, he bent and grabbed two thick branches from top of the stack. As he turned to place them onto the fire, he glimpsed an odd shape emerging from the darkness, approaching the camp near where the injured man lay.

Immediately, Kamua tossed the branches to the ground, slipping the rifle from his shoulder. A moment later, he stifled a laugh as a savanna hare—long ears held straight and high atop its head—slowly hopped into the light of the campfire. When the animal noticed Kamua, it stopped. In turn, Kamua smiled at the hare, placing his rifle down by his side.

Bending to one knee, Kamua extended a hand in greeting. Ears twitching, nose wriggling, the hare moved no closer. Waiting to see what the animal would do, Kamua sat down on the grass and crossed his legs. To his pleasant surprise, the hare immediately hopped a few paces closer. Stretching its torso long and flat along the ground, the animal inched forward, sniffing the air as it drew near. When the creature reached the injured man lying on the ground, it rose up on its hind legs, pausing to study Kamua for a moment before jumping over the man's body. Haunches elevated, chest and forelegs pressed close to the ground, the hare moved next to the wounded man. When the animal rose and placed its two front paws on the man's back, Kamua leaped up to chase it away. But the hare didn't flinch, ignoring the sudden movement as it calmly went about sniffing the man's bandages.

"It must be the honey salve," Kamua murmured as he watched the animal touch the man's back in several places.

As if the hare could understand him, it turned to look at him. Kamua stared into the hare's eyes.

Irises the color of desert sand lured Kamua into a landscape of windswept dunes, smooth-faced ridges of sun-gold powder shifting and tumbling in hypnotic waves. Lured deeper into the orbs' soothing, rolling motion, Kamua felt his awareness drifting with the ever-moving flow, cascading toward a sparkling yellow flare rising on the far fringe of a curling, swelling dune. Mesmerized, Kamua stared at sprays of pinks and orange-tinged white radiating along the light's crest, the feel of an imaginary hand on the back of his neck guiding him toward the intoxicating vision. Suddenly, sand-colored irises turned green. The yellow flare exploded, rose-colored shards splaying past emerald pools, rocketing into darkness. Kamua started to scream, but a hand slid from the back of his neck across his cheek to cover his mouth. Reaching up to pull the hand away, Kamua turned to catch the fleeting glimpse of a woman's face floating beside him in a misty haze. As though caught in a whirlpool of air, the mist began to swirl, pressing gently against his skin, the fragrance of a thousand flowers seeping into his nose. Threads of heady vapor sewing a dewy blanket across his eyes, Kamua slipped into a dream-like darkness, a gentle hand lowering his head softly to the ground.

* * *

Dear God, it's hot, Sarah thought. *I hope the church where we're going has air conditioning.*

"It shouldn't be too much longer, Sister. Some sort of military higher-up being escorted to the French Embassy, from what I can gather. Once they pass through, we should be at the diocese in a few minutes."

Sister Sarah looked at Father Gebre from the back seat of the old, box-styled Renault, trying to decide if she was going to take a liking to the thirtyish, goateed, smooth-headed, very black-skinned man sliding into the driver's seat. He seemed to know everything about everything, she'd concluded. Including how God interpreted the way Djibouti built roads, the airport, the docks, and the decrepit railway system. At this rate, she thought, Father Gebre would probably locate Sister Claire all by himself—and within the hour. She laughed.

"You find sitting in a traffic tie-up amusing?"

Sarah cleared her throat and placed her hand to her lips as if she had just accidently spit bits of food out of her mouth.

"I was just thinking I've been sitting and waiting for what seems like two days," she told him, glancing between the street outside her open car window and his inquisitive dark brown eyes. "I guess I find it amusing I am made to sit and wait yet again."

"God's way of allowing you to see the country you have traveled so far to get to and get a sense of its people."

He smiled at her through the rearview mirror.

"He is amazing in the ways He works. Do you not agree, Sister?"

"Indeed, Father. As He has always been and will continue to be," she replied, returning his smile.

Watching him shift his attention out the windshield, she hoped they'd be moving soon. For the air was thick and hot, smelling of salt and dirty sand. It made her wonder if where she was headed was going to be like this place—hot, dry, and smelly—if all parts of Africa she would be traveling to would be the same.

"I might suggest, after we stop in the diocese and deposit your bag in the rectory, we walk to Hotel Rayan to see if Mr. Savage is there, having what I am told is his customary late afternoon alcoholic beverage."

He turned around and smiled at her once again.

"Or, better I say *beverages*," he told her, accentuating the *s*.

The distinctive sound of automatic gunfire made Sarah gasp and jolted Father Gebre's attention back to the street in front of them.

"Afar!" Father Gebre shouted. "Quick, get out of the car and find—"

Bullets strafed the car ahead of them, Father Gebre ducking sideways as the vehicle's back window shattered, splaying the Renault's windshield with broken glass.

"What's going on?" Sarah screamed.

"Get out of the car, Sister!" Father Gebre yelled. "Get to a side street!"

And then all hell broke loose.

Gunfire exploded, seemingly from all around her, the sound deafening, terrifying, confusing. Bullets fired from every direction. In a state of shock, Sarah stared straight ahead, trying to process everything she was seeing: Five bare-chested, very dark-skinned men with flowing black hair, dressed in white robes with large, curved knives strapped to their waists, running in their direction from the far side of the boulevard, firing machine guns. Bystanders in the line of fire shot, screaming as they fell to the ground. Glass shattering, cars honking and driving onto sidewalks as drivers tried to escape. People, panic-stricken, running and shouting, diving for cover.

And for some reason, Sarah found she couldn't move.

Sarah sat wide-eyed, her mouth open in a silent, paralyzed scream. The windshield of the Renault blasted inward, a big shard of glass flying toward her head, slicing open a gash just above her left eyebrow as it rocketed past. In a daze, she watched her hand shoot up to her forehead, her fingers red and wet when she pulled them away, blood dripping from the tips. Her breath accelerating, throat constricting, muscles tensing, a scream barreled up inside her. Then a hand grabbed her shoulder, squeezing the muscle attached to her neck. Pain shot down her back as the hand pulled at her collarbone. Panic stricken, she slapped at her assailant, kicking at the seat of the car as she curled herself into a ball and screamed.

"Sister!"

The voice was angry, awful, accusatory, and loud. A dark form loomed over her.

"Sister! Calm down! Let me help you out of the car!"

Shaking, her entire body feeling as though it was collapsing inward, she tried to focus on the dark shape reaching for her, frantic to understand what was happening. *White, white, white!* her fragmented thoughts screamed. *A ring of white!* She stared at it, locked onto it, fervently reached for it, gasping in terror and relief when she felt the stiff white fabric of the collar between her fingers.

"Yes, Sister, that's right! It's me, Father Gebre! Come on, come on, let's get you out of the car!"

Like a blubbering child, Sarah slid from the backseat and fell into the arms of Father Gebre.

"Now let's get out of here!"

Just as Sarah nodded and looked up into the man's smiling face, the car ahead of them exploded, front end lifting off the ground, frame screeching backward. A fireball shot into the sky, pieces of metal and glass flying through the air. Sarah covered her ears as streaking shrapnel screamed past. Then a second explosion rocked the ground beneath her feet. Father Gebre's body lurched sideways, Sarah dazedly watching him fall to the ground. Fire was suddenly everywhere—smoke, the rushing whoosh of spreading flames making it hard to think, to breathe, to see.

"Father!" she screamed, dropping to her knees and pulling at the man's body. "Father! Where should we go? Father! Father Gebre!"

She didn't understand at first, didn't know what the liquid pooling by the man's neck was—but then his white collar turned crimson. Suddenly dizzy and weak, she stared into the growing pool of blood by Father Gebre's head, the urge to vomit rushing up her throat. As she fought to gain control over the heaving wave of nausea, the gunfire became eerily distant, as did the screams of the people around her. Overwhelmed, she covered her face with her hands and sobbed.

Metal crashing against pavement sent her sprawling forward as the blue Renault was hit by gunfire, tires exploding, rubber shredded by bullets. Scrambling to get away, Sarah tripped over Father Gebre's feet, her hand landing in the pool of blood as she fought to keep her balance. Retching, gagging, her breathing reduced to shuddering gasps, she found herself on her hands and knees, arms shaking as she struggled to keep her body from collapsing.

Gas! some voice from deep inside her screamed. *There's gas!* The fumes were overpowering. She turned to see liquid pouring out the rear panel of the Renault, a river of it flowing toward the curb with her in between. Flames engulfed the car in front of the Renault and spread back, jumping from one puddle of fuel to the next. *Run! Run!* her head screamed. Sarah scrambled to her feet and staggered away.

Igniting with a roar, the Renault's gas tank exploded, hurtling shock waves outward, leveling everything in a radius of twenty feet. Sarah was propelled into the side of a building, her shoulder smashing into a wall, pain shooting down the side of her body, breath knocked from her lungs. Disoriented, terrified, one arm hanging limp by her side, she somehow kept her feet beneath her, half running, half stumbling ahead.

Breathe, breathe, breathe—why can't I breathe? Move! Run! Oh, God! Breathe! Smoke—so much smoke! Fire—fire everywhere! There—there—out in the street—an opening! Go! Escape! Go!

Sarah ran onto the Boulevard de la République, another earth-rattling explosion causing her to stumble. As she fell roughly to her knees, bullets raked the ground beside her in an arc. Bringing her arms up to cover her head, she glimpsed a man running toward her, a large, curved knife in one hand, a gun of some sort held in his other.

"Give me your hand!" a voice shouted.

She saw an arm reaching down toward her. Startled, she looked up to find a man in a blue uniform standing next to her. Grabbing his outstretched arm, Sarah felt herself lifted and then flung to the side, the man suddenly lurching backward, spinning awkwardly, blue uniform turning purple as he fell to the ground.

A scream—primal, violent, fanatical, menacing. Sarah looked up, trying to make sense of what she was seeing. Flowing black hair; long, curved knife held at shoulder height; brown eyes—innocent-looking but crazed; a mouth twisted with rage. A deafening blast, a blinding flash, the stench of burnt sulfur rushing up her nostrils. She gagged as something wet and hot sprayed her face. The man with the flowing black hair staggered backward, the long, curved knife tumbling through the air in slow turns.

"Are you fucking crazy?" a man's voice screamed into her ear.

Stunned, Sarah felt herself being pulled toward the far side of the street. Staring at objects rushing by her, she tried to make sense of what was happening. A pistol jerking upward, a flash exploding out of the barrel, the booming sound of the weapon reverberating through her head, the smell of sulfur again—and gunpowder—overwhelming her senses. Her thoughts became clouded, dizzy.

"Stay behind me!" the male voice shouted.

Hands grabbed her shoulders, pressing her against a wall. Wincing from pain shooting down her side, she numbly stared at the man's neck while he raised something up to his face. She heard something whirring, and then a click, click, click. The man turned around and smiled. She saw stubble on his chin and the incredible blue of his eyes. Pressing her head against the man's shoulder, she sighed.

"I don't know what the hell you're doing here, Sister," Dirk Savage said. "But let's get you off this street.

8

"I DON'T LIKE this."

"Then turn around and close your eyes."

Akmir wrapped one end of his black-and-white keffiyeh across his shoulder to cover the bottom of his face.

"If Adiam finds out, he'll be angry."

"Adiam," Akmir scoffed. "He is getting old in the mind. What are we, Bin'ka, businessmen or Bedouins?"

He smirked.

"What was it Susenyo always said? Everything has a price, so everything is for sale? Yes? Remember?"

"Susenyo was a fat *khanzeer*," Bin'ka remarked.

"Pig or no pig, the man knew how to make money."

Bin'ka shrugged his massive shoulders, fastening the middle button of his chocolate-colored Armani suit coat. With a scowl on his face, he watched a procession of dark shapes moving through stacks of crates.

"Selling people." Shaking his head, he gazed out over the Gulf of Tadjoura. "It's not like selling *things*. It's—troublesome," he told the smaller, thin-framed man.

Even without turning to look, Bin'ka could feel Akmir's dark, hawk-like eyes studying him.

"I have a cousin who works in the administration office at Cairo University," Akmir said. "Perhaps you would like me to call him and see if there's an opening in the philosophy department."

Akmir pushed the sleeve of his *thawb* up his arm, checking the time on his rare Paul Newman vintage Rolex watch.

"In another few minutes, these *abeebs* will be on the path to their rightful place amongst the only true people of this world. They are as nothing, Bin'ka. As it has always been with those of black skin."

"Ask the General of the Adal what he thought of the *nothings*, as you call them, in 1527," Bin'ka countered. "True people of the world," he sarcastically added. "If the black goo pooled beneath the sands of your deserts weren't there, most of your true people would still be riding camels and picking sand fleas out of each other's asses."

The two men looked at each other in silence. Bin'ka watched Akmir's hand disappear in the folds of his white *thawb*, where he knew the man kept a knife.

"It is the Serpent's trade," Bin'ka went on, stepping closer to Akmir so the bulk of his powerful body pressed against Akmir's shoulder. He glared down into Akmir's eyes. "Selling souls will haunt you to Jahannam."

"Please," Akmir lightly countered, stepping away and drawing his hand out from the folds of his robes, "you speak of trivialities, my friend. We are just businessmen. Nothing more."

Lifting his arms outward from his chest, he faced his palms to the sky.

"See them, Bin'ka. Look what we sell. They are nothing but impoverished, ignorant orphans who would likely perish within a year. They should thank us," he told him with a definitive nod.

Bin'ka grunted and shook his large, rounded head. "You are *majnoon*. There are more than just street urchins and orphans there," he said, nodding toward the dock. "I am not blind. There are two Afar girls there you sell. You are begging to have your throat slit by one of their curved blades."

"Wandering goat herders," he said with a dismissive wave of his hand. "They are nothing that concerns me."

"They are warriors," Bin'ka argued. "Didn't you hear of the attack today on the Boulevard? Seven of the Afar assassinated the commander of Lemonnier and six of his guard. And two policemen and a dozen bystanders," he went on, his voice rising with intensity. "Is this what you call goat herders? Is this nothing?"

Shaking his head, he looked at Akmir with a troubled expression.

"*Majnoon.* If that is what you say is nothing, then you *are* crazy."

"Fanatics on a suicide mission," Akmir calmly replied. "None escaped with their lives. And for what? To kill a colonel or a general—someone who has already been replaced?" Akmir shook his head. "No, Bin'ka," he disagreed, his small, round eyes squinting to slits, "these are not men to fear. They have no strategy, no design. Men like that—they will never know how or where to find me, or if I even exist."

"It does not take a fool to follow the path to this port. They were in the city today."

Bin'ka did a slow search of the dock: ships' running lights and giant spotlights mounted on cranes and loading platforms created a patchwork of shadows within large areas of glaring brightness.

"Some could be here right now," he said, as he watched two dozen murky figures of human cargo hurried across an open area along the pier, "sharpening their knives."

Akmir turned his attention to the dock, his attention focused on one of the smaller transport ships moored some hundred meters from where they stood. As he pulled his keffiyeh away from his face, the hint of a smile appeared at the corners of his lips.

"If the Afar are here, then they best hurry. For the loading begins."

Bin'ka followed the path of Akmir's pointing finger. The ship—white with a dark green keel, flying an Egyptian flag—lowered the ramp of its aft loading bay. As the thick metal plate clanged against concrete, Bin'ka watched the cargo of slaves hurried onto the ship.

"You see, Bin'ka. For all your misgivings, they are herded into their stalls without incident—like the sheep they are. *Abeebs*—slaves—they know where they belong."

Sighing, he smoothed the sleeves of his *thawb*.

"It is done. Let us go to our meeting with Adiam."

With a grunt, Bin'ka turned and began walking with Akmir toward the white Mercedes limousine they'd arrived in. Abruptly, both men stopped.

"Is that Muhammad?" Bin'ka peered at the dark shape of a body lying next to the Mercedes. "Is he asleep?"

Akmir said nothing in response as he produced a shiny handgun from the folds of his robe.

A sound—like an empty paint can bouncing across an asphalt floor— came from a point off to their left, some thirty paces from where they were standing. Bin'ka pulled an Uzi from the inside of his Armani suit coat, extending the rear stock adapter.

"There," Akmir whispered. "Standing near that loading crane."

Bin'ka shifted his attention to a mammoth piece of rust-colored machinery resembling half a truss bridge. Near the bottom of the closest support column, Bin'ka saw her. Or saw what he thought was a woman. For the person was dressed in a hooded gray robe, locks of white or blonde hair visible from the edges of the material hiding the person's head. From where he stood, Bin'ka couldn't tell much else.

"Can you see what uniform the man is wearing? I can't tell from this distance."

"Uniform?" Bin'ka scanned the area around the woman, thinking he had missed seeing someone else. "I don't understand."

"No matter," Akmir said. "He's a dead man."

The figure suddenly bolted to a stack of nearby shipping containers, disappearing behind them.

Akmir touched Bin'ka on the shoulder. "Go left," he said, motioning with his shiny gun. "Let's be done with this quickly." And then he was off, moving ahead and to the right, his footsteps quick and deliberate.

Bin'ka went left as Akmir had instructed, but his pace was more cautious. There were too many hiding places along the dock to be careless, he knew, too many places where more than one person could be holed up, waiting to spring an ambush. He had seen but the one figure standing by the loading crane. Yet, from what Akmir had said, there were two: a man in a uniform and the woman in a flowing gray robe. If that was the case, then what had happened to Muhammad? Who had knocked *him* unconscious— or was he dead? Perhaps there were many unseen persons about. Gripping the Uzi with both hands, Bin'ka moved guardedly ahead.

Nearing the stack of shipping containers the figure had run to for cover, Bin'ka stopped. Crouching, he shuffle-stepped to the farthest edge of the lowest container and peeked around the corner. Akmir was twenty paces ahead, facing into the opening between two pallets of crates, gun pointed straight ahead, chest-high. Bin'ka squinted, turning his face ever so slightly to the right. Was Akmir talking to someone?

Fog suddenly appeared, swirling around Akmir's feet. Bin'ka looked out to the gulf to see thick, white waves of mist rolling in off the water as if pro-pelled by a stiff wind. But there wasn't any wind this night.

"*Iblis!*"

An eerie flash exploded within the fog enveloping Akmir.

"Akmir!" Bin'ka shouted, sprinting toward him. "Are you all right?" he yelled. "Who are you shooting at?"

Bin'ka faltered to a stop. He couldn't see Akmir. Tentatively sticking out a hand, he waved it from side to side, trying to separate the dense fog. But it was as if the mist was made of sand, for the vapor immediately closed upon itself with his every motion.

"Akmir," he said in a low voice. "Akmir—where are you?"

Deep and menacing, the growl of a big cat—a lion or a leopard—burst outward from the opening between the crates. Eyes the color of flames appeared in front of him, low to the ground. As the growl swelled to a roar, Bin'ka engaged the Uzi's trigger, firing a suppressed round into the space. Staring intently into the mist to see if he had killed the beast, he pulled out the empty ammunition cartridge, replacing it with one clipped to the back waistband of his pants. Once he'd reloaded, he aimed the Uzi straight ahead and waited.

"Bin'ka!"

Bin'ka turned at the calling of his name.

"Did you get the *jasoos*?" Akmir shouted, running up to him.

"How did you get there?" Bin'ka asked in disbelief. "Did you chase whoever it was you were shooting at?"

"Shooting at?"

Akmir stopped a few paces from Bin'ka.

"Now who is *majnoon*? I haven't fired my weapon." Akmir held the sil-ver-plated Colt .45 flat in the palm of his hand, "Smell," he told him, seeing the doubting look on Bin'ka's face.

Bin'ka leaned forward and sniffed the barrel.

"But I saw—"

"Yes? What did you see?" Akmir pressed when Bin'ka fell silent.

"I saw—" Bin'ka looked back at the opening between the crates.

The fog had disappeared.

"You fired your weapon there," he told him, nodding to the opening. "I saw the muzzle flash in the fog, heard the shot."

"You *are* crazy," Akmir laughed. "Look at the night sky, my large-headed friend. There is not a cloud or a whisper of a cloud. There's been no fog." Eyeing Bin'ka with suspicion, he offered, "Perhaps it is all this gibberish about losing one's soul. Your mind is clouded."

"But I saw— And you yelled—"

"This is a trick to make me stop selling *abeebs*, isn't it?" Akmir narrowed his eyes to slits before shifting his attention to the near crate shredded with bullet holes.

"And what were you firing at that your bullets would be so near to the ground—a *fahr fara* of some kind? One with pointy teeth," he mocked, "and glowing red eyes? Save your attempts to dissuade me. Slaves are gold."

Akmir twirled the silver-plated Colt .45 around his finger, a harsh, glaring look on his face.

"And I like gold," he emphatically stated. "Best," he went on, shifting his eyes to the gun in his hand, "you keep your objections to yourself."

As if to underscore his words, Akmir raised his weapon and swung it outward, firing a round into the crate.

"There, now I have fired my weapon. Now you can—"

"Akmir! Bin'ka!"

Both Akmir and Bin'ka turned with the calling of their names. Muhammad was running toward them, an Uzi in his grasp.

"I heard the shots and came as quickly as I could. I was speaking to Adiam on the cell phone in the car," he explained, short of breath. "Otherwise I would have been here sooner," he went on, adjusting his suit coat as he came to a stop next to them. "What are you shooting at?"

Bin'ka watched Akmir's expression change from surprise to doubt, his hawk-like eyes scrutinizing the man as though he was potential prey.

"You've been in the car?"

"Yes," Muhammad answered with an embarrassed shrug. "I've been listening to the BBC broadcast of the top British music hits of the past week. I have a fondness for—"

"And what did you see from your seat in the car?" Akmir pressed. "Did you see anyone?"

"No," Muhammad replied, sounding a bit perplexed. "It has been quiet since we arrived. The only people I've seen are the two of you." Muhammad looked at Bin'ka and Akmir with furrowed brow. "When you walked past the car and split up and rounded that stack of containers," he told them with a nod back over his shoulder.

"A trick?" Bin'ka grunted, giving Akmir a pointed glance. "Now what do you have to say about losing your soul?"

Akmir shifted his eyes between Bin'ka and Muhammad several times before turning his head to study the bullet-riddled crate.

"So what was it?" Muhammad asked, seeing what Akmir was staring at.

"It was nothing," Akmir vehemently hissed, glaring at Muhammad. "Nothing," he repeated, addressing Bin'ka. "Let's get to the meeting."

"Yes," Muhammad remarked, stepping behind Akmir as the man headed in the direction of the car. "He's wondering where you are."

As the two men walked away, Bin'ka stared after them, his face a collection of conflicting expressions. Nothing made sense. It was as if everything he and Akmir had experienced since watching the people—the slaves—loaded onto the ship had been an illusion. Yet, when he heard Akmir shout *iblis*—devil—and fire his weapon.... He shook his head. How could it have not been real? He closed his eyes, picturing everything he had witnessed. *Was* it an illusion?

"Bin'ka!"

Opening his eyes, Bin'ka found a gray cat sitting next to the bullet-riddled crate, the animal's candle-flame yellow eyes staring up at him.

"Zanzibar," he muttered, touching his face where she had once scratched him. "The Lion," he whispered.

"Are you coming, Bin'ka?" he heard Muhammad call out to him. "Or should we leave without you?"

To the sound of Muhammad's laughter, Bin'ka jogged toward the waiting car, a sinking, hollow feeling haunting his every step.

* * *

"So the woman—this nun—she is resting now?"

Adiam moved a black lacquer, gold-trimmed bamboo tray closer to Dirk's side of the desk, noting the man's widening eyes and suppressed smile. With a nod to the long, carved ivory pipe perched over the flame of a small oil-burning lamp, he said, "Please—indulge. It is quite pure—and quite potent."

Adiam wanted to laugh when he saw how quickly Dirk took the pipe from the stand—nearly singeing his fingers on the metal coupling of the bowl—but refrained. He knew such a display would serve no purpose, embarrassing the man over his many addictions. No, better to understand his tendencies, Adiam conjectured, gain a semblance of insight, recognize what pushes and pulls the individual rather than throw his shortcomings in his face. So he watched with detached interest as Dirk placed the tip of the ivory pipe between his lips and drew deeply, almost feeling the vaporized opium filling his own lungs as Dirk inhaled.

"I find it all very intriguing, this aspect of a trust fund worth several million dollars awaiting a signature by the one the Lion calls Sister Lady."

He took note of Dirk's already drooping eyelids before continuing.

"And the different parties interested in seeing that signature occur. It is a vast sum of money, is it not?"

Dirk blew a stream of smoke from his nose. "You have the order of nuns; Akmir; you; that oafish warlord, Alba; Sister Lady herself; even her mother, perhaps—all seeking the money released for vastly different purposes."

Adiam allowed himself the hint of a smirk as Dirk's face took on the look of one experiencing a blissful dream.

"Some good, some bad, some selfish, some even cruel, perhaps."

Adiam rapped his knuckles upon the smooth, polished top of his black-wood desk.

"And now these nuns send one of their own. Sister Sarah, you say she is called?" Adiam rapped on the desktop a little louder. "Dirk—yes—Sarah is her name?" he pressed, raising his voice. "Sister Sarah—yes?"

"He— He wants—"

Adiam wondered how long it would take Dirk to corral the words floating inside his head.

"By *he*, you mean Akmir?"

Dirk grinned, nodding after a few seconds had passed.

"Yes. He wants to sell her. Says she must be a virgin." Dirk chuckled. "Some sultan or prince in some hellhole stretch of desert is willing to pay a hundred grand for a white-skinned virgin." Dirk laughed a little louder and a little harder. "Can you imagine? Like any virgin is worth that."

Adiam detected the man entertaining some troubling thought, for Dirk suddenly sat up straight in his cushioned chair, his lips silently mouthing some unintelligible words.

"I've got to get back," he abruptly told Adiam in a troubled voice. "He'll probably try to steal her. She could already be gone," he went on, a touch of paranoia in his tone.

"Be at ease," Adiam told him when Dirk started to rise from his chair. "I have Marlene and Amar watching your room at the hotel. I guessed that is where you have her, yes?"

"The hotel—my room—after those madmen blew up half the street."

Adiam watched Dirk's eyes focus on the pipe in his hands.

"Why did they do that? Why was she there? She was just kneeling in the street," he dazedly explained, as though he was having a hard time believing what he was saying. "Praying? Is that what she was doing?"

Adiam remained silent.

"She was a mess. Cuts and scrapes, one hand covered in blood. Kept muttering something about a father. Did she mean her father?"

Adiam motioned for Dirk to place the opium pipe on the bamboo tray.

"She never really explained," Dirk went on, his voice questioning. Moving his arm as if it were under water, Dirk reached out and deposited the decorative ivory pipe onto the lacquer tray.

"The blood—I had some peroxide and gauze. Gave her a sleeping pill. Put her in bed."

"No one has gone in or out of your room since you left the hotel," Adiam informed him, though he wasn't quite sure the man would be able to process the information.

"She smelled," Dirk blurted out, visibly quivering when he spoke. "Blah. Who would pay money for that?"

"I am sure she just needs a bath. Two days of travel and then subjected to an assassination: rocket-propelled grenades, AK-47s, cars exploding. I'm certain it all added to the deteriorating state of her hygiene."

Adiam reached out and slid the opium tray back to his side of the desk. "You say you shot one of the Afar at point-blank range? I'm sure that in itself was traumatic—not to mention messy."

Dirk ran a hand through his uncombed hair, a perplexed look on his face.

"But she smelled," he repeated with a shake of his head. "And Akmir wants to sell her? Do all slaves smell like that?"

"There are no slaves," Adiam replied with a touch of reproach in his voice. "Just unfortunate souls kidnapped and sold—to people who mistakenly believe they are entitled to own another human being. Perhaps what you smell on this Sarah woman is nothing more than the fear and despair *you* would feel if *your* freedom was suddenly threatened with an indefinite future of chained servitude."

Adiam carefully unscrewed the bowl from the pipe's grooved fitting and screwed another one in.

"Akmir," Adiam began with a disturbed shake of his head, "foolishly believes one class of person is better than another. He embraces the notion that a person's skin color—or religion, or sex—deems them inferior. Of course," he continued, placing the pipe back onto the custom-built platform in the middle of the tray so the flame of the small lantern touched the metal coupling, "according to Akmir, there is only one true god—Allah—and one true people—Muslims—and all other gods and all other civilizations are inferior or false. But history shows us that way of thinking is not only misguided, but folly."

Adiam twisted the gold, jewel-encrusted lion-head ring on his finger while he thought.

"The Romans, the Mongolians, the Umayyad Caliphate, China, Spain, England—ah, the British, with the empire where the sun never set—the world has watched all of them rise and fall. And each," he paused, adjusting the height of the flame with a small turn of a dial protruding from the lamp base, "had their different gods, their different-colored people, their different religions. And who's to say which one of them was better, or best, or true?"

He shook his head.

"Akmir plays a fool's game—the Serpent's—and he will no doubt pay for it someday soon by an Afar jile cutting off his head."

Reaching out, he gingerly placed the tip of his finger on the pin-sized hole atop the pipe's cylindrical bowl.

"He thinks it is a secret he sells two Afar girls on this trip. He, of all people, should know there are no secrets along the docks."

With a nod to the opium pipe, Adiam pushed the bamboo tray back across the desk so Dirk would be able to reach it.

"And poor Bin'ka, lost within a world of shifting equality while grappling with his own newfound freedom. Susenyo reminded him daily he was nothing but a big, black slave. So much so that he came to believe it himself."

Adiam gestured for Dirk to take up the opium pipe.

"And now he finds himself attached to a man such as Akmir—someone who he shares business with, but who sees him as nothing but a nuisance, a person of vast inferiority he is forced to interact with on a daily basis."

Adiam smiled as he watched Dirk draw another hit of opium vapor into his lungs.

"And now, tonight, he finds himself standing right beside him as people just like he himself once was are loaded onto an animal transport to be ferried up the Red Sea and sold. It must be very difficult for him. A dilemma, one might say."

Adiam saw Dirk's eyes glaze over.

"But this nun, this Sister Sarah—she will not be sold as these others are. No, I think it better she accompany you to find your Sister Claire. The Lion will be much more receptive if she is with you when you eventually find them. I doubt the Lion of Djibouti will be happy to hear Sister Lady is wanted back in the U.S." Nodding with the observation, he added, "This nun of yours—she may be quite valuable to you in ways other than monetary."

Entranced, a curling stream of smoke accompanying each slowly annunciated word, Dirk managed to say, "The—Lion—of—Djibouti."

"Yes, Dirk, the Lion of Djibouti. You must find him. For where he is, this Sister Claire will surely be."

"Sister Claire. Find her. Take her to America. The Lion—won't be happy. Seven million—"

Adiam recognized the signs of a full-blown stupor taking hold of the man.

"Seven million dollars is just a start, my friend. I have been doing some checking." Adiam chuckled when Dirk closed his eyes. "I wondered how much more her mother might be worth." Bending low to the desk, he whispered, "It makes seven million look laughable."

He saw Dirk's eyes flutter open, nearly laughing out loud as he watched the man try to focus.

"Do you think she'll smell too? Do you think all nuns smell that way?" Dirk smiled, closed his eyes, and started to laugh. "Because if they do…"

Adiam waited for him to finish his thought, but Dirk said nothing further. He stared off into space as if the words he wanted to say were drifting somewhere in the air in front of him. Seeing this, Adiam got up from behind his expansive desk and walked the length of the long, narrow room to the door at the opposite end. Pushing it slightly ajar, he clapped his hands three times in quick succession and then walked back, stopping at an area where a couch, two armchairs, and a coffee table were arranged along the room's outer wall, the matching blue, deeply cushioned furniture placed between two rectangular windows facing the waters of the gulf. Adiam took a moment to admire the swath of glittering moonlight floating on the gulf's surface. The smell of perfume brought his attention back to the room.

"Talia."

The woman entering Adiam's private living quarters was closer in age to a girl, but the seductive curves of her body and the way she carried herself cemented her stature as a woman—young, sensual, disarmingly beautiful. Her face held a mixture of Asiatic, French, and Arabic lineage, features defined and exotic; her beauty had caught Adiam's eye the moment he had first seen her begging for handouts in a slum outside Khartoum some eight years earlier. Since that day, Talia had not only become Adiam's concubine, but also a business partner, a confidant, and a friend.

"Opium?" she asked, sniffing the air. "A little early, I would think."

Her dark hair flowing down to her waist, Talia walked past him, moving slowly toward the desk. Watching her slender hips sway beneath a thin layer of yellow chiffon, Adiam suddenly wished he didn't have a meeting to attend.

"I have a task for you," he told her, nodding to the stupefied figure of Dirk sitting like a statue in his chair. "There is more opium and some hashish in the top drawer," he told her when she turned to look at him. "And you know where the wine and liquor is kept."

Adiam watched her move slowly to where Dirk was seated, shaking his head when he saw her reach down and stroke the man's groin.

"I have heard that he is big," she purred. "What should I do with him?" she teased.

Dressed in a sand-colored suit coat with dark pants and an open-collared white shirt, Adiam pulled at his sleeves as though he were adjusting their length. He gave Talia a knowing smile.

"What you need to," he told her, his voice kind but businesslike. "Keep him here the entire night."

Turning to leave, he hesitated. Glancing back at Talia, he added "And may you both enjoy the pleasures of each other's flesh."

* * *

Five minutes later, Adiam was down on the second floor of the three-story building he owned off Avenue Marechal, sitting at one end of a long table. Among the five other men seated near to him were Akmir and Bin'ka.

"As-salaam alaikum," he said to the gathering with a touch of his fingertips to his forehead. "I thought it best we meet this evening to make certain everything is set for tomorrow's shipment. As you are all aware, we are not only shipping out twice the amount of merchandise as is our normal quota, but also packaging four tons of ivory stored in three separate containers in a different area within the hold of the freighter. Needless to say, every aspect of this operation must go smoothly."

Adiam looked at each man at the table before continuing.

"Bin'ka, you are certain our people in customs will be on duty when loading begins later tonight and through the day tomorrow?"

Bin'ka nodded his head. "Schedules were altered through normal channels. And in the one instance where there was some doubt, we handled it with a broken ankle. When the shift changes, our longest-tenured employees will be working. I've also arranged extra precautions in case the army or police decide to spring a last-minute spot inspection."

Bin'ka glanced at the other men at the table, offering an uncertain laugh. "The Afar men are quite taken with the American-made RPGs we sold them. I promised them a half dozen more at no cost as long as they are willing to provide us with an armed distraction if we see even one uniform show up on the docks."

Bin'ka rolled his massive shoulders and sighed as the men around him nodded their approval.

"Excellent," Adiam said. "And when we reach our destination? How is it on the American end, Akmir? Is everything in order? Has there been any trouble with the new woman you spoke of at our last meeting—this assemblyperson, or whatever government post she holds?"

Akmir pulled at the sides of his keffiyeh, his small dark eyes darting from face to face.

"As you are aware," he began, "Newark Seaport is not Djibouti. We do not control each and every employee of customs and we have only a fair number of the police on our payroll."

He held up a hand when a few men grumbled.

"What we do have however, is the mayor of the city accepting our cash gifts, as well as two local police commanders and the head of the New York, New Jersey Port Authority. Yes," he concurred as the others around the table nodded with satisfaction, "we are as well positioned as we can be. We also have made deep inroads within the organization known as the Family. They are our main facilitators on the other end, taking care of security, local transportation, and intelligence. It is a troublesome area," he explained. "Different gangs, different organizations, different nationalities all trying to gain control of the docks. Many would see profit funneled into one pocket instead of several. Not a bad idea," he said, laughing, looking around at the men seated at the table. "Ten times the profit if that was accomplished. Perhaps more than ten," he added, making a widening gesture with his out-stretched arms. "Yes—quite a profit would there be." Placing the tips of his fingers to his silver-tinged beard, he conjectured, "Perhaps scores of millions per month."

Adiam waved down the excited outbursts from the men around the table.

"And those millions of dollars would disappear as soon as a gang war erupted and the federal authorities or the army was brought in to secure the facilities. No," he told them, challenging them with a hard look, "it is enough we control what part of the seaport we do and allow the other countries, other organizations, to carry on business in the same manner. There is no need to upset the balance of commerce as it is now. We all benefit, yes?" he asked them, nodding his own answer. "We all coexist. We all benefit. We all generate massive profits. Would you have this change?"

As Adiam expected, there were mutterings and grumblings. But no one, as he had anticipated, voiced a differing opinion.

"It was just a thought, Adiam," Akmir offered, laying the palms of his hands face-up atop the table. "Just thinking aloud. Surely we are all aware of the potential trouble any infighting amongst the different organizations might cause. And yet," he said, laughing as he looked around the table, "it is an intriguing idea, is it not?"

"Intriguing and reckless," Adiam replied. "Think of the loss we would incur if even one shipment were impounded—this one in particular. Would you be willing to risk the fifty-million-dollar payload our ship will be carrying to the States if the Newark Seaport was in the midst of a power struggle?"

Pausing, Adiam waited to see if someone would speak up. With a pointed glance to Akmir, he went on to say, "Let us end this fruitless discussion and focus on the matter at hand. We still need to go over distribution, banking, communications, and the report on our suppliers in Afghanistan. So let us proceed."

* * *

After the meeting concluded, Adiam was tempted to go back up to his third-floor living quarters, but he quickly pushed the thought aside. Talia would not appreciate the interruption; nor was she in need of any help in keeping Dirk occupied for the remainder of the night. So instead of heading up to the third floor, he went down to the ground level, to the small café he'd opened with funds from his personal savings. A drink and a smoke were in order, he decided—and then a visit to Dirk's hotel room.

As it was on this night, as it had become increasingly so as of late, the café Adiam owned was filled with a bustling, eclectic crowd, talking, laughing, singing, smoking, and drinking away whatever cares they might have. Catching the eye of one of the waitresses he personally hired, he nodded toward the front door. Stepping through the archway to the café's sidewalk patio, his eyes fell to the sparkling waters of the gulf.

No matter where Adiam found himself in the port of Djibouti, the air smelled of ocean, the lower edge of the Red Sea and the Gulfs of Tadjoura and Aden surrounding the jagged peninsula on which the port city had been built. After decades of living by water, everything the sea embodied—salt, wind, sounds, currents, essence—had become part of him, the ocean's influence inescapable.

As-salaam alaikum—peace be unto you. Contemplating the greeting, Adiam interpreted the phrase to mean so much more when viewed in the context of the sea. For the sea—the oceans—touched every shoreline of every continent on the planet. Someday the Consortium would do the same, he envisioned, countries interconnected through commerce, sharing the same goals, philosophy, principles. Respecting individuality, treasuring ethnicity, encouraging innovation, all the while acknowledging existence within an all-encompassing, superbly crafted society unfazed by the ebb and flow of evolution. A vast, unfathomable expanse of humanity linked by the simple phrase *as salaam alaikum*—peace be unto you.

Staring at twinkling drops of moonlight dancing upon the surface of the water, Adiam envisioned the world much like the vista spread out before him, the wavering tiny beacons of light afloat on a dark-flowing mass sparking visions of the planning and ingenuity needed to accomplish the task of unity. Taking a seat at an empty table overlooking the port's original dock, he brought a pack of Camel cigarettes out of his coat pocket. A tumbler containing three fingers of amber liquid simultaneously delivered by a slender, weathered hand.

"Ah—*shukran*, Monica—thank you," Adiam said with a slight bowing of his head. "Jim Beam?" he asked, bending to sniff the aroma rising from the glass. "Oh no, I see. You have given me the good stuff, as they say, yes?" he teased with a smile. "The Turkey 101."

"There is no fooling you, boss," the waitress quipped, slipping a small ceramic ashtray from one of the deep pockets of her apron and placing it on the table by the pack of cigarettes. "You are a true connoisseur of American whiskey." With a kind laugh, she withdrew a shiny metal lighter from the same apron pocket, flipping open the lid while offering a polite, "May I?"

Adiam took a cigarette from the pack and placed it between his lips. Monica engaged the striker wheel with her thumb, putting flame to the end of the rolled tobacco. Taking a deep drag, Adiam sighed.

"I'll make sure to check on you every so often, boss," Monica said over her shoulder as she turned to go back inside.

Adiam raised the lit cigarette in the air as if to say "thank you" or "don't worry about me" or "I appreciate it" or, perhaps, a mixture of all three. Left to his thoughts, he reached for the tumbler, savoring the aged Kentucky bourbon as he took the first sip. Closing his eyes, he concentrated on soft burn of the alcohol sliding down his throat, his plan for the world placed temporarily aside.

* * *

The terrain ahead changing, the green flower beetle with the purple circle on her outer wing came to a sudden stop. The others behind her did the same. The forest having come to an end, her sensors had begun relaying abnormal stimuli: mounds, hills, and gargantuan protrusions looming in their path.

Not understanding the configurations, she extended the range of her feelers, sweeping for information in a slow-moving arc.

West, north, and east, she gauged steep formations rising upward, blocking their advance. Accessing her sensor banks, she searched for any similar likeness stored within her receptors—height, width—but there was no information to draw from. How wide and far did these protrusions run? She didn't know, none of her kind—as far as she was aware—having ever been this far north. Slowly sweeping her front antenna left to right, she gathered what stimuli were available, hoping a feeling or an awareness of some sort would be conveyed, alerting her to a passage she could not yet discern.

Although west appeared somewhat less dangerous than north or east, west was not a direction in which she wanted to travel. Yet, she sensed it the better of the three choices presented. For both north and east she could see massive domes of ultraviolet light and smell the pungent stench of the animals radiating the energy. Through the soil, she detected rumbling motions and the hum of contained electrical currents. North and east, she understood, lay a large number of hunter-gatherers—defilers, polluters. North and east, therefore, were not wise options.

Yet north, north was the direction she and all the others traveling with her had been heading since the pre-dawn morning in the rain forest when the calling was first transmitted. She had felt it—the summoning—begin in the soil, each particle of dirt part of a message she could not ignore. The plea accentuated through the surrounding foliage, pheromones bursting forth from every tree and flower, showering her in elements containing the most primal instinct—survival. She had answered the call to move northward immediately—as had every other beetle of her kind. They had been on the move ever since, losing track of cycles of sun and moon. North, ever northward they had traveled. Yet, as she surveyed the terrain ahead, she was at a loss as to how to proceed.

A strong gust of wind rattled the limbs of trees and bushes above and around her, leaves blowing sideways from a surge of rushing air. The atmosphere suddenly filled with moisture, pure and fresh, not fully formed, bursting with molecular energy, not yet tainted with gasses and chemical residues. And electricity—raw, unstable—its churning presence within the clouds above her unmistakable, so unlike the controlled currents she'd sensed through her feet and abdomen.

Looking skyward, she witnessed the first strike of lightning shooting down out of a massive black cloud trimmed silver-white. The air roared with the crack of jagged, unharnessed energy. The ground trembled; the sky rumbled in rolling waves of echoing thunder. The downpour—a streaking rain of translucent black—gusted with a howling wind, the squall pressing her body closer to earth. Cluster lightning exploded, serrated white fingers hurtling in every direction, illuminating the terrain around her, ghost shadows appearing and disappearing along rocky formations.

As suddenly as the storm formed, the cloudburst dissipated, remnants of the furious outbreak of wind, rain, and lightning funneled into an opening behind a ridge. In the storm's wake, sunlight returned, gold rays sparkling against energy lingering in the air. Pinpoints of color began to gather, the flower beetle opening her elytra, stretching her inner wings as a rainbow formed. Following the path of the expanding arch of brilliant colors, the green flower beetle watched the rainbow bend into the same opening the black storm cloud had entered. Slapping her elytra closed, she moved forward with determined purpose, millions upon millions of other feet moving behind her.

9

"LOOK—I'M NOT READY for—you know—anything." Yutanda picked up her glass of sweet tea and took a sip.

"Who said anyone was? I think you've got this all twisted. Me coming around here—as you say, all the time—is just something that's kind of happened." Noah shrugged his shoulders, his face a mixture of innocence, surprise, and disagreement.

"I mean, what do you want me to do? Your dad's lost up here—taking care of your kid while you're off playing detective. And you're going to have to explain what you mean by—*you know, anything.* Far as I recall, it was you who wanted to meet *me* that first time at the Met."

He frowned.

"So I don't know where this idea of yours is coming from, thinking I'm looking for some kind of relationship. 'Cause the words haven't come from these lips," he said, pointing to his mouth.

Yutanda ran a hand over her close-cropped hair and stood up from the beige corduroy couch where she and Noah were seated. Dressed in a loose-fitting boho-style tunic boasting a colorful African print against a background of yellow, she crossed over to the only window in the room and looked out through the venetian blinds. Feeling the scrutiny of Noah's piercing brown eyes on the back of her head, she fanned herself with her hand, suddenly feeling warm.

"Look," she began as she turned back to face him, "I'm sorry if I've got this all wrong. I certainly don't mean—" She shook her head and glanced at the floor. "I mean," she sighed.

Placing her hand along the side of her face, she looked at him and chuckled.

"Shit, Noah—I don't know what I mean. All I know is that you seem to be a part of my life now. And I don't know if I'm ready to have—or want—someone to be a part of it."

The lines of her square, chiseled face softened, her eyes widening.

"Does that make sense to you? Can you understand where I'm coming from?"

"Not really," he replied. "Only reason I'm here right now is because your dad called and asked if I would come over and watch the Celtics–Rockets game while he and Lizbeth watched your kid—again—for the hundredth time," he added, a little testiness in his tone. "And I can't help it if your mom thinks we have something going. Which is why they always rush out of here after you get home from wherever it is you've been."

He picked up a lone baby back rib from one of a half dozen Styrofoam boxes arranged on the long, low coffee table set in front of the couch. After a cursory look, he put it back down.

"Just where were you this time?" he snidely inquired. "Some heroin drop-off by the river, trying to catch the dealer?"

"You sound like my father talking," she fired back. "Is that what you two do while you're watching some stupid basketball game, talk about me? Make fun of what I'm trying to do? Belittle my efforts in trying to clean the scum out of this city?"

Folding her arms, she turned her back.

"Stop being so uptight. Nobody's making fun of or belittling you." He ran a hand over his head. "Shit," he said in long exhale. "Your old man's just worried about you—so's your mom. Your boy's starting to see your folks more than he sees you."

"You leave my son out of this," she snapped, whirling back around. Jabbing a finger in the air, she added, "Just leave Menelik out of this entire conversation."

She felt an anxious shiver wiggle down her spine, dismissing the tears welling in her eyes by gritting her teeth. Noah raised his hands up in the air over each side of his head in a sign of surrender.

"Whatever you say, Mrs. Big Boss Woman," he joked. "Or should I call you Mrs. Shaft?"

Yutanda quickly turned away with a frustrated sigh. "That how you see me, Noah?" she asked, the tone of disappointment in her voice unmistakable. "That how my parents see me? As some over-the-top TV character?"

When she heard him laugh, she winced.

"Well, what do you see yourself as? It's Sunday, Yutanda. You know, day of rest, day off, day with your family—if you're lucky enough to have one."

Some snippet of sadness she heard in his voice made her turn and face him.

"I mean—Jesus, woman—you just can't seem to leave it alone."

She saw from the expression on his face that he was trying to understand.

"You got a son, a family. And yet, you'd rather spend all your time snooping around places you shouldn't ought to be." He shook his head and looked down at his feet. "I know this city—same as you. You shouldn't be showing your face in some of the places you been showing it. It's going to come back at you and bite you hard."

Lifting his head, he looked her straight in the eye. "But you already know that."

She took a step toward him.

"And you still go."

She stopped and closed her eyes. "Who else— I mean— I don't know." She opened her eyes to stare at him, her thoughts as disconnected as her words. "It's just—it seems—nothing's being accomplished. Like it's all just getting worse: drugs, junkies, crime. I just don't see it getting any better— until someone—until *we*—change the way things are done."

She pulled at the frayed threads of her cutoff denim shorts.

"Like tonight," she continued, moving back to the couch and sitting down a cushion away from him. "Two young men murdered—gang related—Bloods and Ñetas, from the evidence."

She saw Noah's eyes grow wide.

"That's just what I mean," he told her, disapproval evident on his face as well as in the tone of his voice. "And you want to get in the middle of that?"

"Want to get in the middle of it?" she repeated, somewhat incredulous. "*Want to* and *already am* are two entirely different viewpoints. When all—all of us," she explained, swinging an arm out in a semi-circle, "are already in the middle of it. There's no choice here, Noah," she pointed out. "You might see tonight's killings as just two more meaningless, worthless punks snuffed out with bullet holes in the back of their heads, but I see two young men who lost their lives because they were driven to the wrong side of life because of neglect. Their lives taken from them because nobody gave a damn about them when they were screaming for someone to care."

She clasped her hands together, twisting her fingers. "And now they're dead—somebody's child, somebody's son."

She paused.

"A part of this community, this city, died with them tonight. And now their killers—their killers, Noah—they're still walking on the same sidewalks as you and me, driving down the same streets, buying cereal from the same store."

Tilting her head slightly to one side, she eyed him with wariness.

"And you think I have a choice whether or not to be involved? Maybe I am Mrs. Shaft," she said, half laughing. "Maybe I am over the top."

She shook her head.

"But from where I'm sitting—if you want this place to get better," she nodded to what lay outside of the walls of her apartment, "then you better get off your ass and do something about it."

"You get all this shit from your ex-husband?" he shot back, his expression of disapproval unchanged. "You think if he were here right now—knowing he had a son he was responsible for—that you wouldn't be the one asking him why the hell he was down in some back alley looking over two corpses instead of being at home spending time with his family? Is that where you'd want him to be?"

Bunching one hand into a fist, he smacked it into the palm of his other hand.

"Knowing it could follow him home some night?"

Menelik. Yutanda still couldn't wrap her head around the thought he was gone. Dead. That was the State Department's official stance—but they'd never found the body. The remains of the pilot—what was left of them—they'd identified his. And the crash site—yeah, there was no disputing the helicopter had crashed, from the photographs she had seen. But Menelik himself—his body, clothes, ID—not a trace of him had ever been located. As if he had never been on the helicopter when it was shot out of the sky. But people had been witness to him getting on it; Jim Stokes, the ambassador's assistant, had personally watched him take off. And then the delayed reports from the relief camps had come in—officials from the Red Cross and Christian Aid, documenting his visits. And finally, the report from the pilot himself, early on the morning of the day—the day they were all telling her he died—calling in his flight plan to the Air Force base in Djibouti, Camp Lemonnier, saying they—*they*—were heading north into the highlands of Ethiopia. What was anyone left to think, but that Menelik had been on the helicopter, that he was one of the *they*. But still, even after all this time, she couldn't—or wouldn't—come to terms with him being—god, she didn't even like thinking of the word—dead. And now, here Noah was, throwing him in her face. Using him like he was nothing but a word to sway her from doing what she felt was right—what Menelik himself would have agreed was the path to take.

"How dare—"

"What makes you think it was Bloods and Ñetas?" he asked, cutting her off. "They leave a calling card of some kind?"

She could feel the blood rushing to her face, anger tightening the lower muscles of her stomach.

"I'm serious. A gang war's nothing you want to screw with."

He said it in such a way Yutanda actually felt he had her best interests at heart. All the anger suddenly seeped away. For a fleeting moment she wondered what she'd be saying to Menelik if he *were* sitting here telling her he was sticking his nose in between two violent gang organizations.

"Look, I get where you're coming from. I really do," she told him, offering him an uncertain smile. "And you may be right. Least partly," she added when she saw him raise an eyebrow. "Maybe I wouldn't be so happy with a husband who disappeared a little too often. But," she raised an open hand in front of her chest when she saw he was about to interrupt, "I'm pretty sure he'd look at me and ask 'If not me, then who? Who is it you think is going to change things? Some stranger you dream about? Some fictitious comic book character come to life?'"

When she saw Noah shake his head and twist his body to get up, she reached over and placed a hand on his leg.

"He'd say there's no one but you—you and me. Don't expect change just because you want it. I can hear him saying it now."

She laughed, her eyes drifting to the ceiling.

"What's so funny?" he wanted to know.

"Oh," she replied, softening her laugh to a giggle, "just thinking of what he'd say after that."

"And what would that be?" he asked after she hesitated.

"Just that he'd probably look at me and say: and don't expect it at all. Change—if it even comes—will be a surprise. Because change has always been a blowing grain of dust in a river of sand."

She saw Noah studying her.

"Bloods, Ñetas—nothing to screw with," he offered. "Nothing you or anybody else is going to be able to change."

Abruptly standing, he took a few steps toward the door.

"Hey, I didn't mean for you—"

"So how do you know it was gangs? What kind of evidence was there?"

"The two with—the two who died—were dressed in red T-shirts, red beads around their necks, a pentagram drawn on the sleeve of their right shoulder."

"Bloods, all right," he said with a nod. "But—"

"And when they turned them over, they each had a hand—the index finger—tied to the middle finger so it was pressed over the back."

She fell silent for a few seconds, running one hand over and around her other.

"Around each of their wrists, a bandana."

"A bandana doesn't necessarily mean—"

"Replicas of the flag of Puerto Rico. Ñetas," she stated. "You want to say it was someone different?"

"Shit, if it's true, that could mean some big trouble for this city."

He looked over at the door as if he was thinking of leaving.

"Cops got any ideas of why?"

"The bomb at the seaport's the only thing that sprung up in anyone's mind. Though putting a bullet in the back of two people's heads seems a little harsh for that."

"Why do you say that? I recall seeing in the paper, they searched the ship and found a stash of drugs, right?"

"Yeah, that's right," she told him as she watched him move around the coffee table and sit back down on the couch.

"And what was the street value? Somewhere around seven million?"

"More like fifteen million."

She drew back with a start when he slapped his thigh and groaned.

"And you think offing two punks as payback for losing fifteen million in merchandise is harsh? Jesus, Yutanda."

He clapped his hands together.

"Wake up. These guys run a multi-million dollar business. And anyone who they even think is screwing around with their livelihood is going to pay."

"I appreciate your concern, but—"

"Don't go down there again. Don't show your face down at the docks. You've got to know it will bring you a lot of hurt. Promise me," he urged her, reaching over and grasping her forearm. "Don't go back to the seaport."

"Noah, you're not my keeper," she told him, wrenching her arm free of his hand. "It's really none of your concern."

"Like it was none of my concern when those three punks assaulted you and would have probably raped you if I hadn't been there?" He shook his head. "You could be dead right now," he dismissively added. "None of my concern," he muttered with a grunt. "You have one short memory."

"Dear god, Noah—just relax!" she snapped, exasperated, pushing off of the couch, taking a few steps into the middle of the room. "It's all taken care of, okay? We've got people down there now. I'll be fine."

"People?"

He looked at her in a way that made her think he didn't believe her.

"What do you mean, it's all taken care of? You'll be fine?"

"You know," she coyly replied with a shrug of her shoulders. "People," she said, raising her eyebrows. "People who've been—you know—trained."

"What? Undercover cops—is that what you mean? Jesus," he hissed, "you've got yourself involved with an undercover operation?"

"Be more than that soon."

She saw the shocked look on his face.

"Got the council to pass funding for security cameras to be installed."

She felt a tinge of redemption when she saw him close his eyes and mutter, "Good god."

"Already have the security firm lined up to install them. Should all be operational within a few weeks."

She looked down at him with a big smile.

"So there's no need to worry about me. I've got it all covered."

She watched him place his head between his hands and look down at the floor.

"I'll be fine—really."

Her smile disappeared as soon as he thrust himself off the couch.

"You'll be fine? You'll be fine?"

She didn't understand his anger.

"God, Yutanda! Two punks were executed tonight! And you think putting some cameras around the docks is going to stop that from happening again? Are you really that naïve?"

"Why are you so upset?" she yelled. "What is it that—"

Her head snapped around when she heard the jingling of keys on the other side of the door to the apartment. A moment later, the doorknob turned, the door swinging inward a crack. When the top of Ed's silver-haired head edged around the corner, Noah chuckled.

"Safe to come in?" Ed inquired as he pushed the door all the way open. "Land sakes, you two sound like an old married couple," he joked, giving both Yutanda and Noah a sheepish glance. "Hear ya shoutin' at one another clear down the hall."

Before she could respond, Yutanda watched Noah walk swiftly by Ed and out the door, saying a passing goodnight to her mother, who was obviously standing just beyond. A moment later, Elizabeth Taylor stepped into the room with Menelik fast asleep in her arms.

"We stayed away as long as we could," her mother said as she looked questioningly toward Ed. "But ice cream only lasts so long," she offered, looking back at Yutanda.

"Oh, Mother," Yutanda sighed shaking her head. "There's really no need to be leaving me and Noah alone."

"Well, why in tarnation you say a thing like that, girl?"

Yutanda felt her face twist into a defensive scowl.

"Maybe it's lost on you that you got a son over here," Ed continued, nodding toward Menelik, "who ain't got no daddy. And a momma," he went on, pointing a finger at her, "who ain't got no husband."

Ed ran the back of his hand across his upper lip and sniffled. Looking past Elizabeth out the open door of the apartment, he finished by saying, "And there just went one hell of a young man."

* * *

Yutanda. Jesus, he thought. *Insufferable bitch!* He'd felt like slapping her when she preached to him about the two Bloods who'd been killed. Spouting that crap about them being dead because they were neglected when they were younger. What a bunch of shit! Like that was the reason they joined a gang? Because they were neglected when they were what, five years old?

Popping a Miller Genuine Draft tall boy, he laughed. *Neglected.* He took a long sip of beer and shook his head. *Like who hasn't been? Self-righteous bitch, thinking she can change the world—change gangs!* He laughed again and took another long draft from the sixteen-ounce can. *Neglect, like you're doing to your own son! Hypocrite!*

Chris leaned forward over the small metal desk, hitting the Rewind button on the closest cassette deck. While listening to the soft whine of the rewinding tape, he plugged in the set of earphones resting next to the machine. Taking another long sip of beer, he placed the earphones over his head, adjusting the headband so the sound cups fit snugly over his ears.

"Let's see if anything went on while I was away," he muttered, hitting the Play button.

As he waited for the tape replay from the tap on Rue's phone line to begin, he gave the small studio apartment he used as one of his several safe houses a lookover, wondering how much longer he'd have need of it.

The metal desk, the chair he was sitting in, a duffel bag of clothes, toiletries, a coffee maker, a can of Maxwell House, paper plates, plastic cups, plastic utensils, and whatever scraps of takeout food remained in the refrigerator—not a whole hell of a lot to write home about, he thought. *Home.* He grunted. *Neglect—like you'd know anything about neglect, with the parents you have. Uppity bitch.*

Leaning forward, Chris checked the progress of the tape. Already a quarter of the way through, and so far, nothing but an empty hiss in his ears. Wondering if Rue had even been in his office today, he gave the other seven cassette recorders he'd run the feeder line through from the router box an apathetic smile. Listening to twelve hours of blank tape wasn't his idea of a fun night. With that thought in mind, he pressed the Fast Forward button and ran the tape ahead. After taking a long swig of beer, he hit Play. Still nothing.

"Yeah," he suddenly heard in his ears.

"It's me," a different voice said.

"You're calling early." Rue's voice, Chris was certain.

"I'm leaving for the evening and thought it best to touch base." Chris concentrated on the new voice. European? It certainly wasn't American. "There is a meeting later. And I have business at the dock first."

"Ah—the new shipment. Will everyone be attending?"

"*N'am.*"

"Speak English, would you? What the hell does *n'am* mean?"

"After all this time we do business, you still do not know one word of my tongue."

Chris chuckled. The man seemed genuinely pissed.

"It means 'yes,' you fat asshole," Chris muttered, recognizing the Arabic word from his time in Africa.

"Akmir—please—can we just stick to the business at hand?"

Sounds like these two like to rattle each other's chains, Chris observed.

"Americans," Akmir grunted over the phone. "So ill-mannered, so arrogant in the way you perceive yourselves in relation to the world."

"Yes, as you've pointed out a number of times before," Rue answered with a touch of disdain. "So is it yes or no? Not that it makes much difference, I suppose. The meeting will go on whether everyone is there or not, I would guess. Right?"

"*Kuss ummack*," Chris heard the man—Akmir—say in Arabic.

"And what does that mean? 'Go to hell' or some such insult?" Rue inquired.

Chris heard sardonic laughter on the other end of the phone.

"Perhaps," Akmir replied. "And perhaps not. You see what a disadvantage you are at because you haven't taken the time to show respect to another culture. It will be your undoing—you Americans. The disrespect you show the world will be your downfall."

"Fine. I'll take some Arabic lessons as soon as I hang up the phone. Now, can we get back to business? You called me, remember?"

"Indeed," Akmir said with a click of his tongue. "I have called to see what developments there have been since we last spoke. All will be calm in a week's time?"

"That when it's due to arrive?"

"Fair weather permitting."

"In a week?" Chris heard a pause. "I would think things would be by then."

"There is hesitation in your voice." Chris caught the apprehension in Akmir's tone. "What has changed? What is different?"

"Talk on the street about a hit coming. Seems our Hispanic friends are seeking a pound of flesh for the little incident that cost them their shipment."

"Pound of flesh?" Chris heard Akmir's confusion. He could see him grappling with the meaning. "Cutting off someone's leg or arm? Is this what you mean?"

Rue chuckled for a moment.

"Revenge; it means they're seeking revenge."

"I see. So there will be a killing."

"That's the word I'm receiving."

"They already did it—killed two punks," Chris mumbled.

"People die all the time," Chris heard Akmir casually reply, as though he was commenting on the weather. "This is of no concern. Your police will investigate for a day or two, and then it will be over, yes?"

"I suppose—unless there's a retribution killing in return. But that doesn't mean it will affect the seaport. The Bloods and our Hispanic friends can kill each other just about anywhere in the city."

There was a long pause then. Chris started to wonder if the call had been somehow disconnected. But then Akmir's voice returned.

"There is something else, then, something that is more cause for alarm? You hide something in your silence, I think."

"Surveillance cameras are going to be installed. Not right away. The mayor's going to do his best to drag his feet on signing off on the council's resolution."

"Cameras?" The pitch in Akmir's tone reflected his concern. "This could be problematic. How did this come about?"

"The Arbagna woman. And there's more."

"Yes. I'm listening," Akmir hissed.

Chris pictured the image of a snake.

"One of my contacts on the force—apparently they have inserted or are about to insert an undercover police officer into one or more of the shift crews. —Or they'll try," Rue said, chuckling.

"Are you laughing at this? Why is this amusing?"

Chris lifted the ear cups a quarter inch away from his ears. This Akmir had a temper, he noted.

"Because anyone new joining one of the shift crews is going to stand out like a sore thumb. Won't be anything undercover about him. Just a waste of time."

Chris imagined Akmir grinding his teeth, staring at the phone.

"Still, the presence of the police and the introduction of surveillance cameras speaks of a heightened threat to our operation. This woman—she has become troublesome. I think it is time to stop trying to manipulate her and simply kill her."

"Now, hold on there, Akmir. Let's not do anything drastic. This all sounds worse than it really is. Surveillance cameras can be neutralized or vandalized, and when we know who the undercover pigs are, we'll feed 'em so much false information we can have the police farther away from our little piece of the dock than we ever thought possible."

Chris took a sip of beer and nodded. Rue's line of thinking made sense.

"Items of concern that we never have had to think about before."

Chris tilted his head and raised his eyebrows. What Akmir was saying was also true.

"What if there is more? What then? What if the woman persuades Customs to double the number of inspectors? Is this something you would say sounds worse than it is?"

"I can't see that happening. Every government organization is strapped for funding right now. I doubt they could find the money to hire more inspectors, even if they wanted to."

"Did you foresee surveillance cameras and undercover policemen?"

Chris laughed at the vehemence in Akmir's voice, picturing Rue's face as he listened to the voice on the other end of the phone, yelling at him.

"Foresee or not foresee," Akmir continued in a nasty tone. "We should not have to be concerned with either one! And what is the cause of this newfound concern? A *sharmuta*. Why have you not killed her already?"

"Because, Akmir, that would bring a whole lot of—"

"I did not hesitate when you asked me to kill her husband!"

Chris almost fell out of his chair.

"And he is dead. As I told you he would be. So why do you argue now? Are you not capable of doing this thing? Should I take care of it myself?"

"Simmer down, Akmir. I'm telling you it would be more trouble than it's worth. Killing a state assemblywoman will bring the feds down on us. And I know you don't want that. Nobody does."

"No, that wouldn't be smart," Chris muttered as he waited for Akmir's reaction.

"Why would anyone care if she is killed far from the docks? At her home, let's say—by intruders, or a freak accident of some sort. You have no imagination, I fear. You think murder must always be carried out using a gun or a knife. Another American fault."

Chris couldn't help but smile as he waited for the punch line.

"A lack of creativity in the ways of attaining death. But I suppose one cannot blame a country that has only been in existence for a few hundred years. It is unfair of me to think that your United States could even slightly compare to the Arab dynasties that have ruled this earth for thousands."

This guy's got a definite superiority complex, Chris thought. *No wonder he and Rue somehow hooked up. They were made for each other.*

"Save the rule-of-Islam crap, okay, Akmir? You always get off on that tangent. Not going to help the Arab dynasty much once the world uses up all the oil you fuckers are squeezing us with. Just might find yourselves back in the Stone Age once it's all gone."

Score one for the reverend. Chris couldn't wait to hear Akmir's response. This was better than TV, he thought.

"We stray from our common problem."

There was a long block of silence. Chris bent forward and looked at the tape. It appeared there were a few minutes left. He hoped the conversation would be over before he had to switch to the next cassette recorder in line and rewind the tape.

"What about this operative of yours? This person you have referred to as the black tiger?" Akmir asked.

"That's black cat—and he's been able to weave a relationship with the woman. He's provided some useful information, confirming what my other sources have also reported. From what I gather, he's over at the woman's residence now."

He must have a set of eyes on her place, because no one's been tailing me.

"He is capable of carrying out a sudden end to this woman's life, yes?"

In the silence before Rue's reply, Chris felt his body tense.

"More than capable, but that wasn't the job I hired him for. And since he's been seen with her on a number of occasions, I doubt he'd want to make himself vulnerable to any investigation that would follow such an extreme course of action. It is as I have told you: the woman can be handled, played. She's just a nuisance, nothing more."

Chris felt his body relax. *No, I wouldn't put myself in that position. I'd be the first person Ed and Lizbeth would bring up to the cops as soon as I disappeared from their lives.*

"This conversation has disappointed me. You assured me all would remain smooth on your end. There is too much at stake to leave things to chance. I see now that I must—"

Chris lurched forward in his chair when the tape reached the end of the spool with a climatic click. Feeling a need to hurry, he slid the next cassette deck over and hit the Rewind button. The whir of the tape was lost on him as he contemplated what he'd already heard.

Akmir had had Yutanda's husband killed at Rue's request. How the hell did he orchestrate that? Seeing—as far as Yutanda had told him—his helicopter had been shot down by a ground-to-air missile by some rebel faction in some remote area of Ethiopia. *Talk about connections*, he thought. And now this Akmir seemed intent upon killing Yutanda. The prospect of her dying bounced around in his head. Surely he didn't care, he thought.

Chris felt a jolt of adrenaline shoot through his body when he heard the rewinding tape reach a clicking end. Slowly, he reached out his hand and pressed the Play button: silence and then a brief hiss.

"There's no need to do that."

It was Rue's agitated voice speaking. Where was Akmir's? *There must have been a few seconds lapse as the machines switched over! Shit!*

"It is settled."

What's settled?

"I must leave for business now. We will speak soon."

"Akmir! You don't need to send—"

"It is settled. I will take care of it. Do not worry. Goodbye."

Chris heard the click of the disconnecting phone.

"Shit," he heard Rue exhale.

And then there was another click.

And then silence.

* * *

Mirko Haddad had emigrated from Lebanon in 1980. As with a large number of Middle Eastern immigrants, he'd settled in Detroit. Modified his first name to Mark, and began a career in marketing with an import company with multi-pronged ties to a vast conglomerate of Arabic companies exporting goods to the United States. Mirko's particular area of marketing expertise was edible commodities: pita bread, hummus, coffees, tahini—staples of the Arab diet where the sight of a traditional label conveyed home, and desirability. Although Mirko found marketing commodities somewhat boring, the industry was stable—ever-expanding with a steady influx of Middle-Easterners—the pay sufficient. The job also offered a few nice perks, such as tickets to sporting events. Of which Mirko had attended many—the Detroit Lions, Tigers, Red Wings, and Pistons providing many an afternoon and evening of exciting entertainment for himself and his clients. More recently, the access to tickets had given him the opportunity to take his wife and their twin six-year-old boys out for some special family time. Especially fond of the basketball team, the Detroit Pistons, Mirko even owned a Bad Boys T-shirt he would wear to the games—much to his wife's chagrin.

But of course, like many people who had emigrated from Lebanon or Syria or Iran or Palestine, Mirko had left an entirely different life behind. Unfortunately for him, it was one that had followed him across the ocean by way of a recent long-distance phone call.

*

"I have a job for you," the voice on the other end of the telephone had said when Mirko's wife, Gabrielle, had handed him the receiver.

"I'm sorry. What did you say?"

"Your mother and father are well, yes?"

"What do you mean?" he had asked. He could still feel the mixture of anger and fear as he spoke. "Who is this?"

"A friend of a business partner. One you owe favors to. One you made promises to in return for safe passage out of Lebanon."

"Look," he had started to say.

"Do not waste my time—or your parents'. They are still tending their grove of olive trees, yes? Utilizing the honored practices handed down from generation to generation, is this not so? Their prized donkeys as much a part of their lives as the olives the beasts haul for them? Is this something you wish to see change?"

Mirko had felt perspiration start to bead on his forehead, anticipating what was coming. He had been too good at his old job, the job he had been doing in Lebanon since he was twelve. He'd smuggled the Desert Eagle into the U.S. when he emigrated, stashing it under a floorboard beneath the bed he and his wife shared. He'd hoped he'd never have to use it again.

His shoulders slumped when he asked, "When?"

"The sooner the better," had been the reply.

"I just can't—"

"Your mother seemed frail today. She had to lean on the side of one of the pack animals as she came in from the olive grove."

"Where," he had asked with gritted teeth.

"Newark, New Jersey."

"Who?"

"The name, address, and instructions are in an envelope on the driver's seat of your little red Ford Escort parked in front of your house."

"I swear to God," he had blurted out.

"Better you pray to Allah. Don't make me call you again."

He remembered his balls feeling like they might explode as the line went dead.

* * *

Bongo was flying solo, parked in the lot of Perry Funeral Home across the street from Yutanda's apartment complex. Normally, he'd be hanging with Twister—or Griper if circumstance called for it—but he was okay with being on his own tonight. It wasn't too bad a night—not too humid or too hot, for July. And the parking lot was quiet. And it felt pretty good having the windows rolled down and breathing in some fresh air. If he hadn't had peeping-Tom duty, as he called it, he would have found a basketball somewhere and walked two blocks over to Saint Benedict's Prep School to shoot hoops on one of their outside courts.

Gotta love prep schools, Bongo thought, *especially Saint Benny's. Got all the good shit.* Tartan track, basketball courts, tennis courts, baseball fields—shit, some prep schools he'd seen even had football stadiums with cement bleachers. Schools he'd attended—when he'd bothered to attend class back in the day—were lucky if they even had toilet paper in the stalls. Forget the athletic shit. Weren't no money for that. He sometimes wondered—when he was younger—what it would have been like to be a student at one of those prep schools. But wondering didn't change anything, he'd learned, and his days of daydreaming about those kinds of things—where he was a rich kid with fancy clothes and parents who dropped him off in front of school in a big Cadillac—ended pretty quickly. When you didn't have lunch money most days, the thought of attending a prep school—with their uniforms and polished shoes and such—well, you might as well just dream about becoming Superman—or James Brown.

Bongo pulled on the lip of his Yankees cap while checking the rearview mirror. All was quiet—as it had been since he'd pulled in. The only cars in the lot besides the old Saab he'd hotwired to make the drive across town were parked near the funeral home's side entrance. And where he'd parked—behind a row of trees separating him from the prying eyes on Mercer Street—he and the Saab were as inconspicuous as they could be. Figuring the two other cars belonged to a couple of night employees, he didn't think he had anything to worry about. He imagined they—the employees—were too preoccupied looking over their shoulders to see if a zombie was popping out of a coffin to take notice of him and the Saab.

Just thinking about working at a funeral home gave Bongo the heebie-jeebies. But working the *night shift* at one? Hell, he couldn't even imagine that. Frigging dead people lying all over the place dressed like they were going to a fancy party gave him the creeps. All stiff and ghost-like, eyes wide open, staring off into space like they could actually see where they were heading. *Shit, shut your eyes, motherfuckers, they don't work no more! What you staring at? Act like you seen a ghost.* The thought making him laugh, he slid a little deeper into the front seat of the car and tried to make his laughter sound like crying. Cause that was going to be his excuse if anybody got near enough to the car to ask him what he was doing there.

"I'm crying. Done lost a loved one, you know," he would say. "Just sittin' here collectin' my thoughts, remembering all the special moments. You mind leaving me alone?" he'd ask with a sniffle.

Yeah, the funeral home parking lot was a good place to have picked to watch the assemblywoman, he thought. But he checked the side mirror just in case. Just in case some zombie was crawling up behind him.

Bright headlight beams from a large, dark car swung across his face as the vehicle turned into the funeral home lot and drove across the asphalt at an angle toward the building's side entrance. Following its progress through the rearview mirror, Bongo took note of the car's closed rectangular back. A hearse, he guessed, making a delivery. His assumption was confirmed when a band of light appeared from the funeral home's side door. Absently, he wondered if the hearse was carrying the two Bloods he had heard about, the ones who'd been executed. Them two boys getting the big sleep made him think of the line from the Marvin Gaye song.

"Brother, brother, brother—there's far too many of you dying"; he could hear the man singing in his head.

You got that right, marvelous Marvin. Brothers be dropping like flies. Open season. Seems like we've done been labeled to be exterminated. Now, even you be dead, my man. Say your daddy shoot you. Fuck—what's going on? Ain't that what you said? And now here I am keeping an eye on this black sister. What is going on?

She'd be dead soon enough, he figured, the assemblywoman bitch. Fuckin' with the goods—the merchandise—get you in a world of trouble, he knew. Tough place, this world. Checking the rearview mirror again, he saw the murky figures of two men opening the back of the hearse. How soon would it be before he was the one they'd be sliding out of the back? Pulling on the lip of his cap, he looked away from the eyes peering back out at him from the car's rearview mirror.

* * *

"What are you and I going to do?"

Yutanda's question came with a heavy sigh. Part of her wished Menelik was old enough to open his sleeping eyes and answer her with some sort of innocent, childlike words of wisdom. Out of the mouths of babes— wasn't that the saying? It sure would be helpful if he *could* talk, she thought. Maybe he could point her in the right direction, because lately, she sure as hell didn't know what direction she should be going.

Her thoughts drifted to the little figures on the wall beside his crib: hand-painted pink elephants, blue giraffes, yellow stars, and brown-trunked, green-leafed palm trees. Suppressing a laugh, she thought, *Are there palm trees in Africa?* Surely there had to be—didn't there? Certainly in Egypt, right? Surrounding an oasis? Blowing air out between her lips, she shook her head. *How little I really know about Africa*, she thought. Pink elephants and blue giraffes. *Maybe I am crazy*, she observed. Studying the animal's painted faces, she suddenly wondered, *Are they mocking me?*

When she heard the door behind her open, she turned to see her mother's face peeking into the room. "We're leaving," she saw Elizabeth silently mouth. Yutanda held up a finger to signal her mother to wait. Looking back down into Menelik's peaceful, sleeping face, she carefully adjusted the blanket away from his chin before turning and leaving the room.

"Sleeps real quiet-like, doesn't he?" Elizabeth whispered to her daughter as Yutanda eased the door shut behind her. "Don't you want to leave it cracked?" she asked, eyeing the closed door.

"I'm going right back in," Yutanda whispered, moving past her mom to head down the short hallway toward the living room. "I don't want to wake him," she added.

When Yutanda stepped through the archway to the living room and saw her dad with his faded green and yellow Southern Railway hat in his hands, she lowered her eyes and came to a stop.

"He still asleep?" Ed tentatively asked.

Yutanda nodded, lifting her face to meet his eyes.

"He's a fine boy," Ed offered. "Real even-keeled, he is. You should be proud," he told his daughter with a nod of his head. "Yes sir, real proud."

"Then why don't I feel that way?"

"Land's sake—what is it girl?" her mother asked, stepping up behind Yutanda to give her a hug. "What's wrong?"

"I don't know, Momma." She covered her face with her hands. "I guess—I'm just tired is all. Too much going on, I guess."

"I think you do know."

Yutanda jerked her head up at her father's comment.

"You've seemed out of sorts ever since we got back. Just what was it you and Noah were going on about? Could hear you going at each other as soon as we stepped into the hall from outside."

Noah? Is that what this is all about? Noah? She slowly shook her head. It wasn't him, she didn't think. Was it something he'd said? What was it they were raising their voices over?

"And I guess I should say I'm sorry, about you not having a husband. That weren't right."

Yutanda glanced over her shoulder to the hallway leading to Menelik's room.

"Your father's trying to apologize, Yutanda," Elizabeth gently offered. "Did you hear what he said?"

"What if he isn't?"

"Why, whatever do you mean?" her mother asked, turning her by the shoulders and looking up to her face. "Course he means it when he says he's sorry."

"Oh, not that," came Yutanda's distracted reply, her eyes darting around the apartment for a moment before coming to rest on her father. "What if he isn't dead? What if they're wrong? There's no proof."

Yutanda saw her mom and dad exchange confused looks.

"They never found a body, belongings, clothes—nothing," she went on. "Why did I just accept that it was true?"

Her eyes drifted to the floor.

"'Cause I was having his baby? Just the shock of hearing them say he was dead?" she muttered. "But what if he isn't?" she asked in a heightened voice, her face shifting between her parents. "What if he's over there somewhere—?"

Her forehead wrinkled, then smoothed, her eyes flitting from side to side as if they were keeping time with the thoughts spinning round in her head.

"Wouldn't be the first time," she expounded. "Memory loss, shock from the crash—getting hit on the head. What if that's what really happened?"

"Yutanda, what— I don't— The State Department—"

Ed took a step toward her, his hands absently twirling his old railroad hat. "They say he died." He looked over at his wife. "That was over a year ago now. I don't understand."

"You feelin' all right, Yutanda?" Elizabeth added. "Somethin' happen today to make this—this revisiting Menelik's death—"

"But that's just it, Momma." Yutanda took a step to her mother, her eyes wide. "No body, no proof, no nothing—why would we think he's dead? Because some stranger from the federal government's told us so?"

She clasped her hands in front of her chest.

"God, what a fool I've been." She shook her head and loudly exhaled. "Getting lost in work, in the programs Menelik and I started before he left—instead of focusing on him."

She looked at both of them then, her expression determined.

"Believing in him, his will to survive."

"Whoa, whoa, whoa now, girl," Ed interrupted, motioning with his hands for her to slow down. "What is all this? Just what are you trying to say? I don't get where this is all going."

"Oh, Daddy, you were right. I guess I do know what's wrong." She took a step toward him. "And yeah," she went on, her voice tinged with excitement, "it was something Noah and I were debating. Something about what Menelik would have said if he were here right now."

"And what might that be?"

"If Menelik were here right now, Daddy, he'd tell me you have to put the past to rest before you can take a step away from it."

"I don't understand," he admitted when she didn't explain. "What does that mean?"

"It means, as soon as I get this dock business squared away, me and the baby are moving down with you for a time."

Her face beaming, she went on.

"And then when he's a little older—maybe a few more months—we're taking a trip to Ethiopia, to find his father, to find Menelik. To square away the past."

"But what about your job, your position?" Lizbeth asked.

"I know it's sudden, Momma. I'd probably sound as perplexed as you do if the tables were turned. But I realize my place isn't here right now. I'll just have to step down." With a smile and a shrug of her shoulders, she added, "I'll tender my resignation next week."

10

TEIMBAKA WINCED WITH the jarring recoil of the rifle shot. Several paces behind him, someone laughed.

"We are not dove hunting, Teimbaka," came the chiding, good-natured voice of Tengene. "Maybe you should aim at the ground until you get the hang of it."

Laughter erupted from the three men standing behind him, but Teimbaka knew Kamua, Selam, and Tengene meant it all in good fun. With a smile and a quick glance over his shoulder, he slid back the loading bolt, ejected the spent shell casing, and placed a new round inside the breech before shifting the bolt closed. As Selam had instructed, he stood straight, raised the rifle to his shoulder, bent his head to the sight, aimed the barrel an inch lower than the target he wanted to hit, held his breath, and squeezed the trigger. This time, expecting the jolting recoil, he absorbed the gunshot's blow without a flinch, the Lee Enfield barely jerking upward. Fifty yards in front of him, the slender trunk of a dead scrub tree exploded.

"Impossible!" he heard Kamua exclaim. "It's only his second time!"

"You fire the weapon as though it has been a part of you for years," Selam called out to Teimbaka. "Surely you have used one before."

Somberly, Teimbaka studied the weapon in his hand, remembering the lament in Untello's voice when he spoke of the ways of the old Africa fast becoming abandoned. *So it has come to this.*

"Why do you look so pained?" Tengene asked as Teimbaka turned and walked toward the three men gathered behind him. "I would be jumping up and down if I could make a shot like that."

"Beginner's luck," Kamua stated, eyeing Teimbaka with doubt.

"Thank you for instructing me," Teimbaka said, handing Selam the rifle. "You are a thorough teacher."

"What were you seeing when you looked at the rifle?" Selam quietly asked him. "The man who took the whip to you?"

"No—not him," Teimbaka thoughtfully replied. "Something worse."

"I don't know how that could be. George Henry is the devil himself."

"And now you can put a bullet through his head," Kamua interjected.

"We must get you a gun," Tengene added. "I'm sure the captain will give you one of the older rifles. We could use a shot like yours out here in the bush."

Teimbaka surveyed the terrain: shoulder-high brown-tinged bush grass and spindly, grey-trunked, sparsely leaved scrub trees. Though no animals were apparent, he knew both predator and prey were using the foliage as cover, engaged in the never-ending struggle of survival. Yet, here they stood, casually speaking of killing. What was happening within the Mother? he wondered.

"I wish it—the weapon—was something I would never use."

The words left him before he realized he had spoken.

"A gun—a rifle—the ways of the Mother are being lost," he explained with regret. Searching their faces, he asked, "Is there no way back?"

"Back? Back to what?" Kamua wanted to know. "Back to spears and arrows and clubs, when bullets and rockets kill dozens at a time? Is this what you mean by *back*?"

Kamua gave Teimbaka a harsh look.

"My village was slaughtered by grenades and machine guns and put to fire by men with flame throwers. And you speak of weapons from the Stone Age as a way to combat these?"

Teimbaka studied the face of the teenager as it took on a fierce look of defiance.

"Those pitiful ways are dead. Dead and gone, like the laughable notion of your Mother—of Africa."

"She is not dead," Teimbaka was quick to say, his voice barely a whisper. "Nor is there humor in what She was or is—or what She will become. These changes—" he said, looking at the rifles each of them held, "they are not of

Her. Yet they have been brought here—here, as you say—to kill, nothing more. This is not what She wants, Kamua. This way of killing is not Hers."

"You are mad," Kamua harshly responded. "You speak as though you can talk to this Mother, as though you—"

Selam grabbed him firmly by the arm and gave it a shake.

"What?" Kamua demanded. "You don't think he is touched?"

"Be still," Selam commanded. "You are young. What do you know of the real Africa?"

"I know its hate," he spat. "Young," he scoffed, slapping the stock of his rifle. "I wish I was too young to know the savagery that has taken over this country. You speak of Africa as though it is something to be cherished, or holy. When butchers run rampant across it, killing without purpose or reason."

Kamua looked at each of the older men around him, his face slowly changing from one of defiance to one filled with remorse.

"Africa is lost. Perhaps it was something more once, something better— but there is no good here any longer. The real Africa," he said, turning his attention to Selam, "whatever you remember it as, has been overrun by evil."

"No," Teimbaka quietly said. "That is not so, Kamua. There are those that are here," he explained, extending a hand out toward the savanna, "those that you see and those you cannot, who will not give in to the Serpent. Evil will not claim the Mother. As long as there is one who will stand by Her and hear Her voice, Her children will not be devoured by darkness."

"You talk—"

Before Kamua could say anything further, Teimbaka walked away. As the others watched him make his way toward the Land Rover parked at the edge of the small clearing where they'd stopped to rest, Kamua looked at Selam and frowned.

"Serpents, the Mother—he talks of folklore and myths, stories told by old women around a fire. Next he will want us to believe—"

"A savanna hare turning into a woman?" Tengene teased. "How do you explain the gashes from the whip having already healed?" Tengene placed a large hand on Kamua's slender shoulder and smiled. "Do you believe the bloody mess on his back was healed overnight because of honey salve?"

"A tabib," Selam said. "A shaman. You saw her yourself, Kamua," he told the young Kenyan. "There are still those who walk the path of old

Africa. And he is one," he added with a nod to Teimbaka. "Africa—her spirit, her mystery, her ways—she is strong within him. Do you not feel it in his presence?"

Kamua looked over at Teimbaka and remembered.

*

Violent shaking had awakened him. And as he opened his eyes, the blaring call of an elephant had rattled his head. With a pang of fear, he'd pushed himself off the ground, his hands tight around his rifle. Looking wildly about for the cause of the rumbling earth, he saw the man they had cut down from the tree; he was squatting next to the low-burning flames of the camp's fire, edging a tin coffee pot closer to the heat.

"Is it an earthquake?" Kamua had asked, his voice near panic.

The man had turned his head and smiled. Kamua looked to Selam and Tengene, wondering how they could still be sleeping when the land beneath them felt as though it was about to burst open.

"So you feel the tremors?"

"Yes, I feel them," came Kamua's quick reply. "How can you not?"

"They are leaving."

"Who? Who's leaving?"

A smile had broken out on the man's face as what sounded to be the trumpeting of a massive elephant blared through Kamua's head. It was then that Selam and Tengene had awoken.

"Is that coffee I smell?" Tengene had asked, sitting up and rubbing his face.

"You changed his bandages without our help, I see," Selam added, looking squarely at Kamua.

It was then that Kamua had noticed the bloody, salve-soaked gauze lying in strands upon the ground. With a nod to the dirty bandages, he looked at the man tending the coffee pot, demanding, "Did you do that?"

The man shook his head no.

"Then how?" Kamua pressed. "What is your name?"

"Teimbaka," the man said. "Do you have but the three cups? That's all I could find in your vehicle. Coffee's ready."

Over coffee and strips of spiced antelope jerky, Teimbaka had relayed the story of being taken to the camp of the ivory poachers and brought before their leader, a bearded, heavyset man who called himself George Henry. When George Henry had asked him why he had come to his camp, Teimbaka had told him the truth: spirit elephants had led him there to stop any more of their kind from being killed. George Henry had studied him for a time, his brow furrowing, stroking his beard. And then he had burst out laughing, causing the entire group of thirty-some armed men gathered near him to laugh as well.

"'It is the Serpent's bidding you do,' I told him. 'You will be devoured by his evil.'

"'Silence!' George Henry roared. 'God speaks through me! He has blessed the killing of the beasts! The ivory is His to give—and He has told me to take it!'"

George Henry had stood up from the chair and glared. Teimbaka described how the man's body had gone rigid, his forearms flexing as he clenched and unclenched his fists.

"'The elephants are children of the Mother,' I replied, 'The ivory a gift from Her to them. The spirit elephants have made it plain this must stop.' Looking over to the ivory stacked on the perimeter of the camp, I asked, 'Do you not hear it in the wails of the beasts when you cut it from their jowls and see it in their eyes when their tears turn to blood?'

"George Henry took a few steps toward me then, pulling a thick knife from the sheath tied about his waist.

"'The Father has no voice in the giving of their tusks,' I said to him as he approached me. 'It is the Serpent's words you hear. Have you not felt the coldness of the coils slither across your shoulders as he whispers in your ear?'"

George Henry unleashed a terrifying, guttural scream, Teimbaka told them. Then watched as a knife was thrust toward his neck. Teimbaka touched a spot on his throat, as though the point of the blade was pressing against his flesh.

"I do not know why he did not shove it through my neck."

A puzzled expression took hold of Teimbaka's face as he paused.

"Or what stayed his hand. But when he drew the knife downward, the blade sliced open the front of my shamma, exposing the scars from the lion wounding."

Teimbaka felt his chest when he recounted this, his eyes taking on a faraway look.

"It sparked something in him when he saw the jagged pink lines. And before I realized what was happening, several of his men grabbed hold of me and dragged me to a tree."

Kamua remembered the pained expression that had taken hold of Teimbaka's face.

"They turned me to the tree, bound my wrists and ankles to the trunk, and pulled my robe away from my shoulders and back. And then George Henry shouted to me: 'Let us see who is stronger—your African wench, or God!'

"There came laughter then, and the crack of the whip as it snapped an inch from my ear. I said to him: 'You are of Her, George Henry. You are one of Her children. Why is it you forsake Her? Surely you must know that the Father and the Mother speak to one another. What must they think of you?'"

Teimbaka's body had shuddered then. Kamua remembered seeing him squeeze his eyes shut, watching his face turn into a mask of hardened wrinkles.

"'God speaks to no one but me!' George Henry roared back.

"And with the first bite of the whip, he screamed: 'Do you hear?' And thereafter, each lash sent my mind numb with pain. While he screamed the same question: 'Do you hear?' After a time—" Teimbaka fell suddenly quiet for a moment. "I lost count of the number of times he screamed this to me. Soon, only the crack of the whip could I hear. And the pain ripping into my flesh."

There had been a long silence then. Kamua had stared into his coffee as Teimbaka gazed into his cup.

"How is it you are alive?" Kamua had dared to ask after a minute had passed.

Teimbaka had looked at him then, and Kamua was surprised when he saw a slight smile touch the corners of his lips.

"The young spirit beast—the one whose mother was killed near the glittering lake—the baby spirit elephant that has been with me since before I—"

The smile slowly faded from Teimbaka's face, departing with a heavy sigh before he continued.

"It appeared not five paces away from me. Staring at me, flinching with each strike of the whip. It started to cry. Tears I lost myself in. Tears that absorbed my pain."

He had looked at each of them, his gaze slowly moving from Selam to

Tengene and finally to Kamua. He sipped his coffee and said, "And that is how I awakened—remembering the tears of the spirit beast."

"And your wounds?" Selam had asked.

Teimbaka had set his tin cup of coffee on the ground, stood, and removed what remained of his tattered shamma. And they all gasped when they saw his wounds. For what had been deep, raw, swollen lacerations when they had wrapped them with gauze were now scars, resembling the smooth pink lines etched across Teimbaka's chest.

"How is this possible?" Kamua had shouted. "You are healed! But—but how?"

"You had first watch," Tengene had interjected. "And you never woke me for mine. Did he wake you for yours?" he had asked Selam. And as Tengene watched Selam shake his head, he stated, "You must have fallen asleep."

"No. I was awake. And then—"

"And then?" Selam had pressed him when he fell silent.

"A hare," he had whispered. "A bush hare."

He had quickly glanced at each of their faces.

"It came into camp. Its eyes—they shifted like the sands of the desert."

"A hare came into camp and got so close to you, you could see into its eyes?" Tengene sarcastically questioned. "Are you saying a hare healed his wounds?"

"The eyes," he'd started to explain.

Kamua observed Teimbaka studying him as he spoke, as if noticing something he had missed seeing before.

"They—a woman's—green, like emeralds—glittering with rings of fire."

The calm of the morning had been broken by Tengene's deep laughter.

*

"I am ready!" Teimbaka called out.

Kamua shook his head, awakening from the memory.

"Ready for what?" Selam called back.

"To find George Henry!" Teimbaka replied, climbing into the back seat of the Land Rover.

"Hurry—before his tracks are lost."

"He may well be in Sudan by now," Selam told him as he began walking toward the vehicle. "We cannot follow him there."

"Then take me as close to the border as you can, if you would," Teimbaka calmly replied. "The Mother has healed my wounds. I must try to do the same for Her."

"But it is madness to seek out George Henry." Tengene said, giving Teimbaka a quizzical look. "You will be killed if you fall into his hands again."

"What would you have me do?"

Teimbaka looked westward, his eyes drifting across the savanna as a gust of wind stirred the grasses.

"The Mother is in need," he said to Tengene. "Will you not help me reach Her?"

* * *

Eden ran as fast as she could, her thin, taught legs like those of a spry gazelle as she bounded down the backside of a rock-strewn ridge, run-jumping between outcroppings of stone resembling the broken walls of an earthquake-shattered temple. Hurrying after John Too and Sister Lady, she tried her best to keep up as they ran from the sound of approaching vehicles.

On the move for four days since leaving the waterfall on the Tekezé River, they'd neither heard nor seen any sign of Bacha Alba and his men. And though none of them would speak of it, they knew they hadn't been followed because of John, because of what he had done so the three of them could escape. What danger the bouda must be in, Eden had thought to herself numerous times. What sacrifices he must be making, offering his life in return for their safety as he had done when he and the hyenas charged the warlord's camp to free Tabib. What hold did she—this Sister Lady—have on the bouda? Eden wondered. Whatever spell she had cast upon him, it was certainly powerful, she thought. Tabibs, boudas, abdars—what in the world had she gotten herself into?

"Quickly!" John Too shouted over his shoulder as he scrambled down the steep incline. "The vehicles are getting close. It's the warlord. I can feel it."

"But—there's—no road—down this ridge—John Too," Sister Lady called down to him. "Whoever—it is—won't be—able—to follow."

Eden heard the labored breathing of the woman. The tabib was winded, she realized. Struggling with the rough terrain, Eden guessed. But having been tied up in a tent for a week or more, how could she not be? Outrunning the warlord—if that was who was behind them—no, that would not be possible with the tabib in such a weakened state. This was all going to end very badly, Eden thought—yes, very badly.

"Listen," John Too harshly whispered.

Eden tried to listen, but the pebbles dislodging as she made her way down to where John Too waited kept her from hearing anything but the steady sound of rocks bouncing against stone.

"Quiet!" John Too hissed. "They will hear."

Who will hear? Eden thought as she turned and craned her neck to try to see the crest of the ridge they'd been travelling down the past hour. This abdar—this John Too, as he went by—he was an odd one. Always giving orders. Like he was an elder. But he was only a boy. Younger than her, she guessed. She shrugged her shoulders. *He is abdar; what do I know?*

"They're here!" she heard John Too shout. "Hurry!"

"Quiet—listen—they will hear—hurry," she muttered, giving him an angry look. "Make up your mind."

A bullet splintered the face of a boulder not ten paces from where she was standing.

"Eden!" Sister Lady screamed. "Run, Eden! Run!"

Eden looked down to see the tabib holding out her hand, frantically motioning with her other for her to move toward her. Bullets blasted into the loose, rocky soil, some hitting dangerously close to Sister Lady. Miraculously, as suddenly as the rain of bullets began, it stopped. Eden took hold of the tabib's hand as a voice called out to them from above.

"Sister Claire!"

Claire's name echoed between the ridgeline they'd descended and the one some half kilometer west across the valley floor. John Too hurried them behind a large, square-shaped outcropping of stone.

"There is nowhere to go, Claire Waterman!" the same voice shouted down to them.

Eden glanced at the worn face of Sister Lady before turning her attention to the area around them. The floor of the valley was flat, the soil—or dried sand as it looked to Eden—lined with cracks from lack of moisture, with a few dead-looking scrub bushes dotting the way across to the far ridge. The bushes would offer no cover, she knew. And even if they could cross the open space to the next elevation, they would be easy targets, climbing slowly upward. She looked quickly north; the ridge ran as far as she could see, an unbroken barrier keeping them pinned in the valley. South, formations of stone and tufts of vegetation ended quite abruptly, hinting at an opening of some kind before another section of elevated stones and sparse vegetation arose farther past. How big the opening might be in the ridge face, Eden could only guess at. But looking across the valley, she saw the same gap existed in the opposite ridge, leaving her to wonder if there wasn't a gorge blocking their way if they chose a southward route.

"It's him," she heard Sister Lady say. "It's Alba. What does he want with me?"

"Your mother sends a message to you!"

The word *you* reverberated against the rocks as though a dozen people were shouting at the same time. Eden watched Claire's face go ashen.

"My mother," Claire whispered. "How is that possible?"

"Your letters!" Alba shouted as if he had heard her question. "She wants you to come home!"

Eden saw John Too move to the edge of the rock and peek his face around. The tabib, she saw, was muttering something, casting a spell or a curse of some kind, Eden imagined.

"Some of his men are coming down," John Too said with urgency. "We must move."

From Sister Lady's expression, Eden could tell the woman heard nothing of what the abdar was saying.

"Your father!"

The two words echoed over and over and over: *your father, your father, your father.* "He's ill!" *Ill, ill, ill, ill, ill:* floating all around them, dwindling to murmurs absorbed by stone.

She saw Sister Lady rise from her crouched position and stumble forward, face pale and frightened, as though she had seen a ghost.

"Where are you going?" John Too asked, grabbing her arm and pulling her close to the wall of stone.

"My father," she uttered, dazed.

Eden saw her look at John Too as if the boy was a total stranger.

"Why didn't you tell me?"

What is the abdar doing? Eden wondered. Why is he closing his eyes? They needed to run, to escape. The warlord would not treat them with mercy if they were captured. She had seen the butchered government soldiers on the road. She did not relish the thought of having a blade ripped across her throat and her stomach sliced open.

"I will see you home!" the voice of Bacha Alba boomed. "Your father needs you!"

Sister Lady tried to push away from the wall of stone, but John Too pressed her back using strength Eden would not have believed he possessed.

"It is a trick," he said to Sister Lady. "His words are not true. We must go."

Eden noticed the twitch in Sister Lady's forehead, her eyes blinking several times. Her shoulders trembling, John Too grabbed hold of the tabib's hand and raised it to her neck. There he placed the small silver cross into her fingers.

"Ask the Father," John Too told her. "Close your eyes and hear him tell you."

"I can't," Claire snapped, thrusting John Too away. Skin flushed, her eyes pooling with tears, she blurted, "I can't think, I can't hear, I can't—anything! My father!"

"Why are you like this?" Eden demanded when Claire sank to her knees and covered her face in her hands. "And why do you let her be this way?" she scolded John Too.

"They are going to kill us!" she yelled at Sister Lady. "And you act like we have all the time in the day to decide whether your father is ill or not!"

As if punctuating her point, several bullets raked the ground behind them, the burst of the automatic weapon booming across the valley like the roar of swift-moving storm.

"Now will you move?" Eden screamed at Claire. "Because I don't want to die!"

John Too bent and took hold of Claire's arm.

"Sister Lady. Come. We must leave," he told her.

"But where?" Claire sniffled, wiping tears from her eyes. She looked up into John Too's face. "There's nowhere to go."

Eden folded her arms across her chest and grunted. Hearing Sister Lady's reply, she shook her head, tempted to pick up a stone and throw it at her head.

"*Anti ghabiya*," she muttered under her breath.

"She is not stupid!" John Too yelled.

Eden cowered away at the sound of John Too's voice. For she had awakened some spirit in him, she feared, his voice not that of the boy she had been traveling with for the past several days. Immediately, she bowed her head.

"Forgive me, Abdar," she quickly offered. "It is only that I am afraid."

"Which way?" Claire asked. "John Too—how can we escape?"

Eden looked up to find Sister Lady rising to her feet, strength radiating from her face. And there—*when she looks at the boy as though she is his mother*—something powerful—magical—a twinkling of light shining in the amber speckles of her eyes. *Tabib is strong*. Eden could see that now. The revelation brought a smile to her lips.

"Why don't we fly?" she suggested.

"What do you mean? How can we fly?"

"Surely you know a spell," Eden innocently replied. "Between the two of you," she explained, casting her gaze between Claire and John Too, "you must know how to fly."

"My men will reach you soon!"

Claire, Eden, and John Too looked up toward the top of the ridge.

"I will let the boy and girl leave unharmed! It is only you, Claire, that I want."

Eden glanced at Sister Lady to see what her reaction would be.

"Your father cries for you! He is begging to see you! Come freely, Sister Claire. Or do you want the boy and girl to suffer?"

As the taunting laughter of Bacha Alba filled the air within the valley floor, Eden saw Sister Lady's expression change from one of strength to one of doubt. When Claire tried to move past her, Eden thrust out an arm.

"Do not listen to the *ebob caca*," she told her. "His words are lies. He will kill us. Whether it is in front of you or after he has taken you away, Abdar and I will be killed. Don't be *ghabiya*," she said, giving John Too an impish smile. "We must all go."

An explosion rocked the earth beneath their feet, the concussion from the blast knocking them to the ground. Eden frantically crawled to the base of the boulder, pressing her body flat as a shower of dirt and debris fell upon her. A torrent of gunfire quickly followed, shards of stone exploding into the air as bullets riddled stone above them. Eden covered her ears with her hands and saw Sister Lady and John Too do the same. And then the day seemed to blink, sunlight dimming to a shadow, the air suddenly still except for a swooshing whir of wind that seemed to be gaining strength.

The howl of some tormented beast accompanied a massive black cloud racing up the southern end of the valley. And as the cry of the beast faded to a distant echo, the air became alive with flapping wings, the sun nearly obliterated as a gathering of birds drew closer.

"Quelea," Eden whispered, lifting her head.

And as she watched the birds come streaming up between the ridges, she marveled how they flew as one. Changing shape from a dark cloud to a black fist to the shape of a wavering gray puddle, erupting into a silver funnel swirling up the face of the ridge they'd descended before zooming back down to the valley floor. There, like a swarm of angry bees, the flock hovered not an arm's length above their heads, wings beating in a tight-packed cluster, creating a living dome.

"Run! Now!" John Too shouted.

Before Eden could even think to reply, the tabib pulled her to her feet. Together, they raced after John Too, running south. Behind them, the sound of gunfire erupted.

Eden felt the sky come alive, for the quelea flew right above their heads. What Eden thought must surely be tens of thousands of the birds churned the air, kinetic energy pulsing in every direction. *So this is what it is like to travel with a tabib and an abdar!* She eyed Sister Lady and John Too with a smile. *How clever they are! How creative! And to think I suggested we fly. And they pretended not to know how.* She giggled. *So they call upon a sky full of birds instead. Is there nothing they cannot do?*

Hearing the grating, raspy breathing of Sister Lady, Eden realized the gunfire had stopped. Panic bunched in her stomach when she looked up and saw the birds no longer above her. *Where did they go?* she wondered. Glancing over her shoulder, she glimpsed the back edge of a dark, moving mass speeding over the crest of the opposite ridge. The birds gone, they were exposed once more. *Why did Tabib and Abdar not ask them to stay?*

"What is it?" Claire asked when John Too came to a sudden stop.

"A gorge," Eden told her, slowing as she reached Claire's side.

"A deep break between plateaus," John Too said, turning briefly around to answer Claire. "Where the highlands begin to give way to the plain," he explained, pointing to the other side.

"Have you been this way before, Eden?" Claire asked, giving Eden a questioning look. "Traveling with your father on his way back to Sudan?"

"I have never been to Sudan. He said it was too dangerous for little girls to go there." She grunted. "Where is it not dangerous?"

Claire giggled, squeezing her hand. "Perhaps we will run across him." Claire smiled and took a deep breath. "And find Thomas and the others— and your mother," she added, hugging Eden to her side.

Eden gazed across the gorge, wondering how they would cross, the distance too far to try to jump. She guessed, even without looking, that the depth of the break would kill a person falling into it; certain the ravine—a sudden, unexpected break along the floor of the valley—had claimed many lives before. Looking to her left, she saw the gap between the eastern ridgelines ran several hundred paces before ending at a sheer wall of rock. Turning her head in the opposite direction—west—she spied a narrow ledge running the length of the gorge as far as she could see. Venturing a quick look behind her, she groaned; five of the warlord's men had reached the valley floor. *I am dead,* she thought. *I knew this would end badly.*

"There is nowhere to go!" Bacha Alba's voice shouted to them from above.

Eden heard the sound of vehicles—the warlord and his troops moving into a new position, following them.

"Let this be over, Sister Claire!"

Eden picked up on the change in the warlord's tone. The playful edge he'd exhibited was gone.

"Give yourself up! I'm sending you home!"

Eden looked at Sister Lady; the woman mouthed the word *home,* staring off into space. Eden yanked on her hand.

"I told you not to listen to him," she snapped. "There, Abdar," she said to John Too. Motioning with her chin toward the ledge running aside the western ridge, she yelled, "Go!"

* * *

Where it began, the ledge was wide enough for three people to enter abreast. And for the first hundred paces, they crossed in this manner, John

Too nearest the edge of the ravine, Eden rubbing against the cliff face on the other side of Sister Lady.

Eden could see she'd been right—the drop-off of the gorge was deep. Half a kilometer straight down, she guessed, wide where they were now—at the top—but narrowing at the end where the plateaus closed against one another. She shivered at the thought of falling into the crevice. It would not be a pleasant way to die, she thought. No, not quick and painless as everyone always said they hoped death would be. No, this would be a painful and perhaps drawn-out death, especially if the initial fall didn't kill you and you were trapped at the bottom of the gorge with no way to escape. What if only your legs were broken? she thought. You would starve and die of thirst, or vultures would find you and peck out your eyes and then feed upon your— She gave her head a good shake. *Stop thinking this way! Stop it!*

"Slow!" John Too barked.

Putting his arm out to keep them back, John Too moved ahead, motioning for Sister Lady to come next, Eden to follow.

"Only room for one to pass at a time," he said over his shoulder. "Hurry."

Coming to a bend in the ledge, Eden pressed her body against the stone and began to shuffle around the crest. Once past the apex, she stopped, gazing in wonder at what she saw.

The plain seemed endless, stretching outward as far as she could see, not a mountain or a ridge rising up from the land to block her view to the western horizon. The sky a fathomless blue, the landscape below, varying shades of green, dotted with clumps of trees and tracts of golden brown savanna grass. Southward, she spied sunlight twinkling off the waters of a twisting river, gold-hued flocks of birds gliding overhead. Massive herds of animals grazed near the river's shores, drawn to water's edge to drink and take refuge from the heat.

A gunshot shattered her moment of reflection, the bullet blowing a chunk of rock out of the cliff face just above her head.

"Eden!" Claire shouted. "Keep moving!"

Claire grabbed her by the shoulder and pulled her to her side.

"Why were you just standing there?"

Why is the tabib so upset? she thought. *The warlord's men are only a few hundred paces behind. I will be dead soon.*

"Keep moving!" John Too yelled to them.

John Too was halfway around the new section of ledge, Eden saw, hugging the cliff face where the stone walkway narrowed and curved inward. Looking across the crescent-shaped indentation, Eden could see the ledge narrowed once more before disappearing around another bend. What would they find if they could make it there? she wondered. Surely, the warlord's men would shoot the boy and her before they reached the next bend. They would be easy targets once the *ebob caca* reached the spot where she was standing. Two hundred or more paces to go, she guessed, and she and the tabib were not yet a quarter of the way across.

"We will die."

"Nonsense," Claire admonished her. "John Too will lead us—"

"They will just shoot us." Eden shrugged. "It will be easy. We will be over there," she explained, pointing to the other side of the inward-curving ledge, "when they reach this spot. Would you not just shoot me and the abdar if you were them?"

"Get in front of me," Claire told her. "No one's going to shoot you. Not unless they're going to shoot me too."

Claire carefully ushered Eden around her body until the girl was in front. Eden felt the tabib's hands take her shoulders and prod her forward.

"Hurry, child. We must catch up with John Too before they get here."

Though she felt there was no purpose in trying to flee, Eden did as the tabib instructed, shuffling as quickly forward as the ledge safely allowed. Halfway to the abdar, Eden heard the first of the warlord's men reach the bend where she and the tabib had just been standing.

"*Wa-kif!*"

Eden tried to turn her head when she heard the command to stop, but Sister Lady kept her moving forward. John Too, she saw, still a dozen paces ahead of them.

"*Wa-kif! Yamuutu!*"

The short burst of gunfire from the man's automatic weapon sounded like an avalanche, the ear-splitting boom of shots sending tremors through Eden's body down through her feet. Instinctively she squatted to a crouch when a shower of rock and dust fell upon her, shards of stone biting into the skin of her arms and hands as she placed them over her head to try to protect herself.

"John Too!" she heard the tabib scream. "Get close to me! Now!"

Another burst of automatic gunfire raked an area ahead of them, Eden staring at the exploding clouds of rock, unable to block out the vision of her body being shredded by bullets.

"Eden—climb up and put your arms around my neck!" the tabib commanded her. "And wrap your legs around my waist! John Too, place your back to the rocks and grab hold of my blouse! Quickly."

"*Sharmuta! Wa-kif!*"

"What's he saying?"

Eden reached up and placed her arms around the back of Claire's neck, wrapping her legs around her waist so her feet were crossed around her back.

"He called you a—um, a bad name—and told you to stop."

Eden felt John Too press against her backside as he took hold of the tabib's tunic.

"Tell him— Oh, never mind. John Too, move when I move."

Eden turned her head to the side so she could see what lay ahead of them. But as they started forward—Sister Lady carrying her, John Too shuffling along, mirroring the steps of the tabib—she couldn't help but let her eyes drift down the depth of the ravine.

Enormous plates of smooth-faced rock ran from the top of the gorge to the bottom, resembling giant blocks stacked atop one another, seams running in sloping angles. At the bottom of the gorge, she spied massive boulders intermingled with sharp-edged stones, the image of the two conflicting dangers making her wonder if the ancient god who'd created the fissure hadn't had a sense of humor, betting with other gods on the chances those falling into the ravine would either be impaled on the sharp-pointed rocks or bludgeoned by the impact of landing on rounded boulders.

When the booming eruption of an automatic weapon sounded once more, Eden felt Sister Lady's body go rigid. Bullets tore into the stone by the tabib's feet, chunks of it falling into the deep chasm. Staring at the falling rocks, Eden knew she be would be next. The notion made her shiver.

"Enough!"

Eden turned her head at the shouted word to see two more of the warlord's men joining the first. One of them spoke English.

"Return now, woman! Or have the ledge you walk on shot out from beneath your feet!"

Eden felt the tabib take a deep breath.

"And what will your master say when you tell him you killed the prize he seems to want so much? What will you say to him when he pulls the knife sheathed to his leg and puts it to your throat?"

Ah—the tabib is smart. Eden watched the men begin to whisper amongst themselves.

"Keep moving, John Too," Claire said. "Go."

Just as they started to move again, Eden saw two of the warlord's men hand the third man their rifles as they drew knives from their belts. One of the men gave Eden an evil smile as he took his first steps toward her.

"They're coming—with knives!" Eden exclaimed.

"Hurry, John Too!" Claire barked.

"It would be quicker if I went ahead without clinging to you."

"No!" Eden shouted. "Another has arrived," she hurried to explain, her attention focused on the men behind them. "This one has a long rifle with an eye-piece on the top. He's aiming right at us."

Eden pulled her face away as Claire jerked her head around, the quick motion shifting the slender chain around Claire's neck. Curious as to what sort of adornments a tabib might wear, Eden stared at the cross, captivated by its smooth, shiny surface. A miniature reflection of her face looked out at her. She smiled. Her reflection smiled back. She blinked. Her reflection did the same. And then something strange happened—something Eden was not expecting. The coffee-brown eyes looking out at her from the surface of the cross turned emerald green, a flare of yellow light flowing out from the centers, trailed by sparks of rose-hued pink.

"We're almost there, Sister Lady!"

At the sound of John Too's voice, Claire turned her head back the other way. Her necklace shifted with the movement, the cross falling behind the collar of her tunic. Eden left to wonder what she had witnessed.

"They're catching up!" Claire replied. "We only have a minute!"

The tabib sounded frantic. Perhaps she was realizing how badly this was going to end, Eden thought. She and the abdar would be put to death. But by what means? she wondered. Would it be the knife, or would they be thrown off the cliff? The prospect of dying by a mixture of the two crept into her imagination.

Five paces from the bend in the ledge, John Too dashed ahead, the crackling boom of a rifle shot sounding nearly at the same time. The bullet exploded into the rocks just behind his neck, forcing Claire to stop until the cloud of debris fell clear.

"John Too!" she screamed.

"Hurry!" Eden heard the abdar shout from the other side of the bend. "There's a way across!"

Without hesitating, Claire shuffled the final few steps. Taking a quick look behind her, she carried Eden around the point.

"It must be an old shepherd's crossing."

Eden followed John Too's eyes to the length of ropes running across the span of the gorge. She almost laughed when she saw them, for the ends of the three frayed, weather-worn ropes were tied to the trunk of a half-rotted tree. Looking across the gorge, she could see the ropes on the opposite side buried at a point on an earthen landing. More worrisome than the ropes was the single plank of wood—rather, several planks of wood laid end-to-end and attached with vines—serving as a footpath across. The whole bridge—if that's what it was supposed to be—looked like a frail, limp V. Gaping disbelievingly at the flimsy construction, Eden shook her head.

"Probably used in older times," John Too said, "when herdsman cared for no more than a dozen or so, and placed the goats or sheep on their shoulders, carrying them across one by one."

Eden looked at John Too like he was insane.

"Hurry," she heard Tabib say. "Go first. And you right after," she said, grasping Eden by her arms and setting her down.

"No," John Too argued. "I should be at the end to protect."

"They would just shoot you in the back," Eden offered.

"She's right, John Too. Go. Now. Hurry."

No sooner had they started across the bridge than Eden realized they were doomed. With the three of them crossing together, the structure sagged lower by the height of two men. To keep from falling to an instant death, Eden placed the support ropes under her arms, placing all of her weight upon them.

"Stupid woman!"

Eden almost lost her footing when she felt the support ropes beneath her arms begin to sway. The warlord's men must be pulling on them, she thought. What words would they say to the tabib to make her stop? she wondered.

"Solomon is an excellent shot! He never misses at this range!"

Eden felt a dribble of pee slide down her inner thigh when the booming explosion of a rifle sucked the breath right out of her. She didn't see the exact spot the bullet hit, but the cloud of dust lingering at the end of the bridge was an arm's length below where the ropes gathered. Realizing each of them would need to climb upward to reach the landing, she understood John Too would be the first exposed. She would be second. *So I am to die by a bullet to the back of my head.* She felt Sister Lady stop behind her.

"We have to go back," she heard the tabib say. "I don't see any other way out of this."

"Call the birds back," Eden urged her, twisting her thin frame around so she could see Claire's face.

"Eden—I can't," Claire replied, her expression one of despair. "I don't know how they came to appear the first time."

"Well, someone called them," Eden pointed out. "Maybe it was the green-eyed person in your cross."

"The what?" Claire confusedly asked, lifting a hand toward her neck.

"Ah—they glow. The sacred beetles," Eden said, her eyes fixated on the bracelet around Claire's wrist. "Why do you pretend?" she innocently asked, shifting her gaze back to Claire's face.

"*Dhab'a! Dhab'a!*" one of the warlord's men excitedly shouted. "*Dhab'a!*"

Eden looked past Sister Lady to see one of the soldiers pointing farther down the ledge. Twisting her body around, she searched for the cause of the man's screaming, smiling when she saw the running figures of four hyenas. *The tabib is indeed a clever one*, she thought. She has summoned the bouda; guessing one of the four hyenas racing up the narrow ledge was he.

The sudden boom of the gunshot sent a shiver down Eden's spine. Much to her embarrassment, she felt another dribble of pee slide down her leg. With the sharp echo of the shot pounding in her head, she followed the track of the bullet to see rocks exploding just to the inside of the lead hyena's chest. The voices of the warlord's men became animated, the men muttering curses in both Arabic and Amharic. Twisting back around so she could see the soldiers, she saw the one who was called Solomon frantically ejecting a shell casing from his long rifle and slipping another bullet into the chamber. Just as he raised the weapon to his shoulder and bent his head to look into the eyepiece attached to the gun, she heard John Too say, "Hurry!"

As the bridge began to sway, another gunshot boomed, the sound of a squealing animal quickly following. Twisting back around, Eden watched the lead hyena tumble headfirst into the ravine. But the three others raced onward, fifty paces from the soldiers. She smiled when the cursing of the warlord's men became louder and frantic.

"Follow John Too," Tabib instructed her.

And when she felt a slight nudge to the back of her shoulders, she turned and did as she was told. Ten heart-pounding steps later, Solomon's rifle boomed again, the agonized yelp of an animal following. Hesitating, Eden fought back the tears forming in her eyes. *Please don't let it be the bouda.*

"Keep moving, Eden. We're almost there."

Enraged snarling erupting behind them made her turn.

"The hyena is leaping!" she gasped.

And she saw a hyena pounce atop the man with the rifle—Solomon—both of them falling hard against the face of the cliff.

"No!" she cried when Solomon pulled a knife from his waist and stabbed the animal in the back. Anguished, she found herself smiling when the hyena clamped its jaws around Solomon's arm. But Solomon kicked out at the beast, pushing it off the ledge. Stomach churning, Eden watched the animal struggle to find its footing, jaws still clamped around the man's forearm.

"Eden!" Claire shouted. "Keep moving!"

"But the—"

Stunned by the sight of the hyena pulling the soldier over the side of the ledge, Eden couldn't finish what she was trying to say.

"Hurry, Eden. Take John Too's arm."

Eden looked away from the falling man and animal to find the abdar offering his hand, his expression turning grim as he glanced behind her.

"What is it?" she asked him as he helped her up to the earthen landing.

"One is crossing," he told her. "And more are coming," he added.

Eden jumped up next to John Too, turning to see the remaining hyena attacking one of the warlord's men. To her dismay, she saw the two other soldiers beginning to make their way across the flimsy bridge, knives clamped sideways between their teeth.

"Hurry, Sister Lady!"

And as Claire took hold of John Too's hand, Eden watched the last hyena lunge, locking its jaws around the knee of the remaining soldier. In turn, the man delivered a wicked knife thrust across the back of the animal's neck before thrusting the blade into the beast's side. The howling squeal of the wounded hyena was paralyzing; Eden covered her face with her hands.

"Bouda," she gasped. *He's dead! We're lost—lost!*

"Cut the ropes, John Too," Claire gasped, setting her foot down upon solid ground. "Hurry. Before they reach us."

As John Too pulled his knife from the sheath tied to his waist, he froze—as did they all—when a tormented howling blared across the ravine.

"Bouda!" Eden shouted.

And her smile grew wide as she watched the man-beast drop from the rocks above the soldier tending to his injured knee, ramming the impala horn through the man's chest. Before she could blink an eye, the bouda shoved the man's body into the ravine and leapt to the rope bridge.

"What is he doing?" Eden cried.

She looked to the tabib, her expression desperate. She didn't understand. Bouda would die.

"John!" Claire screamed. "No!"

But it was too late. John cut one of the support ropes through, the bridge jerking sideways and down. Eden watched one of the soldiers crossing fall to his death, his scream piercing the air until it abruptly stopped.

"Go back, John!" Claire shouted. "Climb back to the ledge!"

Eden shared the tabib's horror as John cut into the second rope.

Bullets strafed the face of the cliff just below them. Another burst ripped into the formation of rocks behind them. More of the warlord's men were arriving, Eden could see. Eden felt someone grab her shoulder as she watched the second support rope fall away. The bouda was hanging by the remaining length with one hand! To Eden's utter shock, she saw him begin to cut into that.

"Through the narrow passage!" she heard the tabib shout.

And as strong hands turned her around, she heard the scream of what she hoped was the second soldier falling to his death. As another round of gunfire erupted, Eden was ushered through the narrow passageway between two monolith stones.

11

THE ROAD TOWARD Perpetual Commitment had been long—and was getting longer by the day. What in the world was she doing here? Sarah thought. She kept telling herself she was fulfilling the last task set before her before life in the service of the Lord Jesus Christ could be attained. But in the back of her mind, she couldn't quite quell the notion she was on a road to oblivion.

"It would have been best if you had just returned to Paris."

Sarah glanced over at Dirk and smiled. How many times was he going to say that? she wondered. Ever since their impromptu meeting with that man, Adiam, in the hotel room after she'd woken up, he'd been saying the same exact sentence over and over and over.

"We've been through all of this, Mr. Savage. I was sent here to fulfill a mission. And that's what I intend to do."

Sarah ran a finger around the collar of her powder-blue shirt. Although the sun was setting—the air becoming noticeably cooler—the searing heat of the day still lingered, rising off the paved road like steam in a sauna. She toyed with the idea of undoing the top buttons of her blouse to relieve some of her discomfort, but she'd caught Dirk looking at her breasts when Adiam had explained the route he'd mapped out for them. She had since come to realize Dirk Savage was a lecher. The distinct odor of sex on his skin when he had stumbled into her—his—room when she'd awakened had been disgusting. She remembered her face flushing with anger. Not wanting to think about the subject of sex—the repulsive smell of mixed male and female body fluids—she quickly glanced out the passenger side window.

"When do you think you might call me by my first name?" she heard him ask. "It's going to be a long trip." He chuckled. "You know, it would have been best—"

"If I had returned to Paris?" she snapped, turning with a scowl on her face. "You mean Le Mans, don't you? Or have your frequent bouts of debauchery whittled away your mind?"

"Testy, testy," he remarked.

She felt a new surge of anger at his flippancy. Didn't he understand where an existence of drugs, alcohol, and frivolous sexual behavior would lead? Surely Satan was just waiting for his despicable life to end so hell could claim his soul for eternal damnation.

"Are all nuns so threatened by the behavior of men in the real world? And what do you mean, frequent? Have you been making inquiries about me behind my back?"

She found his smug, mocking laugh infuriating. It tempted her to lean across the front seat of the big jeep-type vehicle they were riding in and slap him hard across his face. But she settled on clenching her fists and silently asking God for patience.

"And what do you consider to be the behavior of men of the real world, Mr. Savage? Ones who prey on the flesh of little girls who can't protect themselves? Or, perhaps, ones who supply drugs and alcohol to young women with the intent of defiling their bodies?"

Sensing him about to turn his head to stare at her, she folded her arms across her chest and looked out the windshield.

"I'm sorry you feel that way, Sister."

His voice was remarkably calm, she thought.

"Nothing could be further from the truth."

She ground her teeth when he laughed.

"It's usually the other way around. And there is nothing defenseless about them."

She gazed into the long shadows of the darkening terrain in an effort to distance her thoughts from his glib remarks.

"A woman can turn a man inside out."

What does he mean by that?

"Especially when she knows she has the power to do so."

"Power?"

She bit down on her lip, not having intended to say the word out loud. She felt his eyes upon her again. She shivered.

"Love."

Was he being sarcastic? Or was he being fatalistic? She waited for him to explain.

"Have you ever been in love, Sister?"

"The love of the Lord Jesus Christ is the entire purpose of my life, Mr. Savage. But please don't compare my love of Him with one of your tawdry obsessions. That kind of love—if that's how you want to phrase it—does not compare to the pure and selfless love of the Lord."

"Don't be so quick to judge, Sister."

She swung her head around to glare at him.

"Love—no matter how one might wish to view it—is consuming, don't you think? Would you be here, riding in this Land Cruiser with me across some of the most desolate terrain in Ethiopia, if it wasn't?"

"I'm simply following—"

"What *wouldn't* you do in the name of Jesus Christ, Sister? What hasn't already been done in his name throughout the ages?"

"Do not belittle my devotion to Jesus Christ with some generalization of history, Mr. Savage. There are many whose love for Him is untainted. I do not bear the sins of those whose love of Him has gone astray."

"How noble of you, Sister. I'm sure the tortured souls of those who were butchered at Antioch will be glad to hear you carry no burden of the sins committed there in the name of Christianity."

"What has taken place, I cannot undo, Mr. Savage. Only through prayer and the charity of the Lord can there be forgiveness for what has been done in his name."

She started to look away, but stopped when she heard him spit out the window.

"In the name of God, I burn you at the stake," he mocked. "In the name of Allah, I cut off your head."

His laughter hit her like a fist to the stomach, knocking her breath out, making it hard to breathe.

"In the name of Zeus, Apollo, Jupiter, and Tengri, we pillage your lands, rape your women, and defile your temples."

She felt an immediate coldness in her loins.

"It's all such hypocritical nonsense when you think about it," he droned on. "You'd have to agree, wouldn't you, Sister."

The darkness from the closet pushed in on her, constricting her throat. She slapped at the hands she felt encircling her neck, the same ones that had placed a blindfold across her eyes.

"What is it—a bug?"

What is it? How many times had she been asked that? *What's wrong?* Fingers wrapping around her wrist made her lash out. She struck at the hand pulling on her arm, slapping it several times before it released its hold.

"Hey! You having some sort of seizure or something?"

The baying call of some mocking animal seeped into her awareness. Frightened and disoriented, she looked from side to side, not quite certain where she was.

"Just a hyena."

"What?" she gasped. "What did you say?"

She felt a sudden rush of relief as she focused on the face of the man looking at her. It was Dirk. Dirk Savage. *Oh, thank God.* She exhaled.

"Don't look so terrified," he told her in an even-toned manner. "You'll get used to them."

"Them?"

"I suppose—where did you say you were from? Massachusetts? They're like squirrels back where you grew up. They're everywhere here. Or so it seems, anyway. Though, I guess, their calls are a bit different than a squirrel's."

When he patted her on the thigh just above her knee, she quickly shifted her legs in the opposite direction.

Sunset called to her then. Reds and purples with ribbons of orange interlaced, weaving a tapestry on the western horizon, turning the sky above the looming mountain range ahead of them into a painting of living colors she could not seem to take her eyes off of. In the distance, somewhere far behind her, she guessed, the intermittent rumble of thunder could be heard rolling across the arid landscape. A storm, she thought. So she turned back to the east to see what it might look like—a thunderstorm in Africa. But to her surprise, she didn't see any dark clouds or bolts of lightning shooting down from the sky. Just an occasional flash of orange-tinged white, the somewhat brief occurrence of each seeming more like the flaring of a match when first lit.

"Is that a normal storm for this part of Africa?" she asked out of curiosity.

"Storm?" Dirk replied, briefly turning to take a quick glance out the rear window. "I suppose you could call it that. But you won't find any rain there."

"I don't follow," Sarah said, turning back to face him.

"It's war you're seeing, Sister. Not a storm."

She didn't quite understand why he was shrugging when he explained.

"Though the Ethiopian government wouldn't call it that. To them, it's just civil disobedience, dealt with in the harshest manner."

"You mean—"

"It's been going on for decades. Brutal—violent—hundreds of thousands displaced. Hundreds of thousands more killed. Each side has sustained heavy losses. It's—" he shook his head. "That's why we didn't take the sea road up past Assad like the Reverend Mother told you you'd be doing. All fine and well that Christian Aid has many workers there who could help you on your way to Mek'ele. But it's lunacy to travel north in that area. That's why Adiam suggested this route."

When he looked over at her, Sarah couldn't help but think he was trying to scare her.

"At least we won't be killed right from the start. We may even get close to where this elusive Sister Claire might be found before we face any real hostilities."

"And she's—she was there?" Glancing quickly over her shoulder, Sarah shook her head. "In the middle of all that? Why? Why would she go there? What would she be doing?"

"Doing?" she heard him scoff. "Have you read any of the letters she wrote?"

"Why, no. Just parts of the one you gave the Reverend Mother. And I only—well, I guess I just skimmed over it."

"Not interested in what a real nun might be doing?"

"What's that supposed to mean?" she shot back.

"No need to get so defensive. It takes all kinds, doesn't it?"

"Don't patronize me. Each of us is called to follow our own path in serving the Lord. We can't all be running off on our own to end up in some remote location where the order has no knowledge of what we're doing."

"Pity. The world might be a better place if you did."

"You know nothing of what the order is or what it has accomplished," she vehemently argued. "For centuries it's been teaching and caring for the poor in many areas of the world. We can't be everywhere, Mr. Savage. But where we are, we make a difference. A real difference in people's lives. Can you say the same about yours?" she demanded.

"No—no, I can't say the same, Sister."

Again, she thought, his voice was remarkably calm. *Why does that make me so angry?*

"But I'm not a nun," he said.

"Ugh!" she growled.

Thrusting her arms out away from her body, she tilted her palms skyward, bunching her fingers so they looked like claws.

"Are you going to be like this every day?"

"Relax, Sister," he chuckled. "No need to give yourself a heart attack. I realize some people are more suited for office work. Or, in your case, cloistered in some safe haven of tile floors and polished wood with candles and crosses to remind you of the sacrifices you've endured in the name of God."

Sarah pressed the palms of her hands over her ears and screamed.

"Should be interesting to see what you're like out of your comfort zone!" she heard him shout.

With that, she curled herself into a ball and let her head fall against the back of her seat. Squeezing her eyes tightly shut, she waited for him to assail her further. But, to her gratitude, he didn't say anything more. *Thank you, God,* she thought. *I just need to gather my thoughts.* She let her mind go blank, not wanting or needing to ask why she was in a car with a man she barely knew in a remote part of the world. Or what she thought she might be able to accomplish by riding in a jeep with the sex-starved half-in-the-bag journalist. She was on the road to oblivion, as she'd deduced. That much was clear. What would she find at the end of that road? she wondered. Thinking about the answer could wait, she told herself. Right now, the serenity of nothingness was where she needed to be.

*

When Sarah finally decided to open her eyes, uncurl her body, sit up straight, and look out the windshield, the long shadows of sunset were gone, replaced by the total darkness of night. Except for the beam of the headlights from their own vehicle, she could see no form of manmade light. It was as though she and Dirk Savage—and the car they were driving in—were the last remaining objects on earth. The notion the world had suddenly come to an end while she was taking refuge in her blankness made her uncomfortable. What if it really had come to an end? she wondered. What if judgment day had already occurred? What if she and Dirk *were* the last humans alive? Was this to be her punishment? To be stuck in a car in the dark with only him to talk to? Or was this God's way of rewarding her for all that had happened in her life up till now? That she was alive. On her way to some grand adventure. Sharing the quest with a man she found— She pressed her fists into her crotch and bit into the side of her mouth.

"She started two orphanages."

"What?" Sarah dazedly replied, peering into the darkness on either side of them with the hope of seeing something, anything that might tell her she was thinking crazy thoughts.

"Apparently one—the first one—was destroyed by mercenaries working for the Mengistu regime."

"What are you talking about? What was destroyed?"

After a slight pause, he said, "Never mind."

She tilted her head to the side and listened. She could hear nothing but the sound of the tires on asphalt and the hum of the car's engine.

"Where are we?"

"On Highway 1 heading toward the Mile Serdo Wildlife Reserve. Why do you ask?"

"Because—because there's nothing around us. No lights, no other cars—I can't even hear any other sounds. It's like we're the only things left in all the world."

"Don't be fooled just because you can't see them. They're out there. Probably staring at our headlights right now, hoping we'll stop to get out to take a piss."

"Can you please get your tongue out of the vulgarity it so normally is accustomed to? And who are *they*?"

"The animals," he unapologetically replied. "Snakes for certain—like a haven for them. Kind of like what I might picture hell to be, in certain respects. You definitely don't want to go taking a—uh, have to relieve yourself—out there in the dark," he went on with a nod at what lay on the other side of the windshield. "Least not without a powerful flashlight and someone standing close to you with a gun."

"A gun?"

"It's like I said. They're not the squirrels and rabbits and the occasional deer you're probably used to. Hyenas, wild dogs, snakes—maybe a lion; they're all happy to wait while you're taking a—uh—are preoccupied, before closing in for the kill. Makes it easy for them. I've witnessed it myself a few times. It's what they do, you know," he glibly remarked, flashing her a smile.

Sarah looked out the side window with a new perspective on the country she was traveling in. Shuddering just thinking about what Dirk had said, she wondered if she had to urinate. *When was the last time I did?*

"But don't worry," he offered, as though he could read her thoughts. "There's a ranger station about an hour's drive ahead. We'll be stopping there before we start the drive northward. Might be the last friendly faces we see for a while."

"What do you mean?"

"How much do you know about Ethiopia, Sister?"

"I, uh—"

"Did you ever read or ever hear anything about the famine that's decimated this country? Do you have any knowledge of the years of civil war that's brought it to its knees? Or is the news of people suffering in remote areas of the earth not welcome within the sanctity of the walls you've been hiding behind the last several years?"

Sarah felt her body trembling with rage. *How dare he! How dare he belittle the Lord!*

"I would have thought, after living through that little Afar assassination ordeal the other day, you might have gotten an inkling as to what you have gotten yourself into."

She saw him then—the man with the flowing black hair standing over her with his large, curved knife. She'd been confused, though, because the man seemed kind. She could tell when she had looked into his eyes—just as she was picturing them now in her memory—just before the bullet blasted a hole in his chest. But his face had been gripped with anger. She hadn't had time to ask him why. *Why was he so angry? Why did he want to kill me?* She hadn't had time to think about the *whys*. Everything had happened so fast. She remembered Dirk. Remembered falling into his arms, remembered him carrying her to a room. But the sound of the guns and explosions followed. Even when he—when Dirk— closed the door, it was as though the deafening onslaught and shuddering eruptions of weapons were still taking place. And the smells: gasoline; burning flames; black, choking smoke—she could taste them on the pills he'd made her swallow when she was sitting on the edge of a bed. And then the room had started to spin, blood appearing on the inside of her eyelids when she closed them. The sight of it pooling was terrifying as she remembered the sensation of gagging when she fell toward it. And then someone lifted her up, pulling her by her shoulders. But she couldn't tell who. It was just a big, dark form. Father Gebre! She remembered trying to scream his name. But she'd started to choke. And then someone thrust fingers inside her mouth, pulling on her tongue, frantically trying to clear it, unfurl it from her throat. And she'd gasped and spit. She could still feel her chest heave when she'd sucked in a deep, panicked breath of air. And she'd jerked up, pushing against the hands trying to keep her pinned down. And then she'd sunk lower, slowly lowering onto a soft pillow. She remembered now, her head eased onto a pillow by a gentle hand. But Father Gebre was dead! It was her last memory before her mind went blank. But one last thing—touching her forehead as the snippet came rushing back to her—a kiss. Someone had kissed her on the brow and wished her sweet dreams. Her fingertips brushed her skin where lips had touched. Looking over at Dirk, all the rage she was feeling dissipated. She started to tremble, but not because she was angry. She was trembling because Father Gebre was dead. And she had just remembered. She should be dead too, she realized. How close had she come to dying? Feeling a few tears sliding down her cheeks, she touched them to see if they were real.

"Are you crying?"

She covered her face with her hands, her body heaving as a flood of emotion overwhelmed her.

"Jesus fucking Christ, Sister. You should have gone back to Paris."

* * *

Claire stared into her silver cross, turning her head from side to side as she studied the reflection within. A green-eyed person, Eden had said. *What could she have possibly meant?* Claire saw nothing but the blurry image of her own face framed by wavering outlines of flames. Pressing the cross between her thumb and index finger, she looked across the fire John Too had insisted they build, relieved to see Eden sleeping, a swath of her violet dress bunched beneath her face. Letting her gaze fall to the flames, she shivered with the thought that Bacha Alba and his men were somewhere out in the dark, closing in on them. She hadn't wanted to stop, hadn't wanted to build a fire. But John Too had been adamant.

*

"The warlord and his men will be at least a day behind us now," he had assured her.

And soon, he explained, they would be leaving altogether the sphere of lands he controlled.

"Besides," he had added when she'd started to disagree. "We need to give John time to catch up."

"Catch up," she mumbled.

She closed her eyes, picturing John's face as he had cut the final section of rope. She hadn't told Eden or John Too what she'd seen. They had already passed through the opening between the monoliths when she'd looked back. It was as if John had known she was going to turn one final time, the impala horn poised a foot or so above the rope, his gaze focused on her. And when their eyes met, she glimpsed the blur of the horn, the rope cut. John's fall instantaneous.

But as she recalled the image now—sitting crossed-legged on the ground, staring into the fire—it was as though the moment had occurred in some frozen snapshot of time. John's face stoic, unafraid, challenging. She'd watched him wrap his free hand around the length of rope before plunging downward toward the unforgiving wall of the ravine. She'd held on to his gaze as long as she could. But he was gone in an instant, falling into the chasm before she could even blink. And then bullets strafed the huge stone by her shoulder. She had turned and run.

John was dead. She didn't have the heart to tell Eden or John Too. *Why did he do it?* It was the same question her thoughts had been crying out since she had watched him fall. *Why didn't he save himself?*

*

"You should sleep, Sister Lady."

Startled, Claire gasped, jerking her head around. John Too gently placed a hand on her shoulder. Forcing a weary smile, she took his hand in hers.

"The day will be upon us before we wish it to be," he softly remarked.

"The day," she murmured. "What was it Teimbaka said? When will it end?" She searched John Too's eyes. "How many years ago was that?"

She felt John Too squeeze her hand.

"And still it goes on." She shook her head. "When will it end, John Too?" Her eyes blurred as she asked, "When?"

John Too searched amongst the silhouettes and shadows dotting the foothills. Beyond lay the beginning of open land—miles of tall grasses, pockets of woodlands and scrub—the terrain they would have to cross to reach the border of Sudan.

"When we no longer wish to carry it," he quietly remarked. "Etiyopiya knew this when he asked," he added, a mischievous smile breaking out on his face. "I think he has known all of his life. Perhaps he was asking to hear what your answer would be."

Claire tried to recall what she had told Teimbaka the evening he had asked her about the day. But she could only remember John being by her side, clinging to her when she'd started to tremble, as if the boy could sense the raw emotions running through her. John was just a child then, hardly able to understand what she and Teimbaka had been saying. And now he was gone. What more would the day ask?

"Are you ready to stop?"

"Stop?" she asked, not understanding.

"Trying—making where you walk a better place. Are you ready to stop hoping, someday, the Mother and the Father will forgive us?"

Taking a moment to reflect, she shook her head.

"No."

"Then it is best the day does not ever end," he said with a nod. "Do you not see this?"

"Forgiveness. The cost in lives—does the day need to ask for so many?"

When John Too didn't answer, she sought solace in the fire. But the flames had grown weak, barely flickering amongst the branches and sticks they'd gathered. She could feel darkness creeping closer. As if the scream of a haunting ghost sounded just behind her, she suddenly turned her head, her face stricken with fear.

"What is it?" John Too whispered, crouching, his hand wrapped around the hilt of the knife strapped to his waist.

"Something—something Teimbaka once told me. I—I didn't mean to alarm you." She reached to touch his arm. "I'm being silly."

She tried to giggle, but it sounded more a whimper. John Too stared at her.

"About spirits—those that fear fire. I was—" She glanced at the dwindling flames. "The fire grows smaller."

John Too stood and surveyed the surrounding darkness. Claire could see the stringy muscles of his arms and legs go taught, then slowly relax as he finished examining what was, or might be, around them.

"They are not here," he told her. "I will get more wood."

"Wait," she said when he started to move away. "Where is—?"

He furrowed his brow.

"Do you—? Never mind." She looked down at the silver cross between her fingers. "I'm being silly again."

"He is where he is needed, where he has been called. The great herd is near to him." John Too looked west, toward Sudan, before letting his gaze drift southward. "They will help him if they can."

"Is he all right?"

"How can he be?" John Too innocently asked.

"I—I don't understand, John Too. Why can't Teimbaka be all right?"

"Because it has not ended."

"You're not making any—" She shook her head and sighed.

"The killing. He must end it."

"The killing?"

"The elephants—their tusks."

"But how can he do—?"

"It is what the Mother asks of him. Even the boy has asked me why it cannot be stopped."

"John Too, please. I've told you not to speak about— I mean—" Claire rubbed the back of her neck and closed her eyes.

"He has told me that when men no longer kill elephants for what is not theirs to take, there is a chance for the killing of each other to stop."

"John Too," Claire pleaded. "Please don't—" She buried her face in her hands.

"Why are you so much like Thomas in the story?"

Claire lifted her head up at the saying of the name.

"Why do you not believe?"

"Don't do this, John Too," Claire begged, her voice choking. "I can only see—"

"Blessed are those who have not seen, yet believe, Sister Lady. Is this not something you know?"

"John Too," she pleaded, tears streaming down her face.

"I will gather more wood," he told her. Touching her on the top of her head, he said, "Sleep now, Sister Lady. You are tired."

* * *

Teimbaka surveyed what remained of George Henry's camp, wondering what caused the lines of scorched earth scarring the soil with black ash and foul-smelling ooze. What machine or weapon did the warlord have that could create such burning destruction? Looking at the rifle in his hands, the one Tengene had given him, he thought about what Kamua had said about weapons. What could a spear or arrows—or even a rifle—do against a weapon that could burn the earth? He shook his head. He didn't know.

Atop the blackened soil, tracks made by the warlord's vehicles indicated the mercenaries had headed west—as Selam had forewarned—toward the border into Sudan, a country where they—Selam, Kamua, Tengene—had no jurisdiction. Apologetic but unyielding, Selam had given Teimbaka the rifle and departed, the rangers heading northeast, where they were due to check in at the Shire Wildlife Reserve. Selam said it would take them a few days to reach the ranger station. And he didn't know when, or if, they would return. Teimbaka was not expecting to see them again. He was alone. He'd been grateful for the gift of Tengene's Lee-Enfield and the box of ammunition. But as he looked upon the swaths of charred earth, he was no longer certain the weapon would do him much good.

"They went south."

Teimbaka turned at the frail-sounding voice. A hunched figure cloaked in a gray robe stood some twenty paces from him, brown bony hand extended from a drooping loose sleeve. The figure scratched the blackened soil with a crooked, weather-bleached stick.

"The tracks lead west."

"They will turn."

"You saw them go?"

The person seemed to stiffen at his question.

"Watched, smelled, listened—prayed they would."

He observed the figure jab the stick into the ground, raking it atop the surface of the soil as though slashing open a wound.

"Everyone's dead. You are too late."

The voice was a woman's, Teimbaka realized. And though he felt a pang of guilt at what she had said—that he was too late—it did not seem to him that she said it in a way to make him feel guilty. She simply seemed to be stating a fact.

"A dozen—slaughtered—east of here," she said, pointing with the gnarled length of wood. "The last of a family—gone."

"What are you called?" he asked her, taking a few steps toward her. "And where is it that you live?"

"Live?" she repeated, straightening her body to stand.

She circled the stick above her head.

"This is my home," she told him. "Is it not yours as well?"

"I come from—"

"Why are you wasting time?"

The scars on his back began to tingle.

"There are a dozen families there, several hundred that he will kill to build his army—and you stand here talking to me. Do I need to show you the twelve faceless bodies before you decide to do something?" she assailed him. "Have you not seen enough dead elephants already?"

The sadness in her question pulled at his memories, his stomach twisting as he revisited the faces of the dead spirit beasts he had walked amongst. The image of their hollow eyes sent a shiver down his spine.

"I've seen more than you know," he told her.

"Have you?" she shot back.

A bell, small from the sound of it, jingled somewhere near. Or was it near? he wondered. For as suddenly as it had begun, the sound ceased. The hooting laughter of a hyena took its place, turning him full around.

As he searched for the animal, for the bell, whispers from the spirit children reached him. Drifting on an easterly breeze—from the highlands he'd left—their voices troubled and anxious as they murmured his name. When he looked back toward the mountains, the whispers suddenly quieted to silence. Was he going mad? The notion was unnerving. He turned to answer the gray-robed woman.

A cheetah—muscles tensed, bunched at the shoulders—studied him as he turned. Thinking the beast was preparing to pounce, he slowly raised his rifle, taking aim. The eyes of the cat narrowed. To his utter bewilderment, the animal turned its face to one side, gagged, and then spit upon the ground. As Teimbaka lowered his weapon, the big cat darted across the open space between them, briefly looking up at him as it passed. With eyes as green as emeralds, the cheetah disappeared, loping into the tall grasses where the tracks of the warlord's vehicles led.

Staring after the beast, Teimbaka found the hold of the animal's gaze enthralling. Beckoning him forward with the vision of sparkling green pools showered in rose-hued flames. Shouldering his rifle, he secured his bow and arrows across his back. Grasping his steel-tipped spear, he set out to find the mysterious beast, mist-shrouded forms of a thousand spirit elephants at his heels as he pushed through the first stalks of shoulder-high grass.

* * *

Sarah jolted awake to the grinding sputter of some gargantuan machine. Lifting her head from the duffel bag she was using as a pillow, she experienced a momentary stab of panic until she saw Dirk sitting in the seat ahead of her, his gaze focused out the side window above her.

"You're awake."

"Yes—I—"

Sarah covered her ears as the grinding squeal grew to a grating crescendo. "What's happening?" she shouted.

Dirk smiled.

"A tank!" he yelled.

A tank? She tried to get her mind around the concept. Pushing her upper body off the middle seat of the Land Cruiser, she twisted around so she could look out the window, catching sight of the back end of the massive machine as it moved past.

"What's it doing here?"

"What? What did you say?"

"I said, what's it doing here?" she shouted, turning her face away from the window so she could look at him. "Why is it here?"

"To enforce the government's war! Sorry!" he added when he saw her wincing.

"Thank the Lord we're headed in the opposite direction," she remarked, glancing out the rear window as the squeaking rumble rolled farther down the road.

"Unfortunately, we're headed where it's going," he told her, a grim nuance in his tone.

Sarah looked around the interior of the Land Cruiser for a moment.

"But we're facing the other way."

"Just a little insurance we wouldn't be stopped."

"What do you mean?"

Dirk was about to reply when a truck drove past, the open bed behind the cabin carrying a dozen armed soldiers. Sarah turned her head to peer out the window. One of the soldiers in the rear of the truck took notice, poking his elbow into the side of the soldier next to him. The second soldier laughed, bending forward and down to look at her.

"They're used to seeing people moving away from conflict," she heard Dirk say. "If they saw we were heading where they were going—especially in a vehicle like this—we'd be stopped, searched—"

Sarah studied his expression. Saw him avert his eyes.

"Stopped, searched—and what, Mr. Savage? What aren't you saying?"

He stared out the front windshield for a moment before closing his eyes, his brow wrinkling into deep lines.

"Let's just leave it as 'and god know what,' shall we?" He rubbed his face with his palms before turning to face her. "Sometimes it's best not to think about what could happen."

A shaft of sunlight appeared a short distance in front of the car, and Sarah dazedly watched the beam's slow progression westward onto the road. Sunrise. Glancing at Dirk, she realized he must have driven all night. With a tired sigh, she shifted her gaze back to the widening band of sun, placing a hand over her mouth when she saw what the light revealed.

Wisps of smoke floated upward from a burned-out wreck on the other side of the two-lane asphalt highway, mangled splinters of jagged black metal sprouting up from a vehicle's half-melted frame, skeletal remains of some horned creature littering the area around it. Beyond the charred remnant of the vehicle, a line of zombie-faced, stick-like figures walked in a slow procession. To Sarah, they looked as if they were trudging to their deaths, an air of hopelessness about them. The doom awaiting them conveyed in bent heads and shoulders, hinted at in the way their feet barely lifted off the ground as they stepped. Most of the people were elderly or very, very young. Some of the old men and women had baskets strapped to their backs. Others carried nothing at all. The young—children no more than three or four, held on to the bright-colored dresses of elderly women or the loose-fitting pants of wrinkled, gray-bearded men. They followed along in a trance, eyes wide and round, faces frightened and uncertain when a few glanced across the road to find Sarah ogling them. Where were the adult men and women? Sarah wondered. The mothers and fathers? And the other children, those who would have been old enough to help with the young—where were they? Looking farther down the makeshift line, she could see no one resembling those age groups—only the very old and the very, very young, the line stretching farther than she could see. Reluctantly, turning her head in the opposite direction, she saw the procession had no beginning—or end.

"Hard to comprehend, the first time you witness it."

"Where—where are they all going?"

"Hard to say," he quietly replied. "Most don't want to go anywhere."

"But you said—there's war where the tank's headed—where they're coming from. Why would they want to stay?"

"Because it's their home," he told her, shrugging his shoulders. "Wouldn't you want to stay? If this was Massachusetts? And you were one of them?" he asked, nodding to the line of refugees.

"But—" Mouth agape, she stared over at the endless line of—misery, she decided. "But they have nothing." She shook her head. "How can you go anywhere to start over if you have nothing?"

"They're alive."

Quite unexpectedly, Sarah felt a sudden urge to reach across the seat and embrace Dirk, needing, wanting to feel his arms wrapped around her. But something kept her from doing so. The embrace would be misconstrued, she thought. Or maybe she didn't trust herself. She wasn't sure. So she focused on the blank faces of the refugees, doing her best to push Dirk from her mind.

"Where are the parents—of the little children?" she found herself asking. "And the older ones—the ten-and twelve-year-olds, teenagers—I only see toddlers and babies."

"Dead," he replied, seemingly without even considering his answer. "Or worse."

"Worse?"

"Sold as slaves or prostitutes. Or compelled to fight against their own people—or be put to death if they won't."

"Slaves?" she repeated, incredulous. "That's— That's—"

"What happens here," he told her. "Been going on for centuries." Dirk ran a hand through his uncombed hair. "I imagine slavery's worse than death, don't you?"

"I— I never—"

She looked over at the line of refugees, a lost expression on her face.

"What will they find when they reach where they're going?"

"What do you think they'll find, Sister?" came his terse reply.

She felt the vibration of the engine run through her body as Dirk started the car.

"Will they survive?" she asked him as the car eased forward. "Is there hope for them?"

Dirk turned the steering wheel hard to the right, the beginnings of a 180-degree turn setting them on a northward course, placing them on the road the tank and the truckload of soldiers had taken. Sarah leaned forward, waiting for him to answer. Staring at the faces of the toddlers as the car rolled past, she wondered what would happen to them all. A full minute elapsed before she realized Dirk had nothing to say.

12

TIRED. WEARINESS EVERYWHERE: her feet, legs, and body—even the joints of her inner and outer wings. How many cycles of moon and sun had occurred? She'd lost count. How many more would she experience? There was no way of knowing; she felt this. No way of knowing what was driving her—driving them—onward, northward. Compelling her and the millions behind her to keep moving, keep pressing forward. No matter what the elements placed before them. No matter how, sometimes, the temptation to stop—to rest, eat, mate, lay eggs—intermixed with the urgency to hurry. The conflicting instincts caused confusion, an unsettled state she was not used to. She sensed a similar mood swirling within the multitude following her. Although the calling they had answered was still strong inside them, their journey had been long, their destination undefined, the compulsions of their life cycles at odds with their purpose.

Having no way to calm the feelings running through her, the green flower beetle unfurled her outer wings and rubbed her front feet over her face. As she probed her receptors for information, she felt life around her go still. Nothing moved. There were no sounds. Even the earth—the activity held beneath its surface—had quieted.

Sun and moon—a melding—bathed her in a soft, luminous hue. Sparkling particles of each essence enclosed within an approaching spherical form. Incandescent, shining brighter as the sphere floated nearer; the flower beetle bowed her head to shield her eyes. In that moment, the illumination extinguished. The sphere transformed into a translucent creature with pink-red eyes, ultraviolet light swirling inside the shifting outline of its body. The female flower beetle extended her elytra and whirred her inner wings. The shimmering entity trumpeted a response, its call awakening stillness, voices of life returned.

The female flower beetle studied the young creature, a constricting ache forming in her abdomen when it began to drift away. As if walking on a bed of mist, the shimmering beast headed northward, each step placed and taken in utter silence, as though the creature's feet were made of air. With a single click of her mandibles, the green flower beetle flew down from the yellow-veined leaf she been perched atop and began to follow. Soon, the tremors of millions of other feet marching behind her set the sensors in her abdomen abuzz.

1 3

BONGO STARED UP at the short-barreled pistol, eyes fixated on the hand holding the stock, frightened by the rivulets of bright red blood oozing from the knuckles. Running his tongue along the inside of his mouth, he tasted thick, salty fluid leaking between his teeth where the man's bony fist had struck him. Afraid to look up into the man's face, Bongo kept his focus on the gun, knowing that if he dared glance into the man's eyes, he'd only make the man angrier. And he didn't want that to happen. The gun could easily go off and blow a hole in his face. He knew the man to be unstable—more so when he was liquored up and high like he was now—so curling himself into a ball and taking whatever beating the man decided to inflict upon him was about the only course of action he knew to take. He knew this for a fact. Because this wasn't the first time the man had pointed a gun at his face and beat on him. And it wouldn't be the last. The beatings would continue until the day the man—his father—decided to go cold turkey and get clean, or until Bongo was old enough to get himself out from under the man's roof. Bongo didn't know which scenario would come first. But he wasn't betting on his father getting clean.

"Don't tell me you didn't take a dime bag out of my stash and sell it to one of your fuckin' friends! I know it was you!"

The bulging, bloodshot eyes peering into Bongo's were filled with fury, the snub-nosed revolver wavering an inch from his forehead. Bongo closed his eyes.

"Look at me, you little fuck! Where the money? Where you hidin' what's mine?"

Bongo winced as a current of air rushed down the side of his face; he curled his body tight, preparing for the blow he knew to be coming. But when the toe of his father's steel-toed construction boot found the soft area in his side just below his elbow, he couldn't help but cry out, the crushing pain of the kick forcing the air right out of his body. Gasping, writhing in spasmodic attempts to breathe, he tried to crawl out of the corner of the room his father had boxed him into, only to be shoved back so hard the back of his head slammed against the joint where the walls of the room came together. Dazed, bloodied, nearly incapacitated with shooting pains in his head, back, and side, Bongo slumped to the floor, tears streaming from his eyes.

"What I tell you 'bout cryin'?" his father screamed.

Bongo felt as though his arm was being ripped from his shoulder as his father jerked him up and pressed the barrel of the gun against his face.

"This is what you get when you steal from me! Now tell me where my money is, boy! Or I'll stick this gun up your fuckin' nose and pull the trigger!"

Bongo jerked his head back when the barrel of the gun penetrated his left nostril. Terrified, he looked up into his father's face. Wild, unfocused eyes glared back at him. He tried to speak, tried to tell him he hadn't taken the pot. But he could only manage what sounded like a croak. His father shook him by the arm and threw him down on the floor.

"Shootin' you's be too easy!" he shouted. "I'm just going to beat it out of you!"

When he saw his father undo his belt and pull it from the loops of his jeans, Bongo frantically looked for a way to escape—an opening where he could possibly scoot past the man and reach the front door of the family's one-bedroom apartment.

"Where's the cash, boy?"

The crazed tone of the question came with the metal edge of the belt buckle whipped into the side of his head. Bongo wailed, throwing his hands out and up to try to block the next strike, the belt buckle cracking against his wrist.

"What the hell you doin' to our child?"

It was his mother screaming now. Slamming the door shut behind her, rushing into the room, throwing a McDonald's bag onto the only piece of furniture they owned; a stained, chocolate-brown, three-cushioned couch with a hole in the back where his father had repeatedly kicked it one night when he'd lost a week's paycheck betting on a football game. As the aroma of french fries enveloped Bongo's senses, his mother—a slight-framed, tan-colored Puerto Rican woman in her mid-twenties—punched his father in the jaw and began slapping him across the back of his head.

"I told you never to hit him!" she screamed, her arm flailing.

Bongo saw his mother shaking, her eyes laden with tears, her slaps growing weaker until they stopped altogether. The final intended blow suspended in mid-strike, her body trembling so violently Bingo thought she was having a stroke. And when his father unleashed a twisting backhand against the side of his mother's head, sending her flying across the room, Bongo leaped up from the floor and grabbed hold of his father's gun.

"You gonna kill me now, boy?" his father roared.

Bongo felt the muscles in his father's arm relax. Confused, he looked into his father's face; the man was eerily calm, almost melancholy. Bongo released his hold on the gun and took a step back.

"Take it, then," his father said, nodding to the gun.

The pistol lying flat in his open palm, he offered the weapon to Bongo.

"Take it," he softly told him.

Bongo stared at the gun for a moment before shifting his gaze to where his mother was slumped against the wall, sobbing.

"You wanna kill me—don't you?"

The words were spoken as a statement more than a question. Bongo gazed up at his father's face. The man seemed lost. Bongo thought he saw tears in the man's eyes.

"Take it, then," his father quietly prodded. "Take it."

He felt a nudge to his shoulder, the gun placed right in front of his face. What sounded like a bag being ruffled open was followed by the smell of french fries.

"Take it. Yo—Earth to Bongo. You in there, nigger?"

Griper laughed, nudging Bongo's shoulder with the butt of the snub-nosed pistol he was holding.

"It ain't the biggest gun in the world, but it'll do in a pinch."

Griper gave Twister a questioning glance. Twister shrugged his shoulders and stuffed a handful of McDonald's french fries in his mouth.

"Yo—Bongo boy; take the gun."

Bongo blinked his eyes and smacked his lips.

"Haven't had nothin' to eat," he muttered. "Fries smell good."

"Tell ya not to smoke that shit," Twister laughed.

Bongo wanted to tell his father how hungry he was, how it had been more than a day since he and his mom had had anything to eat. She felt so bad about it—about having no food in the apartment—she told Bongo she was going to do something about it. Something his father wasn't going to like. She never said what. The french fries smelled so good he could almost taste them. But it wasn't his father's face grinning at him when he decided to tell him how long it had been since he and his mother had eaten; it was Twister's.

"Here, munch on some," Twister said, pushing the McDonald's bag into the crook of Bongo's arm. "I super-sized two orders cause you're such a fuckin' mooch," he said, laughing.

"And here."

Bongo felt something heavy slipped into the right side pocket of his Hammer pants.

"Just keep this for later—after you snap out of whatever trip you be fucked-up on."

"You boys about done with this little skit of yours?"

Bongo turned his head around at the sound of the voice. What the hell was Super Freak doing here? he wondered. *When did I get here? Where the fuck am I?*

"Why don't y'all sit at the table and eat your fries," Super Freak suggested as he eased down on the edge of the bed. "While I finish filling you in on what's going down."

Dazedly, Bongo took a look at his surroundings. He, Twister, Griper, and Super Freak were in a small box of a room with a bed in the center. A door to his right led to a small bathroom. Other than a night table on one side of the bed and a TV in the corner on a rollaway stand, the only other furniture in the room was a cheap Formica table with metal legs placed against a wall. Bongo took a seat in one of the three orange, molded plastic chairs set around it. As he reached into the bag of fries, the room started to shake.

"Turnpike Motel," he heard Super Freak say, laughing. "Place earns its name."

Bongo took a fry and put it in his mouth, the taste of salt and cooking oil snapping him out of his daze. He nodded his head. *Fuckin' dump of a motel*, he thought. *No wonder I started thinking 'bout the ghetto room I lived in*. Without realizing it, he ran a finger up inside the rim of his Yankees cap and felt the scar on the side of his skull where the belt buckle had hit him all those years ago. His hair had never grown back in the spot where the metal had cut him, the scar smooth to the touch. Sighing, he shoved his hand back into the McDonald's bag and grabbed a handful of fries.

"You want I should call room service for some Cokes?" Super Freak sarcastically asked.

"They got that here?" Bongo innocently replied.

"Shut up, fool," Griper admonished him. "Let the man get on with business. And stop making so much noise."

"Coke be good right now," Bongo mumbled.

Shrugging his shoulders, he took another handful of fries and shoved them in his mouth.

Griper gave Bongo an angry look, while across the table Twister was doing his best not to laugh.

"Now I gave all of you the Cobras because they're easy to conceal," Super Freak explained.

"Snakes?" Bongo asked in mid-chew.

"The guns, asshole," Griper said, rolling his eyes. "Like the one I slipped in your pocket."

Bongo felt the heavy object weighing the pocket of his pants down.

"Oh, yeah, right. Solid," Bongo told him with a pat to the weapon.

"No need to point 'em at anyone," Super Freak went on. "But if you run into any trouble tomorrow night—this way you have something to protect yourselves, just in case."

"Serial numbers filed off, right?" Twister asked, tipping his chair back so he could rest his broad shoulders on the wall behind him.

Bongo saw Super Freak nod his head and raise his eyebrows like he was saying "Of course."

"Tomorrow night?" Bongo shot a quick glance at Griper. "What's happening tomorrow night?"

"You *fuckin'* with me?" Griper hissed. "Where you been the past five minutes?"

"You can fill the blank spots in his brain later," Super Freak interjected. "I have other places I need to be." Looking at the flashy, jewel-encrusted gold watch on his wrist, he grunted.

"Our ship's due to tie up about 10:00 p.m. tomorrow. Across the channel, at the Maher, one of our competitor's ships is due to arrive an hour or so before. That's where you boys come in."

"What you mean?" Twister pushed off the wall so the chair came to rest on all four legs. "That's where we come in."

"Just a little diversion," Super Freak assured him. "In case the pigs got something planned I'm not aware of."

"Shit, man—there be Bloods over there and some of those spic boys from that Rican gang. I don't want no part of that shit, man."

Twister adjusted his silver-framed sunglasses and rubbed his chin.

"Diversion. Count me the fuck out, man."

"Be cool, brother," Griper was quick to say when Twister started to get out of his chair. "Ain't no way we gonna have no face time with anybody. S.F.'s talkin' about makin' some noise so the piggies be busy with what going down over there, 'stead of where our shit's comin' in. You dig?"

"Now, Mr. Griper, if Twister here wants no part of the ounce of pure I'm sending your way as payment, no need to try and persuade the brother."

"An ounce? Of pure?"

Bongo stopped the handful of French fries he was about to put into his mouth.

"Shit! Fuck, man. That's like fifteen grand."

"More," Griper chimed in, "when we cut it."

"Solid that, my man!" Bongo excitedly replied, giving Griper a fist bump.

"Can't spend it if you be in a ditch somewhere," Twister grunted.

"Only die once, motherfucker," Bongo laughed.

"Mr. Bongo's right, Mr. Twister," Super Freak remarked. "Ounce of pure this shipment—maybe two the next," he added, a Cheshire grin breaking out on his face. "We do this right, could be an ounce for each of you every time a shipment loads off safe. How's that fly?"

"Ounce apiece? You shittin' me?"

Bongo slapped an open palm down onto the table.

"You hear that, Twist and Shout? Fuckin' A! I could cut a demo! Shit—I could cut a hundred demos!"

With a disbelieving shake of his head, Bongo stuffed more french fries in his mouth and started to chew.

"Well, I'm glad I could make your day, Mr. Bongo," Super Freak coolly stated as he stood up. "I'll expect you brothers at the port by dark tomorrow night," he continued, addressing Griper. "I leave the particulars of the—diversion," he said, chuckling, "to all of you. But something loud and colorful would be nice."

Super Freak swept the locks of his long black hair back over his shoulders, buttoned the middle button of his gray pinstripe suit coat, adjusted his Wayfarer sunglasses, and stepped over to the door leading to the parking lot outside. As his fleshy hand took hold of the doorknob, he hesitated.

"We all have a lot riding on tomorrow's shipment," he said, giving Griper, Twister, and Bongo a quick serious look. "Don't fuck this up."

In one fluid motion, Super Freak opened, stepped through, and closed the door behind him. Griper opened his mouth to say something, but he had to wait, the rumblings from a convoy of big rigs rolling past the motel room making it impossible to hear. Finally, when the eighteen-wheel vehicles lumbered far enough down the turnpike, he looked squarely at Twister, asking, "You in?"

"Yeah—I'm in," Twister grumbled, sounding none too pleased.

"Cool."

Griper stood up and pulled his black Levis up so they didn't fall off his waist.

"Let's blow this dump."

"Right behind you, brother," Bongo chimed in, pushing his chair away from the table.

"Yeah," Twister halfheartedly agreed, "whatever."

* * *

There was a sense he was late. He needed to hurry. He wasn't running fast enough, hadn't traveled far enough. Wasn't going to reach his destination in time. Urging his legs to pump harder, Chris was sprinting by the time he reached the puddle-dotted side street that ran between Mercer and

Springfield. Slowing to a walk, he surveyed the structures on either side of him: a house of god to the west, a house of death to the east. He took note of the near-empty parking lots, guessing that the one car he saw in each belonged to some lonely soul toiling through the night shift.

Gazing at the garish cluster of lights illuminating the names of each establishment—neon green and yellow in the case of the funeral home, bright white for the church—he wondered if the owners of the two vastly different businesses hadn't built an underground employee lounge where the people who cleaned and polished the accessories of worship and death went during their breaks to have a smoke and share a laugh. Maybe sit in red velvet chairs while some stoned-out DJ on some underground local FM station played music from artists no one had ever heard of. Not likely, he decided, though a tunnel between the church and funeral home might expedite matters when someone needed to be put to rest. But speeding up the process of lowering someone into a grave wasn't the focus of either business. No money to be made if there wasn't a show. No reason for people to pay them if there wasn't some extravagance for onlookers to gawk at. No ceremony, no flowers—no scripture reading from some dude in a robe you didn't know, depriving all the good people from having something to chit-chat about when they were stuffing their faces with finger food and sipping wine at the reception following the burial? No, that wouldn't fly. Pigs in a blanket while sipping chardonnay from a plastic glass was part of the American way, wasn't it? As much a part as exchanging memories about the deceased was—whether poignant or meaningless. As long as the *remember whens* and the *I remembers* flowed, the host would keep the liquor and the food coming until, finally, when the last bottle of booze was empty and the final finger sandwich devoured, people would stroll to their cars commenting on what a lovely affair it had been. Or what a nice job the funeral home had done preparing the corpse for the viewing. And for many, the memories of the deceased would quickly fade. Forgotten, filed away in the recesses of their minds. But the reception, or the flower arrangements, and maybe— just maybe, if the family had enough money to splurge—the beautiful voice the singer possessed, those would be memories recalled in vivid detail.

"Wasn't it lovely the way the singer performed 'Over The Rainbow'?" someone would remark as they opened their car door.

"Oh my, yes," another would reply. "It brought tears to my eyes."

Extravagance, pomp, ceremony, organ music, words bought and paid for; money. The almighty dollar—maybe the church and the funeral home shared a joint bank account.

Chris wiped the clutter of useless thoughts from his mind when the headlights of a slow-moving car turned off Broome Street onto Mercer. Instinctively, he squeezed through an opening in the tall boxwood hedge on his left. Careful to stay concealed, he edged forward toward Mercer, where Yutanda and her little boy lived.

As the car neared the first cluster of the low buildings, the vehicle came to a stop. Chris could see one person in the red subcompact: the driver, wearing a baseball cap. The person looked at a map, bending down and sideways a couple of times to peer out the passenger side window. Naturally suspicious—especially of anyone who was out and about at 3:30 in the morning—Chris wondered who the man was and what he was doing. Just as he began to edge a little closer to the street to try to get a better glimpse of the man's face, the car began to move. A red Ford Escort, he noted, with Michigan plates.

For a moment, Chris recalled the phone conversation he'd taped between Rue and Akmir. But he dismissed the notion that the person in the red compact was some kind of hit man. As soon as Ed had called him and told him the news that Yutanda was resigning her seat and moving out of New Jersey, Chris had told Rue that Yutanda wasn't a player anymore. She'd seen the light, so to speak; she was out. And none too soon, he thought. Drug shipments were ramping up, the money changing hands mind-blowing—stakes phenomenally high, hired muscle at a peak. And the gangs, they'd become more violent as their involvement in dealing and distribution had grown. Shit, even the cops were on the take. Local, federal, customs, all the way up to the politicians themselves. Mayors, state representatives— wouldn't surprise him if a congressman or a senator was involved—all of them with their hands in the drug-money jar. And even though the public outcry over the amount of illegal drugs hitting the streets and turning a generation into zombie-eyed addicts was at the forefront of loud political speeches, the private take on the whole sordid affair was to keep the drug machine running. Because the machine was putting cash in everyone's pocket. No way this multinational conglomerate was going to be stopped, especially by a single state assemblywoman from New Jersey. Anyone who had the idea of putting a halt to the flow of drugs entering the U.S. by way of the Newark Seaport had better be prepared to give up their lives, he conjectured, because the drug cartels, the gangs, the cops, and the politicians were all part of it. And that left little room—if any—for stemming the tide of drugs. Money and the good life far outweighed the addiction of a generation. The fact that most of the lost souls were black, living in projects or on ghetto streets in the big cities, made it easy for everyone involved to turn a blind eye, fueling the drive to bring in as much cocaine, heroin, and marijuana as possible. Money talked—its voice loud and convincing.

Chris slipped out of his hiding place and walked to the end of the unmarked asphalt lane that ran between the church and the funeral home, catching the taillights of the Escort turning right onto Martin Luther King highway. An out-of-towner, he guessed. Otherwise the driver would have taken a right turn two streets before MLK onto Lincoln. MLK highway used more by people looking to head north toward the river or south where it connected with I-78, opening up possibilities to go just about anywhere in the tri-state area. Not a local, Chris decided. But who would be driving around this section of town at this time of night? The question gnawed at him as he crossed the street.

*

The layout of Yutanda's block-wide apartment development brought 1978 and the streets of Kolwezi rushing back to Chris. The maze of square, squat buildings reminded him of the death, the fires, and the brutal savagery he'd encountered in the Zairian city. Every turn of a street corner greeted him with corpses: beaten, burned, shot, mutilated. The massacre a product of the disjointed forces of the rebels of the FNLC—Front Nationale pour la Libération du Congo—and the locals of the Katanga province recruited to help take control of the strategic mining city.

The siege of the city had spiraled into a bloodbath. Greed and ineptitude—rampant within the Zairian government—influenced the joint operation conducted by French, Belgian, and Zairian forces tasked with saving the European inhabitants of the city. A clusterfuck of an operation, Chris viewed it as—or as the men in his Legionnaire unit referred to it, *le groupe niquer*.

When Chris's Foreign Legion company parachuted into Kolwezi to help free three thousand European hostages, they initially encountered heavy resistance. But as the Legionnaires probed farther into the city, fighting grew sporadic, the rebels seemingly able to vanish into the dizzying array of streets lined with box-like mud and wooden structures, only to reappear out of nowhere to unleash a barrage of heavy machine gun and mortar fire before disappearing again. Because of internal bickering, miscommunication, and duplication of objectives between the French, Belgian, and Zairian forces, the fighting in Kolwezi lasted a prolonged three days; hence *le groupe niquer.*

He remembered reading about the plight of the hostages in a newspaper article a week or so later. The counter-offensive to retake the city launched by French and Belgian forces was two days too late, the article reported, especially for the European women who had been captured. Made to dance and strip naked for their captors, the women—girls as young as five—were repeatedly raped until near death. The lucky ones—the lucky; he couldn't fathom how any of them had been lucky—died from the ordeal. The unlucky were tortured, scalding metal rods placed inside the most sensitive areas of their bodies, or mutilated an appendage at a time. He'd read in the newspaper account that the women's screams could be heard for miles. The butchering had gone on for two days. And by the time he—Third Company—had entered the building, the killing was over, the hostages dead, piled in corners of the lobby of the Impala Hotel, some nailed to the walls with spikes.

Chris didn't know what had taken place in the Impala Hotel before he'd entered with his unit. He only knew the aftermath. Beyond comprehension, he kept telling himself as he and the rest of his unit tagged and carried corpses out to the courtyard gardens to be identified. He hadn't known at the time he'd encounter another unfathomable display of atrocity in Kolwezi.

Between the Belgian paratroopers and the French Foreign Legion, most of the heavy fighting for control of Kolwezi was over within two days. The Belgian army—having flown transport planes into Kinshasa and ferried them to the Kolwezi airport after the facility had been secured—took responsibility for evacuating the European and Moroccan hostages. Third Company—Chris's—was sent east of the city proper on day three to a shantytown to ferret out any remaining rebel strongholds and free any other hostages who might be hidden there.

He'd spotted the woman running. White, European, carrying a child in her arms, a peculiar mixture of fear and relief on her face. Chris didn't understand it at first—the odd expression on her face. But then he saw a group of soldiers giving chase behind her. And that was even more confusing, because the soldiers were wearing the uniforms of the Zairian army that had been sent into the city to protect and extract the very people this woman was surely part of.

Twenty yards from where he and the six members of his patrol were positioned, Chris caught the blurred movement of a figure on the rooftops. The figure was a soldier, a Zairian soldier with a torch in his hand. Before he or any of his patrol knew what was happening, another soldier rushed out of a narrow passage between two buildings and threw a bucket of liquid onto the fleeing woman and child. The woman stopped and gagged, fluid streaming down her face. Just before she started to scream, Chris smelled gasoline. In the moment his stomach knotted into a ball of sickened disgust, the lighted torch fell atop the woman. She burst into flames instantaneously, dropping the child to the ground while frantically trying to wipe the fire from her face. But she couldn't. Chris smelled her burning flesh before he could react. She and the child were engulfed in flames before the first Legionnaire could reach them. The handfuls of dirt they threw weren't delivered fast enough to make the slightest difference, the woman and child burning to death at their feet. Their tortured, wailing screams mixed in with the animated banter between the approaching Zairian soldiers, sent him into a rage.

The MAT-49 submachine gun Chris and his fellow Legionnaires were armed with carried thirty-two rounds of 9mm ammunition. On full auto, the clip could fire six hundred rounds per minute. Aiming up at the roof, Chris fired a prolonged burst up into the crotch of the soldier peering down at him, the man grabbing hold of his groin, screaming before falling forward and toppling to the ground. Swinging the submachine gun out in front of him, Chris opened fire on the group of men wearing the uniforms of the Zairian army, shredding the chests of two of them before his magazine emptied. The ensuing firefight was short and brutal. The seven soldiers who had been pursuing the European woman were cut down before they could fire a shot, most dead before they fell to the ground.

An eerie silence ensued after the MAT-49s ceased firing. It was in that moment of calm that his corporal took a bullet in the chest, the shot coming from a narrow passageway between two houses fifteen yards away. As the members of his patrol bent to the corporal's fallen body, Chris sprinted toward the point of fire, snapping a fresh ammo clip into his weapon.

Rounding the corner of the house, Chris caught sight of a fleeing Zairian soldier and fired a short burst from his weapon. The man rolled to the ground, clutching one of his knees. As Chris drew near, the distinct odor of gasoline assailed his senses, the smell making him crazy.

Pulling a ten-inch Legionnaire-issued knife from the sheath on his belt, he fell atop the soldier, plunging the blade into man's ribcage on the right side of his body. The blow not intended to kill, inflicted for optimum pain. Puncturing one of the man's lungs, rendering him incapacitated.

"Why?" Chris screamed into the soldier's face, placing the point of the blood-smeared knife below one of the man's bulging eyes. "Why'd you set fire to that woman?"

"Orders," the man gasped, his face twisting with the struggle to breathe. "Orders."

"Orders?" Chris punctured the skin of the man's cheek with the knife. "What orders?" Chris pressed the knife a little harder.

"Incident!" the man cried. Coughing, gasping for breath, he struggled to get out, "Inter—national—incident. Bring att—" he gagged, twisting his head to the side, spitting out blood. "Attention."

He tried to look at Chris but his eyes wouldn't focus.

"Mobutu—world help—him." He coughed, his chest heaving. "Stay in power," he whispered.

"You burned a woman and child alive for your fucking president to stay in power?"

Chris raised his face to the sky and screamed.

Rearing back, Chris rammed the knife into the man's face without mercy, smashing and driving the blade until there was nothing left resembling the features of a human being. When he was done, after methodically wiping the blade clean in the dirt beside the man's dead body, he walked slowly back toward the road. Reaching the corner of the house where he first gave chase to the soldier, he stopped, a sense of utter detachment taking hold of him. Confused, angry, dispirited, he stared at the lumps of burnt human remains for a few minutes before turning and walking away. He never looked back. And as far as he knew, no one had ever been sent to find him. The account he read in the newspaper listed six Foreign Legion troops as missing in action in the conflict. Chris assumed he was one of the six.

He remembered boarding the train out of Zaire thinking he was leaving everything behind: war, killing, death, savagery, hopelessness. But soon found he hadn't—or couldn't—because there was nowhere he could go where the past didn't haunt him. The images of the Impala Hotel and the squat, square buildings of Kolwezi he could never rid himself of. And now, as he walked through the apartment complex where Yutanda and Menelik lived, those images returned as fresh as ever.

*

Chris pulled the hood of his black sweatshirt up over his head as a light drizzle began to fall. His running shoes made no sound on the cracked sidewalks as he made his way through the expansive pattern of buildings, searching the dimly lit openings between each. *All clear*, he said to himself when he reached the last cluster. *Not sure why I thought I was late in getting here.* Exiting the back side of the block-wide compound onto Court Street, he stuffed his hands into the pockets of his snug-fitting sweatpants, shrugged his shoulders, and took a right turn. He decided to make a slow pass down Court Street before reentering the apartment complex at the corner of Broome, where he'd begin another walk-through.

As normal, Court Street was lined with cars. There wasn't an empty space along either curb. Parking was—as he himself had become all too aware of on the several trips he'd made to visit Yutanda, Ed, and Lizbeth—a problem; too many vehicles, not enough spaces. Plenty of room in the church and funeral home parking lots across Mercer Street, but the tow truck drivers made a living off those properties. The *No Street Parking Allowed* signs posted at the entrance of each lot diligently enforced. If you left your car unattended overnight or at off hours, you could pretty much bet your vehicle wouldn't be there when you went to retrieve it. Forcing Chris to park a half mile away on multiple occasions when he drove over to Yutanda's around dinnertime. Making him feel like some second-rate boyfriend when he would bring takeout over for dinner and have to carry the bags and boxes of food several blocks. The whole ordeal making him feel domesticated—*pussy whipped*, wasn't that the phrase?

The smell of engine exhaust brought him to a halt, the odor fairly strong, prompting him to take a harder look at the cars lining the street. The windshields and side windows of the vehicles nearest him were covered in a sheen of water, none looking to have recently been driven. Some ten yards ahead of him, however, adjacent to the empty space along the curb next to a fire hydrant, wet tire tracks ran crossways over the sidewalk leading to the opening between two buildings. Quiet and slow, Chris walked to the entranceway to find a car parked in the middle of the walkway: a red Ford Escort with Michigan plates.

Peering through the rain-slicked back window, Chris tried to see if the driver was sitting in the car, but he couldn't see through the film of water covering the glass. Giving the car a wide berth, he rounded the vehicle from the front, his eyes locked on the side window. Satisfied the driver wasn't slouched down in his seat, Chris stepped over to the front of the car and placed his hand on the hood. The metal was warm. Akmir's voice drifted into his thoughts: "I will take care of it."

Turning at the next cluster of buildings, Chris sprinted down the side-walk, eyes shifting right and left as he ran, the drizzle becoming a steady rain. Suddenly reliving night patrol on the streets of Kolwezi, he slowed to a fast-paced walk, scrutinizing each shadowy crevice. If the driver of the red Ford Escort was hiding between one of the buildings, he didn't want to be taken by surprise. Hearing footsteps—soft, hurried—he stopped and peered into the rain.

A figure holding a flat, square object rounded the corner of the near-est cluster of buildings. When the figure turned toward Chris, the person hesitated, shuffling back a step, head turning left and right as if the person was thinking of running. When the figure started walking right toward him, Chris felt a surge of adrenaline.

Instinctively, Chris flexed the muscles of his upper body and placed his weight on the balls of his feet, widening his stance. Locking his eyes on the figure's face, he saw the person approaching was a man. Searching for any subtle signs that might tell him what to expect, Chris watched for the quick movement of a hand, a curling lip, or a twitching shoulder before shifting his attention to the object the man held.

"Why they do this?" the man shouted in heavily accented English. "They think funny?"

Chris caught the faint smell of pizza as the man lifted the rectangular, red delivery pouch up toward his face.

"I be home—sleep," he complained, tilting his head sideways, closing his eyes and snoring. "You buy?" the man asked, blinking his eyes back open, looking at Chris with a near demanding expression.

Middle Easterner, Chris deduced; scruffy beard, dark eyes, hawk-like nose, and the accent. Chris tried to keep a blank expression on his face, but he couldn't help but smile.

"I ain't hungry," he replied, doing his best to sound annoyed.

"You buy—yes?" the man pressed, giving Chris a harsh look.

The man opened the front of the delivery pouch and pulled the front of the pizza box out.

"Still hot," he stated. "You buy. Ten American dollar."

"You best back the hell off," Chris warned when the man pushed the pizza box into his chest. Chris stepped back and to one side. "And get out of my face."

Acting as though he was going to hit the man, Chris raised a fist up to his shoulder. The man cowered back and crouched low. When the man realized Chris wasn't going to attack him, he began walking in the direction of the red Ford Escort, turning his head to shout curse words in Arabic. Having picked up a few phrases from his time in North Africa, Chris heard him yell "*Hamite zarba!*" (Black shit!) and "*Mos zibby!*" (Suck my dick!). Insults that would have normally roused a quick and physical response from Chris, but tonight made him laugh. A pizza deliveryman, he chided himself. What other foolishness would he fall prey to while playing this stupid charade of being Yutanda's friend?

Chris pulled the hood of his sweatshirt closer to his head as the rain began falling a little harder. A sudden flash of lightning illuminated the low-hanging clouds along the eastern horizon. Thunder rumbled in the distance. Soaking wet, Chris silently cursed the day he'd ever agreed to meet with Rue Thompson.

* * *

Mirko Haddad slid into his red Escort, placing the pizza delivery pouch on the passenger seat. Taking the Desert Eagle Mark I handgun from the back waistband of his pants, he slipped it into an open metal box lying on the floor. When he was certain the finely crafted weapon was secure within the custom depression he'd cut out of the box's foam lining, he closed the lid and slid the box backward. Feeling the magnets on the sides of the seat frame latch onto the metal, he straightened, lifting a ring of keys out of his jacket pocket. Finding the one he wanted, he placed it into the ignition, lightly pumping the gas pedal as he turned the key. The engine sputtered to life. Before shifting into reverse, he leaned to the side, opened the delivery pouch, and slid the pizza box out. Mirko opened the lid and placed a hand beneath one of the tepid slices of pepperoni pizza. Lifting it to his mouth, he took a bite. Slipping his free hand under his jacket, he extracted a switchblade from the light harness strapped beneath his right shoulder and hit the switch for the windshield wipers to engage. He pushed the blade's release button and waited, half expecting, half hoping the man would appear. Best to deal with the stupid black man with the knife, he reasoned—if the *aswad* was dumb enough to follow him to the car. Adrenaline surging, Mirko took another bite of pizza and waited. But nothing appeared in the frame of the windshield except drops of rain. Satisfied the *abeeb* hadn't followed him, Mirko put the half-eaten pizza slice on top of the box and slid the padded pouch out from underneath. Keeping one eye focused on what was going on outside the windshield, he slipped his hand deep inside the pouch until his fingers felt the specially designed zipper baggie containing strands of C-4 plastic explosive. He gave the contents a respectful touch and slid his hand back out. Returning the switchblade to the shoulder sheath, he picked up his slice of pizza, depressed the clutch, shifted the manual transmission into reverse, and eased the car backward.

Taking another bite of pizza, he backed the car out to the middle of the street before braking to a stop. Shifting into first gear, he put his foot to the gas pedal and started down Courte Street at a leisurely pace. After a quarter of a mile, Mirko switched on the car's headlights and checked the rearview mirror to see if he was being followed. Then he checked the small, rectangular magnetized clock mounted on the dashboard: 4:15.

Calculating time and distance, he figured he could be in Queens before the teeth of rush hour started. He might have to wait a half hour or so before some of the Middle Eastern delis and restaurants opened up, but it would be worth the trouble and the drive—having a traditional Lebanese breakfast with real Lebanese coffee. Besides, he thought, he was in no hurry. He didn't need to be back in Newark until late afternoon. And he'd be returning long before then, before the rush to get back out of New York City began. After breakfast, he would go and see an early showing of the new movie starring the crocodile man from Australia. He'd noticed a theater in Astoria offering a ten o'clock showing of the film when he'd scanned a copy of a New York paper while waiting for night to fall. The movie would allow him a chance to relax and, perhaps, catch a quick nap. The trailers he'd seen of the film made him laugh. And the few people he knew who had already seen the motion picture told him he would find it funny.

"I'll put another shrimp on the barbie for ya, mate."

The line in itself wasn't that humorous, but the way the Australian actor delivered it in the TV commercial made Mirko chuckle. And Mirko needed some humor in his life today. He didn't like killing anymore. And murdering someone he didn't know made it all the worse. At least in Lebanon he knew why he was killing a particular person. But he knew nothing about this job, just an address on a piece of paper and a woman's name. Yutanda Taylor-Arbagna. He wondered what she'd done. And wondered why an icy voice out of his past had called and ordered her dead.

A flash of lightning spread through the clouds along the eastern horizon, briefly turning the dull gray sky an eerie shade of greenish-white. Emptying his mind, Mirko depressed the clutch and shifted into second gear.

14

E D CAST HIS line into Branch Brook Lake, sighing like a man who'd found his rightful place in the world.

"Pretty, ain't it?"

Glancing into the stroller, he nodded; baby Menelik was fast asleep.

"No need to answer," he whispered. "You just keep doin' what you're doin'." He chuckled. "Better chance the fish be comin' round to see us if you just keep quiet." Raising an eyebrow, he added, "Not like the other day, when you 'bout scared every one of 'em to the other side with all that hollerin' you be doin'."

Ed shifted his attention back to the lake and located the red and white bobber attached to his line. Studying it for several seconds, he waited, hoping to see it tugged upon from below. Or better yet, disappear altogether beneath the surface of the slate-colored water. But it didn't move.

"You think they be bitin' better on ham or bologna today?" he casually inquired as he started to reel the line back in. "'Cause I got both—and some cheese too."

Ed looked out at one of the small islands in the middle of the lake, spotting a night heron in the shallows along the near shoreline.

"There be one patient fisherman," he quietly observed with a nod toward the bird. "Learn a lot from animals," he went on, giving the baby a knowing look. "You remember that as you get older."

Ed smiled when he saw the heron's long, pointed beak slice into the water and come back up with a small fish wiggling at the tip.

"See that?" he admiringly asked. "Don't need no bait, that one. Been around 'fore God even thought about creatin' us. Knows how to fish, that one." He shook his head and chuckled. "Yes, he sure does."

The sun wasn't quite up over the horizon yet, but Ed could tell it was close to sunrise by the amount of light starting to reflect off the water's surface. Glancing to the sky, he noted the previous night's storm was clearing out. But the humidity remained. Wisps of fog or steam—he wasn't sure which—drifted off the lake but clung to the shorelines. Needed a couple hours of sun for the mist to clear off the islands, he reckoned.

"Lot of moisture in the air still," he remarked. "Probably have another round of boomers come late afternoon or early evenin'."

Ed looked up and spotted some breaks in the clouds. Pale, washed-out blue—closer to milky white—peeked out between scattered openings. The same color sky he'd see above Fauquier County, he guessed—if he were there—but he wasn't convinced of the notion. Too much pollution up in this corner of the country, he felt. Drained the color out of things. Even the trees seemed a washed-out shade of green. Least that's what he kept telling himself—and anybody else who'd listen. But he was prejudiced on the subject. And he'd admit to it—when no one was within earshot.

"Nothin' like the Virginia countryside," he'd say. "Rollin' hills, running streams, green grass, and stands of Sycamore trees everywhere you look," he'd tell anyone who asked.

Which wasn't a lot of people. Noah, usually; a couple of Belinda's—Yutanda's—aides; sometimes even one of those people who called on the phone around suppertime and wanted to sell some kind of insurance.

"Yup. Sure be nice to get back home."

After reeling in the rest of his line, he checked the rolled piece of bologna on the hook. Satisfied the bait would last for another go under water, he took a couple steps away from the stroller and cast his line out. The two-ounce weight attached to the nylon pulled the baited hook along as it arced toward a spot Ed hoped would be near twenty-five yards away. He knew the bigger fish would be there—in the deeper water farther away from the shore—and hoped to catch a few of them: a couple of black bass or some large lake trout. They'd be tonight's dinner—food reminding him of home. He was tired of takeout from restaurants and fast food places. Had a hankering for fresh fish dusted with seasoned flour and then quick-fried in oil, with corn bread and green beans on the side. And though the cornbread

Noah sometimes brought over for dinner was pretty good, it weren't nothin' compared to Lizbeth's.

"Yep, little Menelik, be mighty fine to get back home." Sighing, he looked out over the water. "And I know you gonna like it there, too."

Ed looked up and down the shoreline before letting his gaze wander back out to the islands situated in the southern part of the lake.

"Can't say it ain't pretty here and such. But it's contained, you know? Man needs to stretch his arms and legs and breathe the fresh air. Like where your daddy come from, I guess."

He turned and peered into the stroller.

"Though I can't rightly say. Didn't know him long enough or well enough to learn what his country was really like."

Ed hung his head a little, his face taking on a melancholy look.

"'Bout the time I learned you were comin' into this world"—pausing, he took a moment to study Menelik's face—"your daddy was killed."

Ed pinched his eyebrows together, the wrinkles on his face deepening.

"Say it was a terrible accident. Least that's what the government says."

Ed removed his Southern Railway hat and rubbed the side of his face with the back of his hand.

"But I don't know how you call it that when his helicopter was shot out of the sky. Seems like that be somethin' entirely different than an accident."

A shaft of sunshine broke out of the clouds about the same time Ed felt a definitive tug on his rod. Quickly turning, he located the bobber on his line just in time to see it disappear beneath the surface.

"Land's sake, boy, feels like we got ourselves a big one!" Ed exclaimed, slapping the cap back on his head.

With a quick jerk of the rod toward his right shoulder, Ed took a few steps closer to the water. Coming to a stop, he gave the rod another pull before pressing the strike pin on the side of the reel so the fish couldn't pull any more line out of the spool. With one final pull on the rod, he began to slowly reel in the fishing line—and what was hooked on the end.

"Come to papa," he muttered, a surge of adrenaline awakening every cell in his body.

Like the echo of distant thunder, a low rumble sent a tremor through the sky. Ed passed the sound off as a remnant of the previous night's storm clinging to whatever energy still lingered in the air. But as the rumbling grew deeper, louder, and closer, Ed turned around and looked up.

"Not now," he muttered with a shake of his head.

A 747, flying low, was headed right in their direction. Ed recognizing the make of the plane by the shape of the nose and expansive cabin shell at the front of the body. It was a big, lumbering behemoth of a machine; the roar of the jet's engines on ascent could rattle a brain, burst an eardrum, and shake a house. And Ed gauged it would be passing right above him and Menelik in a matter of seconds. Already he could sense Menelik stirring.

"Not now," he repeated.

But it was too late. The first wail from Menelik shattered what was left of the peaceful morning as the building rumble of the 747 began to resonate in Ed's bones. With a look of desperation, he glanced back at the lake while taking a hesitant step toward the stroller. Menelik wailed louder, a steady grating cry piercing Ed's head like the screech of a cat whose tail is caught beneath the rail of a rocker with a three-hundred-pound man sitting in the chair. Cringing, Ed stumbled forward, thrusting his arms out in front of him. The whistling roar of the 747 nearly directly overhead, Ed fell to his hands and knees, the rod slipping from his grasp. In a moment of frustrated angst, he saw the rod slide back toward the lake, his fingers trying desperately to grab hold of the narrow tip. Above him, in the stroller, Menelik's cries turned into choking coughs. With the earth shaking beneath him, Ed pushed himself to his feet. Scooping baby Menelik up into his arms, Ed pressed one ear of the child against his chest, covering the other with his hand.

"Ain't no harm, ain't no harm," Ed hurried to say. "Grandpa ain't gonna let nothin' happen to you," he told Menelik in a soft, reassuring voice. "Plane be gone in a minute. See," he said, glancing to the sky, "already passed us by. Be quiet again in a minute."

Twisting his body left and right, Ed gently bounced Menelik in his arms.

"So you just calm yourself, little one. Just be calm." Glancing over his shoulder, he said, "And then we can get back to—"

Ed froze, the sight of his rod disappearing into the lake leaving him speechless. As if to mock him, the silvery form of a fish jumped out of the water near to where he had cast his line. A ten or twelve pounder, the fish looked to be—a monster.

"Guess we be done fishin' for the day," he said, sighing and placing a kiss on Menelik's forehead. "Suppose I'll call Noah when we get back to the apartment and see if he knows where there be some fresh fish for sale. *Fresh fish*," he emphasized to Menelik, holding him out and away from his body so he could look into the child's face. "*Caught today.* Goldarn planes," he muttered, casting a disapproving look eastward, where the form of another plane was heading toward them. "Can't wait to get back to Virginia."

Ed fell silent as he looked back at Menelik. The boy's eyes were bright with life, soft brown like his mom's. Had her chin and cheekbones too, he noticed, square and proud. Boy's gonna be a handsome child, he thought. His daddy would have been proud. What did the future hold for his grandson? he wondered. Yutanda saying she was dragging the little boy off to Africa didn't seem right. No good news coming out of that continent lately, he observed, especially Ethiopia.

"Best we head on home," he announced, giving Menelik a hug. "Maybe we get lucky and the bus back to Ferry Street be waitin' for us when we get to the stop."

With a parting glance at the peaceful waters of the lake, Ed placed Menelik back in his stroller.

"Goldarn planes," he grumbled, picking up the small bait cooler from the ground while gazing upward at the winged silhouette veering off to the south. "Goldarn place."

With a tug on the brim of his cap, Ed took hold of the stroller's handles and began pushing Menelik toward the bus stop located at the entrance of Branch Brook Park.

* * *

"What you going to do with everything else?"

Lizbeth looked around the apartment's rectangular living room, her eyes sweeping over the duffel bags and suitcases sitting on the floor.

"Haven't really thought about it," Yutanda replied, folding a pair of Menelik's pants and placing them in a large blue backpack with an aluminum frame. "Lease runs another three months."

She glanced over at her mother and shrugged her shoulders.

"Put it in storage, I guess. Or have someone keep an eye on things until I can get back up here."

Lizbeth frowned.

"Maybe Corporal Stilton or someone from the office," Yutanda offered with a half- hearted smile. "I wouldn't worry about it," she told her mother. "I'm not."

But she could see her mother was worried.

"I just don't understand why it all has to be so quick. Seems like you haven't thought this whole thing out. Your son's not even six months yet."

Lizbeth took a step toward the front door, her hands moving from her hips to the bun in the back of her hair as though she was trying to decide where they would do her the most good.

"And you want to fly him over to some country you don't know nothing about."

"Plenty of time to learn," Yutanda countered, picking up a pair of Menelik's socks and holding them up so her mother could see how tiny they were.

"They wear socks over there?"

"Momma!"

"Well do they? You even know?"

"Shame on you for saying such a thing." Yutanda gave her mother a shocked look. "Course people in Ethiopia wear socks," she admonished. "People wear socks all over the world."

"But you don't know for a fact," Lizbeth challenged.

Yutanda stuffed the baby socks into the blue backpack and let her body go limp.

"Momma."

"But you don't, do you?" Lizbeth pressed. "Just like you don't know for certain what you'll find when you get over there."

Yutanda could see by her mother's expression that she was going to make her point—whatever that point was.

"Your own government told you he's dead," Lizbeth said. "And here you are," she went on, sweeping her arms out toward the array of baggage on the floor, "ready to fly halfway around the world on some dreamed-up notion that your man's still alive. And what, Yutanda? Wandering around with amnesia or some such cockamamie condition?"

Yutanda watched her mother's expression change from harsh to one of confused concern.

"I don't understand what you're doin'. That country's not safe. I've been reading up. Drought, famine, disease, poverty, refugee camps—civil war in about every part of the country. Just what is it you're expectin' to find when you get there?"

Yutanda put down the baby T-shirt she was holding and took a deep breath.

"I'm expecting to find," she said, her arm extended, palm open, facing upward.

Lizbeth raised her eyebrows.

"I'm expecting—"

Yutanda dropped her arm down to her side, her eyes drifting to the floor.

"I don't know, Momma. I don't know what I'm expecting to find," she admitted in a weary tone. "All I know is that they never found his body. So you tell me what I should expect. Because, yeah, as far-fetched as it may seem, cases of people having amnesia after surviving some head-jolting accident aren't unheard of. So you tell me, Momma," she repeated, her voice taking on a combative tone. "Should I just forget about him? Just accept he's dead even though there isn't a body? Or because the government—the government," she said, exhaling sarcastically, "says so? Even though they can't produce any evidence to verify what they're telling me?"

"Yutanda," Lizbeth countered, raising a hand in front of her chest as if she was motioning for her daughter to stop.

"Don't you think it's strange, Momma? Why wouldn't his body have been in that wreck if he were dead? Dead bodies don't just get up and walk away."

"They do if a wild animal done carry 'em," Lizbeth quietly offered.

"Oh my God! I can't believe you just said that!"

Yutanda placed a hand over her mouth and looked away.

"How could—" she took her hand away from her mouth so she could steady herself on the back of the blue tweed chair she was standing behind.

"Because it happens over there," Lizbeth unapologetically replied. "Lions, hyenas, wild dogs. I hate to think about it—hate myself for sayin' it—but you got to realize it could've happened. It's Africa, Yutanda."

Yutanda gave her mother a wary glance.

"I saw the same pictures of the wreck as you. It would've had to have been some kind of miracle for anyone to have survived that." Lizbeth took a hesitant step toward her daughter. "I'm just worried sick about you, is all. God would have had to have sent the angels themselves for Menelik to have been able to walk away from that crash."

Yutanda watched her mother's eyes search the floor.

"What does your heart tell you, girl? Surely you don't want to take your child over there if Menelik's—"

Yutanda rounded the back of the chair, pushed the pile of baby clothes she'd been folding to one side of the cushion, and sat down.

"Don't know what my heart says—or feels. Shut the door on it the day I got the news, I guess. And haven't bothered to open it since." Reluctantly, she raised her head and met her mother's gaze. "Only thing I keep thinking about is: What if he *is* alive? What if he *did* survive the attack?" Yutanda picked up a few items of baby clothes and stared at them.

"He'll never know he has a son if I don't try—if I don't try to find him," she explained. Looking up, she forced a weak smile. "So that's what I've decided to do. Whether you or Daddy agree with the decision or not."

"Land's sake, Yutanda, your daddy and I are just worried about you. You understand? First you get yourself all wrapped up in this assembly-woman business—getting assaulted, taking on drug dealers and criminals and such—and now this?"

Lizbeth crossed the space between them and rested a hand on her daughter's shoulder.

"You gotta admit, seems like you bouncing hard one way and then doin' a complete circle the other. Ed and I just wonder if learning about Menelik's death"—Yutanda shot her mother an unwelcoming glance—"and then having his baby, hasn't mixed up your thinking."

Abruptly, Yutanda rose from the chair and took a few steps away, keeping her back to her mother.

"Well, after tonight, you won't have to worry about the assemblywoman stuff. And I'm sorry you believe Menelik's dead and you both think I'm being crazy." Turning to face her mother, Yutanda wiped tears from her eyes and took a deep breath. "But I'm intending to go to Ethiopia with my son to find his father—or at least his uncle. Boy's got a right to know who his father is," she said with conviction. "And has a right to get to know the country and the people where his father was born."

The two women stared at each other for a few moments as if each was judging what the other had said, each wondering if there was something more that needed saying.

"I'm going to make some tea," Yutanda offered, breaking the impasse. "You want a cup?"

Yutanda studied her mother's expression, understanding from the years she had spent growing up with the woman that she was trying to decide if her daughter was being foolish. But when she saw Lizbeth bend down and start to fold the same baby T-shirt she had been holding when their conversation had taken on an air of disagreement, she smiled.

"Cup of tea sounds good," Lizbeth softly remarked as she placed the folded T-shirt in the blue backpack. "Little extra sugar if you would. Gonna need a little zip in the old joints to get through all this packing."

Silently clapping her hands out in front of her, Yutanda twirled round with a smile on her face and headed toward the kitchen.

* * *

Rue Thompson undid the buttons of his grey Nehru suit coat and removed the stiff, white clergy collar from around his neck. Closing his eyes, he fingered the large, gold crucifix resting on the upper portion of his rotund stomach. Running a thumb over the figure of Christ, he thought about the run-in he'd just had with the female reporter from the *Star-Ledger*.

*

"Still a *practicing clergyman*, Reverend Thompson?" a female voice had asked as he exited the Abyssinian Baptist Church.

He remembered turning with anger on his face, insulted by the woman's mocking tone of voice.

"And whom do I have the pleasure of speaking with?" he politely inquired.

The woman was young, hair tinted red, groomed in cornrows to each side of her face with a part down the center. Rue could see her eyebrows had been plucked for the most part, what little left shaved close to the skin, enhanced with red-tinted make-up to match the color of her hair. Her forehead and cheekbones were rounded and smooth, her full, round eyes an alluring light brown. Rue was just letting his eyes wander to the ample curves of her body when she'd replied.

"Felicia Brown, Newark *Star-Ledger*. And were you addressing the congregation as a practicing reverend just now?" she asked, nodding toward the church door.

"I was speaking as a guest of the minister. Sitting in on a neighborhood discussion on troubled teenage youths. Specifically, young teenage boys that have no father figures in their lives."

"Offering yourself as an example of what not to do when you attain the trust of the people?"

He smiled when she pulled out a small microphone attached to a portable cassette recorder from her oversize denim shoulder bag and pushed a button. Leaning toward the microphone, he responded.

"Offering the path to the Lord when sin has been the only door that has thus far been opened in the life of a young person will always be the road I advocate, the road where love and education can foster the dreams of the misguided. Perhaps your newspaper would like to run a story on the subject. I believe the reading public would find the topic compelling and timely."

The words flowed smoothly from his lips. He could tell however, by the sour expression on Felicia's face, the young woman was not happy her barb had not thrown him off balance.

"Do the people of the neighborhood believe that a man who was forced to resign his state office because of federal charges of corruption and bribery is the proper role model for the youths in this neighborhood? Some would say—and have said—that you set an example that should be steered clear of."

He had been tempted to slap her then, just reach out and slap her across the face to wipe the self-important grin from her lips. But his years of addressing the public and the lessons he'd learned from those years kept him calm. Instead of slapping the woman, he simply ran his hands along the side of his head, pretending to smooth his hair.

"The good people of this neighborhood are not swayed by the propaganda of the government and realize the charges levied against me were contrived by a political and social system run by a white bureaucracy. As the subscribers of the *Star-Ledger* will soon come to know, these fictitious and slanderous charges will be dismissed and I will be completely exonerated. So as you—"

"Then why did you resign, if all the charges—as you say—were erroneous?"

"So as not to inflict any more unnecessary pain upon the good people of this community," he said without missing a beat. "This city still reels from the riots of '67, Miss Brown. The healing it so desperately needs to experience—has cried out for, for the past twenty years—has been purposely stunted by the white man's policies. My personal situation was and is meaningless compared to the suffering this city's had to endure. Even now we are the brunt of nationwide jokes: drugs, poverty, the racial divide between education and housing an epidemic—all of it growing worse."

A smile came to him when he remembered the blistering, condemning look he had given her.

"Would you—and the white establishment you work for—rather I had remained in office so the white government flunkies could parade their three-ring circus of misinformation and misleading stories on the evening news and place Newark in the headlines of the white-controlled media?"

Clutching the gold crucifix in his hand, he shuddered.

"So are you saying that you bear none of the responsibility for the state of this city? That your time in office didn't contribute to the drug epidemic that is killing off a generation of black Americans? That your part in all of this—taking bribes, siphoning money from projects earmarked for urban housing projects, receiving kickbacks from companies you voted for on the floor of the state assembly that turned out to be shells for organized crime— you're saying it's all a contrived plot by the white politicians on the state and federal level to have you removed from office?"

Rue kissed the crucifix before answering.

"Who do you think is responsible for decimating this city with the towers of crime and shame that have been built where neighborhoods once stood? Where superhighways were maliciously allowed to rip through entire sections of this city and displace its residents, condemning them to live in those same urban housing projects that have become a cesspool of human degradation? The very same housing projects you and the white establishment touted as being an answer to all of the black man's woes."

Rue took a step forward, imposing his girth upon the woman.

"The proliferation of the white man's sins toward the blacks in this community is only compounded by their refusal to accept the responsibility their own actions have caused where it pertains to the preponderance of drug use within the scope of the misguided youths of our time. Drug abuse is up and flourishing, not diminishing, as the politicians would have you believe. *Crime* from the drug trade is on the rise. Addiction, homelessness, and hopelessness run rampant. The starry-eyed do-gooders elected to take my place are unable, unwilling, and incapable of stemming the tide and bringing this vicious soul-killing epidemic to an end."

"Are you stating that the efforts and policies put forth by your successors since vacating your office have been failures?"

Rue paused to stroke his chin.

"*Failure* is a word suggested by you. And I do not choose to place labels or spin rhetoric upon people who—though they may be unqualified and inept—are doing what they tell us is the best they can do with what they have to work with. But facts speak for themselves. Our roadways are filled with cars and buses carrying cocaine, marijuana, and heroin; our railways used as a means to distribute drugs to New York City and points north, south, east and west. Young black men are dying in the streets. Young black women are being turned into prostitutes. A generation of black children robbed of their right to succeed by an educational system that allows them to drop out of school or ushers them from one grade to the next though they can't add, subtract, read, or write. It's tragic what the white man has done to our race since we were so called *freed*. And what's worse is that someone like you, Felicia Brown, someone who is obviously educated and has risen above the societal bars raised up before you on your path to attaining the American dream, believes the white establishment when they point the finger at a black man who's done nothing more than try and lay bare the glaring discrepancies between the black and white races. Shame on you for being here today to try and rile me into some sort of inflammatory statement so you can have a by-line in tomorrow's paper instead of writing about the lost dreams of black America, dreams stolen by the same white race that once enslaved us. Shame on you, Felicia Brown—shame on you for pretending you're black."

He had watched her eyes scramble for a place to hide, hardly able to contain his laughter when he saw his barrage of racially themed pomposity had elicited the intended effect. Felicia Brown was questioning herself, he knew, asking herself if she was black enough, if she even understood what being black in Newark, New Jersey, in 1986 meant. When she pushed the button on the cassette recorder to stop the tape from rolling and lowered the microphone to her side, Rue decided to finish her off with a few well-chosen final words.

"Shame is a tool the white race has used against the black man since the beginning of time, sister Felicia. You need not wallow in self-recrimination over your failure to abide by your people. A way out," he explained with an expansive wave of his arms to encompass the city around them, "of poverty will always be the false treasure the white man dangles in front of our race, sister. The placebo of equality a means by which he seeks to keep us under control, while coveting our enslavement. But what the white man won't tell you, won't ever whisper to you as he watches you struggle to pull yourself out of the immorality he has created for our people to endure, is that you can't wash color from your skin."

He'd almost laughed when he saw her glance at her bare arm.

"You're a black woman, Felicia Brown. Black when you were born, black when God receives you into His heavenly kingdom. How you choose to live your life in between is up to you. But you'll never be white. And that's the ultimate weapon in the white man's world—that they'll never accept you—even though they will lie to your face and say they will."

He had waited for a few seconds to see if she had anything to say. But when she'd just stared at him with her lower lip slightly trembling, he had grasped the gold crucifix dangling on the chain about his neck, raised it slightly toward her and said, "May the Lord walk with you on the path to enlightenment, sister. Let Him help you find the way."

*

Rue eased back in his office chair and sighed. Checking the gold Rolex on his wrist, he saw it was time for lunch. Contemplating between choosing the baked pork chops at the Seaport Diner or a McRib sandwich and fries from the McDonald's a little farther down the street, the telephone rang.

"Yes?" he said into the mouthpiece.

He thought he could hear the ocean pulsing on the line as he waited for the caller to respond.

"Be ready," an all-too-familiar voice replied.

"Everything is set on this end," he responded.

"No. Be ready."

"Must you always pretend to be Ali Baba, Akmir? Just say what you mean, for once."

Rue heard the pulse of the ocean for a moment, and then heard the line go dead. He gave the phone a questioning look.

* * *

To keep track of the millions upon millions of intermodal shipping containers crisscrossing the globe, each corrugated steel box loaded onto a freighter is branded with a designation consisting of a series of letters and numerals denoting owner code, equipment category identifier, a serial number, and a check digit, the latter of which validates the recording and transmission accuracies of the owner code and serial number.

Packed aboard the Saudi Arabian–owned freighter *Jameel*—which had embarked eight days before out of the port of Djibouti, sailing under the country convenience flag of Liberia—were several containers bearing the FLLU owner code–equipment category letters, designation stamp placing ownership to a company registered under the name Freightliner LLC, operating out of London, England.

Freightliner LLC—a relatively new company appearing in the Bureau of International Containers (BIC) registry—had begun appearing in BIC logs within the past five years, consistent with bi-monthly shipping paper entries with the registry beginning in the latter part of 1980 to the bi-weekly registrations the company was now logging in the early part of 1986. The documented history of the BIC registry also showed most—if not all—FLLU containers exclusively shipped aboard the freighter *Jameel*, port of origin Djibouti, with regular scheduled stops in Alexandria, Marseilles, Barcelona, and Gibraltar before embarking on its cross-Atlantic journey. Final port: Newark, New Jersey.

Checking the BIC history of the *Jameel*, however, had never occurred to any singular person or law enforcement entity over the span of the past five years, because the freighter, without fail, had always adhered to the Law of the Sea conventions and complied with the multitude of up-to-date certifications and documentation required by the world shipping community for a cargo vessel to cross international waters. And, as the *Jameel* was categorized in one of the smaller bulk-cargo classifications—Feedermax, able to load in a little under three thousand containers, outfitted with its own on-deck cranes—the ship offloaded quickly, usually within several hours. Due to the efficiency of the *Jameel*, the dock master at the Newark terminal was less inclined to make offloading of the vessel's cargo a matter of interest. He tended to leave the ship to its business so its place at the terminal could be utilized by another waiting vessel—of which there were always many. After all, the more ships the dock master could accommodate in a given period of time, the more money the port generated. It was simple business. Tariffs, dockage fees, wharf fees, time allotment fees, water, electricity, truck fees—more ships docked at the terminal equaled more profit. So the *Jameel* was always a welcome sight to the dock master of the Newark terminal. The ship—with a crew that never took shore leave after offloading—could be counted on to be a quick turnaround. Efficient, trouble-free—that was the freighter's reputation. And, therefore, the dock master was very happy.

After leaving the port of Newark, the vessel normally sailed directly to Wilmington, Delaware, according to its shipping log. There it would most often allow the crew a twenty-four-hour shore leave before taking on shipments of machinery or containers of iron and steel and embarking on the long voyage back across the Atlantic to the port of Djibouti via the Suez Canal. It was a two-week round-trip journey, sailing from Djibouti to Newark and then back again—and that was if the weather cooperated. If the vessel encountered storms along either passage route, the voyage would take longer. A longer round-trip voyage, of course, meant an interruption in the flow of commerce. And an interruption in commerce meant a reduction in net profits. As an influx in business dictated a more expeditious transatlantic crossing than the two-week period the freighter had been adhering to for the past two years, Freightliner LLC was seriously considering the purchase of another ship to accommodate the organization's blossoming commercial activity. In fact, the shipment of containers the *Jameel* was carrying on this voyage—assuming the vessel arrived in port with all cargo safe and accounted for—was going to facilitate the purchase of a second freighter. So it was imperative the *Jameel* make port in due course and deliver its payload without incident.

In the lower hold of the freighter, three 40 x 9.5 x 8 foot shipping containers bearing the FLLU code sat side by side. To the curious eye, there was nothing out of the ordinary about the three rust-colored containers, for they were of standard height and length and looked exactly the same as the thousands of other containers carried by the ship. Yet, if a keen-eyed customs agent ever had cause to open one of the FLLU-stamped containers, he or she might take notice that, although the height of the steel container was listed as nine feet, six inches, the measured height inside the three FLLU containers was seven feet, ten inches, leaving one foot and eight inches of space unaccounted for. To the naked eye, the unaccounted one foot, eight inches of space wasn't a glaring issue. It only became one if one of the three specially built containers was opened up alongside any other normal container. Even then, because the reinforced flooring of the FLLU containers was duly noted and documented on the Container Safety Convention (CSC) plate—designating them for heavy machinery use—there was never a cause for suspicion. Suspicion might have been aroused if a person pounded the flooring with a sledgehammer. Only then might a discerning ear hear the echo of a hollow space beneath the surface of the flooring. And that hollowness would only be heard if the space below the flooring was empty—which it wasn't on this voyage. For the containers bearing the designation letters and serial numbers FLLU8945621, FLLU8947251, and FLLU8943321 were packed with ivory tusks. By the Consortium's calculations—at thirty sets of tusks per container, times an estimated one hundred and twenty-five pounds a tusk, at a wholesale price of a thousand dollars per pound—the cargo of ivory would gross the organization twenty-two million, five hundred thousand dollars. And that was in addition to the several other FLLU containers loaded topside of the freighter packed with one hundred kilos of cocaine and one hundred kilos of heroin—street value, between eighteen and twenty-five million dollars, given the going price when the merchandise hit the street. All in all, it was the biggest payload the Consortium had ever put together in one single transaction. The possible take for the shipment carried by the freighter: fifty million American dollars.

As both Adiam and Akmir had been lobbying the other members of the Consortium for a second freighter over the past several months, the windfall of fifty million dollars reaped by the shipment aboard the *Jameel* was to be their final swaying argument in the procurement of a second vessel, overriding the other members' long-standing concerns relating to cost and upkeep.

Presently, the *Jameel* was navigating the waters of Lower New York Bay, heading toward Upper Bay, where it would veer portside through Kill Van Kull Straight before veering hard starboard to enter Newark Bay. At its present speed of five knots per hour, the vessel was due to make the headwaters of Newark Bay by 8:00 pm. Then, given the amount of freighter traffic ahead of them and the dock master's schedule, the *Jameel* would more than likely tie up at the Newark Terminal somewhere between 9:30 and

10:00 pm. All systems on the ship were green—weather clear, waters calm, a diminishing southwest wind blowing port side.

*

Seven thousand miles away, Akmir and Adiam paced the floor of Adiam's third-floor residence on Avenue Marechal. Each man was smoking a cigarette, glancing at the phone on Adiam's African blackwood desk, waiting for it to ring, waiting to hear Rue Thompson's voice on the other end of the line announcing the *Jameel* had made port and was offloading without incident. But each man knew it was too early for the phone to ring. Although it was 2:00 a.m. in Djibouti, it was 7:00 p.m. eastern United States time. And while each man was tired and in need of rest, neither one was thinking of sleep, or entertaining the notion of trying to rest. Too much was at stake, they knew, the amount of money involved in the operation staggering. For Akmir, however, there was a second matter keeping him from contemplating rest.

* * *

Mirko parked his red Ford Escort along Prince Street to begin the final phase of his assignment. Surveying the numerous trees running parallel along the curbs, he concluded the location he'd chosen served his purposes well: easy to access, easy to exit, the foliage providing ample cover from curious eyes. And upon his return, he wouldn't have to worry about some emergency vehicle or police car driving up the road, blocking his escape. Or taking notice of him walking away from what was surely going to be a very large explosion. No, he wouldn't have to worry about that aspect of his plan, because Prince Street was a one-way thoroughfare heading away from the woman's apartment complex.

Mirko took a deep breath and smiled, the aroma of pepperoni pizza a pleasant reminder his mission was nearly done. And though the job he had been given was not one he wanted to undertake, much less complete, the smell of the charcuterie reminded him of makanek sausages, and, of course, Lebanon, the country where he was born and raised, the country where his mother and father still resided, tending their beloved one-hundred-year-old olive grove in the same manner as had been followed from generation to generation. Devoted to cultural traditions and beliefs, his parents' life was rustic and peaceful—semi-spiritual in some respects—and Mirko intended it would remain that way. Even though the voice from his past was one to be feared, he knew there was also a foundation of time-honored trust he could count upon from the people from his country. If he did as instructed, no harm would come to his parents. Of this, he was certain. So the woman—whoever she was and whatever she had done to aggrieve the voices from his past—would have to die.

Blocking everything else from his thoughts except the job at hand, Mirko placed three pyrotechnic blasting caps into the back of the pizza pouch and slid the pizza box snug against them. Closing the pouch, he patted the outer pocket of his red jacket with the emblem of a black domino on the back, making certain the pair of needle-nosed pliers was secure. With a brief touch to the switchblade in the light harness under his arm, he took a quick look around before bending down and pulling the metal box from the magnetic holder beneath the driver's seat. With a mixture of dread and excited anticipation, he opened the lid of the box and extracted the Desert Eagle handgun and the weapon's suppressor. By his calculations, the few drops of hydrofluoric acid solution he'd applied to the natural gas line feeding into Yutanda's apartment early in the morning should have eaten through the metal an hour ago, allowing for a small amount of natural gas to escape and begin to build up beneath the structure. The insertion of a blasting cap into the C-4 he had used to block up the hole around the gas line feeding into the apartment building was the final step he would need to take before creating a terrible accident. Checking the handgun's magazine, Mirko placed the weapon in the rear waistband of his trousers and placed the suppressor in the empty outer pocket of his jacket. Taking one last look at the area where he had parked, Mirko got out of the car with the pizza pouch balanced in one hand. As a safety precaution, he locked the car before heading to the apartment building on Mercer Street.

* * *

Chris reminded himself to tip the guy working the counter at the Popular Fish Market next time he was there, the guy deserving an extra twenty for having the brains to pack everything in ice before allowing Chris to leave the shop. Because finding a parking spot near Yutanda's residence was proving to be every bit as difficult as it usually was around this time.

He'd been tempted to tell Ed he couldn't make it for dinner, that he had a meeting out of town or needed to attend some previous engagement. Why he hadn't offered any of those excuses still a bit of a mystery, because it meant sitting through a family dinner he wasn't a part of. Why put himself through it? he wondered as he scanned the streets for a parking spot. Why sit through an evening of idle chatter; tolerate a fidgeting, crying baby; and have to look across the table at a woman who thought so much of herself she actually believed she could change the course of organized crime all by herself? *Naive! Stupid! Egotistical!* Shaking his head, he grunted, perturbed for being perturbed.

"Chill, dude," he muttered.

One more night, he told himself—just one more night. With a sigh of resignation, he took a right onto Prince Street with the hope of finding the ever-elusive parking spot. If he couldn't find one on this stretch of Prince, he'd decided to take the next left onto West Kinney and begin the loop around Yutanda's complex all over again. And driving around an extended city block—navigating one-way streets, traffic lights, and double-parked cars clogging up traffic—was something he didn't have time for. Already running late, he'd made up his mind if didn't find a spot, he'd take a chance and park his car in the church parking lot, run the fish across the street, and then get back to his car before the tow trucks could haul it away. And if he still couldn't find a spot after that, he'd just leave. What did it matter to him anyway? he asked himself. It was time to end this stupid charade. Besides, the ruse wasn't even necessary anymore. Yutanda would be gone in couple of days, leaving Newark for good, as far as he knew. So the end of the deal he'd made with Rue Thompson—as far as he was concerned—was happening tomorrow. *Time for the fat-ass to pay up—and time for me to blow this scene,* he thought.

A flash of red in the corner of his eye caught Chris's attention. Turning his head, he caught a glimpse of a black-and-white spotted domino on the back of a red jacket. *There's an easy answer for dinner,* he noted. *Pizza. Not like all the hassle of getting fish.* He briefly wondered if the pizza delivery guy was the same one he'd run into at four in the morning. But he dismissed the thought altogether when he reached the intersection of West Kinney and saw an open spot along the curb some twenty yards up on the right side of the street.

15

T HE MASSIVE STUMP rose jagged-edged out of an emerald pool,
sharp-pointed shafts of splintered wood thrusting upward toward
the sky. The near face of the stump—smooth girdled, covered in
a thin layer of green moss dotted with blue flowers—was crowned by three
uneven steps: increments of gray-weathered wood cut by the blade of a
sharp-edged axe. Roots thick as elephant legs fanned outward from the base
of the stump, bending to the pool in sculpted contours, intertwining near
the surface to form bulbous, gnarled knots. Vines, wispy and delicate, laced
with ghostly white tubular flowers, hung as a backdrop to the aged stump.
Around the edges of the glass-smooth water, blooms of purple flowers—
centers hued in varying shades of yellow and red—swayed atop graceful,
wispy stems, attendants to clusters of pink, star-shaped water lilies massed
where roots and water met, petals aglow within ribbons of soft moonlight.

"*Etsgenet*," he whispered. "*Mekdes*."

At the saying of the words "heaven" and "holy place," John Too heard
the sound of water flowing over rocks. Yet, as he searched for a waterfall,
he could not find one or detect any movement upon the smooth surface of
the flower-ringed pool. Songs of birds suddenly became apparent, soothing and melodic, their voices keeping time with the swaying purple blos-
soms. A light—like the flame of a candle cupped between the palms of
interlocking hands—began to glow in the water beneath the stump—a filtered yellow-orange aura encased in emerald. Above him, from some hidden place amongst thick-leaved branches, the deep *gwok-gwonk-gwokwokwok* of a night-hunting owl sounded. Turning his attention skyward, John

Too searched for the bird, but instead found himself captivated by glittering specks of gold floating within beams of pale white moonlight.

A rush of air against the back of his neck and the sound of feathered wings drew his eyes back to earth. To his delight, he looked upon a single ibis—white feathered, black highlights on tail and wings—as it came to rest on the lip of the stump. Spindly, stork-like legs performed a graceful dance of balance as the bird folded its wings against its long, slender body. John Too bowed his head in deference and whispered, "*senay*"—"gift from above"—while placing his hands in front of his chest as though in prayer. At the second sounding of the owl's call, John Too lifted his face, his eyes widening as specks of floating gold fell in a mist atop the ibis. Each glittering droplet adhered to the next, the bird soon covered in a translucent cloak of color, as though a veil of sunlight had been laid upon its shoulders.

"He said you would come."

John Too stared at the ibis, thinking the bird had spoken. Closing his eyes, he tried to remember where he had heard the voice before. A woman's—old but youthful, harsh yet compassionate, welcoming or brusque, depending on the way you interpreted her words. And though he was certain he knew the voice—timbre, tone, and inflection—he could not place it. It bothered him that he did not understand why.

"And now you are here."

John Too opened his eyes. The gold-shrouded ibis was no longer perched atop the stump. Instantly, he felt a great emptiness, as though he had lost something cherished, something he would lament forever. With fading hope, he searched for the bird, looking right and left, skyward and then to the water. But nowhere was the ibis to be found.

A third time, the night-hunting owl hooted: *gwok-gwonk-gwokwokwok*. John Too stared up into the trees, suddenly overcome with the feeling he needed to see the bird.

"What is it you are looking for?"

John Too snapped his attention back to the tree stump, certain the ibis had returned. For the voice speaking was the same voice he'd heard before. To his dismay, the bird wasn't there.

"He didn't tell me you were mute."

John Too noticed her then—a hooded figure bent near the ground. A bony hand extended from the sleeve, fingers pulling at something between stems of flowers.

"I am John Too."

"So you say."

He watched as she pulled some type of flora from the earth and put it in the folds of her robe. He could see strands of hair—white or blonde, he couldn't tell—peeking out from the edges of her hood as she bent closer to the ground.

"How is it you are here?" he asked. "Did you see the ibis?"

"Ibis?"

"A bird—large and white. It was there on the stump," he told her, pointing.

"Ah—you are looking for a bird, then?"

"Yes."

"There are many," she replied with a wave of her hand. "Choose any. They are all equally beautiful."

"But the ibis"—he hesitated, fumbling for the right words to say—"seemed special."

"Special?" she questioned. "How so?"

"The gold—a cloak of gold upon its shoulders."

"Gold," the woman repeated, shaking her head, cupping the bloom of a purple flower with her hand. "So it is treasure you seek."

"No," John Too was quick to say, taking a step toward the woman. "No—it's just that the bird seemed to carry some meaning."

"Meaning?"

"Because of the gold that came to rest upon its shoulders."

"Probably just the sun," she dismissively replied. "Even so—why equate color to meaning?"

John Too saw her turn her head his way. But when he bent to try to get a look at her face, she shifted her attention to the vines adorned with white, tubular flowers.

"What would be more meaningful to you, then?" she asked, raising and twisting her open hand. "Here or anywhere—what color holds more importance?"

John Too parted his lips as though the answer to the woman's question was on the tip of his tongue, but then found he had nothing to say, the thought of one color being better than another suddenly seeming quite strange and altogether wrong. *Even if I say I am partial to the browns of an animal's fur, or the soil, or of Sister Lady's eyes, why does my preference hold more meaning than the greens of the forests, the blues of the waters and sky, the gold of the sun, the radiant sapphire of the stars?*

"I misspoke," he admitted. "It was not the color of the ibis's cloak. It was a feeling the bird relayed. No," he told her, shaking his head. "It was something I felt when I saw the ibis, a sense that the bird was—special— like I said before."

While he waited for her to respond, he saw the glowing light in the water beneath the stump begin to move, drifting toward the front of the pool.

"Some believe they are sacred," he added when she seemed not interested in talking.

"Sacred?" she scoffed. "Sacred to whom?"

So quick did the woman arise from her crouched position to stand that John Too took a step back.

"Do the other birds think this?" she pressed, her voice raised, back turned toward him, arms lifted, hands opened to the branches above. "Or the animals? Or the sky?" she asked, incredulous, her voice crackling like a current of static electricity. "Sacred," she said in a way that caused John Too to feel a pang of deep despair. "Too many gods, so much confusion. Kill an animal and call it sacrifice."

He saw her look to the ground, her arms disappearing into the sleeves of her robe as she lowered them to her side. It took him a moment to realize her skin was different shades of browns, ringed in even proportions, growing lighter from hand to elbow.

"How is it—?"

"I don't know why he made you," she sighed, her voice tinged with confusion. "Or why he makes the boy bother with the lot of you."

"The boy?" John Too took a few steps toward the woman. "You know the boy?"

"The girl calls you Abdar," she responded, reaching for one of the white tubular flowers. "Are you?"

John Too watched the flower the woman touched emit a soft light, as though a dollop of moonbeam had been placed within its petals.

"I am not abdar," he said in a quiet voice.

The flower lost its glow as the woman took her hand away. John Too watched her shoulders slump.

"Abdar is just a word," he offered.

He shifted his gaze from the woman to the pool of water, curious as to why the light beneath the surface was now moving in a zigzag pattern.

"What—or who—are you, then?" the woman asked.

"I am John Too."

"That is just a name," she told him, carefully stepping between the purple flowers to stand by the edge of the pool. "*Who* is John Too?"

John Too pursed his lips while adjusting the straps of his bow and the satchel of arrows on his shoulders. Wearing a shamma of earth-colored brown with a pattern of violet and green diamonds interwoven through the fabric, he furrowed his brow, taking stock of himself.

"He is—"

He shook his head.

"I am—I was an orphan," he offered. "But now I have—"

"I did not ask you what you were or what you have," she interrupted, kneeling to the side of the pool. "When you were shot in the hand, sharing the same wound as the boy, how was it that it came to heal?"

"How did you know I was shot?" he asked. "You were not there."

"Wasn't I?"

"But I—"

"Didn't you?"

He watched her dip her hand into the emerald water, not at all surprised when the yellow-orange light beneath the surface immediately moved to it.

"Your hand," she repeated, her voice reaching him as a whisper, "tell me how it healed."

"There was a surge—a feeling," he began, his eyes focusing on the glowing light. "I felt a link to a power. Sun and moon—the colors—I could see them. Like wings of birds intertwined, looping and swirling, alighting on my shoulder before sliding down my arm to my bleeding hand."

"You could see this?" she inquired as she rose to stand.

"Yes."

"Was that unusual for you—to see this *power*, as you call it?"

"No," he replied. "I have seen the same colors when I have spoken with the boy. And other things," he added, somewhat disappointed when he saw the light in the water recede. "People, places—sometimes what has not yet taken place—sometimes what I wish I—"

"You feel what is happening, yes? Heartbreaking sometimes."

"That is why the ibis—"

"Ah—now I understand," she confided in the same instant a gust of wind rustled the leaves of the trees, sending ripples across the surface of the pool. "Gold and white, yes; this is what you saw."

He said nothing in response, content to watch her move closer to the stump, one slender, bony hand extended as though she intended to touch it.

"What is it you see now?"

Before he could ask her what she meant, the woman leaned over and placed her hand against the stump. John Too edged backward as he tried to fathom the tree now towering over him. But a moment later the tree disintegrated, the image bludgeoned by an enormous steel ball, its trunk plucked from the ground by a metal arm. In the trunk's place, a vast forest appeared, trees as tall as mountains spread out before him as far as he could see. But in the next instant, the woodland began to disappear, one tree at a time cut down by faceless men with loud, smoke-spewing saws, sheared of branches before being loaded onto long, double-hitched, flat-bedded trucks. Miles of sky-scraping timber laid to waste, the forest turned into a barren landscape, jagged-edged lightning shooting down from black, swift-moving clouds, tree stumps exploding, catching fire. The remnants of the forest set to flame, a haze of churning gray smoke obscuring the sky.

When the smoke cleared, John Too found himself standing on top of a ridge; below, a tranquil blue river weaved through a plain of golden savanna. Elephants, a herd of fifty or more, moved toward the water, great bulls—tusks glinting in the late-day sun—both leading the way and protecting the weak and young lagging behind. Ominous, the grinding *thump-thump-thump-thump* of helicopter blades slicing through air assailed his ears, two flying machines swooping in over the elephants from opposite sides. Gunshots erupted, a massive bull at the head of the herd crumpling to the ground, its agonizing cry of pain and rage echoing over the plain. An army—staggered rows of uniformed men, dark brown faces grim and hostile—rose from the cover of the savanna grass to ensnare the fear-stricken herd from behind. Rifles raised and ready to fire as the helicopters worked in tandem to turn the elephants back toward them. And then John Too saw him—Teimbaka—alone, armed with a rifle, a spear, and bow, running out of the water, firing round after round at the hovering helicopters. Bullets from his gun struck one pilot in the head; the flying machine spun out of control before crashing on the far side of the river. Two jeeps—long-barreled weapons mounted to their frames—raced out of the grass, Teimbaka turning at their approach, taking aim and firing several rounds into the windscreen of the closer.

John Too was overcome with panic when Teimbaka's rifle seemed to run out of ammunition; tears began to well in his eyes. The mounted guns on the two jeeps rained a barrage of bullets upon Teimbaka as he tried to reload. His flesh ripped apart by heavy-caliber ammunition, his bones shattered, the soil turning crimson with his blood. John Too sank to his knees as Teimbaka's shredded body fell lifelessly to the ground. The jeeps swerved toward the elephants, their large guns turned upon the animals. Gunfire boomed. Elephants fell. John Too burst into tears.

"Teimbaka!" he screamed.

Filled with rage, John Too pulled his bow from his shoulder, nocked a feathered shaft to string, and let the metal-headed arrow fly. An instant later, he saw the arrow embedded in the wood of a tree stump, the *gwok-gwonk-gwokwokwok* of the owl sounding for a fourth time. Drawn to the call, he looked to the trees once more, confused when he saw but one lone tree, branches withered and stark, save for an eagle-sized owl staring intently down upon him. Seeing its perch discovered, the owl unfurled its wings and took flight.

Behind him, in the direction where he had left Eden and Sister Lady in search of firewood, he heard a woman scream. Glancing back to the tree stump, he saw the hooded old woman was no longer there, nor the pool of emerald water with glowing light beneath its surface, nor flowers or vines or flecks of gold floating within moonbeams. Only an old tree trunk in a barren spot in a break in the grass did he see, and an arrow he had loosed in vain lodged within weathered, fire-ravaged wood. The image reinforced the feeling he had lost something cherished—something he would lament for the rest of his days. With the silhouette of the owl circling above, John Too sprinted back to where he had left Eden and Sister Lady.

* * *

Claire sat up with a start, her body trembling. Breathing shallow and rapid, she sought the flames of the fire she and Eden had built, a moment of panic shooting through her when she found nothing but a few red sparks smoldering amongst the charred remnants of wood. When something grabbed her shoulder, she screamed and rolled away.

"Tabib," came a familiar voice. "What is it? Why are you afraid?"

"Eden," Claire gushed, arching her body back so she could look into the girl's face. "Eden," she said leaning forward, taking the girl into her arms and squeezing her tight.

"What did you see in your sleep, Tabib? You're shaking."

"Sleep," Claire muttered. "A dream. It was just a dream," she said, sighing and releasing some of the tension in her grasp. "Thank God."

"John Too has not returned," Eden said, gently pushing away from Claire. "Should I look for him?"

"No," Claire quickly replied, her hands sliding down Eden's arms. Grasping Eden's hands, she stammered, "I— I— The darkness—you'll get lost."

An odd, haunting call sounded in the distance. Claire stared into the night's shadowy landscape. Clouds—high above, gray-white with silver edges—moved swiftly across the face of a three-quarter moon.

"An owl," Eden offered. "Perhaps carrying a message to you."

"A message?" Claire questioned, confused.

"Or does it wait to hear what you wish to say?"

"What I wish to say."

Claire furrowed her brow as she recalled the question posed to her moments before, the memory murky and fleeting. But the more she concentrated, the clearer the dream became.

*

"Must I repeat the question? Or shall I give the order to fire?"

"They're children!"

She looked down at the boys' expressionless faces, wondering what they must be feeling. She recognized some, Thomas amongst them, pretending not to be afraid. But knowing him the way she did, she knew he was terrified. Yet, he stared at the ground like the other seven boys on either side of him, seemingly resigned to his fate. Trying to meet his death, she thought, with what dignity a boy of eight or nine could muster.

"What do you wish to say?" the voice asked again, its tone harsh, as if the man who was speaking was impatient and in a hurry.

Claire tried to turn her head to see who the man was, but found she couldn't move. As though some silent command had been given, she saw a dozen faceless soldiers appear behind the boys, rifles pointed at their heads.

"Please don't do this," she begged. "They're children. You must set them free."

"Free?" the voice bellowed. "That is why they will be shot! Because you tried to set them free!"

"But they're children!" she cried.

Mocking laughter echoed inside her head.

"They are slaves," the voice calmly explained. "Bought and paid for. Deserters now. Their punishment—death."

"But I—"

"Sentenced to die because of you."

"No!" she wailed. "No!"

Laughter erupted once more. But the sound of it was different than the laughter she had heard before, closer to crazed howling. Still unable to turn her head, she found she was able to spin her body around, finding John and four hyenas standing behind her. Injured—half of John's face bludgeoned, the hyenas barely able to stand, their legs disjointed, bodies covered with bloody wounds—the animals paced back and forth, cackling, sneering muzzles matching their taunting tone. As Claire extended a hand in an effort to reach John, the hyenas sprang forward, snapping and snarling, lips curled, teeth bared. Claire pulled her hand back, looking to John for help. But John did nothing, neither speaking nor moving. Passively watching all that was occurring as the distance between he and Claire widened.

"John!" she called out. "Help me!"

But John receded, disappearing into nothing as she watched. The hyenas howled, moving toward her. Claire backed away, holding her arms out in front of her to ward off an attack.

"You should never have left."

"Father?"

Claire's father, dressed in full foxhunting attire, top hat perched at an angle in the crook of his arm, stood where John had been but a moment before. Claire gazed into his pale gray eyes, a feeling of sadness coming over her when she saw them filled with regret. An instant later, the hyenas turned on him, her father offering no resistance, silently staring at her while the beasts pulled him to the ground and dragged him away.

"Father!" she screamed.

She tried to follow, tried to run after the hyenas to free her father from their jaws, but she couldn't move one of her legs. Looking down, she saw her ankle shackled by a thick, rust-colored chain fastened to a large silver cross, hilt buried halfway in the ground.

"So be it."

Jolted by the voice, Claire looked up to find Bacha Alba's yellow eyes peering over the top of a black scarf, his gaze shifting to the faceless soldiers standing at attention behind the kneeling boys. As Claire looked on, he raised his arm as though issuing the command to fire.

"Wait!" she screamed. "There must be another way!"

"There is a way," a child's voice meekly offered. "Sacrifice yourself."

Looking down at the line of kneeling boys, Claire found Thomas staring up at her, his face sad and gaunt, his eyes tired, without hope.

"Excellent idea!" Bacha Alba exclaimed.

With a clap of his hands, the faceless soldiers handed the rifles to the boys. Rising to their feet, the boys took aim at Claire.

"They will make fine soldiers, don't you agree?"

Bacha Alba pulled the scarf away from his face and smiled.

"Anything you wish to say? Before you die?"

Claire tried to answer, but found her mouth wouldn't open. Frantic, she looked at Thomas, hoping he would see the terror in her eyes, praying he would understand she was unable to speak. But at the sound of clapping hands, Thomas, along with the other children, raised their rifles to their shoulders and pulled the triggers. Bullets exploded from the barrels in a rush of smoke, Claire watching the projectiles speeding toward her in a paralyzed stupor. *So this is how it will end*, a hollow voice inside her thoughts whispered. But then something curious occurred. A hand appeared in front of her face, blocking the bullets from reaching her. A voice spoke into her ear.

*

"Are you sick?"

Eden's face slowly came into focus, her expression questioning, confused.

"What is happening to you?

"Eden." Claire blinked her eyes. "How did you get here?"

"How did I? Ugh," Eden growled. "Where is Abdar? You are losing your mind."

The haunting call they had heard moments before sounded once again, the distinct, *gwok-gwonk-gwokwokwok* sharp and clear. Eden looked up and saw the dark form of a large bird circling overhead, broad wings passing intermittingly through bands of silvery moonlight and shadow cast by swift-moving clouds.

"An eagle-owl," Eden said, her voice tinged with awe. "My mother said they are the messengers between here and the spirits."

"An eerie-looking creature," Claire muttered.

"That is a strange thing to say," Eden sarcastically responded. "*Tabib.*"

"Stop calling me that. You know I don't—"

"Sister Lady!" a boy's voice called out.

Claire reacted with a start, pushing her body across the ground as the sound of feet trampling dry grass drew near.

"I heard a scream," John Too said, panting, his eyes darting from side to side. "What was it?" he asked, surveying the area around them as he tried to catch his breath.

"A dream," Eden told him.

"A dream?"

Eden shrugged her shoulders, nodding to Claire.

"It has left you now, your dream?" he asked Claire, his voice filled with concern. "For we must go."

Claire studied John Too's face, not understanding the urgency in his voice.

"Nonsense," she told him. "It's dark. And where is the wood for the fire? Where have you been all this time?"

The eagle-owl cried out once more, the call so near and loud Claire covered her head with her arms.

"Please, Sister Lady," John Too implored. "We must go before—"

"Before? Before what?" she asked.

He said nothing at first, Claire noticing wrinkles forming upon his brow as he followed the flight of the owl. She was about to ask him again—ask him why they needed to leave and where it was they would be heading—when she saw his shoulders slump.

"Teimbaka," he sighed.

"Why do you say his name?" Claire asked, rising to stand. "Is something wrong?" she probed, placing her hand upon his shoulder. "Is he hurt?"

Claire grasped John Too by his arms and looked straight into his face.

"What is it you've seen?"

John Too lowered his gaze to the ground as a dense formation of clouds passed across the moon. The sudden darkness left Claire to wonder what emotion she thought she had seen in his eyes. In the interlude of silence while she waited for him to reply, she heard the rush of feathered wings. Briefly turning her attention upward, she was both relieved and puzzled to see the eagle-owl flying off. As she wondered where the bird was heading and why it had been circling overhead, she heard a sound that pulled at her heart.

"I saw him die," John Too whimpered.

The words entered Claire's consciousness as parasites, innocuous at first, seemingly innocent and of no consequence. But the longer they were left to explore the crevices of her thoughts, the more damage they caused, until their bloated, grotesque forms became screeching aberrations anchored inside her head. In a dizzying moment of crushing disbelief, she dropped to her knees, a choking breath caught in her throat.

"Where?" Eden pointedly asked, moving swiftly to Claire's side. "Breathe, Tabib," she sternly instructed, pulling Claire's hands away from her throat. "Where did you see him die?" she pressed John Too, giving him an angry glance.

"I don't know where," he answered, his tone bewildered, his gaze fixed upon Claire. "Just that he—"

"Ugh! Why say it, then? Look at her," Eden snapped. "Does she need to hear this?" she admonished. "She is already half-mad this night."

"John," Claire dazedly muttered. "And now Teimbaka."

"John? Why do you say *his* name?" Eden demanded, poking Claire's shoulder. "Why?"

Deep within the clutches of her daze, Claire slowly moved her head from side to side, trying to focus.

"I didn't want to tell you," she began.

Shifting her eyes from Eden to John Too, she continued.

"At the ravine—I—I saw him fall." Her face awash with grief, her voice cracking, she told them, "Dead—he's dead."

"No!"

Eden's scream was earsplitting. Her shrill voice shattered the calm of the night, awakening sleeping birds and beasts who answered with roars, hoots, and cries as equally unnerving. Claire fell onto her side, John Too bending to her, one hand grasping her arm.

"You are wrong!" Eden shouted.

Startled by the anger she saw in the girl's face, Claire extended a hand to offer a comforting touch, but Eden slapped it away, folding her arms in a huff.

"Did you watch him fall against the rocks and split his head open?" Eden took an abrupt step to the side, but then stepped back. "And you!" she yelled at John Too. "Are you telling us about a vision? One that's already happened?"

Claire thrust her arm out to block Eden's path as the girl stepped toward John Too with a look of fury on her face.

"Or was it one that is yet to come?" she assailed. "One placed inside your head by Zār to make you weak?"

"Eden—stop," Claire pleaded. "Don't make this any harder than it is."

"He is bouda!" she defiantly screamed. "He is not dead!"

Again, Eden's scream pierced the night, the animals—even the flora—of the savanna reacting with startled uneasiness; cries of alarm sounded over rustling grasses bent sideways in a rush of wind. Claire stared up at the girl, not knowing what to say.

The silver-gray night suddenly became an eerie orange, the faces of Claire, Eden, and John Too cast into masks of artificial light and shadow, the bursting flare captured in their eyes. Claire immediately felt the past rushing up through her as she turned her face toward the shower of exploding light.

"Gunstard," she mouthed, the memory of the night the butcher had come with flares, mercenaries, and mortars overwhelming. As she tried to block out what had happened to her afterward—after the flares had long been extinguished, after the children had been slaughtered—she began to violently shake. For the memory of addiction and forced prostitution cut through what little of her she had been able to reclaim since the night Gunstard had attacked the camp. The feelings of being captured, imprisoned, the helplessness, the defilement, pushed her to the precipice of an uncontrolled panic.

"Gunstard!" she screamed, her hands frantically clutching the fabric of John Too's shamma.

"No," John Too forcefully told her, grabbing her wrists. "He is dead, remember? He can't harm you anymore."

"But what he—what he was," Claire stammered, trembling. "It's still there," she told him, pulling at his sleeves, her eyes wide with fear. "I've—"

"What is wrong with you?" Eden screamed, bending forward to look at both Claire and John Too. "Get up, Tabib! Pull her, Abdar! We must run—now!"

With John Too using what strength he possessed, and with a swift kick from Eden to Claire's rump, Claire struggled to her feet as another flare rose into the night sky.

"It looks to be less than a kilometer away," John Too offered. "Do you think they know we are here?"

"It's Alba," Eden hissed. "*Ebob caca*," she spit. "He must have heard me yelling at the two of you," she said, offering a look daring them to speak.

"It's useless," Claire whined. "Useless to—"

"Ugh. Tabib! Why are you so stupid?" Eden scolded, her face glowing a freakish orange as a second flare exploded. "How did the bouda come to give you something so special?" she asked, shaking her head.

Lifting Claire's right wrist, she looked at the bracelet of pulsing green beetles.

"Would they be glowing if all was useless?"

Heaving a sigh, Eden let go of Claire's wrist, taking another look at the sky.

"Tabibs, abdars," she dismissively muttered.

Raising her eyebrows, smoothing the wrinkles of her purple robes, she looked at John Too and said, "Bring her. We go."

"Go?" Claire numbly repeated. "Go where?"

"The way of the owl," Eden replied. "South."

* * *

Dawn found Eden a good twenty paces ahead of Claire and John Too, every so often stopping to look over her shoulder to make sure the two were behind her. For the terrain of shoulder-high grass they had traversed during the night had changed, transformed to a mixture of shrubs, stunted thorn trees, and thick clumps of grasses with narrow openings of gravelly soil interspersed. Their escape became a twisting ordeal of finding a clear path southward, Eden forced to turn east or west at times before locating a break in the vegetation allowing her to move south again. So stopping every so often to make certain the abdar and the tabib were still behind her had become as necessary as paying attention to the changing maze of the landscape.

They—herself, Tabib, Abdar—were in a precarious position, she knew; the way forward an uncertainty with a possible morbid, depressing ending, if what John Too had said about the man they were searching for was true. The way back, a certainty holding the promise of imprisonment and death—death, at least for the boy and her. The tabib? Her fate was entirely different than theirs. Eden didn't know what would happen to Sister Lady, as John Too continued to call her, if they were to be captured by Bacha Alba and his men. No, she couldn't fathom what would happen to the tabib if they were caught. But she knew the woman wouldn't survive. That much she was certain of.

Tabib was on the edge of a nervous breakdown. That's how Eden saw it. But she didn't understand why. The woman had so much to be thankful for—yet, she seemed incapable of appreciating what she had been given. An abdar and a bouda as devoted friends, ones who would risk their lives to save her—did she not realize this was not normal? Oh sure, she thought, people always said, "I would give my life for you." But in reality—and she knew this from her own experiences—most people would never sacrifice themselves if the opportunity presented itself. Which in this land, occurred almost daily. Eden had seen mothers and fathers sell their children into slavery for a steaming plate of stew and bread. And she had witnessed men stand off to the side while their screaming and pleading wives were taken away by soldiers to be used for sex, then go about their business as though nothing out of the ordinary had happened. Even her own father had left her and her mother to go fight in some endless civil war in another country, leaving them to fend for themselves; and look how that had turned out. And the bracelet—how could the tabib not treasure a bracelet made out of sacred beetles? Did she not understand when the beetles pulsed that a power greater than what any of them could fathom was at work? *Oh Tabib,* she mused, *you are blinder than a man with no eyes.*

Eden studied the terrain in front of her as she waited for John Too and Claire to catch up. Although dawn had arrived less than an hour before, the sun was already hot, the sky a cloudless expanse of the palest blue. The day was going to be unforgiving, Eden observed. They would be hard pressed to travel very far, especially if the tabib was going to have a nervous breakdown. If that were to occur, she figured the warlord and his men would indeed catch up to them and take them prisoner. And that would be the end of her—of that she was also certain. *They will slit my throat and watch me bleed out into the dirt. Ebob caca! I will not let that happen.*

"Eden."

Awakened from her thoughts by the sound of John Too's voice, Eden saw the boy waving to her, the tabib leaning on his shoulder, her steps slow, uneven.

"Sister Lady—she needs water."

Eden raised her arms away from her sides, turning her palms skyward. Shrugging her shoulders, she sarcastically asked, "And food, I suppose?"

John Too stopped several paces from Eden, his face scrunching into a scowl.

Just as it seemed he was going to respond, the dull pop of distant gunfire erupted in the direction from where they'd traveled. She and John Too exchanged hurried glances. Without a word spoken between them, they moved southward, Eden almost breaking into a run as she led the way forward.

* * *

Three hours later, Eden was in a full sweat, the fabric of her purple robe clinging to her body, beads of perspiration rolling down the sides of her face. The sun was unrelenting—as she had foreseen. Shade—what little there was—found in small pockets beneath low-hanging branches of thorn trees, the lowest of which were so near the ground one would need to flatten themselves onto their stomach or back to slide into it. Not so troublesome if one were a rabbit or a jackal or a child, Eden mused. A little more difficult, however, if you were a full-grown woman with a flowing knee-length skirt, as the tabib was. Even if the woman could lie as flat as a round of injera and wriggle into a patch of shade without the thorns of the tree shredding her skin, Eden didn't think the tabib would have the strength to get back up. Even now—as Eden turned yet another time to check on the tabib's and John Too's whereabouts—she could see the woman waning. Her face pasty-white, yet flushed fiery red, her lips dry and cracked, her movements unsteady, as though her limbs were encased in mud. No, Eden didn't think the woman would last another hour without water or rest. And the prospects of either one of those occurring didn't seem likely. For there had been no signs of water—no congregating birds or larger animals heading in a like direction. And the ever-present dust devils she had noticed following them—off in the distance but gaining ground—gave her little reason to believe they would be able to stop anytime soon to find something to quench their thirst. *No,* she thought, *this is going to end badly. This time I'm sure of it.*

"Keep moving!" she implored them.

But she didn't know why she even bothered wasting the energy to shout. The tabib was going to drop to the ground anytime now—she could feel it. And she and John Too wouldn't be able to get her back up. *Ebob caca,* she cursed. *Why did I ever come with them?* Weighted by her own misgivings, she hung her head. Her eyes drifted to the soil, certain it would soon be stained the color of her blood.

Startled by the presence of a large savanna hare sitting on the ground in front of her, Eden stiffened and shuffled to the side. As if mimicking her movement, the hare hopped with her, rising up on its hind legs. In a blur, the animal darted forward, Eden feeling the pull of its nails on her robe as a paw swiped at her leg. Somewhat confused, she watched the animal scamper back several paces before stopping, where it rose up on its haunches once again. Ears erect, nose twitching from side to side as it sniffed the air, the animal gazed into Eden's eyes. Eden felt herself drifting forward, drawn in by the creature's gaze, wondering if she wasn't going mad when she saw a stream of yellow sparks flowing from the center of the creature's emerald eyes.

"What are you?" she whispered.

To her dismay—her voice seemingly having startled the hare—the animal dropped to the ground, hopping several paces farther away before glancing back over its shoulder.

"I'm sorry," she hurried to say, taking a few steps to follow. "I won't talk anymore," she offered, extending a hand.

But the animal scurried away, darting into an opening between two thorn trees. Eden started to rush forward to catch up to it when John Too yelled, "Wait!"

Reluctantly, she stopped and turned to face him.

Thunder, Eden thought, thunder propelled by a roaring wind funneled between two mountains. John Too cowered low to the ground, eyes wide, pulling Sister Lady to him as though protecting her from being struck in the head. Eden had seen a missile once before, streaking across the sky, traveling in a shallow arc, a wide plume of white vapor trailing behind. She remembered the occasion very well, having witnessed the missile being launched from a position on a ridge held by government forces, the weapon aimed at the village she and her mother had just fled. The violent shudder of the ground upon impact, the deafening roar of the explosion, the burst of flames, the cloud of black foul-smelling smoke rising into the sky—she remembered it all. A chilling display of the government's power, she had thought at the time. As were the stories of the soldiers' viciousness following the missile strike, when what few survivors from the brutal attack on the village had wandered into a makeshift camp where she and her mother had taken refuge and told of the slaughter of innocent women and children. But Eden didn't want to think about those stories at the moment, didn't want to lose herself in memories with no bearing on the present. Because the missile she was looking at now, the one streaking through the sky over her head, was dipping toward the earth, heading straight for the columns of dust trailing them since dawn.

The explosion came as a sudden flash of light, followed by a staccato rumble, the billowing dense cloud of gray-black smoke rising skyward accompanied by a slight trembling of the earth. An instant later, she found herself lying face first on the ground, spitting particles of soil from her mouth.

"What are you doing?" she hissed when she realized John Too had jerked her down by the front of her robes.

She noticed a glimmer of sunlight shimmering within the outer rings of his irises as he motioned for her to stay quiet by placing a finger to his lips.

"What's so funny?" she snapped, angry he was smiling.

Even as she watched his eyes shift away from her to gaze off to the side, she saw the tawny-colored shape of the savanna hare move into her sphere of vision. The animal was no more than a few inches away, statue-like, eyes fixed upon an object near John Too's feet. Following the animal's stare, Eden realized the hare was studying Claire.

The tabib seemed to be unconscious, Eden observed, her body motionless as she lay on the ground, her pallid face pointed skyward, glassy-eyed, staring straight into the sun. Was the tabib dead? she suddenly wondered. With a shake of her head, she closed her eyes. She didn't want to know—if Tabib was dead. For it would mean they had traveled all this way for nothing. Squeezing her eyelids tighter together, she held her breath, entertaining the fanciful notion that she was in the middle of some intricately constructed dream.

When she felt the sensation of moisture sliding down her cheek, she silently admonished herself, thinking the moisture a tear, that in a moment of weakness she'd started to cry. But then she felt another drop, this one landing on the bridge of her nose. Confused, she opened her eyes, pulling her head back with a start when she found the face of the hare peering into her own from no more than an eyelash length away.

"What—?" she started to ask.

With the flick of a paw, the hare sent a few drops of water off the tip of one of its ears into Eden's face. Then, in a blur, it darted to Sister Lady, rising on its hind legs to bend over the face of the tabib, one tiny paw placed upon the woman's neck as the animal peered into her eyes.

"*Wuhu*," John Too whispered, his hand drawing a circle in front of his face.

Ignoring the boy with a dismissive glance, Eden looked back to the hare. Blinking, she turned her face sideways to assess the glistening sheen of moisture clinging to the fur around the animal's head. How could she have not noticed it before, she wondered, when the animal had been so close?

"But—"

"Shhh," he told her, placing a finger to his lips.

Eden watched the hare meticulously scrape every drop of water from its fur onto Sister Lady's face. Then it carefully bent its head to the side until the tip of an ear touched the tabib's lips, depositing droplets of water into the woman's mouth. With a final look into the face of Sister Lady, the hare dropped to all fours and darted back toward Eden and John Too. Pausing to look into their faces, the animal scurried past, jumping into an opening between two thorn trees. In the distance, Eden heard the sound of gunfire.

"Help me," John Too said. "With Sister Lady," he added when Eden looked at him with a blank expression on her face.

"To do what?"

"To find water," John Too replied, looking to the spot where the hare disappeared into the brush. "And a place to wait for darkness," he added, looking up at the sun.

Claire's eyelids fluttered as John Too slid a hand beneath her neck and raised her head off the ground. Bending to the woman from the opposite side, Eden placed her arm under the tabib's shoulder and helped lift her until she was sitting in an upright position.

"Help me get her to her feet now," John Too said.

"But where are we going?"

"Where the Mother is strong," John Too replied, nodding to the thorn trees. "We follow the hare."

16

*S*AINT MICHAEL, DEFEND *us in battle; be our defense against the wickedness and snares of the devil. May God rebuke him, we humbly pray, and do thou, O prince of the heavenly host, by the power of God, thrust into hell Satan and all the other evil spirits who prowl about the world seeking the ruin of souls. Amen.*

With a deep sigh, Sarah bowed her head and made the sign of the cross.

"And Father?" she murmured aloud. "Bless us this day—if you would."

Morning dawned blood-orange, the sun a giant ball of crimson fire cresting over the eastern horizon as though it had passed through hell on its way to ushering in the light of a new day. Clasping her hands together, Sarah watched the flaming orb with a mixture of awe and dread, the same interlaced emotions she'd felt when she saw the first flare burst upon the night sky.

*

"What's that?"

"A flare," Dirk replied, his tone nonchalant.

But then he pulled the Land Cruiser off the road, turned the lights off, and shut the engine down, raising his hand for silence when she opened her mouth to speak. They'd sat quietly for what seemed like five minutes or more. And when the second flare had shot into the sky, Sarah was certain the lines appearing around Dirk's eyes, mouth, and forehead were caused by worry, especially when they heard a burst of gunfire.

"What's happening?" she had whispered. "Are we in danger?"

She remembered how foolish she felt as soon as she asked—about being in danger—his raised eyebrows and the smirk on his lips making her feel doubly naïve. *Danger—when haven't we been in danger? He must think I'm an idiot. And he might be right. On the road to nowhere,* she reminded herself, *how perceptive of me to have realized where this was all leading from the beginning.*

*

It had been three days—or was it four? She couldn't quite remember—since they had driven north following the government tank and truckload of soldiers. The line of refugees they passed along the way endless. Even when she had talked herself into believing it wasn't possible all the people she was seeing had been displaced by civil conflict, more would appear, dragging what belongings they owned behind them, toddlers struggling to keep up. Worst of all were the babies she saw, some crying from hunger, others abnormally subdued—stricken with despair, Sarah imagined—their faces a reflection of the hopelessness they'd been born into. She would stare out the Land Cruiser window at the endless parade of downtrodden faces and wonder how there could be anyone left in the north. What was it they were all fighting about, anyway? And who were they? She didn't know, she realized, didn't have a clue about the country she had come to in search of Sister Claire.

They hadn't traveled more than a few hours that first day when Dirk pulled the Land Cruiser off to the side of the road after passing a particularly desperate looking family—or what Sarah thought to be a family—Dirk muttering something about getting information when he swung open the door after bringing the car to a stop. The family he went to talk with consisted of an elderly man wearing a red baseball cap, body bent at the waist, his crooked, protruding spine draped by a loose white T-shirt. One of his shoulders was heavily bandaged, the wrapping stained with blood. A silver-haired woman wearing a rainbow-colored dress walked behind the man, the stick she used to help her find her way tapping the ground in front of her. Her face tilted skyward, her eyes fixed upon an object in the sky Sarah couldn't find when she followed the woman's unfocused gaze. Two little girls followed the woman. Twins, Sarah thought, no older than four or five, clothed in bulky burlap tunics, their legs disfigured with raw swaths of pink-red skin dotted with clusters of yellow blisters.

Reluctantly, she'd slid out the passenger side of the Land Cruiser. She'd been intrigued when she heard Dirk speaking what she supposed was the family's native language, and somewhat touched when she saw Dirk slip money into the elderly man's trembling hand. She remembered Dirk's voice being soothing and calm as he spoke; she'd been curious as to what he and the man were speaking about when the man looked over at her and seemed to study every piece of clothing she was wearing. When his eyes came to rest upon her silver cross, the old man gave Dirk an assuring nod. Dirk smiled in return. Then the man pulled at Dirk's arm, pointing to the legs of the two little girls. Sarah remembered tears welling in her eyes when she saw the man begin to cry. Deeply moved when she watched his hardened, time-worn features transformed into a quivering mix of pleading sadness.

"Get back in the car," Dirk abruptly snapped, pushing away from the pleading man and heading toward the Land Cruiser.

"But what about—?"

"Do as I tell you," he had gruffly told her, grasping her arm and turning her around. "Go."

No sooner had Sarah gotten into the passenger side of the vehicle than the Land Cruiser lurched forward. Before she could even get her side door fully closed, Dirk executed a sharp, 180-degree turn, then proceeded to head back in the direction they had just come from.

"What was that all about?" she asked several times after he had turned the car around. "Why was the man crying? What did he want?"

Dirk had sat stone-faced, unwilling to answer her or meet her eyes, his attention fixed upon the highway or checking the rearview mirror. Doing anything he could think of, so it seemed to her, to keep from having to deal with her persistent questions. It wasn't until an hour or so later, when he saw a sign bearing the name Gashena and took a right turn, that he gave her the courtesy of a reply.

"He wanted medicine—whatever we could spare—for the girls' burns."

"Do you have some?" she had carefully asked, not understanding why he had put off answering.

"In the med kit. In one of the duffels in the back seat," he replied matter-of-factly. "You learn to pack anything you might need when you travel into the bush."

She remembered her face feeling flush as she turned in her seat to face him.

"By the love of God, why didn't you give it to him?" Her anger still lingered—even now, three days later, as she thought about the exchange. She had been incensed when she blurted, "What in the world is wrong with you? Did you see those girls' legs? They must be in misery!"

"Wish you were somewhere else?" he had coldly responded. "Somewhere where Italian marble makes a fine backdrop for the prayers spoken on behalf of the poor and downtrodden?"

"Oh my God," she had uttered in disbelief. "Oh my God. You're a— You're—"

"Brilliant? Intuitive?" he'd said, chuckling.

"A monster!" she shouted. "How in good conscience could you—?"

"We would have never gotten out of there."

"What?" she had asked, incredulous, mouth agape. "What kind of lame excuse is that? Those people needed help!" she'd screamed.

He had given her a look then, turning his face toward her—to gauge her anger? Or was he trying to judge the sincerity of her emotions? She couldn't tell. But the momentary interlude seemed to take the smugness out of his tone.

"Everyone you see walking along the side of the road needs help. When you get to a city—if we ever get to a city again—every beggar, street urchin, orphan, petty thief you'll run across needs help."

He had paused then. Sarah thought, perhaps, he was revisiting some memory, because when he spoke again, there was sadness to his tone.

"And if you dare to visit a hospital or a relief camp or a place where the do-gooders have set up shop to try and cure the plague that's beset this corner of the world, you'll understand that once you have medicine to offer— or food, or water, or shelter—you'll never have enough. Because the ones you say *need help* will devour all you can give them, all that you are—until there's nothing left of you. And in the end—"

She watched his face as he struggled for what to say next; his eyes blinked a few times, his lips trembled before tightening to a thin line, a hand ran up and over his forehead through his hair as though he was pushing what memory he had recalled back into the recesses of his thoughts.

"They'll take that too."

He'd sounded—*defeated*. Was that the word to describe what she was hearing? she had thought at the time. But his words—whatever feelings he might have been conveying in his tone—had stayed with her, made her think. She was on a road to oblivion—she had known that for a while now. But what he was saying was that, even on the road to nowhere, everyone she was going to run across needed help, everyone—it seemed—in danger. And now here they were, four days—or was it three?—from the start of their journey and the quest to find this elusive Sister Claire had already taken them hundreds of miles in different directions. But they were no closer to finding her than when they had left Djibouti. They had crossed deserts, forests, and mountains. Seen burned-out vehicles, tanks, truckloads of soldiers, and an endless stream of refugees. But it was only when the flares had risen into the night sky that she started to understand what he meant when he used the word *plague* to describe what was happening to this land. Evil was here—sinister and soul-killing—as it has been throughout time, she supposed, as it was everywhere. What form would Satan take today? she'd wondered.

*

Immersed in the color of the apocalyptic sun rising higher into the sky, Sarah's thoughts drifted back to the prayer she'd recited. She was hoping—sincerely hoping—Michael the Archangel was indeed watching over her, ready to do battle, ready to come to her aid if need be. Armed with the prayerful hope God would not forsake this land, she gripped the cross about her neck and closed her eyes.

"Wishing you're somewhere else again?"

"No!" she retorted, nearly hitting her head on the frame of the door at the intrusion of his voice. "I mean—" Sighing, she rubbed the back of her neck with her hand. It was already quite hot, she noted, and it was only mid-morning.

"I'm sorry," she apologized, giving him a quick glance. "I didn't mean to snap at you. I guess I—*we*—didn't get too much rest last night."

"No. No, we didn't," he agreed, placing a pair of binoculars up to his eyes for the twentieth time, she calculated.

"What are you expecting to see with those? And why have we stopped *here*?"

She looked out at the harsh landscape below the hill where Dirk had parked the Land Cruiser, wondering what he was expecting to find in the incomprehensible maze of thorn trees and inhospitable mounds of thick-stalked grasses stretched out before them.

"Are you keeping something from me that that old man said to you to make you think Sister Claire headed this way?" She glanced out the windshield. "I can't imagine why she would," she remarked. "Seeing how desolate this place is."

"Not a place you would choose to vacation in? Not picturesque enough?"

"Do you have nothing better to do, Mr. Savage?" she quipped. "Than to try to irritate me? Paint me as some sort of porcelain shut-in who's going to crack into a thousand pieces at the slightest inconvenience?"

She turned her face away from his, her eyes focusing on the columns of dust rising into the air several hundred yards away.

"You don't know me, Mr. Savage. You know nothing about me."

"This was part of a great forest once."

Reluctantly, she looked back at him, relieved when she saw him peering through the binoculars.

"And why is that of interest?" she baited.

"Just following what you were saying. Just now"—he lowered the binoculars, turning his face so he could look into her eyes—"when you spoke about me not knowing anything about you, or," he continued, nodding out the windshield at the landscape around them, "not knowing anything about a place. What it might have once been. Before—"

Dirk's eyes wandered from hers to look out past her shoulder. When he began to raise the binoculars to his face, she reached out and placed a hand atop them.

"*Before?*" she inquired, giving him a look of disdain. "Or is it too much to ask of you to complete a sentence?" she added, pressing the binoculars down toward his waist.

She could tell he didn't want to take his eyes off of whatever he was looking at. But after a few seconds of her not flinching, he relented, shifting his attention back to her with an audible sigh.

"Before us," he said. "Before the great societies of the world decided to grace this continent with their lofty presence to extract whatever they could get their filthy, greedy hands on. Like this desolate place," he went on with a dramatic nod of his head toward what lay outside. "I believe it was the Italians—but it could have been the Brits—who needed all the wood from what was a beautiful pristine forest so they could fuel their railroad engines to enlarge their empire." He motioned with his hand to what lay outside. "Empires," he scoffed. "At whose expense? Raped, gouged, burned, and enslaved for the good of king and country—or was it queen then?"

A tortured soul, Sarah thought as she listened to him talk. Reverend Mother had warned her. But she had been entertaining other thoughts about Dirk Savage when Reverend Mother had told her what she had found out about him. Impure thoughts, she reminded herself as she turned her face away from him, thoughts that would prevent her from attaining Perpetual Commitment if she allowed them to resurface. She pressed a fist into her groin.

"Do you ever wonder what it would be like?"

What did he just say? Is he asking me a question?

"When I see what we've done to Africa, I'm given to wonder what it would be like in the remotest parts of the world where man has never set foot. Where the wind hasn't had to smell our stench, the water not been fouled by our waste, the earth not—"

"In the name of God," Sarah gasped, making the sign of the cross. "What is that?"

*

Seeing the frightened look in Sarah's eyes, Dirk turned to follow her gaze.

"Holy fuck," he muttered when he saw the streaking plume of white vapor shooting low across the sky. "Who the hell is shooting off a ground-to-ground missile out here in the middle of nowhere?"

"Why are you asking me?" he heard Sarah shriek.

"Calm down!" he shouted. "I wasn't asking you," he grumbled, turning the key in the ignition.

He saw her cover her ears with her hands and shake her head.

"It sounds like a tornado!" she yelled.

Dirk watched the missile begin its descent, noting the trajectory. Impact took place in the proximity of the columns of dust he had glimpsed while talking to Sarah. And as his mind began to work out what was transpiring—the flares and gunfire from the previous night, now a missile launched from the opposite direction—the missile reached its target, the flash of the explosion so bright it forced him to bring a hand to his face to shield his eyes.

"Oh my God!" Sarah screamed.

When she pulled at his arm, he grabbed her wrist and squeezed, hoping the sensation would keep her grounded, keep her calm. But when the tremors from the explosion reached them and the sound of gunfire erupted, he pushed her arm down to her lap and reached for the steering wheel. In one fluid, frantic motion, Dirk depressed the clutch, shifted the gear stick into reverse, hit the gas pedal, and maneuvered the Land Cruiser backward in a swerving arc. Just as his left foot found the clutch again and his hand grabbed the knob on the end of the floor-mounted gear lever, the roaring staccato of an automatic weapon erupted. Bullets strafed the ground near the front of the Land Cruiser, a shower of dirt and debris splattering against the windshield.

"Shit, shit, shit!" he cursed.

Sarah's shrieking screams forced him to glance sideways just as a two heavily armed men in camouflage uniforms rose out of the underbrush some twenty yards away. Dirk tried to see if they were wearing recognizable insignias on their berets or shoulders, but Sarah launched into a fit of hysterics, screaming, "Get us out of here! Get us out of here!" while slapping at his arms. In a moment of pure reflex, Dirk depressed the clutch, shifting into first gear. Sarah's screeching wails grew to a crescendo just as another round from an automatic weapon fired at close range. Dirk cringed, looking in the direction where the sound originated to find another soldier stationed on his side of the car, little wisps of smoke escaping from the barrel of his weapon. The man—grim faced, an AK-47 pointed right at Dirk's face—jerked the rifle upward toward his chest, Dirk understanding the motion to mean he was to get out of the car. Offering the grim-faced soldier a wide smile, Dirk nodded his head and slowly took his hands off the steering wheel.

When the Land Cruiser suddenly sped forward, Dirk didn't understand what had happened until he felt something push against his shoulder and found another foot pressing on the gas pedal next to his own.

"Sarah!" he shouted, trying to elbow her away while kicking at her ankle with the edge of his boot. "What are you doing?" he yelled, looking down into the well of the floor to see how he might gain an advantage over her foot.

When he heard someone shouting, he lifted his head to see where they were heading, flinging his arms up in front of his face as the windshield exploded inward. The boom of the gunshot blast roared into his consciousness a split second later, Sarah's pain-filled scream nearly simultaneous. The car lurched to a jolting stop; his door was flung open. Strong arms wrenched him from the car, throwing him to the ground. What felt like the tip of a steel-toed boot kicked him in the side, and then kicked him again when he tried to move. Dazed, struggling to breathe, pain shooting down the side of his body, Dirk found himself jerked to his knees by the collar of his shirt.

"*Raweenee edeek! Raweenee edeek!*" an angry voice screamed.

"What are you saying? What are you saying?" Dirk hurried to say, vaguely recognizing the words as some form of Arabic. "I have a papers from—"

With a sharp groan, he grasped the fingers pulling on his ear, awkwardly staggering to his feet before the appendage could be wrenched from the side of his head.

"*Raweenee edeek!*" the same voice commanded, the barrel of a rifle thrust beneath his armpit, nudging upward.

"Raise my hands?" he rushed to say. "Is that what you're saying?"

"*Eskoot! Eskoot!*" came the response with a slap to the back of his head.

Violently pushed forward, Dirk slammed into the doorframe of the Land Cruiser. As he hung on to the lip of the cabin's roof to steady himself, his eyes just began to focus on the pool of blood near Sarah's slumped body when a sharp blow to the small of his back crumpled him to the ground, turning everything inside his head tingly white.

* * *

Dirk jerked back to consciousness with a searing pain spreading through the soft tissue just above his left hip. Reflexively, he tried to touch the area, but found his arms unable to move. Blinking his eyes into focus, he found he'd been stretched outward, his wrists and ankles tethered to metal poles with leather straps, his shirt removed.

"Good. You awaken," a male voice said.

Dirk felt intense heat on his skin just before something incredibly hot pressed into the soft flesh above his right hip. Recoiling, his body shuddering from pain, he bit down on his lower lip.

"Painful, yes?" the male voice mocked.

Dirk could smell his burnt skin as he looked at the man standing in front of him, thinking he knew who he was from the description Adiam had given him.

"Yellow-brown eyes," Adiam had told him. "I know of no one else who has such an odd-colored pair."

Dirk studied the man's irises for a moment more before focusing his attention on the steel rod clutched in his balled hand, its chalky-white tip crusted with what looked to be curled bits of flesh.

"Bacha Alba," Dirk muttered in a raspy voice, nearly choking as he tried to get the words out of his throat.

"So you know who you spy on, sending coordinates of my position," he snarled, placing the hot steel close to Dirk's lips.

"Spying?" Dirk questioned, shifting his head back and to the side.

"Who's paying you?" Bacha Alba demanded, pressing the tip of the steel rod against Dirk's neck. "Ah, no longer hot enough, I see," he remarked when the metal did not singe the skin. "A moment while it is made—suitable."

"The Consortium," Dirk offered as he watched the warlord turn and place the end of the metal rod into the flames of a fire burning on the ground several paces away.

Swallowing dryly, Dirk took a quick look around. When he saw he was in the middle of a stone-ringed area on some nondescript ridge top surrounded by a few dozen well-armed men and tied spread-eagle to metal poles, he suddenly wished he was back in Adiam's office smoking opium and lying with Talia.

"Adiam. Akmir," he croaked when Bacha Alba seemed not to have heard what he said before. "The Consortium."

He watched the warlord pull the steel rod from the fire to examine the tip. Slowly rolling the rod to and fro, Alba eyed Dirk with a sardonic grin before replacing it in the flames.

"A slight delay," he quipped. "Perhaps the feel of a blade while we wait for the metal to heat."

"Didn't you hear me?" Dirk rasped when he saw Bacha Alba extract a long, thick-bladed knife from the sheath strapped to his ankle. "I was sent—"

He began to cough, jerking on the leather straps securing his wrists, when the man walked toward him.

"The girl," he gasped, his eyes fixated on the knife in Bacha Alba's out-stretched hand. "Sister Claire."

A small line of blood appeared on the underside of Dirk's arm where the warlord skimmed the tip of the blade. Dirk entertained the notion the man was insane as he watched the first crimson drop fall toward the ground.

"I was sent to get her," Dirk struggled to say, trying to swallow. "Papers—in my boot. You told Akmir you had her."

"You lie! Akmir knows I no longer have her!" he shouted, his yellowish eyes glaring into Dirk's. "Who are you spying for? Who fired the missile?"

Dirk cringed when he felt the tip of the knife slide across his abdomen. He squinted against the reflection of the late-afternoon sun as the warlord raised the blood-stained edge of the blade up to his face. He heard some of the men nearest to him laugh.

"Water," he rasped.

"A dying man asking for water!" Alba shouted, eliciting a new round of laughter from his men.

"Water," Dirk repeated with a wheeze, suddenly feeling the effects of the burns, the cuts, the beating, and the heat. "Information."

Dirk studied the warlord's face with raised eyebrows and a slight nod, hoping the man understood the subtle physical inflections of bartering a deal. When the warlord smiled at him, however, he wasn't at all sure it was a smile he could interpret as agreeable. But when the man placed the knife back in its sheath, clapped his hands, and barked "*Wuhu!*" Dirk felt as though he gotten through to him, that he would be given water. And then, Dirk hoped, perhaps Bacha Alba would calm down a degree or two so he could explain why he and Sarah were sitting in the Land Cruiser when the missile launched.

"Sarah," he muttered, his thoughts suddenly flooded with the vision of her slumped sideways in the front seat of the car.

In one violent motion Dirk's head was yanked back, a ring of hard metal shoved into his mouth, his hair pulled so hard on the back of his head he could feel the strands separating from his scalp. Water rushed down his throat, clogging his windpipe, blocking oxygen from his lungs. Liquid spewed from his nostrils. Gulping, choking, trying to swallow, thrashing his head sideways, Dirk sensed the water threatening his life; his lungs tight-ened, his vision clouded, his thoughts became disjointed, spinning into a vortex of panic. Blackness began to settle over his eyes. And then suddenly it was over, his head thrust forward, a final gush of water spit from his mouth, oxygen pulled into his lungs in frantic gasps through bouts of choking coughs. Laughter assailed him from every direction. When his vision cleared, when he regained some of his faculties, he found Bacha Alba standing in front of him, the white-hot tip of the steel rod pointed at his right eye.

"Who are you spying for?" the warlord screamed.

"The Consortium!" Dirk shouted, turning his face as far to the left as possible.

"*Ayreh feek!* And the same to the Consortium!" the warlord snarled.

"Tanks!" Dirk yelled as the scalding metal point edged closer to his face. "SAMs! G-to-Gs! RPGs! You want 'em, don't you?"

Dirk tensed his muscles when the heat from the steel rod singed the skin on the left side of his jaw. He sagged with relief when it moved away.

"What are you saying?" Bacha Alba demanded, squeezing Dirk's face in his hand, twisting it frontward. "Speak!"

"In my right boot—a letter—Adiam—the girl—the nun—for arms. A list of what he offers in trade."

Dirk looked past the warlord's yellowish eyes and took a deep breath. The Land Cruiser, he saw, was parked a good fifty yards from where he was staked. Two small tents had been erected close to the vehicle. He wondered if Sarah was in one of those tents—if she was even alive.

"That's why we were parked where your men found us," he explained as Bacha Alba barked a command in a dialect he wasn't familiar with to a soldier standing near them. "I was given information that led me to believe Sister Claire was in this area—along with a little boy and girl who appear to be traveling with her."

Dirk stretched and wriggled his foot as a soldier removed his boot.

"You're familiar with what she is worth, yes? Adiam is aware of your communiqués with Akmir."

He watched the warlord scan the letter the soldier handed him, sensing in him a degree of satisfaction; the man's yellow eyes seemed to brighten as he mouthed the list of arms Adiam was promising him in exchange for the nun.

"*Sihr sharmuta,*" he heard the man mutter to himself. "We have been following her trail," he said, lifting his eyes to address Dirk. "She is—cunning. Here one moment—gone the next. My men think she is tabib—a witch." He laughed, glancing at the faces of the soldiers around them. "But she is just a *sharmuta*, like any other whore. We will find her," he went on with bravado. "And when we do, we will see how much the Consortium is actually willing to give up for her," he said, the clear intent of a threat in his voice. "If," he continued, holding up the steel rod, "I allow her to live."

"But you'll need the armaments Adiam is offering if you want to hold on to the territory you've already taken," Dirk countered. "And from the movements of the government troops I saw on my way here, you'll need the weapons very soon."

"You lie!" Bacha Alba screamed, bashing the steel rod flat against Dirk's rib cage.

"I'm— I— I'm not lying," Dirk sputtered, trying to breathe, wondering if some of his ribs were broken. "Ask the girl who's with me," he croaked, wincing from the blow. "She saw them: tanks, truckloads of soldiers, all heading north, into the Tigray. Ask her," he said, nodding toward the two tents. "Or did your man kill her?"

The warlord raised the steel rod above his shoulder as though he was preparing to strike Dirk again, but then looked to the tents, the steel rod drifting slowly to his side. He eyed Dirk suspiciously for a moment, then barked, "*Sharmuta hulet!*"

To the sound of laughter, two soldiers immediately ran toward the tents.

"So she's alive?" Dirk ventured.

"Wounded," Bacha Alba replied with a shrug. "Bloody, yes. But she lives."

Dirk saw the warlord studying his face, not at all certain what the wry smile suddenly forming on the lips meant.

"She is your wife?"

"No," Dirk said, laughing. "She's like the other one—the *sharmuta*, as you call her. She's a nun."

"A nun?"

Dirk didn't understand why the man seemed so pleased.

"And how much is she worth, this one?" Alba asked with a nod toward the two tents. "Seven million American dollars like *sharmuta* one?"

Dirk was about to scoff at the idea, but then realized he knew nothing about Sarah. Was she from a wealthy family, like Sister Claire? Would she be worth ransoming? *Good lord,* he thought, *is kidnapping aid workers and religious do-gooders going to become the norm?*

Shouting voices and a bevy of activity near the area where the tents were erected jolted Dirk from his thoughts. The two soldiers who were to have retrieved Sister Sarah ran toward Bacha Alba, their expressions alarmed as well as frightened.

"What is it?" the warlord yelled when the men were a dozen paces from where he stood. "Why have you not brought the girl?"

The two soldiers stopped an arm's length from their leader, stood at attention, and saluted.

"She's gone," they reported in unison, their eyes fixed on a spot somewhere above Bacha Alba's right shoulder. "Escaped."

"Escaped?" the warlord raged. "How? How?" he asked, throwing the steel rod to the ground when the men hesitated in answering.

"A slit in the back of the tent," one hurried to say. "And—"

"And?" the warlord shouted when the man fell silent. "Speak!" Alba commanded, slipping the knife from his ankle sheath.

"Tracks," the second soldier blurted.

"How many men?" the warlord was quick to ask, his eyes darting about for signs of an enemy.

The two soldiers gave each other looks Dirk could not discern.

"Must I cut your eyes out to get you to speak?" Bacha Alba screamed.

"There were no tracks of men," one explained.

"Only animals," the other one added.

"Hyena markings," the first one offered.

"Bouda," the second soldier muttered, his eyes nervously shifting back and forth.

"Bouda?" Dirk repeated, familiar with the term. "A hyena man?" He laughed.

But all around him, Dirk could hear soldiers repeating the word amongst each other. And as he looked around at their faces, he could see none were smiling when they spoke the ancient word, nor did they seem amused by the notion of a bouda having taken the woman.

"Bouda," Dirk murmured, scanning the rocks around him. "Why?"

* * *

Kamua's ears hurt. Having listened to Tengene and Selam go back and forth over the number of kilometers they'd traveled since leaving the Shire Wildlife Reserve ranger's station two and a half days ago, a dull ache lay in the recesses of his eardrums, accompanied by a high-pitched whine that wouldn't go away. Whether the distance between the Shire Reserve and Gambela National Park was seven hundred kilometers or one thousand kilo-meters, Kamua didn't care—and didn't want to hear about the subject any longer. He was weary of the two older men's seemingly tireless discussion over the matter. No matter how far they had come or what the weather had been like along the way, the three had finally reached their destination. He hoped the subject was now closed. Enough was enough; he wanted quiet.

Once the old Range Rover had been unloaded and camp set up for the night—fire built, tent erected, canned rations opened and eaten in near blessed silence—Kamua willingly volunteered for first watch. His willing-ness became utter joy when he heard Tengene and Selam begin to revisit the conversation about distance traveled when they retired to the tent as dark-ness began to fall.

"Old men," he scoffed in a whisper as he watched the mosquito netting close across the entrance to the tent, "can talk about nothing forever."

Shouldering his Lee-Enfield carbine, Kamua bent, picked up a stick, and threw it on the fire. Observing the dwindling flames, he realized the blaze needed more wood. Fortunately, Selam had chosen a good spot for camp, stopping a tenth of a kilometer away from a stand of trees; the open area between the campsite and the grove was littered with abundant kin-dling. Straightening, glancing overhead at the first stars of the night, he headed out of camp, grateful for the respite from old men and their petty, argumentative ways.

Kamua decided he'd walk to the tree line first, reasoning that he not only needed to stretch his legs, but that it was wiser to collect firewood on his way back to camp rather than hauling an armful of branches away from it, only to turn back and retrace his steps. Besides, the night was clear, the breeze cooling, the soft calls of the animals and birds settling for the night, soothing.

The journey to the Gambela region had been long and tiresome. The orders issued by their commander, along with alarming reports of a large-scale poaching operation within the boundaries of the game preserve, had come as a surprise. The handful of rangers stationed at Gambela Park was overwhelmed. The rangers needed assistance, their commander had explained. Leave immediately and plan on staying indefinitely, he'd told them. Needlessly adding that the assignment came with a certain amount of risk—as all rangers in all the national parks and game reserves in Ethiopia were well aware of.

Combatting poaching had become an open-ended task. Poachers had become more brazen. Their actions escalated as the market for ivory, rhino horns, pelts, and trophy heads of big cats skyrocketed. Poaching was now conducted on a worldwide scale—as every ranger across Africa was learning. And killing a ranger to secure a commodity for the world's black market had simply become part of the black-market trade. Just as staying alive while protecting animals had become an integral part of a ranger's job. So, for Kamua, taking a few moments to savor the nature he had been sworn to protect seemed a fitting tribute to the beautiful terrain he now found himself in.

Gwok-gwonk-gwokwokwok, came a shrieking call inches above his head. Startled, Kamua dropped the wood he'd been gathering and ducked. Exhaling with a hiss, he kicked out at the branches scattered around his feet.

"Damn stupid bird!" he shouted. "What do you want with me?" he barked, jabbing a fist up at the dark winged form.

Gwok-gwonk-gwokwokwok, the bird called out, swooping so low Kamua covered his head with his arms.

"Do I look like a mouse or a hare?" he hollered. "Go to the trees to find your dinner!" Kamua eyed the bird with disdain as it flew off. "Stupid owl," he grunted. "Can't you see I'm a man?"

To his dismay, the large owl turned in a slow, looping arc. Kamua's eyes widened as it headed back toward him, the bird's body drifting lower, flapping its wings to pick up speed.

"What on earth?" he muttered, slipping the Lee-Enfield from his shoulder.

Feeling threatened, Kamua raised the rifle to his shoulder and leveled it, sighting the onrushing owl. Taking aim, he marveled at the wingspan of the bird, hypnotized by the owl's disk-shaped face and the bird's blazing emerald eyes. Without warning, the owl opened its beak to unleash a piercing screech. Taking a deep breath, Kamua bent his head over the stock of the weapon and placed his index finger on the trigger. He was just beginning to squeeze off the shot when the owl disappeared from view.

"What?" he mumbled, tilting the rifle upward so he could get a better look at what was in front of him.

With a gasp, he glimpsed a blurred movement rising up from the ground just before two outstretched, milk-white feathered legs appeared near the barrel of his weapon. The long talons of the bird grasped the far end of the leather shoulder strap. When Kamua tried to jerk the rifle away, a flurry of battering wing thrusts to his face and a screeching cry sent him sprawling backward, the Lee-Enfield falling from his grasp. Scrambling to get back up, he stood in disbelief as he watched the eagle-sized owl fly off, the rifle dangling by the shoulder strap beneath the bird's feet. Kamua raised an arm in protest, a hollow ball forming in the pit of his stomach. The owl and the rifle disappeared into the stand of trees. He stared after them, bewildered, wondering how he would explain this to Tengene and Selam. They would ridicule him.

"First, Teimbaka is healed under your watch by a rabbit," they would say, laughing. "And now your weapon is taken by a bird," they would tease.

It would be humiliating—and rightfully so. How could he let this happen? What did the owl want with his rifle?

Gwok-gwonk-gwokwokwok.

Gritting his teeth at the sound of the owl's call, he began a determined walk toward the tree line, breaking into a sprint after a few angry steps.

*

What Kamua thought was a small stand of trees—the grove no deeper or wider than fifty or sixty paces in any direction—seemed endless and foreboding, the foliage stretched out before him a tangled collection of massive tree trunks, saplings no wider than the palm of his hand, thick-leaved bushes, and dangling vines. Kamua studied the vines for a moment, a tingling sensation spreading over his skin as his eyes looked upon tubular, ghostly white flowers hanging from feathery, curled vines.

Were the flowers emitting light? he wondered. Squinting, he turned his face from side to side to view them from different angles. Were the flowers glowing? he asked himself again. Or was he hallucinating?

The cry of the owl sounded once more, the call softer, seemingly close by. Lured by the bird's haunting voice, Kamua entered the forest, placing his hand on the hilt of the knife sheathed at his waist. Several cautious steps forward brought him to the edge of a small clearing, where he spied the Lee-Enfield leaning against a moss-covered tree. Surveying the area around him, he started across the small glade, only to stop when a hare appeared around the back of the tree and plopped down next to the rifle. Subtly, the fragrance of a thousand flowers seeped into his senses, the sweet, heady scent casting him into a momentary daze.

"You must hurry," a voice whispered.

Blinking to alertness, he looked across the clearing to see who had spoken. He glimpsed a flutter of gray disappearing into the bushes behind the moss-covered tree.

"You there!" he called out.

But no voice returned his hail. He heard only the soft call of the owl, coming from a place deeper within the forest. Puzzled, shaking his head, he walked the remaining paces to his rifle. Placing his hand around the wooden stock, he sighed, wanting nothing more than to get back to camp, hoping the foolishness with the crazy owl was done.

Plodding tremors shook the ground, underbrush crackling in incremental volume as though something heavy and slow was approaching through the forest. Kamua raised his weapon to his shoulder as the rumbling grew near. Off to his left, bushes began to shake, saplings bending and swaying, each snapping of a limb causing his breathing to quicken. Taking aim at the spot where the flora near the edge of the glade began to violently part, Kamua sighted the massive form emerging from the trees in the crosshairs of his weapon.

The enormous bull elephant burst into the clearing with a blaring, head-splitting cry, Kamua's bones humming from the unbridled power, the earth's shuddering felt through the soles of his boots. Marveling at the sight of the animal, Kamua guessed the mammoth bull to be at least five meters tall, with tusks so long and curled that the beast must be close to—

"The same elephant from before," he murmured, awestruck. "When we found Teimbaka. But—"

Intimidating and monstrous, the great male lion Kamua had seen in the company of the enormous bull elephant leapt into the clearing. Snarling, amber eyes ablaze, the animal loosed an ominous roar as his gaze fell upon Kamua. Gripped by fear, Kamua took aim at the lion, his finger tightening around the trigger.

As though shards of glass were raking across his hand, Kamua felt ripping pain slice into his flesh above his knuckles. Immediately, he pulled his hand away from the trigger guard, swinging his arm up to his face in an effort to fend off the assault of feathered wings.

"*Fala bundi!*" he shouted in Swahili. "*Tomba! Tomba!*" he swore, wincing with pain.

Letting the rifle fall to the ground, he covered his face with his arms and dropped to his knees. Certain the lion was going to attack, preparing for what he thought would be certain death, he closed his eyes and began to recite the prayer his mother had often said to him when he'd been frightened.

"*Baba Yetu, uliye mbinguni, jino lako litu kuzwe, ufalme wako uje—*"

"Thy will be done."

Kamua dropped his arms from his face at the whispering voice of a child.

"On earth as it is in heaven."

Kamua bowed his head, a feeling of contentment washing over him. Air stirred against his cheek, coaxing him to look up. The image of a baby elephant stood in front of him, ghostly in appearance, shades of the sun and moon shifting within the beast's wavering form.

"What are—?" Kamua started to ask before the dexterous lips of the ghost elephant's trunk pressed his mouth gently closed.

Drawn to the animal's pink-red eyes, Kamua was only vaguely aware of the trunk of the ghost-elephant moving to his chest. His heart tingling, he looked down to see a green speck crawl into his pocket.

"You must hurry."

The voice Kamua listened to was that of a young boy, his tone eminently pleasing, soft, reassuring.

"Where?" Kamua asked, looking upward into the branches of the trees, certain the boy was speaking to him from above.

Keeping still, he stared up into the maze of interlocking branches, waiting for a reply. But none was forthcoming. He heard only the rustling of the leaves—and the soft calls of birds as the fragrance of a multitude of flowers filled his senses.

"You must hurry," the voice murmured once more as a spark of light appeared in the center of the clearing.

Kamua gazed at the flickering ember, hoping it would grow, hoping the boy would speak to him again.

"You best hurry."

Kamua furrowed his brow.

"If you don't, it'll go cold."

A nudge to the back of his shoulder brought Kamua scrambling to his feet.

"You fell asleep, didn't you?"

Kamua stared at Selam as if he had never seen the man before.

"I— I—," he stammered.

"And here you volunteered for first watch," the older ranger remarked, a touch of disappointment in his tone. "Go on—get some wood. We need to build this fire up." Sighing, running a hand through his thinning gray hair, he added, "Then I'll take over."

Kamua looked across the stretch of open field toward the small stand of woods.

"Can't sleep anyway," the older man grumbled. "Damn Tengene's snoring," he said with a shake of his head and a nod back across his shoulder toward the tent. "But you get the wood first. Part of first watch responsibility."

Kamua watched the older man's expression change from disappointment to curiosity. And when Selam's hand darted forward and grabbed him by the arm, Kamua pulled away, thinking the old ranger was about to hit him.

"What happened to your hand?" Selam asked. "Those look like some pretty deep scratches."

Kamua followed Selam's eyes to the bloody lacerations on the back of his hand close to his knuckles. Remembering the owl, he looked skyward, then looked to the trees.

"Secret, is it?" Selam queried, releasing his hold. "Best see to it before you go to sleep," he advised, turning to go back into the tent.

Kamua waited for Selam to enter the tent before placing the back of his hand to his mouth. Running his tongue over the cuts, he tasted blood. *Fresh*, he thought, *newly made.* With a quick glance to the trees, he moved his injured hand to his shirt pocket. No sooner had he pulled the pocket open than a green bug flew out, the metallic luster of its body shining in the light of the moon. Kamua stood mesmerized as the bug hovered an arm's length from his face. A moment later, the bug dropped, landing on his leg. As he was about to brush it off, the insect raced away, a blur of silver-edged emerald jumping from the tip of his boot to the ground.

"What's your hurry?" he joked as he watched the bug disappear into the darkness.

A sudden rush of wind gusted against back of his neck, the sound of feathered wings pushing through air causing him to duck. The eagle-sized owl swooped by, the bird's wings flapping hard, gaining speed with every thrust, its silhouette fast disappearing into the face of the moon.

"Hurrying to catch the bug?" he called out, seeing the owl and the insect were both heading in the same direction.

As the distant *gwok-gwonk-gwokwokwok* of the owl echoed through the night sky, a whisper drifted to him upon the stirring breeze.

"*You must hurry.*"

17

S HE DIDN'T LIKE traveling at night. Didn't like the effect of darkness on her sensors: it negated several. Especially alone, like she was now, crossing terrain she had no familiarity with, her limited sensory perception impeding the call guiding her back to where she wanted to go—needed to go. The lack of stimuli—sight, sound, sensory, ultraviolet light groupings—made her journey more difficult than it had already been. And there wasn't much time left—perhaps two cycles of sun and moon, according to the receptors in her abdomen. For they had been receiving rapid transmissions, flashes of gold-white, gold-white. The pattern of color held no other meaning to her—two cycles of sun and moon—a clear impression of time. What would transpire after two cycles ran their course she had no awareness of, the calling to reach wherever she was destined to go superseding all other stimuli. Ignoring darkness, casting aside cautious instinct, she pushed on.

Feeling her way through monstrous stalks of grass, her sensors concluded the terrain she was crossing was nothing like the area where she had left the others. The lush, moist foliage, blooming flowers, and fruit trees—overripe pieces scattered on the ground beneath their branches—were embedded in her short-term retention, relaying the dissimilarities in the landscape she was now confronting. Extending her legs, she pushed her body as high as her appendages allowed. Tasting, smelling, feeling—she sensed no trace of what she yearned to find anywhere near.

*

When the glittering animal had beckoned her to climb atop its dangling trunk, the green female flower beetle hadn't wanted to leave the nectar tube she was feeding upon. But she'd complied with the calling from the animal nonetheless. Why the beast had taken her so far away, far from the others of her kind, far from where she needed to return, she didn't know. But a nagging sense she was not going to be able to fulfill her calling was beginning to gnaw at her, undermining her determination.

And there was water still to come—two wide, swift-moving channels she would need to cross. She remembered these because the glittering beast had carried her across them. But the animal was nowhere to be found. She wouldn't be able to glide across the surface of the water as the glittering creature had done. No, she wouldn't be able to cross the water in the manner of sunlight spreading from one shoreline to the next. Reconstructing air currents, sound dynamics, visual logistics of the waterways, she assessed she wouldn't be able to cross either watery barrier on her own. Isolated, unable to join the others, a feeling of helplessness overcame her. She stopped.

By the time the urgent warnings emanating from her antenna traveled across the synapses to her receptors, the strength of air currents buffeting over her back were so strong her body was pressed toward the ground. Instinctively, she retracted her legs and lay flat. Her torso lifting and sliding in swirling currents, she appeared dead, a dried-out carcass with nothing to offer.

The aura of light radiating from the winged creature setting down next to her hummed with such energy her sensors interpreted the impression as lightning. Pulsing, radiating, bristling with unbridled power, the entity was like nothing she had experienced before.

A sharp mandible took hold of her body, clamping softly down on either side of her abdomen, lifting her from the ground. Airborne, with the sky rushing past, she raised her antenna, extending the range of her sensors to maximum scope. Blinded by moonlight and the aura radiating from the entity holding her, she clamped her pincers around the tip of the bird's lower beak. As she and the winged creature flew closer to the rising moon, the green female flower beetle with the purple circle embedded within her elytra felt the first tendrils of wild throbbing energy surge through her.

* * *

The smell of feces and urine instantly transported her back in time, placing Sarah inside the closet where she'd been kept in her own filth for countless hours. As it had been during that spirit-breaking event in her life, her entire body throbbed with pain. Some searing—needle-like—some numbing, shielding her from the awful ache woven into every fiber of her groin. Fearing she was reliving that same weekend of abduction and rape at the hands of the hooded man, Sarah squeezed her eyes tightly shut and began to whimper.

"You are of the Father?"

It was a man's voice. But it wasn't her captor's.

Sarah bunched her muscles tight and tried to slide away. Sniffing back tear-laced mucus as she tried to distance herself from what smelled like a dead animal.

"Don't hurt me," she sniveled, pressing her arms tight to her body, hands clenching to fists when her shoulder pushed against something solid.

"Are you of the Father?" the voice urgently pressed.

Flinching, moving her fists down to cover her crotch for fear of being punched between her legs as her hooded captor had done to her every time she tried to get a look at him, Sarah fluttered her eyelids open to slits. Before she could scream, the dark-skinned, foul-smelling monster squatting next to her covered her mouth with a hand.

"You wear the same cross," the filthy man-beast growled, his eyes glancing down to a spot below her neck.

"My—my cross?" she stammered when he removed his hand from her lips.

Feeling for her necklace, she clasped her fingers around the small silver cross.

"Are you of the Father?" the man-beast shouted.

Hearing the sudden growls of other animals somewhere nearby, Sarah looked at her surroundings and began to tremble. The walls and ceiling of the shallow cave were black. Bones were scattered across an uneven stone floor. Ash-edged pieces of wood were arranged in a crude circle near the mouth of the enclosure, red embers faintly glowing. Squatting across from her, a man-beast of some kind—but what sort of creature it was, she didn't know. One side of the creature's face disfigured by jagged lines of dark, dirt-crusted scabs, shoulders adorned with the heads of some rotted-mouth, dog-like animal; his upper torso wrapped in decaying, spotted pelts. One hand clenched the base of a sharp-tipped spiral horn. The man, the thing—whatever he was—looked like something she thought could only exist in a nightmare. A beast, she was certain, beset by madness.

"Tell me!" the man-beast yelled. "Are you of the Father?"

"The father?" she asked, both frightened and confused. "You mean the Lord Jesus Christ?"

Sarah looked down at her necklace.

"Yes—yes—I am—a Sister of the Holy Cross. A nun."

"Like Claire," the man-beast muttered.

"Claire?" she repeated, moving to prop herself up on an arm. "Sister Claire?" she was able to ask before wincing in pain.

Sarah eased her body back onto the stone floor, moving her hand to her injured shoulder. Carefully probing the area around her wound, she felt a ridge of coarse stitches laced across her skin.

"Are you—a witch doctor?"

"You know Claire?" The man-beast bent toward her. "You are her sister?"

"Her sister? In a sense," she told him. "I've been sent to find her. Her father, you see, he—"

"Yes!" the man-beast said, grabbing her wrist. "You must call him—the Father," he urged, his expression serious, determined. "He must help. She is in need of him. Call him now!"

"I don't understand what you mean," she hurried to say, pulling her wrist free. "Her father, I'm afraid, has passed on. To heaven, I'm sure," she went on. "But her inheritance—"

"The Father passed on? Dead?"

Sarah fell silent, cowering away when the face of the man-beast looked upon her as though she had just committed some sort of sacrilege.

"He is all! He does not die! You lie!" he screamed, his face contorted in raging disbelief.

Outside the mouth of the cave came the growling of several animals. Sarah's eyes shifted between the creature squatting beside her and the entrance.

"No, no, no—not the Lord," she rushed to explain. "Sister Claire's own father—um, her dad. The head of her family," she went on, not knowing how much the creature understood what she was saying. "Not God in heaven," she said, wincing as she tried to extend her arm upward. "The man who raised her," she slowly expounded, enunciating each word with care.

"Then you are not zār," the man-beast said with a visible sigh. "Good. She will be happy then—to see her sister."

"Do you know her? Do you know where Sister Claire is?"

Sarah watched the man-beast edge over to the mouth of the cave to look outside, gasping when she noticed the battered state of his body.

"You will need to pray through your suffering," he remarked, turning to look at her. "We will be leaving soon."

"Leaving?" Sarah's eyes widened as one of the beasts from outside the cave approached the entrance. "But where?" she absently asked, her gaze fixed to the short, blunt muzzle of the dog-like animal peering in at her.

"Where Etiyopiya waits. Where Claire goes. Something is wrong," he said, Sarah noticing a faraway look in his eyes as he glanced back over his shoulder. "We must hurry."

"Hurry? I don't—I don't think I can move, much less travel."

For a moment, when she saw the creature raise the spiral horn up to his eyes and place a fingertip atop the point, she thought she had angered him and was about to be stabbed. But when he picked up a flat stone off the cave floor and began to methodically rub the tip of the horn across the stone's face, she breathed a sigh of relief. *Maybe he didn't hear me*, she thought.

"Sister Claire doesn't need to go wherever it is you think she is traveling to."

She studied the man-beast's face, wondering if he understood what she was saying.

"I've been sent to bring her home—back to the United States. She needs to sign some papers."

"Home," the creature mumbled, his brow furrowing. "Claire *is* home. *Etiyopiya* is Claire."

"Etiyopiya?" Sarah repeated with a shake of her head. " I don't really know what you mean, but Sister Claire is from Pennsylvania. That's in the United States of America. That's where I've come to take her back to, me and—Dirk!"

"It is time to go."

"Dirk! The man who was with me! Who was in the jeep with me when I was shot!"

Sarah raised her body off the stone floor, propping herself onto her elbows, ignoring the pain shooting down her left side.

"Where is he? Did you see him? Was he with me when you brought me here?"

Near frantic, Sarah waited for the man-beast to answer, her imagination running wild as her thoughts began to focus on Dirk and what had happened to him—if he was still alive.

"Tell me!" she begged, when the creature turned his back on her. "Is he still alive?"

"The dust clouds are moving. They are leaving."

For a brief moment, as the man-beast stood at the mouth of the cave with sunlight at his back, Sarah glimpsed what she imagined as a child to be the form of Satan: body edged in fire, smoldering eyes of the damned perched atop his shoulders, an instrument used to extract souls clenched in his hand. But as the man-beast crouched and approached where she lay, the image of Satan fell away, replaced by a youth somewhat younger than she, afflicted with a limp, his body cut and bruised, whatever part of him she looked upon.

"It is time to go."

"The man," Sarah said, gesturing with a hand for him to stop. "I was traveling with a man," she calmly told him. "A man of white skin. Was he with me when you found me?"

She studied his eyes when he answered.

"There was only you," he told her.

She couldn't tell if there was something more he wanted to say.

"Come," he said, offering her his hand.

"Not until I know what's happened to him!"

"*Toh-loh nah!*" he responded with a clap of his hands.

Sarah drew back when several of the short-muzzle dog-like animals appeared at the cave's entrance.

"Come," he repeated as one of the animals entered the cave to stand by his side. "This is Seh-my," he told her, nodding to the beast. "He will protect you."

"But I—"

"Quiet," he commanded.

Bending to her, the man-beast grabbed the elbow of her uninjured arm and yanked her to her feet. Thinking she should be terrified, Sarah found herself surprised when a feeling of strength surged within her as she looked into the man's soft brown eyes.

"*In eh heedt,*" he gently said to the animal, placing a hand atop the beast's head, stroking it behind its broad, rounded ears.

And then the man-beast left, leaping to the mouth of the cave and disappearing outside. Sarah looked down at the dog-like animal to find it staring up at her. Gently tugging on her skirt, Seh-my led her from the shallow cave.

* * *

"Tell me why you are here."

"I was a slave. Brought here by my buyer—Susenyo. I was young. Taken from the coffee fields near my home in Uganda."

Bin'ka offered nothing more. Content to wait. The waters of the gulf calm and peaceful, the whispers he was hearing arriving in subtle ripples upon the surface, the voice barely audible over the massive loading cranes at work across the channel.

"Why stay?"

"This is home now. I'm free."

"Free?"

"I have money and food," he replied, his eyes brightening as a lone fishing boat—a dhow—sailed into port for the night, bow riding high in the water, laughter coming from astern. "And cars, helicopters, jeeps—planes, if needed."

The fishing boat glided past the end of the rock pier, three Issa Somali fishermen falling silent when they saw Bin'ka gazing down at them. As the deep-green, sleek-hulled vessel neared the berthing slips located farther down the dock, Bin'ka watched with admiration the precision of the men as they scrambled fore and aft, taking in sail, readying casting lines.

"Free," the sea whispered when the wake from the dhow calmed.

"Free," he muttered with a nod of his head.

With sunset nearing, rays of fire-infused light dipped lower in the sky, slipping out upon the turquoise waters of the Gulf of Tadjoura from arid land, transforming its sky-smooth surface into dizzying slivers of auburn, gold, and white. Inland, past Rue de Venice where Rue de Genève ran parallel to Rue de Bir Hakeim calls of *adhan* began, voices of the muezzins amplified from the several mosques clustered in the area. Bin'ka never tired of hearing the call for *maghrib*—the evening prayer—for it meant day was fading, light giving way to darkness. Stars would soon blaze overhead. *Free*, a simpler notion to contemplate then, when darkness fell, for the blemishes of the city he called home—so exposed when the sun was high—would be absorbed by night, hiding the scars of poverty that marked the city's boroughs and alleys.

"Are you?" the water inquired.

Bin'ka stared down into the gold-tinted sea, studying the reflection of his face.

"When Susenyo died, I was freed. Adiam and Akmir—they—we—became partners. We carry on the business Susenyo put in place."

"Selling?"

"Yes," he answered.

As the final amplified calls of the muezzins fell silent, the sun drifted below the western horizon, silver-gold water taking on the color of polished gray. The smell of salt and diesel fuel blew inward off the sea, subtle reminders of eternity and progress, each struggling for Bin'ka to acknowledge their existence as he stared down at his vanishing silhouette.

"Drugs—weapons—animals—people." Each word came to him as a whisper, drifting on puffs of wind blowing in off the gulf.

"We sell everything—for a price, of course," he lightheartedly replied, thinking back to Susenyo's favorite saying.

"Addiction—death—spirits—souls?"

Bin'ka gripped the steel railing in front of him.

"Are you? Free?"

The voice of the sea was closer now, her breath caressing his neck, the skin of his ear. The words the sea had spoken—*addiction, death, spirits, souls*—flashed before him in images. The prostitute—the one they called Sister Lady; Susenyo—a bullet hole in his forehead; the Lion—existing within the form of a cat and a man; the soulless—the line of shackled, nameless people herded onto a ship of slavery. Each image lingered, clamoring to be remembered, reluctant to be dismissed when Bin'ka invited the darkness of night into his head.

"The woman—the nun."

"A whore," he quickly countered, turning to address the voice.

He hadn't noticed fog rolling in off the water, but Bin'ka found he'd been engulfed by it, immersed in thick vapor. An eddying current near to where he stood settled to stillness, as though an object once there had retreated farther into the fog's mass.

"Was she?"

Bin'ka wiped the droplets of moist air from the lids of his eyes, blinking, trying to focus on the slight shifting within the mist when the voice of the sea whispered *she*. The nun—the one the Lion had come for, the one the children called Sister Lady—he remembered holding her down while Susenyo injected the first dose of heroin into her veins. Remembered her young, unblemished face turning pallid and haggard as months slipped by, innocence—so evident in her eyes when Bin'ka first saw her—drained from her soul with each passing day. She had fallen slave to the addiction, doing whatever was asked to satisfy her need.

"No," he relented, his voice quiet. "No, she was not that way when— when—before Susenyo enslaved her."

"You said he was dead," the voice hissed.

"That was after—after he—"

"She suffers."

The mist swirled with the saying of *suffers*, billowing forth in a slow tumbling loop, the word floating within the motion, drifting out over the gulf, where it mingled with the cries of gulls. Bin'ka swept an arm through the fog to create an opening, moving his great girth into the narrow, whimsical passage to confront the voice from the sea. The appearance of a swath of gray cloth—the sleeve of someone's robe—made him hesitate. Following the length of clothing through the break in the fog, he saw a frail hand wrapped around the rust-colored railing, bony fingers curled around the steel bar reminding him of a bird clutching wire.

"What do you know of her?" Bin'ka sharply asked. "Why are you here?"

Far out in the Gulf of Aden, a ship's horn sounded. The woman released her hold on the rail, pointing outward into the fog.

"Lost her way," the woman offered, her voice subdued. "Perhaps she will hear the calling once more."

"Who are you?" he demanded.

"And what of the Lion?" she calmly responded, moving her hand upward where Bin'ka guessed her head would be.

Through the movement of her arm, a brief chasm appeared in the fog. Bin'ka glimpsed a flowing lock of gold-white hair showing beneath the edge of a drooping gray hood. The arm of the woman—slender and taught, muscles smooth, defined—was an array of earth-colored hues: dark as river mud, light as the sun-kissed sands along the Djibouti coast. From her fingers to her elbow, the subtle changes in shade ringed her skin like bracelets.

"The Lion?" Bin'ka repeated.

"Is he free?"

"Yes—yes," he said, remembering the day when Teimbaka—the Lion of Djibouti—carried the nun from the storage labyrinth. "We let him go."

The sound of churning, swelling water rushing toward the pier prompted Bin'ka to stagger back a step. Mist flowed past his head, currents swirling and pulsing, driven by the chaotic winds of an approaching storm. Looking outward in fear, sensing a towering wall of water about to break upon him, Bin'ka rushed forward to the guardrail, wrapping his massive arms around the top bar.

"Hold on!" he bellowed as droplets of water—the vanguard of the wave—sprayed against his face.

"The spirits."

Caught in the vortex of the looming wave, Bin'ka dropped to his knees, bunching his body into a tight ball.

"The elephants."

The churning din of the swell roared into his ears.

"Their tusks."

He screamed as the darkness of the wave fell against his eyes.

"Are they free?"

One hundred meters behind him, he heard the sound of water crashing against the shore. Shaking, unsteady, Bin'ka struggled to his feet. Loosening the tie knotted about his neck, he unbuttoned the collar of his custom-made Egyptian cotton shirt and took a few deep breaths.

"Everything has a price," he answered, though he did not understand why he felt the need to explain. "The tusks—the ivory—fetch more than gold." Fanning an arm out in front of him, Bin'ka tried to part the fog. "Nothing we deal in is free."

"Except you."

"I am not for sale," he was quick to say.

He saw a wavering orb of fog flowing toward him, hovering for a moment in front of his face, spinning one way and then the other before abruptly ebbing back.

"Aren't you?" the voice of the sea whispered, the words tumbling toward the water as though carried by a waterfall.

"No!" he shouted.

From both land and sea, raucous calls of crows and gulls arose, filling the fog-shrouded sky with screeching cries. Bin'ka covered his ears with his hands, his eyes nervously shifting from side to side as he gazed upward. All at once, the birds fell silent, the blare of a ship's horn sounding in the quiet.

"And they?"

Bin'ka felt his hands pried away from the sides of his head, the breath of the sea sweeping into his ears, threads of an invisible web pulling his arms down to his side. Deep and resonating, a ship's horn bellowed so near, Bin'ka felt the vibrations in his bones. Fearing the small pier was about to be rammed by a freighter, he tried to back away, only to find the invisible threads binding him to the rail.

"There."

The woman's voice came with the splashing spray of a wave. Bin'ka wiped water from his face with the back of his hand, the sudden appearance of bright, penetrating lights causing him to squint.

"I can move my arms," he said. Relieved, he grasped the steel bar in front of him, squeezing it hard as he could to feel his muscles flex.

"Are they free?"

As Bin'ka adjusted his eyes to the bright lights, he found the fog had lifted, the waters of the gulf calm, the sky clear of clouds, what stars were visible in the periphery of the glare from the loading dock across the channel twinkling clear and blue. Figures—dark shapes of people walking in a line—brought to his attention by a bony finger pointing in their direction.

"Slaves," he muttered, instantly recognizing the way the group moved: steps slow, synchronized, and halting. "Being loaded."

"You sell."

Not certain whether she was asking a question or making a statement, Bin'ka replied, "Akmir."

"But you watch."

"I don't like what he does. It's not—"

"And do nothing."

"I've told him. Adiam's told him. We've all—"

"And you are—*free?*"

"Listen," he warned, reaching over to grab hold of the woman's arm.

"Is that you?"

Bin'ka whirled round with the question, for the voice had come from the other side of him, the woman in the gray flowing robe pointing across the channel toward the loading dock. The slaves stood beneath one of the mammoth industrial lamps interspersed along the pier, their images clear. Bin'ka noticed a young man—much larger than the others—staring out at him across the water.

"He sends his soul," she murmured. "He does not want it enslaved."

"I—" he feebly replied. "There's nothing I can do."

"Why?"

Bin'ka closed his eyes, ushering in blankness, hiding in its void. Concentrating on the slow, rhythmic flow of the waves breaking upon the rocks beneath him, he sought refuge in the sound, hoping when he opened his eyes the old woman and the line of slaves would be gone.

"Why do you sell yourself?" she asked. "What will you do with the boy's soul?"

Bin'ka pretended not to hear, keeping his eyes shut, pulling on the metal railing with all his strength.

"Will you sell it? Send it in the ship with the spirits of the elephants? Or trade it to the Lion, perhaps, when he comes to ask?"

"Silence!" he shouted, bunching his hands into fists, trembling with the urge to bash the woman across her head.

"He *will* ask."

"Ask?" he raged. "Ask what?"

"Why you are here."

"I told—"

"Why you do nothing. Why you stand and watch."

"Get away, old hag! Go, before I throw you into the sea!"

"Why you are a slave"—the woman hesitated, placing her hands to the sides of her hood—"content with being a slave."

Bin'ka's eyes widened as the woman began to lower her hood, but looked past her when a violent explosion sent a shudder through the early night sky. Taken by surprise, Bin'ka stood mesmerized as a column of fire shot up from the far side of the city. In the distance, the air-raid siren from Camp Lemonnier began to wail.

"How many do you think?"

Several more explosions followed the first, feeding the tower of flames, fueling them higher toward the stars. And though the camp was a good ten kilometers away, the reds and yellows of the inferno splashed atop the waters of the gulf, creating the vision of a sea ablaze.

"How many what?" Bin'ka absently asked, his eyes focused on the column of fire.

"Souls," the voice whispered back as a wave crashed upon the rocks below.

Startled by the force of the water smashing against the pier, Bin'ka backed away from the railing, staring out into the gulf.

"Stop your babbling, hag. I've listened to your—"

"Before the flames are satisfied."

Tires squealing over asphalt made Bin'ka look back toward the front of the pier. A car sped up the service road, its white frame flashing in and out of beams of light shining beneath lampposts.

"Why are you here?"

The long white Mercedes limousine came to a screeching stop, Muhammad flinging the driver's side door open before smoke beneath the tires began to rise.

"Bin'ka!" Muhammad yelled. "What are you doing here? Adiam has been calling for you!"

Bin'ka glanced over to the gray-robed woman as Muhammad ran up to him.

"Hurry—we must go," Muhammad rushed to say. "It's the Afar— they've apparently fired a few of the RPGs you gave them into the old munitions dump. Adiam thought you had them under control. Bin'ka. Bin'ka! Are you listening? What are you looking at?"

"Did you see her?" Bin'ka asked, turning to look at Muhammad. "When you drove up. Did you see her next to me?"

Bin'ka took a step toward Muhammad, drawn to the column of flame dancing within the man's eyes.

"See who?" Muhammad replied.

"An old woman. Wearing a hooded, gray robe."

A new explosion from the direction of Camp Lemonnier infused the night sky with a glaring orange hue.

"There was no one," Muhammad told him. "Unless you mean the cat running past you when I stopped. We need to go. Come on," he urged, grabbing Bin'ka by the sleeve of his suit coat.

"Cat?" Confused, Bin'ka grudgingly allowed Muhammad to lead him toward the car.

"That one there," Muhammad said as he hurried them forward, pointing to a tattered gray animal at the base of a lamppost near a row of flat-roofed buildings. "The one that's always somewhere around here." He laughed, sliding into the Mercedes. "Get in. Let's go."

Bin'ka rounded the front of the car toward the passenger door, his eyes locked onto those of the cat staring back at him. As he felt for the door handle, the sound of a wave rushing toward the pier made him glance back out into the gulf.

"Let's go!" Muhammad shouted with a tap on the horn.

Bin'ka heard the wave crash against the base of the pier, the crest washing over the railing.

"Now!" Muhammad yelled, pounding on the windshield.

Bin'ka opened the car door as the churning water slipped back into the gulf, nothing but a foam-edged puddle left in its wake.

* * *

Sarah wrapped her arms around her legs and rested her forehead against her knees. Shivering, her shoulder throbbing, her feet sore, her body aching in so many places she'd become immune to the pains shooting through her muscles, she focused on what the man-beast had said to her when he'd finally stopped to allow her to rest.

*

"Where—where are you taking me?" she'd asked, out of breath.

The man stared at the cross about her neck as the tawny-colored, black-spotted beasts gathered round him in a circle.

"To Claire."

"But—but where?" she'd pressed, plopping down on the ground.

"Where there are elephants." The dog-like animals began to cackle. "And Teimbaka—Etiyopiya." He held the spiral horn up toward the sky, tip pointing to the stars. "You will call the Father when it is time."

He'd given her a look then, one she did not quite understand. Was he seeing her as a savior of some kind? she'd wondered. Or feeling pity for one he was about to sacrifice?

"Call—the Father? You mean—God?" she'd asked, confused. "I can't—"

"You are his messenger," he'd told her, reaching out to touch the tip of a finger to the silver cross hanging about her neck. "He will come." Nodding to himself, he turned his head to look in the direction they were heading. "He must," she'd heard him say. "He must help the Mother."

"The—the mother?" she'd repeated, barely able to get the words out of her mouth before a fevered chill tensed her jaw shut.

"You are cold."

And he'd swung the pelts of the dead animals from his body and placed them around her shoulders.

"Rest. Pray if you must. We need to hurry."

Before she could reply, he'd walked away.

*

The pelts smelled awful—but offered warmth. Sarah closed her eyes, wondering how long she'd be allowed to rest, hoping—though she knew it wasn't likely—the man-beast would forget about her so she could sleep.

Pray—she wondered how praying would help her. *Why didn't I tell Reverend Mother I wasn't up for this?* She grunted, finding her situation so tragically dire no one would believe her if she lived to tell the tale.

"What do you go by?"

Sarah looked up with a start to find the man-beast standing over her, extending his hand toward her.

"Sarah," she mumbled, trying to blink his image into focus. "And you?" she automatically asked.

"I am John," he told her, pulling her to her feet.

"John," she whispered, swooning, unable to find her balance.

Feeling her body rising off the ground, she curled herself into a ball, nestling into the strong arms lifting her. Vaguely, she sensed air rushing against her face, a slight jarring motion rocking her body. Eyelids fluttering, she fell fast asleep.

* * *

"Why do you insist on turning it over to see if there's anything on the other side?"

Bacha Alba shot Dirk an angry look.

"There are no instructions for how and when these *promised goods*," he said, the words *promised goods* spoken as though they had been dipped in vinegar, "are to be exchanged for the *sharmuta*. This is not—as you *ferenji* say—a good deal," he declared, smacking the sheet of paper with the back of his hand.

"I've told you over and over: once the woman—the *sharmuta*—is in my possession, we'll contact Adiam and you can arrange for the transfer however you want it to be handled."

Out of habit, Dirk tried to run a hand through his hair. Jerking his wrist against his bindings, he winced from the pain shooting through his ribs.

"Why doesn't that make you happy?" he asked with a sigh and a shake of his head. "I can't think of a simpler, easier way for it to happen."

"Just for that reason," Bacha Alba replied, pulling at the hilt of his knife. "It is too easy." Bending toward Dirk, he confided, "There is something smelly in this, something that makes me think I am being cheated."

"I'm just a go-between," Dirk offered, frowning. "I can't give you any assurances."

Bacha Alba drew the eight-inch blade from the sheath tied to his ankle and held it up to his face.

"And remind me again why I need you at all."

"Your country is in the midst of civil war," Dirk replied without hesitation. "And will be for god knows how long."

"Allah—blessed be He."

"Whatever," Dirk dismissively responded. "Point is, to keep the control of the territory you've claimed, you need weapons to hold it—expand it—weapons more sophisticated than what you possess now. Weapons more powerful, deadlier—capable of striking your enemies from great distances. Like the G-to-G missile that struck your position today."

Dirk paused, staring unflinchingly into Bacha Alba's eyes.

"If the missile had been set to the proper coordinates, you'd be dead right now. And I'd be talking to one of your subordinates," he offered, nodding to the scores of men setting up camp for the night, "about weapons to keep *him* in power—to make *him* the new lord of *your* domain."

"That does not explain why I need *you*!" Bacha Alba retorted, taking a menacing step toward Dirk. "I should kill you now and be done with your insolence!"

"You could," Dirk agreed. "But then you'd have to find a way to become white. To renounce Allah, become Christian, and travel across the oceans to collect your reward."

"What are you saying?" Bacha Alba raged. "You speak blasphemy!"

"The *sharmuta*," Dirk calmly replied, "is a sister—a nun. She serves the Christian God, sent by those, like your imams, who direct her in the ways she conducts herself, the way she is to serve. Kill me and you will then need to speak directly to them, acknowledging their god and the power they wield through him. Is this something you're prepared to do?"

Bacha Alba glared at Dirk, twisting the knife in his hand.

"If you're not," he went on, "then even if we find the woman—you get nothing. No weapons, no money, all of this wandering around the country looking for this *sharmuta* while the government solidifies their positions in the Tigray. And for what? So you can say you captured her?"

Dirk offered the man a shrug and a smirk.

"That'll go over big with your men—chasing a *sihr sharmuta* while the territory they've fought and died for—and all the power and perks that go along with it—is lost. What did you say your men called her?" Dirk smugly inquired. "A tabib? It wouldn't take much for them to believe that she had cast a spell over you, would it?"

Bacha Alba lunged forward, the knife pointed directly at Dirk's face. Dirk tried to jerk his hands free from the leather strips binding his wrists to the ringed stake driven into the ground next to him, but to no avail. He felt the knife slice into the flesh of his upper cheek. The blade was extracted and presented to him so he could see blood dripping from the tip.

"There is no need for you to have the use of your eyes," Bacha Alba hissed, "when all that is needed is your tongue. You think your subtle insinuations are too clever for a man of Allah to follow? You pretend to able to look into the future. Only, Allah—blessed be He—has that power! Your punishment for such blasphemy is your sight!"

"Wait! Wait! Wait!"

Half a kilometer away, a portion of the night sky exploded into a sickly luminous green. A moment later, they heard distant bursts of automatic weapons.

"Firefight," Dirk observed.

Bacha Alba stiffened at the remark.

"The patrol you sent out, perhaps?"

Bacha Alba shifted the knife between his hands.

"Supreme Commander!" a voice called out.

Bacha Alba turned at the approach of running footsteps.

"Message from the patrol, Supreme Commander!"

"Report," Alba ordered, exchanging a hurried salute.

"Enemy position: two kilometers south-southwest. SPLA flags. Dodging patrols. Awaiting orders."

"Ready the men," Bacha Alba snapped.

"George Henry," Dirk uttered.

"We're pulling out," the warlord told the soldier. "Go. Now!"

With a quick salute, the soldier ran off. Dirk could hear the man shouting orders in Arabic and Amharic. The men in Alba's command scrambled to mobilize.

"No confrontation with the Sudan People's Liberation Army?" Dirk quipped.

"We each have our own countries and our own battles," Bacha Alba replied, sheathing his knife. "There is no need to spill each other's blood."

"You just going to leave your men out there to fend for themselves?"

"You run your mouth so much you do not hear," the warlord said, spitting on the ground near Dirk's boots. "The gunfire is silent. My men are now in the glory of Allah, blessed be He."

"Where are you going?" Dirk asked with some concern when the warlord turned his back and began to walk away. "Aren't you forgetting something?" he went on, jerking his wrists up as far as the bindings would allow.

Bacha Alba turned and looked at Dirk, a sardonic smile on his face.

"The deal," Dirk said. "Weapons for the woman—me as go-between."

"It is said that George Henry fancies himself as your Christian God," Bacha Alba smirked. "It is also said he despises those who brought ruin to his country—those with the white skin. Many tales have I heard of him burning your kind alive to cleanse the land of the sins brought upon it. So I leave you to George Henry; may your end be one of flaming agony."

With a nod of contempt, Bacha Alba turned and walked away.

"And don't worry about being left in the dark," he heard the warlord shout with a mocking laugh. "We'll build you a blazing fire before we leave!"

* * *

The voices of the birds seemed to come from everywhere: each side of her, above her, behind, in front. Eden wondered how many there were, what they looked like, how each of them could be so different—yet be the same. What god made them all? Was it Allah? she wondered, remembering the teachings of her father. Or was it the Christian god, the one simply known as God? The one—as in the stories the missionaries told—who made all things in the universe in a week's time? Or was it the god her mother had simply called the Mother, the entity the Amharic people of olden times were so devoted to? The Mother: interwoven into the spirit of the people's souls, joining the people with the land.

It was all so confusing—gods—Eden didn't know what to believe. But she recognized the voices of the birds as life, something real, not skewed by emotion or colored with superstitions passed down from generation to generation. As real as the hunger in her belly when she had no food—as real as the tears she cried for all the people in her life who were gone.

Yet, here she was, sitting on one side of a tabib—who seemed to be having some sort of seizure—while across from her sat a youth—an abdar— holding the tabib's hand, telling tales about a boy with sparkling eyes. Were these not real too? As real as the birds, her hunger, her pain, even though the tabib and abdar were people who existed in some kind of spirit world? She stared at the tabib—the woman's quivering lips, the way her eyes moved beneath her lids while she slept, the manner in which her hands twitched as though swatting away flies—and shook her head.

Where are the gods, she wondered, *this Allah, this God, the Mother?* If they were all as unbelievably all-knowing and all-seeing as they were portrayed to be, why had they allowed her country to be in constant pain, constant war—yet allowed birds to sing and chatter as though nothing was wrong?

And what about this hare they had chanced upon? The one that had led them to water, the one the abdar followed through the maze of thorn bushes and stinging mounds of grass to bring them to the safety of this forest. What god should be given credit for the hare? She didn't know, she realized. It was all so confusing. But as she listened to the birds, their voices led her to make one simple observation: although she didn't know what to believe, she wasn't bothered at all by not knowing.

A sudden eruption colored the pre-dawn dimness in orange and red, tremors shuddering the earth beneath her rump. And though the sound of the blast seemed some distance away, the rumbling traveling through the soil made her think the explosion had been massive. When the glare of what must have been a huge wall of flames filtered down through the canopy of leaves and branches to dance across the tabib's prone body, Eden and the abdar exchanged the same look of concern; something was terribly wrong.

"Teimbaka!" Claire shrieked, her hands frantically grasping at the air in front of her.

Eden fell backward at the sound of the tabib's terrified voice, cowering away when the woman's upper body heaved forward off the ground.

"Teimbaka!" the tabib cried out, her eyes manically searching the terrain around them. "Teimbaka!"

"Sister Lady!" John Too shouted, grabbing Claire by the shoulders. "Sister Lady," he said in a calmer tone when she looked at him.

Eden watched the tabib search the eyes of the abdar.

"It's him," Claire whimpered, her face etched in grief. "Tell me I'm wrong, John Too," she sobbed. "Tell me I'm wrong."

The glow of the fiery sky flickered in the abdar's eyes as he gently took the tabib's chin in his hand. Eden sat up, eager to hear what the boy was going to say.

"He is there—where the fire burns," he told her with a nod to the glowing sky. "But I cannot see more."

"Then he's—"

"We must hurry," the abdar said, helping Claire up off the ground.

Eden took a step backward as the tabib rushed by, the abdar close on her heels, hurrying to keep up. Eden was about to follow when a yearning held her still, prompting her to look northward, where the village she had been raised in awaited her return. Standing erect near the base of a slender sapling, she saw the hare, brown fur radiant in the glow of an orange-gold sky.

"*Ahmahseyguhlahnoh, Enat.*"

Startled by the abdar's voice, Eden flinched as he took hold of her hand.

"Come," he told her.

"But—"

Eden turned to take one last look at the hare as John Too pulled on her arm—but the animal was gone.

"Why did you call her mother when you thanked her?" Eden shouted to John Too.

But the abdar was already far ahead, running to catch up to the tabib.

18

"HOW'D HE DIE?"

Chris pretended to be absorbed with the combination of succotash, corn bread, and fried catfish collected on his fork while the stunned silence from the people around the table screamed disbelief. He didn't need to look up at their faces to see what consternation his question had caused. Just the fact Ed's silverware had gone suddenly quiet was all the proof Chris needed that he had opened a door to a subject no one wanted to address.

"That's not a question for the dinner table, Noah," Elizabeth politely countered, breaking the awkwardness of the moment. "That's a subject—"

"Helicopter crash," Yutanda interjected. "Government report's horribly incomplete, however," she added.

Chris glanced up in time to see Yutanda shoot Ed and Elizabeth a defiant look.

"Cause of death was listed as an accident. But the report alludes to the copter he was riding in was shot down by rebel insurgents in a remote desert area. That he died in the subsequent explosion, crash, or fire—or all three."

Chris watched with some amusement as Yutanda picked at the edges of the cornbread pan and nibbled on the hard-baked pieces she worked loose.

"But they never found his remains. Pilot's, yeah. His remains were there—but not Menelik's."

Chris looked at Ed and Elizabeth's concerned expressions as they listened to their daughter talk.

"That's why I think they're wrong," Yutanda went on, stabbing a piece of catfish with her fork, oblivious to the undercurrents of emotions around her. "That's why I've come to believe he's still alive," she said, giving Chris the same defiant look she'd given her parents moments before. "Why I'll be— why *we'll be* heading over there as soon as I can arrange it," she explained with a glance at the crib she and Ed had placed in the living room. "Until someone can show me his body, his remains, there's no reason to think he's not somewhere over there unable to communicate with me for some reason or wandering around with amnesia."

Chris watched her place the hunk of catfish in her mouth, her jaw squared and determined as she methodically chewed.

"So just out of the blue—so to speak—his helicopter was just randomly shot down. Is that what you're saying?"

"Noah, let it be, son," Ed softly, but firmly, implored.

"Yeah, that's what I'm saying," Yutanda quickly replied. "Why?"

"Just seems a little strange, I guess," Chris responded, reaching for the glass of iced tea he was having with dinner.

"What do you mean, strange?" Yutanda challenged, putting her fork on her plate.

"Just the fact that a helicopter flying in a huge open area—desert terrain you said?—would happen to cross the exact spot where a patrol, or whatever, had a surface-to-air missile ready to fire seems—I don't know—a bit of a stretch."

"I don't understand, Noah." It was Elizabeth talking, a grave expression wrinkling her face. "What are you trying to say?"

"Sounds like they were expecting the helicopter to be there at a certain time—least, that's how it sounds to me, anyway."

"Noah," Ed pleaded.

"You know something?" Yutanda snapped. "You saying Menelik was set up?"

Chris didn't answer right away, the half-melted ice cubes in his glass sounding like distant wind chimes as he swirled the drink in his hand.

"No," he finally admitted with a shrug. "Just thinking out loud, I guess."

"Well, think out loud somewhere else, then," Yutanda frostily replied. "Unless you know something concrete—and I don't see how that's possible—you can just keep your thoughts to yourself."

"My apologies," Chris immediately offered with a nod. "It's just—never mind," he told her, dismissing the subject with a wave of his hand.

"Jesus Christ!" Yutanda slapped the tabletop with her open palm. "What the hell is wrong with you? You think—"

"That'll be enough of that kind of talk right now, young lady!" Elizabeth ordered. "You keep a civil tongue, just like you were raised. You hear me?"

Elizabeth glowered at her daughter before turning her attention to Chris. Raising a hand to ward off any response from Yutanda, she admonished Chris, "And that'll close this subject right here and now." She punctuated the word *now* with a shake of her pointed index finger. "*You* hearin' *me?*"

"Yes, ma'am," Chris replied, raising his hands above his head in a gesture of surrender.

The phone in the kitchen rang just as an ornery whine from the crib proclaimed baby Menelik was done napping. Yutanda and Elizabeth got up from the table in unison, mother heading to the kitchen to answer the phone, daughter going to the crib to see to the needs of her son.

"Best not get Lizbeth riled up, son," Ed good-naturedly remarked as he splashed a piece of fish with hot sauce. "And please—and the Lord knows I mean this in the right way—don't go fillin' Yutanda's head with any more ideas about her dead husband." Ed eyed the food on the end of his fork. "Though I rightly can't confirm that he's truly dead," he added, placing the piece of fish in his mouth. "But the government's done stated it so," he went on in soft voice, bending toward Chris. "So best she start believin' it."

Ed licked the tips of his fingers and nodded his head.

"All this going-to-Ethiopia talk is just plain foolishness, if you ask me. What she expect to find in a country she knows nothin' 'bout, anyway?" he offered, suddenly looking at the food on his plate as though he didn't know what any of it was. "And where would ya start?"

"Yutanda." Elizabeth stepped out of the kitchen with a sigh. "It's that female policewoman, Corporal Stilton," she announced, holding her arms out to take baby Menelik from Yutanda. "Says it's important. I told her we were having dinner and that we had company—"

"It's all right, Momma," Yutanda told her, gently placing the baby into Elizabeth's arms. "I'm not very hungry anymore," she said, shooting Chris a sour look.

"Seems like a good time for me to be on my way, Ed."

Chris pushed away from the table and stood up to leave.

"Now, hold on, Noah. Ain't right, you leavin' like this. Not after all you've done for us—for Yutanda."

Chris looked down at the man's lined, worn face, not knowing what to say—or think. *What he had done for them? Shit*, he thought, *everything's been orchestrated—all of it—saving Yutanda from the thugs at the dock, ingratiating myself with Ed and Elizabeth, tapping the house phone, reporting Yutanda's every move to Rue Thompson—the whole charade was just a big pile of horse shit.* But Ed—what did he really see in Ed Taylor that made Chris like him, made him feel sorry for all the conniving shit he was pulling? Something in Ed reminded him of the father he didn't quite remember. Or of something he wished his father had been—if the fuck had ever hung around long enough after he was born for him to get to know him.

"I have to be somewhere else anyway, Ed," he ended up saying, glancing at his wrist to check on the time. "I'll just say a quick—"

"Something big is going down at the port tonight," Yutanda announced as she stepped out of the kitchen.

Placing her hands on her hips, she looked at each of her parents before continuing.

"Police commissioner wants me to be there in an hour or so. Says it would be good PR for the city. Seems like the job requires one more night of me," she added with a self-satisfied smile.

"No!"

Surprised by the vehemence in Chris's tone, Ed, Elizabeth, and Yutanda scrutinized him for a moment before exchanging questioning looks.

"I mean, no—uh, you shouldn't go down there. Not with all the violence that's been taking place there. Sorry, I didn't mean for it to come out sounding so forceful."

"Well, aren't you just full of yourself tonight?" Yutanda sarcastically responded, taking a step toward Chris. "Didn't I hear you say you were just leaving when I came back in from the kitchen?" She gave Chris an unforgiving look. "Well, don't let the door hit you on the way out, as the old saying goes."

"Yutanda," Ed snapped. "Noah's just looking out for you—like he done since the beginning, I might add. And you ain't even have the manners to thank him for the dinner he brought over tonight."

"Well, thank you, Noah Kunda, for supper."

"Yutanda! That's enough of that haughty attitude," Elizabeth reprimanded.

"And get home safe," Yutanda added, forcing a smile.

Before anyone could say a word, Yutanda took baby Menelik from Elizabeth and disappeared into the hallway leading to the bedrooms. Chris, Ed, and Elizabeth traded embarrassed glances to the sound of a door closing.

"Land's sake, Noah," Ed offered as he rose from the table, "I truly don't know what's wrong with her tonight. Never seen her act so rude before. I apologize—I truly do."

"I probably had it coming, Ed, the way I brought up her husband's death and all. So please—no apologies necessary." Chris checked the time on his wristwatch. "And like I said," he hurried to say before Elizabeth could interject, "I have somewhere I need to be right now."

"Noah."

Chris turned at the sound of Elizabeth's voice, thinking for the briefest of moments he was hearing his mother's.

"I'll try to stop by before you all leave for Virginia," he said, crossing the room to give Elizabeth a quick hug. "I'm sure you have a lot of packing to do before you go. Day after tomorrow, right?"

Elizabeth gently broke their embrace to run her hand alongside Chris's face.

"You shaved your sideburns." She smiled, patting his broad chest. "See more of that strong, handsome face of yours."

"You trying to make me jealous, woman?" Ed teased. "Keep talkin' like that, I might start thinkin' you married the wrong man."

With a brief touch to Elizabeth's shoulder, Chris turned and headed toward the door.

"I say something to offend you?" Ed asked, his silver eyebrows pinching together.

Chris opened the door.

Elizabeth reached out a hand.

"Noah," she said.

It wasn't so different from the day he had been inducted into the army.

Chris had looked back from the front door of the apartment where he and his mom lived as he left to report to Fort Dix. She'd said his name just like Elizabeth was saying it now: concerned, laced with a mixture of tenderness and apprehension, trying to convey her understanding him needing to leave—but not wanting him to go.

"Don't let her go to the port tonight," he found himself saying. "Whatever you do, don't let her go."

Chris stepped through the open door, quickly shutting it behind him. He didn't want to hear what Ed and Elizabeth might say in response to his warning. Didn't want to have to explain what he meant. It was just the same the day he'd left his mom standing in their little one-bedroom apartment in Camden so he could go off to Vietnam and become a soldier. He hadn't known what to say to his mother then—when he had closed the door on her without looking back—and he didn't know what to say to Ed and Elizabeth now.

"Noah!"

Before Chris could turn around, Ed grabbed hold of his arm and spun him around. Chris countered with an upward hand block, knocking Ed's grip off his arm with the base of his palm. Ed cried out, clutching his forearm.

"Shit, Ed." Chris hurried to apologize, steadying the man by grabbing hold of his shoulder. "I'm sorry. I—I just reacted. You okay?"

"Learned that in the army, did ya?" Ed replied, rubbing his forearm. "I'll remember that for the next time," he added with a halting laugh.

"Look, Ed—" Chris shifted his attention across the street to the church. "I gotta go."

Ed grabbed hold of Chris's wrist.

"You know something, don't you?"

Chris kept his focus on the church.

"What is it you're not sayin'?" Ed asked, squeezing Chris's wrist.

"Ain't nowhere safe, is there?" Chris nonchalantly remarked with a slight nod in the direction he was looking.

Ed turned and looked across the street.

"Even a church parking lot," he continued as he watched a red tow truck haul a car out.

"What's that got to do—?"

"Trouble find you just about anywhere, anytime."

Ed gave him a curious look.

"What you sayin', Noah? My little girl in trouble? Is that what you're sayin'? 'Cause if it is—"

"Some desert in some far-off country—or just across the street. Sometimes it seems like it's just been waiting for you the whole time. And you were too blind to see it. Too caught up in chasing it to notice it was lying in wait for you. Trouble—you know what I mean?"

Chris glanced at his watch as the tow truck took a left turn out of the church parking lot onto Mercer and disappeared from view.

"I got 8:25," he said to Ed. "You go back inside and keep Yutanda there with you—all night if you can. Least till 10:00; 10:30 if she throws a fit. I don't expect you to understand," he offered, seeing the confused look on the older man's face. "But you served in Korea, so you know just as well as I do. Bad shit happens—but most of the time—"

Chris gently pried Ed's fingers from his wrist.

"It's because someone wants it to."

Before Ed could reply, Chris turned and walked away. Half expecting Ed to grab his arm again, he breathed a sigh of relief when he heard the door to Yutanda's building open and then slowly swing closed. Chris shut his eyes for a moment, hoping Ed would take his advice, hoping he was going back into the apartment to barricade the door and not let Yutanda leave.

She'd be dead if she did. Chris had no doubt the phone call from Corporal Stilton laying out a specific time for Yutanda to arrive at the port was just a setup. Rue's Middle Eastern partner was probably going to have her killed en route, he figured. Make it look like an accident: hit and run or maybe a mugging that went tragically wrong at a stop sign at some particular out-of-the-way corner on some street near the port. *Dumb bitch,* he thought. *Like the police commissioner gives a flying fuck if you're at some big bust. Like he'd want to share the spotlight with you. How stupid can you be?*

Chris exited Yutanda's apartment complex at the corner of Court and Broome Street, stopping for a moment to watch a group of kids playing baseball at the athletic field on the opposite corner. The next thing he knew, he was sprawled across the middle of the road, his head filled with the deafening roar of an explosion, shockwaves buckling the asphalt beneath him.

* * *

Bongo revved the engine of the Honda CR125R dirt bike and smiled. *Shit got some torque,* he said to himself with a nod. *Fuckin' Griper be the man when it comes to lifting shit for a job. Yeah baby,* he thought, giving the throttle another twist, *gonna cause some fuckin' shit with this.*

Tilting his head to the side, he looked across his shoulder, offering Twister a big tooth-filled smile as he revved the motor again. Without warning, Twister reached over and slapped the side of his helmet.

"What the fuck's that for?" he protested, releasing the throttle and throwing up his arms so he could ward off any other unexpected blows.

"Why you always gotta draw attention, man?" Twister complained in a hoarse whisper. "Low profile, remember?" Twister pushed the pair of Ray Ban sunglasses down the bridge of his nose about a half inch to glare at Bongo. "Why don't you just go piss on a Blood's foot or somethin'?"

Bongo thrust his arm out to try to smack Twister's helmet, but the bigger man easily knocked his arm away.

"Better be the best fuckin' blow ever hit the street," Twister remarked as he pushed the sunglasses back up the bridge of his nose. "Some fuckin' diversion Gripe-ass came up with. Shit."

Bongo flicked the kill switch on his bike, sat back on the banana seat, and folded his arms.

"You the biggest bitch in the world, ain't ya? Scorin' a Z of pure? You shittin' me?" he asked, his voice rising in pitch with every word. "Just for shootin' a few rounds off? Fuck, man," he scoffed, imitating Twister by pushing his own pair of Ray Bans down the bridge of his nose so he could glare at him, "easiest payday we seen in a stretch. Put us on easy street, is all. And you sittin' bitchin' like you be—like—uh—bitchin' like you be—uh—"

"Shut up, fool," Twister snapped, leaning over to slap Bongo on the helmet again.

"Aunt Esther! Yeah, man—that who you be bitchin' like!" he said, laughing and balancing the dirt bike with his legs while slapping the handlebars with gloved fingers. "Come on, man. It's funny, right?" Bongo went on, his laughter slowly subsiding. "Why ain't you think it's funny?"

Bongo followed Twister's gaze, looking out across the water of Newark Bay toward the giant cranes positioned along the outer edges of the Maher Terminal. To Bongo, the pier looked like a small city. Bright lights, bustling activity, trucks, cranes, ships, trains—all a part of a self-contained metropolis running to its own schedule, following its own set of rules. Bongo let his eyes drift to the water and watched the rippling currents approach the little stretch of beach he and Twister were situated on. Why the city planners, or architects, or construction people—or whoever—Bongo thought, had decided to leave a stretch of marshland undeveloped in the middle of an area teeming with multilane highways, railroad lines, and an airport was a mystery. Wasn't like it was a wildlife refuge or anything. Just a couple of dirt tracts crisscrossing a grassy armpit of an area that smelled like a can of sardines. Maybe a dirty seagull here and there scavenging for whatever was to be found along the littered shoreline—but it wasn't like the area needed to be preserved for some environmental reason. But then again, what did he care? Couple years of makin' bank runnin' dope and such, and he'd be out. Super Freak and all the other hustlers in the world could have this fuckin' place. Weren't nothin' to him. He was gonna make music.

"I knew one of the brothers."

"Say what?"

"Brothers the spics dusted," Twister said. "The ones got the back of their heads blown off."

"What's that got to do—?"

"San Fran they called him."

Startled by a big shadow passing in front of him on the surface of the water, Bongo looked up to see a freighter sliding by not more than a hundred yards from shore, the ship's running lights blending into the skyline of cranes and taller buildings across the channel in Bayonne.

"Liked the handle California better. Said he was from L.A."

Twister slapped at the back of his neck—a mosquito, Bongo guessed—before he went on.

"Said all the freaks from up north were faggots."

Twister shook his head.

"Yeah, bro, but he was Blood, right? Gang shit ain't cool. He oughta known it was all gonna turn bad."

"Yeah? Well, fuck you! Dude was solid. And he weren't doin' nothin' the night the fucks grabbed him and shot the fuckin' back of his head off. Not like we're about to do tonight."

Even in the fading daylight, Bongo could see Twister's jaw grinding.

"We'll fly right by 'em, bro. Torque these fuckers all out," Bongo said, pantomiming revving the engine. "Fuckin' Bloods or nutty Ñeta motherfuckers won't see nothin' of us but our assholes blowin' by 'em."

"Oh, really, bro—that all there is to it? Just shoot their motherfuckin' dock up, bring the pigs down on 'em, have their stash impounded, and they just gonna forget about two dudes ridin' through on bright red dirt bikes fuckin' up their turf? Shit, man, you got butterflies up here," Twister told him, pointing to the side of his head.

"Whatever," Bongo countered, pursing his lips and shrugging his shoulders. "Bitch."

"Yeah, well, you better pray no gang-bang boys are able to finger us through this shit we got on. Fuckin' black jump suits, black helmets, black shades—ridin' bright red dirt bikes; shit—stand out like two niggers at a Klan rally."

"Bitch, bitch, bitch, bitch, bitch," Bongo mocked. "Man, all we gotta do is follow the plan. Once we clear here, couple miles north on the turnpike, we ditch the bikes and the threads in the Passaic. A few blocks over, we got the ride we ripped earlier today waitin' for us. Why you gotta be so sour, man?"

"Don't see Griper here, do ya? Why you think that is?"

"He's throwin' the flames and got the boom-boom stick. You'd wanna be doin' that? Probably light yourself on fire *and* blow your hand off 'cause the way you be bitchin' so much."

"Yeah, well, Super Freak asshole better be level on the Z," Twister pouted, folding his arms over his chest. "He and Griper—don't trust 'em, man. Always makin' me feel like bait—and they be the fishermen. You dig where I'm comin' from?"

"Griper's got the hookup with the Freak, man," Bongo acknowledged with a shrug. "What's a brother to do? You watch my back and I watch yours, dig?" he offered, extending a closed hand for a fist bump.

Twister reciprocated, giving Bongo a halfhearted tap on the knuckles with his fist.

"When this shit goin' down, man?" Twister complained. "I'm gettin' tired waitin' for Griper boy to start the fireworks."

"He said sundown—whenever that is. Like I be a weather dude or somethin'," Bongo scoffed.

* * *

The freighter *Jameel* passed through the tidal straight, Kill Van Kull, without incident, entering Newark Bay a little ahead of schedule. When the first mate radioed the dock master at the Port Newark terminal about their earlier-than-estimated timetable, the man seemed pleased by the news, laughingly telling the first mate—a seasoned sailor named Ahmed Nazari, who hailed out of Egypt—to dock the *Jameel* at berth 30 on the west side of the terminal, where Calcutta Street ended. When Ahmed asked the dock master—with whom he'd had many exchanges over the past few years—what was so amusing, the man laughed anew, saying, "You know—Calcutta, Egypt; goes together, right? Big city in your country, right?"

Ahmed had taken his finger off the Send button of the radio transmitter, looked at the Sandy Hook pilot, who had come on board before the ship had entered the Kill Van Kull, and shook his head.

"Ignorant Americans," he'd muttered. "Why are some of you so stupid?"

The pilot—on board as a requirement of the Port Newark–Elizabeth Marine Terminal—simply shrugged his shoulders.

In turn, when Ahmed informed the captain of their expedited docking schedule, the captain—a Turkish man named Ali Reza—sent a coded message via the shortwave radio frequency he'd been supplied with before departing Djibouti, alerting whoever the recipient was to the *Jameel's* altered schedule. After receiving the coded response of "understood," Ali Reza issued orders to initiate docking procedures and ready cargo for immediate offloading. Understanding the importance of a smooth transfer of merchandise from the *Jameel* to the waiting trucks and railroad cars at the terminal—and the implications to his life, and the lives of his crew, if any mishap might occur—Ali Reza then joined Ahmed Nazari on the bridge.

"All is good, Ahmed?" the captain inquired as he strode onto the bridge, giving a brief nod of acknowledgment to the silver-bearded pilot standing nearby.

"So far," Ahmed replied, glancing between the busy terminals on the port side of the ship and the instrument panel in front of him.

"Thunderstorms expected within the hour," the pilot remarked, never taking his eyes off the bank of instruments and gauges laid out before him. "Tugs'll have us in before they hit."

In unison, Ali and Ahmed looked port side to the western horizon, a distant lightning strike confirming the pilot's observation. Nodding to one another, they almost missed the sudden appearance of a fireball shooting up from within the city limits of Newark some six miles away. But Ahmed caught sight of the anomaly out of the corner of his eye.

"What is that?" he asked the pilot, pointing at what looked to be a column of fire reaching hundreds of feet into the air.

"I don't know," the pilot responded, barely giving the occurrence a passing glance. "Ain't none of my concern at the moment," he remarked, picking up the radio transmitter. "Tugs nudging us to the dock is," he explained, pushing down the Send button.

As the pilot gave his orders to the tugboat captains, Ali and Ahmed stared at the far-off, wavering pillar of fire. And as the *Jameel* passed the northern corner of the Maher Terminal and began the slow slide toward berth 30 on the adjacent Newark terminal, Ahmed caught the flicker of new flames, these erupting on the south corner of the Maher Terminal near a freighter the *Jameel* had followed through Kill Van Kull.

"By all that Allah holds true," he murmured, "what is happening this night?"

No sooner had Ahmed spoken than the *Jameel's* emergency horn sounded a series of short blasts, alerting the Maher Terminal dock personnel and the crews of all vessels tied up to the pier of fire.

"Are you aborting docking?" Captain Reza asked the Sandy Hook pilot, his face going pale.

"No reason to," the man calmly replied. "Not berthing at Maher," he explained, giving Ali a quick glance. "Tugs proceed as instructed," he said into the radio transmitter.

Ali and Ahmed eyed one another while the radio receiver crackled with static, each man breathing a silent sigh of relief when they finally heard three staggered *aye*s from each of the tugboats guiding them to the pier. Ali looked at the watch on his wrist, checked the western horizon, then made eye contact with the first mate.

"So far, so good," he remarked to Ahmed with a nod.

When the *Jameel* came to a full stop, both Ahmed and Ali watched the crew at the bow of the freighter send the berthing lines over the side. Glancing over to his captain, Ahmed observed the stress of the week's transatlantic voyage begin to seep away from the features of the man. Having made many such crossings with Ali before, Ahmed understood the reason for the man's visible relief, he himself recognizing their accomplishment; bringing a cargo valued in the millions safely to port across three thousand miles of the Atlantic ocean.

"I'm done here," the Sandy Hook pilot announced, stepping away from the instrument panel. "Might see you on the outbound," he said, tipping the brim of his baseball cap as he walked past the captain and first mate.

Ali Reza was just about to reply when what sounded like a burst of thunder coming from the Maher Terminal prompted all three men to rush to the bank of windows on the port side of the bridge.

"For the love of Allah," Ahmed muttered in a bewildered tone as he looked upon the cloud of smoke rising from the midst of the railroad cars stationed in the center of the pier. "What is happening?"

* * *

Griper revved the engine of the same model red dirt bike he'd supplied to Twister and Bongo, zooming into a maze of stacked shipping containers. As sirens blared all around him—from fire, rescue, police, security, and freighters tied up to the pier—he brought the bike to a stop in the center of a narrow passageway. Hitting the kill switch, he shimmied off the back of the bike's banana seat. He reached forward and loosened the cap of the gas tank, placed his black helmet on the handlebars, extracted a switchblade from one of the pockets of his black jumpsuit, cut the skin-tight material open from knees to ankles, unzipped the front of the garment, slipped it off, and threw it on the seat of the bike. He took a red, white, and blue baseball cap— *Norton Lilly* embroidered on the front   from the baggy back pocket of the denim overalls he was wearing, placed the hat on his head, and bent down to the two saddlebags he'd fastened to the back frame of the bike. Positioning his hand directly over one of the leather bags, he lifted out a glass bottle three-quarters filled with gasoline, a dark-blue rag stuffed inside the mouth of the bottle. Pulling a plastic lighter from the pocket of the overalls, he tilted the rag-topped bottle to the side, putting flame to cloth. Edging backward a few steps, he hurled the bottle against the side of one of the steel containers right above the motorbike, turning to run as spraying fluid ignited. The eruption of flames rushing after him like a gust of wind, Griper sprinted for the opening on the northern end of the passageway, reaching the exit as the dirt bike's gas tank exploded.

Jumping to the side, he pressed his body against the end of a container, his heart racing as he saw a car with flashing red and blue lights speeding up Tripoli Street. Instinctively, he slapped the side pocket of his overalls, reassured when he felt the metal handgun strike against his palm. Surging with adrenaline, he pushed his body away from the corrugated steel, running straight for the onrushing car.

"Over here! Over here!" he shouted, waving his arms over his head. "Over here, officers! Over here!"

Griper saw the Port Authority Police Department decal on the side of the car as it came to a screeching halt ten feet in front of him.

"Thank god you guys are here, man!" he shouted at the uniformed men in the front seat.

"Back away from the vehicle," the officer on the passenger side ordered, pushing his door open and drawing his service revolver.

"You gonna need that!" Griper shouted, raising his hands above his head. "Fuckers are crazy," he hurried to say, sounding frantic. "They got guns! One guy looked like he had a bomb under his arm!"

"Bomb?" the officer who was getting out of the car repeated. "You saw this? You saw the guys responsible for this?" The officer glanced at Griper's *Norton Lilly* hat. "Call it in, Pete," the officer yelled over his shoulder, quickly glancing back at his partner. "Possible bomb suspect."

"They were headed that way!" Griper yelled, pointing toward the end of the terminal. "Said something 'bout blowin' up the big freighter moored at the end of the pier!"

Griper suddenly doubled over, placing his hands on his knees, gasping for breath.

"Motherfuckers took a shot at me. Thought I was gonna die," he panted, dropping to his knees. "One fucker chased me on his bike," he went on, his voice growing weaker. Dropping his hands down to the pavement, he struggled to say, "Heard the explosion behind me—don't know what happened."

Gasping, Griper heaved a mouthful of foamy spit to the ground.

"Call for an ambulance, Pete!" Griper heard the officer yell to his partner. "This guy looks to be in shock!"

Griper fell sideways, curling his body tight, panting for air. He tensed

when he heard boot steps drawing near, then breathed a small sigh of relief
when he heard a flurry of gunshots erupt from the south side of the terminal.

"Let's roll, partner!" the officer driving the car shouted. "Leave him! F
and R's on the way! They'll be here in two!"

Griper closed his eyes, letting his body relax. When he heard a car
door close, an engine rev, and tires squeal away, he allowed himself a smile.
Ten seconds later, he lifted his head from the tarmac to take a quick look
around. With the smell of burning gasoline in the air and the sound of two
more gunshots popping in the distance, he calmly pushed himself up off
the asphalt. Slipping his hand beneath his overalls, he reached under the
waistband of his underwear into the crack between his buttocks, removing
the stick of TNT he'd taped between his cheeks. Lighting the fuse with the
plastic lighter, he hurled the explosive as far as he could out toward the end
of the terminal.

As he turned west toward where the exit gates on McLester Street were
located, a sudden gust of wind blew against his face. Glancing up, he saw a
jagged lightning strike come out of the clouds, a rolling rumble of thunder
ominously sounding a few seconds later. Behind him, a sudden jarring blast
echoed through the stacks of truck-size steel shipping containers. Pulling
his cap a little farther down on his head, he headed for the terminal gates,
a second bolt of lightning flashing down from the clouds a little closer than
the first.

* * *

"Time to party!" Bongo shouted when he saw flames erupt on the pier.

After kick-starting their bikes in unison, Bongo let Twister take the lead,
drawing the fist-size Cobra handgun out of his jumpsuit pocket before moving off. Sand from the narrow strip of beach splattered against his sunglasses
as he followed Twister across the shoreline onto the grassy area toward the
chainlink fence surrounding the terminal's perimeter. Spitting a few granules from his mouth, Bongo slowed his bike to a stop as Twister approached
the fence in a tight curving arc, bringing his body parallel to the chainlink fabric. He laughed when Twister pulled away the section of wire they'd
previously cut. Revving his engine, he sped forward, shooting through the
opening, with Twister firing off a couple shots into the air before following.

Speeding up an embankment to the terminal tarmac, Bongo suddenly felt like he was ten years old again, taking a lap around the dirt track the Big Brothers organization had taken him and a group of inner-city kids to for a week's camp. Bongo remembered the time spent at camp as one of the best in his life: learning to ride dirt bikes, helping set up the course for the day, getting lessons from some of the crazy dudes who raced the semi-pro tour, and—the best part—flying without wings! There was something crazy good about "ridin' air," as the dudes called it, even when "going sky", meant crashing his bike in what the dudes called a "gnarly wipeout." As Bongo shot the Honda CR125R airborne over the lip of the embankment, everything he had been taught during that week of camp came flooding back.

At the apex of his jump, Bongo heard an explosion. The reverberating boom of the sudden blast caught him off guard, the bike veering sideways, Bongo nearly losing control. But as his bike began its lazy downward descent, Bongo steadied the handlebars to keep it from drifting. And just before the outer edge of his front tire met asphalt, he leaned back, stood up on both pegs, raised his elbows outward away from his body, and revved the engine with an influx of gas so the bike would accelerate close to top speed when both tires came in contact with the ground.

"Fuckin' A!" he shouted when his tires touched down.

Speeding down the pier, Bongo fired three rounds from the Cobra into the sky. Throttling down from fourth to second gear, he maneuvered the bike into a full 180-degree turn to look for Twister, laughing when he saw him lagging about fifty yards behind, the bigger man struggling to get his dirt bike up the embankment, having to dismount to push it the final few yards.

Another explosion followed by a new eruption of flames toward the center of the terminal caught Bongo's attention, a flash of lightning casting an eerie backdrop to the spires of fire climbing into the sky. Snapping his head back to ground level at the sound of gunshots, he watched Twister making his approach, instinctively wincing when he saw him awkwardly fire off another two rounds while trying to keep control of his bike. A single drop of rain hit the tip of Bongo's nose just as Twister came to a jerking stop beside him.

"Let's get the fuck out of here, man!" Twister bellowed. "Can't believe I ever agreed to this shit!"

"I'm with ya, bro!" Bongo yelled back as he looked across his shoulder at the slew of flashing red and blue lights heading toward them from the north side of the terminal. "We done our bit! Let's bail!"

As Twister turned his bike around and got it going, Bongo fired one more shot into the air. Stuffing the Cobra into the side pocket of his jumpsuit, he twisted the throttle, squeezed the clutch, and shifted the gear lever down with his left foot. Slowly releasing the clutch, he gunned the dirt bike forward with another twist of the throttle. Proceeding through first, second, third, and into fourth gear in quick succession, he sped after Twister.

A bolt of lightning illuminated the murky darkness above the track lights of the mammoth gantry cranes, raindrops suddenly gushing down through halos of yellow light. Water splattered against Bongo's face, his vision instantly hindered by rivulets streaming down his sunglasses.

"Go, man!" Bongo yelled, hastily wiping the rain from his glasses.

Through water-smeared lenses, he saw Twister stop at the edge of the tarmac above the section of security fence they'd cut a hole in.

"What the fuck ya doin'?" he screamed, taking a hurried glance behind him.

To his utter amazement and confusion, he saw Twister duck his head and speed away. Sirens blaring behind him, swaths of flashing red and blue lights racing up the wet asphalt toward him, Bongo revved his bike forward before bringing it to a stuttering, fishtail stop. Looking down the dark embankment, he saw nothing at first, nothing he could see to explain Twister abandoning the plan to exit the terminal the way they'd entered. But in another glimmer of lightning, he saw the outline of a pickup truck, silhouettes of three people standing in the back bed. Before he understood what it all meant, he saw the muzzle flash of a gun. A burning stab of pain ripped into his thigh a fraction of a second later.

"Fuck!" he screamed, gunning the engine. Speeding away from the embankment, he raced after Twister, trying to keep his dirt bike from swerving.

"Twister!" he hollered. "I'm hit, man, I'm hit!"

Powerful spotlights suddenly switched on, a blinding wall of glaring whiteness emerging from a dark crevice between containers stacked four high on Bongo's right. Bongo saw Twister zipping through the center of the wall of light, his dirt bike a shimmering streak of red. A flying silver snake suddenly attacked out of nowhere, Bongo catching a glimpse of the beast's gleaming coils as they wrapped around Twister's face. Bongo raced forward into the barrier of light, flinching when something hard smacked against his chest. He caught sight of the last few links of a thick metal chain as they slithered off his body to the rain-blurred asphalt below. Heart racing, stomach knotting into a ball of panicked fear, Bongo shot out the other side of the wall of spotlights to find Twister's dirt bike lying on its side some twenty yards ahead, a group of blurry figures loosely encircling what looked to be his friend's body.

"Twister!" Bongo shouted, easing up on the throttle, trying to make sense of what was going on.

Then Bongo saw one of the figures turn toward him, arm held straight out. Flopping his upper torso downward, Bongo hugged his chest to the gas tank, water from the front tire streaming into his face as he gunned the bike forward with his head positioned between the handlebars, the sound of the gunshot barely audible over the burping whine of the two-stroke engine.

What the fuck! What the fuck! Twister! We gotta blow! But where? Shit— Twister! Fuck, man! Fuck! What I do? What I do?

Bongo downshifted from sixth to second in a matter of seconds, pulling another 180-degree turn, fighting to keep the bike from sliding out from under him as the back tire struggled to find traction on the heavily puddled asphalt. Pulling the body of the bike beneath him, he came to a stop. Idling, he could see the cops were ten seconds away from Twister's bike, their headlights revealing a group of figures standing around it. Bongo could see four of the five T-shirt-clad guys were wearing red do-rags atop their heads.

"Aw, no man, no," Bongo muttered when he saw one of the gang members point what looked like a sawed-off shotgun down at Twister's head. "No, man. Fuck no."

Pulling the Cobra from his side pocket, Bongo revved his bike forward, firing a round at the gang. But the group of Bloods didn't even notice, the bullet missing high left, the sound of the small-caliber gunshot lost within the rumbles of thunder and the chorus of earsplitting sirens. As the flashing red and blue lights atop the police cruisers came swirling over the Bloods, Bongo saw the muzzle flash of the shotgun. Twister's head jerked off the ground with the impact of the blast before falling lifelessly back to the asphalt. Bongo swung his gun straight out in front of him, doing his best to steady his hand so he could get a shot off at the gang member who'd pulled the trigger. But the group of Bloods was scattering, each man running off in a different direction, rain and darkness covering their escape. Then the cop cars came to a screeching halt, the light from their headlights shining right on Bongo.

"Put down your weapon!" he heard a voice scream from beyond the bank of headlights. "Face down on the ground—now!"

Fumbling for the clutch lever on the left handlebar with the Cobra in his hand, Bongo inadvertently fired off his last round. Hugging his chest to the gas tank, he shifted into first gear just as what felt like an icepick of fire plunge into his ribs on his right side. Flinching with pain, gulping for air, Bongo managed to shift into second when another searing splinter of pain shot through his right kneecap.

"Fuck," he cried, managing to shift the bike into third.

Dizzy, struggling to breathe, shivering from the sudden onslaught of chills running through his body, Bongo drove away from the headlights into a dimly lit thruway he hoped would take him to the exit gates on the north side of the terminal.

* * *

Griper stood outside the multilane entrance of Maher Terminal, one of a couple dozen other men in Norton Lilly uniforms ordered to evacuate the premises by the police and fire department, milling around McLester Street. Griper stood near the back of the group, listening to the conversations taking place around him, wondering if anyone was going to ask him where his ID badge was. From what he'd heard, no one seemed to know what was going on, only that there'd been a couple of fires set, an explosion, and some wild reports of gunshots from the south side of the terminal. Automatic weapon fire, he'd heard one guy recount. And then another guy chimed in that he'd heard there'd been a rocket-propelled grenade fired at one of the freighters.

"Foreign motherfuckers, I bet," he heard another guy say.

The last statement garnered a grumbling of agreement—that whatever was going on, the trouble taking place on the pier was caused by foreigners. Griper almost laughed.

He'd seen a slew of blue and white cop cars racing down McLester Street from the adjacent Newark terminal. They, along with fire trucks, ambulances, and unmarked square-bodied chocolate-brown and black vehicles, poured through the entrance gates. Griper was confident just about every regular uniformed cop and undercover ATF, Customs, and Port Authority officer within a ten-mile radius was either inside the Maher Terminal compound or was part of the blockade of vehicles set up at the north and south gates. Super Freak would be pleased.

Just as the first news van arrived at the scene—a big WNYW-5 decal on the side—Griper heard several excited voices erupt from the front of the crowd. Something was happening, he assumed. From the way everyone started pressing forward, he knew there must be some action going on.

"That must be one of them!" he heard someone shout.

And while everyone either jockeyed to get a better look or voiced opinions about what they were seeing, Griper sprinted back to the ten-foot-high chainlink fence running along the western side of McLester, jumping as high as he could. Gripping the links of the fence with his fingers, he wedged the tips of his sneakers into the holes, twisting his body around so he could see what was going on.

"Stop right there!" he heard someone on a bullhorn yell out from the blockade of cars in front of the gates.

Griper swept his gaze through the beams of the spotlights shining into the first fifty yards of the terminal, his eyes locking onto the black-clad figure riding atop a red motorcycle.

"Stop and throw down your weapon!" the voice ordered through the bullhorn.

"What the hell ya, doin', Bongo?" Griper mumbled, thoroughly confused when he saw the dirt bike shoot forward with a sudden burst of speed.

The salvo of gunfire sounded like a volley of cannons: sudden, booming, frightening, unexpected. It was followed by an eerie moment of silence. Griper watched Bongo fly backward, the dirt bike falling sideways, the metal chassis skidding forward on wet pavement until it hit the side of a police cruiser with a sickening thump. While the crowd surged forward to try to get a better look at the guy the police had shot, Griper dropped down from the chainlink fence. Pulling the Norton Lilly cap lower over his face, he stuffed his hands in his pockets and walked away.

19

MIRKO WAS STUNNED. Gaping open-mouthed at the pillar of fire shooting into the evening sky, he wondered what he'd done wrong. Why had the entire building housing the apartment of the woman he was told to kill blown up instead of just the unit she lived in? Perhaps the gas line configuration in America differed from those in the Middle East, he conjectured. And perhaps, considering the devastation the explosion had caused, the PSI of the gas running through them was also different. Nevertheless, while he slipped his suppressor-outfitted gun into the holster attached to the back of his waist and picked up the insulated pizza pouch down by his feet, he was satisfied he'd accomplished his mission. The voice he never wanted to hear from on the phone from the Middle East would be pleased. Which, in turn, meant his parents would be safe. And now he could go back to Detroit and return to his mundane but pleasing job of marketing hummus and tahini. If he drove through the night—which was his intention—he'd be home for breakfast. It would be good to see his family.

Looking at the burning, almost completely obliterated building he'd detonated, he knew nothing could have survived the blast. And if someone had been lucky enough to live through the initial explosion, the subsequent fire would certainly have finished the job. With that satisfactory thought in mind, Mirko exited Perry Funeral Home parking lot on foot, taking a left on Mercer Street. Crossing over to the perpendicular Mercer Court, he began his hurried but meticulously planned escape to his car just as a flash of lightning lit up the street. Embracing the notion the oncoming storm would help him go unnoticed, he welcomed the first splattering drops of rain.

* * *

Chris was sprinting down Court Street toward the corner of Lincoln when the first bolt of lightning flared in the darkening sky. But he barely noticed. His attention was focused on the tower of flames rising above the area where he estimated Yutanda's apartment building to be. He hoped he was wrong, his calculations amiss. Maybe it was the building next to Yutanda's where the fire raged, or maybe a gas line in the middle of the street near her corner had sparked and exploded. But he knew he wasn't wrong. It was some kind of sixth sense he'd possessed most of his life—locations—where to find something or someone, where something had gone missing, where to locate an explosive, where to place a bomb where it would do the most damage. The trait was one of those nuanced qualities about a person—even the one blessed with it (or cursed, depending on the attribute) couldn't explain it. So he'd stopped trying to figure out how he knew the exact locations of things—places and people. He just knew.

By the time he reached the intersection of Lincoln and Court Street, the first units of the Newark fire and police departments were arriving, uniformed personnel doing their best to block traffic from entering Lincoln from either end. Looking up the street, Chris could see nothing but confusion and pandemonium: people streaming out of neighboring buildings, screaming, yelling, calling out for missing loved ones. Cars lurching out of parking spaces along the curb into the street, only to be waved back by stern-faced firemen who—by the sound of their voices—were not interested in listening to anyone's excuses as to why they should be allowed to exit. But the firemen were having a devil of a time, people not complying with their instructions, either indifferent to or not caring what the firemen needed or wanted them to do. As Chris stood and looked on, the stretch of Lincoln Street between Court and Mercer became a congested mess of honking trapped cars and a shouting throng of anxious people.

Up toward the far end of Lincoln, Chris could see flashing red lights, sirens blaring as a fire truck tried to inch its way down. But the truck was making little headway. Valuable time was being wasted. Unable to completely assess the damage to Yutanda's building from where he stood, Chris nevertheless understood the importance of getting the fire under control. But that didn't seem likely to happen anytime soon. The chaotic scene in front of him was preventing that. Survivors of the initial blast—if there were any—wouldn't last long if the fire went unchecked.

"Why'd I tell you to go back inside?" he muttered, clenching and unclenching his fists.

A gust of driving wind pushed a few large drops of rain into his face, an ominous thunderclap—deep, booming, resonating—rumbling across the sky. Sheet lightning flashed within the mass of deep-gray, fast-moving clouds above him, the eerie pulsing light rendering the scene unfolding in front of him surreal. Onlookers, gawkers, the curious, and the morbid chasers rushed past, an assortment of shapes and sizes dressed in loud, colorful clothes. Each sharing a common thread: eyes and heads tilted upward, locked on to the tower of flames framed by a menacing sky.

"Attention! Attention!"

Chris peered up toward the end of the street as a voice started yelling over a bullhorn.

"All non-official personnel must evacuate this area—now! Pedestrians are to move off this street over to Mercer Court one block over! Those of you in cars—you are instructed to exit Lincoln Street by the south end! Back up or drive out in an orderly fashion! This is a possible gas line explosion! Repeat—possible gas line explosion! Evacuate immediately! Evacuate immediately!"

As a caravan of vehicles and people began moving in his direction, Chris bolted for Mercer Court with the intention of reaching it before a crowd formed. Rain began to fall. Slowly at first, ponderous intermittent drops splashed atop the sidewalk, duping Chris into believing the storm would streak past the intersection of Mercer and Lincoln and unleash its deluge on another part of the city. A moment later, he grunted a self-correcting smirk, the stream of water gushing out of the clouds forcing him to turn his head down and to the side so he could see where he was going.

Screeching brakes, the blare of a horn, and the dull hollow sound of a dense object hitting metal brought Chris to an abrupt stop. Through a sheet of raindrops turned silvery-gold by car headlights, he saw a figure in a red jacket scramble up from the asphalt, a big square object grasped firmly in hand.

"You all right, man?" Chris called out.

Seemingly oblivious to his voice, the figure shouted out *"Mos zibby!"* before bending to search the area around him. One hand continuously patted his lower back—oddly so, Chris thought—while the other swept over the surface of the wet street in an arcing pattern. With a sharp honk of its horn, the car the man in the red jacket had collided with pulled away. As Chris narrowed his eyes to try to get a better look at the man—something about the man's voice seemed familiar—the flash of high-beams of an approaching car illuminated a wide swath of the rain-drenched street, the glaring light capturing a dull metal object on the pavement a few feet from the curb.

"Hey, man! That what you're looking for?" Chris yelled out, pointing to the object.

Just as the man turned his head and noticed Chris standing on the sidewalk, the growing intensity of the car's high-beams defined the object on the ground. It was a gun, Chris saw—an extremely powerful one, from the looks of it. In a blur, the man in the red jacket snatched up the weapon, stuffing it in the back waistband of his pants before turning and running across Court Street.

"The pizza guy," Chris muttered, noticing the image of a domino on the back of the man's jacket. "Why's he packing such a—?"

With a shake of his head, Chris sprinted up Mercer Court.

*

By the time Chris had positioned himself directly across from Yutanda's building, the police had already established a safety perimeter, cordoning off the crowd gathering on the western side of Mercer Court. Hoses were hastily unrolled from the first fire truck as another truck up on Mercer came to an angled stop, blocking travel in both directions. The deluge of rain seemed to be keeping the flames from getting out of control, Chris observed as he watched the firemen getting their equipment into position. But Yutanda's apartment building looked to be a lost cause; there was a gaping hole where the roof should have been, the support frame had disintegrated to charred struts, the windows were blown out, black residue covered what was left of the outer walls, and fragments of wood, insulation padding, and other assorted building materials were strewn over the surrounding area. Edging closer, Chris hoped to hear what communication might be taking place between the firemen on the scene, but the throng of chattering people made hearing impossible.

Futile, futile. What was I expecting to hear, anyway? he asked himself as he gazed at the burning building. *Gas line explosion; isn't that what the fire chief said? The blast must have blown the floor of the building right through the roof.* He hoped Ed and Elizabeth's deaths had been quick. Yutanda's too, for that matter. *Guess the fat-ass reverend won't have to worry about her anymore,* he thought. *All this bullshit I went through—for what?* Grunting, he shook his head. *Died in a freak accident.* Chris turned in the direction of Court Street, suddenly wondering why the pizza man had been carrying such a big gun. And why he had a ten-inch suppressor barrel attached. Chris looked back at the fire scene, shifting his attention to the nearest intact building. *If he carried the gun for protection, a shorter barrel would be best—quicker draw, less cumbersome to holster. Longer would be to cover muzzle flash—and for silence.*

Focusing on the bank of metal boxes attached to the side of the building next to Yutanda's, Chris tried to discern if each apartment housed within the structure had a separate natural gas line running into it. But the rain, the crowd, and the fast-falling darkness made it impossible for him to tell. *Still,* he thought, *a well-placed shot—no—you couldn't count on a bullet penetrating steel pipe from a distance. And if you were standing right next to a gas pipe when you shot into it, you'd be the first one to go in the subsequent explosion. How, then?* Chris studied the ground at his feet, pockets of rainwater reflecting the orange light of the fire back up into his eyes. A nudge to his shoulder stirred him out of his thoughts. When two more people bumped into him, a thread of anger shot through him.

"Hey, watch where you're stepping," he curtly warned.

"Shit—sorry bro," a youth about ten years old, Chris guessed, apologized.

Chris looked down and studied the boy's street-wise face.

"Just loony Lucy pushin' through the crowd, trying to score," the kid offered.

"Say what?"

Abruptly, the boy was jostled sideways by two people trying to get out of the way of an afro-coifed skinny woman outfitted in some skimpy purple tiger-print get-up. Chris assumed she was a prostitute by the way she looked, and by the way she pawed at the men she bumped into as she weaved her way through the crowd.

"See what I mean?"

Chris looked over to see boy flash him a knowing smile.

"You wanna baby, sugar?"

Chris grabbed hold of loony Lucy's wrists as she placed her hands on his chest.

"Sell you one for cheap."

Loony Lucy's brown eyes were watery and bloodshot, pupils no bigger than pin heads. Even in the diffused light of the sporadically placed streetlights, her physical state wasn't hard for Chris to deduce. Her slender—almost sickly—frame, her unsteady gait, the way her unfocused eyes searched his face as if she was seeing ants crawling across it—he knew she was an addict. A heroin junkie.

"Go away," Chris told her, throwing her arms to one side in the hope her body would follow.

"Come on, sugar," the woman responded, pressing her body against his. "You look like the fatherly type."

Surprising Chris with her quickness, she cupped a hand behind his head. Tilting it forward, she whispered in his ear, "Trade ya for two foils, if you're holdin'. Five Benjamins if ya ain't."

She pressed her face into his chest, her wiry mound of hair grating against his neck.

"Get the hell away from me." Grasping her shoulders, Chris pushed her off his body. "Go peddle your junk somewhere else."

"It's a flyin' baby," she told him, holding a finger up in front of her face while wobbling in front of him. "Stroller fly too," she added, cupping a hand over her mouth when she started to laugh. "Though the stroller don't land too good," she said, the words laughingly spit between her fingers.

As much as he didn't want to, Chris found himself chuckling. Shaking his head at the ridiculousness of the situation, he looked at the woman—raindrops dripping from her stiff, over-sprayed Afro; skinny arms adorned with bulbous, shiny, plastic-looking rainbow-colored bracelets; her purple tiger-print dress—or whatever the skimpy piece of fabric she was wearing was called—finished off with black fishnet stockings with runners ripped along each side of her knobby knees. *Freak show,* he concluded. *The girl's just a messed up freak show.*

With a reverberating rumble of thunder, the rain abruptly ceased. Chris looked upward before shifting his eyes to the burning building across the street.

"Ain't got no momma, now," he heard Lucy say, her laughter subsiding. "Suppose she done blew up when her building did."

"Say what?" Chris asked, preoccupied with watching the torrents of water flowing from the fire hoses onto the flames. "What was that you said?"

"So whaddaya say, sugar?" she propositioned, stepping over to him to grind her hips into the side of his leg. "Got two foils for me?"

Grabbing her just below her shoulders, he squeezed her upper arms and pushed her an arm's length away.

"What did you mean—*her* blowing up? Who's *her?*"

"Don't bruise the merchandise, baby," Lucy teased, playfully slapping at his arms. "You like it rough? That it? Ain't no fatherly type after all, are ya?"

With more force than he imagined she possessed, Lucy punched the underside of Chris's wrists with her fists.

"Well, fuck you, then," she spit, her face scrunching into a scowl. "I ain't sellin' you no flyin' baby. Plenty other people around who want it," she told him, her voice rising with anger. "You'll see," she added, taking an awkward swing at his face with her open palm as she tried to pull away.

"Don't be in such a rush," he calmly replied, letting go of one of her arms so he could reach into the front pocket of his pants. "I don't buy nothin' I haven't looked at first."

Pulling out a wad of bills, Chris flipped through the edges until he found what he was looking for. Releasing his other hand from Lucy's arm, he offered her a smile as he pulled a hundred-dollar bill out of the pile.

"What I gotta do for that?" she purred, sliding her hand up his forearm. "You got a place round here, somethin' decent? I ain't no slut, you know," she declared, looking at him as though his face reminded her of someone she was trying to remember.

"Show me this flying baby you got," he said, folding the hundred-dollar bill lengthwise in half and then holding it out in front of her face. "Show me," he repeated, jerking the bill away from her when she reached out to grab it. "Show me."

* * *

Rue Thompson stood at the very end of the Toyota Logistics Services pier, a pair of compact, high-powered binoculars held in one hand, the curved vinyl handle of a closed, dripping-wet umbrella in the other. A contented smile rested on his portly face. As far as he could tell from his vantage point, the operation—one pier away from Newark, two from Maher—was unfolding as planned. The *Jameel* was safely moored, offloading well underway. The feds and local police were busy with the explosions, fires, and gunshots at the adjacent Maher Terminal. The cargo sitting in the belly of the freighter would soon travel along planned distribution routes. The Consortium would reap a huge influx of cash needed to keep their operation growing. He would call Adiam and Akmir as soon as he could, but he was certain they were already aware of the night's success. The captain of the *Jameel* had as much vested in the operation as anyone. Rue was sure that the man's shortwave radio had long since transmitted a coded "all's well," and that the subsequent long-distance call to Djibouti had been placed. For now, he would enjoy the few seconds of solitude. The time to tie up loose ends and plan for the next shipment would come soon enough. As would the time for dealing with the brewing confrontation with the Bloods and Ñetas. A potential gang war wasn't going to help any of the major importers on the docks. *Akmir's playing a dangerous game,* he thought. *Pitting everyone against each other in the hopes they'll just kill themselves off. Fuckin' Arab's going to get us all killed over here—while he sits on a silk pillow under a palm tree in the desert dreaming of a worldwide syndicate.* Rue shook his head—*if he had any idea what it was like over here.*

And then there was the new ivory buyer to deal with. Rue felt uncomfortable just thinking about him. *Lex Taylar—what kind of name is that?* Rue wondered. Probably some vampire-looking dude, he mused, some stiff, creepy old wrinkled white dude in a seersucker suit wearing a silk ascot around his neck. Dealing in ivory—Rue shuddered. What kind of freak makes a living buying and selling bones of dead animals? *At least I don't have to worry about him until tomorrow,* he reminded himself.

Rue shook his umbrella, admiring the twisting pattern of the droplets as they flew in outbound circles toward the ground. His contented smile slowly fading, he slipped the binoculars into his coat pocket before smoothing the synthetic locks flowing over his shoulders.

The headlights of a car suddenly appeared at the far entrance of the vast parking lot situated at the end of the pier. Rue watched the lights slowly and deliberately follow the curve of the railroad tracks as the car headed out toward him. Reaching inside his coat, he flicked off the safety of the .38 Detective Special he had holstered under his arm.

As big as fifteen football fields on the edge of the Newark Bay, the Toyota parking lot had served Rue well over the years, its location offering all sorts of possibilities—remoteness just one. When the lot was filled with cars, it became a maze of brightly colored metal boxes where a person or an item could easily be lost or hidden. And when it was mostly empty—as it was on this night—the lot served as a perfect location to hold a discreet rendezvous and have a conversation no one could overhear. But now, standing alone on the deserted southeastern tip of the pier, Rue suddenly felt vulnerable. Patting the gun holstered beneath his left shoulder, he tried to peer past the headlights of the approaching car.

The glare of flashing red lights suddenly swirling into his face caught him off guard. Reflexively, he swung a hand in front of his eyes, using it as a shield. When a siren from the car briefly blared, he cupped his hands over his ears and took a step back.

"Could you make yourself any more noticeable?" came a voice from the car.

"Son of a bitch. Layla?" Rue sputtered, pulling up the waist of his pants. "Is that you? What the hell you doin'?"

Rue stepped out of the glare of the headlights toward the driver's side of the car.

"And for Christ's sake, can you lose the red twirlers?"

"If your constituents could hear your mouth," he heard Layla mock.

When the red lights atop the police cruiser stopped flashing, Rue lowered his hand, a disapproving frown directed at Corporal Stilton.

"Pretend you're showing me your ID, and back away from the car while I get out, okay?"

"What?"

"You're darn lucky I was the first one to respond to the watch commander's call about a suspicious individual out here looking through a pair of binoculars," she told him, pushing open the driver's side door.

Stepping out of the car, she slid her nightstick into the appropriate slot on her duty belt.

"Your pretend ID, Rue," she said, extending her arm and holding out an open hand.

"What the hell is this, Layla?" he angrily protested.

"ATF spotted you. Thought maybe you were a person of interest, a lookout for one of the cartels. Called it in to his commander."

"Shit," he responded, glancing around the area where they were standing.

"Yeah, shit. So play along. Knowing how gung ho the ATF boys are, one's probably scoping us out right now."

Pulling a flashlight off her duty belt, Layla clicked it on, directing the beam of light to Rue's hands as he reached around and pretended to pull a wallet from the back pocket of his pants.

"ATF, yeah, those dudes are hardcore. They all over at the Maher, though, right?" he asked. "Griper and—"

"Don't tell me any names," she rushed to say. "I don't want to know."

"But they did their jobs, right? Maher's got everyone's attention?"

Layla clicked off the flashlight and reattached it to her belt. Placing her hands on her hips, she stared at Rue, a big scowl on her face.

"I don't want any part of what went down tonight. It isn't what we agreed upon."

"What? Shit, why you sound so angry? What's wrong?"

"Two people are dead."

"Dead? Who? No one was supposed—"

"To die? Really? That collar you wear on Sundays give you the power to see into the future?"

"Just calm down," he told her. "And tell me—"

"This is not what we agreed upon," she repeated.

"Look, Layla, cut me some slack," he replied, taking a step toward her.

"Don't," she ordered, thrusting her arm out. "Stay right where you are unless you want backup to come rolling up this lot."

"Oh, right—being watched, right? Yeah, anyway, hey—I had nothing to do with anyone getting killed tonight. Plenty of that happens on its own, right? Especially down here," he said, chuckling.

"Don't hand me that crap. And it ain't funny," she snapped, pointing a finger at his chest.

"Some kid got his head blown off by a shotgun."

"Who?"

"Who?" Layla barked. "I don't know who! Heard it on the chatter, is all," she explained, nodding toward the police cruiser. "Report said it was point blank."

Layla retracted her finger, letting her arm fall to her side as she began to turn away.

"I gotta go," she told him.

Rue caught the weariness in her tone.

"Layla, wait."

"Make yourself scarce, Reverend," she responded, walking away.

"Arbagna over at the Maher? She there when it went down?"

"No," she replied, placing her nightstick in the car before sliding into the driver's seat.

"You didn't call her?" he pressed.

Rue pinched his eyebrows together when Layla shook her head and resignedly blew a gust of air between her lips.

"You don't know anything, do you?" she condescendingly observed.

"That's what I pay you for," he smugly retorted.

"That can change," she fired back.

"Let's cut the bullshit, Corporal. We can hash out your beef later. Arbagna," he said, taking a step toward the vehicle. "Was she seen at the Seaport tonight like the plan called for?" he demanded.

"She never arrived," she told him, her voice sounding oddly detached. "Came over the radio 'bout the same time all the shit was going down at Maher."

Layla put the car in drive and pulled up a few feet so she could look across at him.

"Gas line explosion on her block," she said in a monotone voice. "That's all I know."

"What, you think—?"

Rue watched Layla drive away, an uncomfortable feeling churning in the pit of his stomach. *Loose ends*, he reminded himself, *loose ends*.

* * *

"You put the kid in a utility closet?"

"Shhh—don't want people to know I got a key," Lucy whispered, bending closer to the doorknob so she could slip the key into the lock. "Don't live here, ya know."

"Then how'd you get it?"

"Got my ways," she said, giggling and wriggling her buttocks. "There."

Swinging the door open, Lucy slipped inside, motioning for Chris to follow. As Chris slipped in next to her, she shut the door behind him.

"Light switch?"

"Better in the dark," Chris heard her murmur as her hand fell atop his groin.

"Shit, that's not why I'm here," he said, pushing her away.

"Come on, sugar. Don't you wanna have some fun?"

When Chris felt her fingers grab his hips he tried to back away, but what felt like a metal shelving unit kept him from moving more than a few inches. Then Lucy pulled his lower body to her, pressing her mouth against the outline of his penis, intermittently running the edges of her teeth along the shaft and sucking side to side like her mouth was an attachment to a vacuum cleaner.

"Goddamn it," he hissed, slapping her across the side of her head.

Chris heard her body fall against what sounded like another metal shelf.

"What's wrong?" she whimpered. "You one of those?"

"One of—?"

"Just pretend I'm a boy, then."

When he felt her hands groping for his crotch, he kicked out with his leg, the tip of his shoe connecting with her body.

"Don't hurt me," she pleaded. "I—I dunno what you want me to do," she cried, her fingers pulling at his pants.

"The baby," he tersely replied, kicking his foot sideways to push her hands away. "Where is it?"

"Oh, forget about the kid for a minute, sugar. There'll be time for that later."

Reaching down, Chris grabbed hold of her wrists.

"You stupid bitch—this was all a bunch of bullshit, wasn't it?"

Thrusting her backward, he turned and fumbled for the doorknob. Finding it, he pulled the door open.

"Where you going?" she angrily shouted.

Chris looked back across his shoulder, the light from the hallway coloring Lucy's face a ghoulish shade of gray. Although her expression seemed angry, Chris noticed a reoccurring twitch at the corners of her lips, her hand trembling as she raised it to shield her eyes from the intruding glare.

"You promised me a Benjamin!" she yelled, pointing an accusatory finger, her body shaking.

"Yeah—to show me this flying kid you said you had!" he angrily replied, keeping his voice level. "Not—not for some cheap trick from a freak-show junkie."

"Wait!" she pleaded when he started walking away. "It's here! It's here," she sobbed. "Come back. You'll see."

Chris tried to block out the sound of her crying as he looked back into the closet. *What a pathetic sight*, he thought, when he found her hugging her shivering body with both arms.

"Where?" he simply asked.

"Light switch—on the wall—inside the shelf," she meekly answered, pointing left of the open door. "Can't blame me for tryin'," she sniffled when Chris turned on the light. "Thought maybe you'd be satisfied with a ride," she half muttered, awkwardly pulling herself to her feet with the help of the shelving units on either side of her. "Sell the baby to somebody else. Make me enough for two, three days of foil."

"Jesus Christ, woman, just—"

"All right, all right, all right," she said in a rush, dismissing him with a wave of her hand. "Fuckin' queer rather have a baby 'stead of having a little fun," she mumbled.

Turning her back to him, Lucy shuffled the couple feet to the rear of the closet, her fingers pulling at the edges of the cardboard boxes stacked within the shelves.

"Now where I put it?"

Standing on the tip of her toes, she pinched down the edge of one of the larger boxes to peek inside.

"Here," she told him, pointing to the box as she turned back around. "It's in here."

"You put it—?"

With a shake of his head, Chris pushed Lucy aside, pulling the box down off the shelf.

"What the—?"

At first glance, the blue blanket decorated with baby pink elephants looked to be nothing more than a dirty mound of stained cloth wrapped around a bundle of old newspapers. But at one end of the bundle he saw an opening, a swath of brown flesh visible within the center. Pulling the folds of the blanket back, he saw the face of a child, streaks of dried blood on its cheek.

"It dead?" Lucy whispered, peering over his shoulder. "I done wrapped it in newspaper to stop the bleeding."

Chris lifted the bundled child out of the box and placed his fingers on its neck just beneath the jawbone. Feeling a faint pulse, he pushed aside the blanket and pulled off the newspaper. Grasping the child around its chest, Chris lifted it to eye level, holding it at arm's length while trying to decide if it was Yutanda's.

"What be wrong with you?" Lucy scolded, placing her hand under the child's chin to support its rolling head. "Gotta support the head. Why you wanna a baby when you don't know how to care for one?"

"How long this kid been unconscious?"

"I dunno," Lucy replied, looking at him like he was crazy for asking. "Done been this way since that woman left him out in front of her building in the stroller, I suppose. You know," she paused, "fore she went back inside. And then—boom!" she described, thrusting one hand above her head, wriggling her fingers as if they were legs of a spider above a flame. "Fuckin' explosion threw me on my ass. And the fire!" she exclaimed, her eyes going wide. "Well, I don't need to say nothin' 'bout that, do I? You done seen that yourself. The whole world done seen that, I suppose," she said, laughing.

"And the woman?" Chris asked, probing the deep scrape on the side of the child's face with the tips of his fingers.

"What woman?"

"The woman who left this kid in the stroller. What happened to her?"

"What you think happened to her?" Lucy admonished, placing her hands on her hips.

Chris quickly moved his hand behind the child's neck to support it.

"Done blew the hell up. Or fried in the fire," she spit, curling her upper lip. "Uppity city official bitch."

"You knew her? Yutanda Taylor? Or Arbagna, maybe?"

"Don't know no names," she hotly replied. "Thinks she better than most—hmph."

Abruptly, Lucy clutched her stomach.

"Pay up," she struggled to say, distressed. "You promised."

Chris shifted the limp body of who he supposed was Menelik Taylor-Arbagna into one arm so he could reach into his front pocket. Extracting the wad of cash, he pulled three hundred-dollar bills from the stack and dropped them on the floor.

"That should get you enough foil to last you for a few days," he said, walking past her. "It's not like I don't know the street price."

Lucy dropped to her knees, scooping the bills up to her chest with a quick swipe of her hand.

"What you do with it now?" she asked, eyeing the child.

"What you should have done in the first place: take him to one of the ambulances sitting a block over."

With a withering glare, Chris pulled the door closed, leaving Lucy in the closet.

"Freakin' junkie," he cursed under his breath.

"Hey!" he heard her shout. "Hey!" she yelled, pulling the door open. "We agreed five Benjamins! Five!"

"I didn't agree to anything," he told her, not bothering to turn around. "Go buy your shit and sit in a dark corner somewhere."

"You son of a bitch," she spit.

Chris heard her footsteps following. The exit door leading out to the street was down a long hallway, a good twenty yards away.

"Uppity, just like her," he heard her snarl. "Show you. Help! Help! Somebody help me! He stealin' my baby! He stealin' my baby!"

Chris ran for the exit door, Lucy's shrill, wailing voice following him like that of some banshee from the depths of hell. One by one he heard doors flying open, voices muttering curses or questioning why they were being disturbed.

"Hey!" he heard a male voice holler. "What the hell's going on? Hey, you!"

Chris turned his shoulder to the fast-approaching exit door, throwing the weight of his hip against the waist-high metal crossbeam containing the locking mechanism. Outside, the night greeted his escape with a straggling line of people heading east toward the fire, their shapes draped in swirling shades of red and blue. Sirens blared; ambulances departed and arrived from different directions. How many other people had died in the explosion? he wondered. Searching for the nearest ambulance, he followed the stream of people, wanting nothing more than to drop the child in the back of one and disappear into the crowd.

"Somebody help me!" Lucy wailed as she stepped outside the building.

"Shit," he mumbled.

"He stealin' my baby! He stealin' my baby!"

Chris sprinted across Mercer Street toward the church parking lot, dodging people as he ran. Lucy's constant cries for help alerted the crowd to his escape. Feeble attempts to stop him followed: arms thrown out as barricades, hands grabbing at his elbows. But Chris bulled his way through.

Just ahead, however, he spotted a very large man moving in front of him, blocking his path. Immediately pushing off the ground with his right leg, Chris turned his body sideways, coiling his left leg as he leaped into the air. He delivered a solid kick to the man's chest with his left foot, and the big man toppled backward with a stunned grunt. Chris barely broke stride as his right foot landed just to the side of where the man's head bounced against the pavement. His path clear, he sprinted into the alley between Perry Funeral Home and the Baptist church. Lucy's screams for help died away as he faded into darkness.

* * *

"He wasn't doing nothin' but ridin' a dirt bike!"

Rue felt the snub-nosed barrel of the gun press deeper into his temple.

"They shot him down like he was some rabid mutt. And where's Twister? Word on the street is the Bloods iced a body on the docks 'fore the cops showed! Weren't no one supposed to die!" he shouted.

"Get ahold of yourself, boy!" Rue barked, glaring into the rearview mirror. "And put that gun away."

"You said they'd be booked for shootin' a gun off and not havin' a permit!"

Rue could see Griper's eyes rapidly blinking in the mirror, his jaw grinding, lips twitching at the sides.

"And that was only if they got caught! They weren't supposed to die, you fucker!"

Rue felt the barrel of the gun trembling against his skull.

"You killed them! Fuck! They were my bros! This is your fault! You and your fucking plan!"

"My fault? You shittin' me, boy? You were the one who explained it all to them, weren't you? Didn't you tell them to just give themselves up if they were cornered?"

Rue turned his head to look out at the bay. When he didn't feel the barrel of the gun follow his movement, he inwardly sighed.

"It's tragic your friends were killed—and we don't know if Twister's really dead, do we? But it's imperative for all of us to understand how trigger-happy the cops are—especially where it pertains to our black brothers."

Rue turned away from the water, shifting his attention to the young man leaning forward from the back seat of his car with a gun in his hand.

"I know it must be painful, Griper," he said in a calm, caring tone. "And it's completely normal to want to—to feel like you need to blame somebody. But trying to pull ourselves out of this pit whitey's put us in takes a toll. Not everyone's going to make it." Rue shook his head. "Not everyone," he lamented, his eyes drifting to the gun. "It's a violent world."

Looking back at Griper, he added, "Tonight's a testament to that violence. Dirty shame it is," he said, offering a sigh and a shrug. "Dirty shame."

"Just shot him down like he was a dog or something!"

Rue could see Griper's eyes fixated on the gun in his hand.

"Like to shoot them the same way. Fuckin' pigs!"

Rue watched the gun slide off the bench seat of his Lincoln Continental as Griper slumped back.

"Won't bring them back, will it? Shooting a cop to even the score," he explained when Griper shot him a surly look. "Still—taking one down would send a message."

Rue looked out of the front windshield to the end of the parking lot, where he'd been standing for the past hour. He could see how he'd been spotted by the ATF agent Layla had told him about. Stupid, he thought, stupid to have exposed his position like that, out on the tip of the pier looking through binoculars. He'd remember for the next time.

"Whaddaya mean, send a message?" Griper demanded.

"Kill a brother, lose a cop," he nonchalantly replied.

"Just randomly shoot some pig on the street?"

Rue saw Griper shaking his head through the rearview mirror, his expression confused.

"Not random," Rue softly countered. "Pointed—a player from the docks tonight. Someone who might've had a hand in how it all went down."

"How you know?" Griper spit. "How you know who was there?"

"Easy now," Rue hurried to say as Griper pointed the gun to his head when he went to reach into his coat pocket. "Just showing you how I know. Binoculars—powerful ones," he said, holding the compact pair up in his hand so Griper could get a good look. "See a lot of shit. Almost makes it like you're there."

Rue studied Griper through the rearview mirror; the young man seemed agitated, lost.

"Seen a black cop—a woman—talkin' to a couple Bloods 'bout an hour before you arrived. Saw the Bloods go runnin' off the Newark pier like she'd told them some news— show back up at the Maher twenty minutes later."

Rue turned around, countering Griper's look of suspicion with an assuring nod.

"Sad to see a sister turn on her own. Just like the pigs, though, isn't it? Using a sister to get a brother killed?"

Griper's voice was icy when he asked, "Who? Who is she?"

"I'd rather not say."

"She the one you talkin' to over there?" Griper asked, motioning toward the end of the pier with the gun.

"You saw that?"

"How you think I break into the back of your car without you hearin'? You two set this whole thing up, didn't you?"

Griper leaned forward, pointing the gun at Rue's head again.

"I ain't stupid, Mister Super Freak. Got eyes, dig?"

"Suppose it could easily look the way you described, Griper. And shit, yeah, if I was in your shoes and I saw me talkin' to a narc, I'd come to the same conclusion." He gave Griper a wary glance. "And I'd deserve to be shot if that was the case," he calmly agreed, shifting his eyes to the gun. "If it *was me* planned Twister and Bongo's killings with the help of a narc pig. Shit—if I were you, I'd have already shot me," he chuckled. "But then I'd be wrong. Maybe not see it for a while, but I'd find out—eventually—that I'd made a mistake. And then I'd realize I had a hand in three of my brothers getting snuffed tonight."

Rue turned his head to gaze out at the Newark Bay, pausing long enough for Griper to begin fidgeting in his seat.

"And the narc would still be sleeping peacefully in her bed, laughing about how stupid I was."

"Then what the hell *was* you two talkin' 'bout?" Griper angrily shouted, gripping the butt of the gun with both hands, his face twisted with rage. "You think *I'm stupid?*"

"Money," Rue replied, keeping an even tone. "I've been paying her for information. Like you probably already guessed. Says she knows how big the operation is. And now she wants a bigger cut—a huge cut."

"What that got to do with Bongo and Twist?" Griper demanded.

"She told me—" Rue tilted his head to the side, lowering his voice to a whisper. "The other cartels are paying her more. Said she tipped the Bloods off tonight to show me she means business. I'm in a fucked-up situation." Rue shifted his head up to look at Griper through the rearview mirror. "And I don't rightly know what I'm going to do to get out of it."

Rue studied Griper's expressions, watching them progress through anger, doubt, enlightenment, and resolve.

"What's the bitch's name? And where she live?"

Rue turned his head away, admiring the lights twinkling on the water.

"I think it'd be better if I didn't tell you. Maybe wait—"

"What her name, Freak?"

Rue felt a chill race up his spine.

"'Cause somebody payin' for Bongo and Twist gettin' burned tonight. And right now, I don't fuckin' care who it be."

Rue felt the barrel of the gun press into his ear.

"Layla. Layla Stilton's her name. She's got a place over—"

"Drive," Griper ordered. "And don't you worry none, Mister Freak. You owe me two Zs of pure now. And I mean to collect."

Rue looked into the rearview mirror to find Griper smiling at him.

"So you can just drop me off a block or two from her crib—and I'll take it from there."

Griper leaned forward and pressed the gun into Rue's neck.

"And then you pay me in full when I come callin'—dig? Bitch be right," he said, laughing, slumping back into the car's leather seat. "Spread the wealth, ya know? Maybe you and I be equal partners after tonight," he chuckled. "Yeah—what you think about that, Mister Super Freak?"

Rue shifted the big luxury car into drive and lightly pressed his foot to the gas pedal.

"Whatever you say, Mister Griper," he casually remarked. "Whatever you say."

20

T HE STENCH OF burning fuel floated on the morning wind, the air saturated with foul-smelling fumes. The ground where he walked and the leaves of the few trees around him soiled with a slick layer of dark residue, remnants of ash-laden smoke spewed from the raging fire. Dismayed by the filth he'd caused, Teimbaka bowed his head and asked the Mother for forgiveness. Yet, even as he asked, he could still see oil-colored plumes rising in the distance from the cache of fuel barrels he'd set to flame before dawn. The pale blue of the eastern morning sky tainted with ominous streaks of black.

Beyond the dingy haze, the sun crested over the horizon, wisps of wavering heat curling along the edge of the fiery dome. Daylight revealed long strands of twisting filth slithering towards him, airborne serpents ferried by winds blowing inland from the Arabian Sea thousands of kilometers away.

"Seeking your revenge," he murmured, eyeing the snake-like formations.

As Claire said you would.

Claire. Mouthing her name, he closed his eyes, conjuring her face. *Where is she?* he wondered. For her features blurred as he tried to picture her, the specks of amber in the brown of her eyes dulled by a thin veil of water. The smoothness of her skin, the smattering of freckles on her nose— these too were unclear, shrouded in mist, leaving him to struggle with an image of a woman who seemed suddenly cold and aloof.

Wiping his eyes with the back of his hand, he blinked away his tears. Longing for the ridges and plateaus of the Simien Mountains, he looked northwest, wishing he were cradled within the Palm of the Mother, Claire by his side. But the subtle sound of an approaching helicopter intruded on his thoughts, making him painfully aware the Palm of the Mother was far from reach. He was alone. Battling an army of fanatics. Capture imminent. Death a likely probability. Today. Sometime today, he reasoned, the Mother would call his spirit back to Her. *Perhaps that is why Claire's image is so blurry,* he thought. *Perhaps she senses I will die today. Perhaps that is why she would not come when I wished her to. Perhaps—*

He shook his head, smirking at his self-pity. *What does it matter if I die?* he asked himself. *I have failed the Mother. The carcasses of the butchered elephants I have seen since traveling here are proof. Blowing up a fuel depot will not stop George Henry and his men from slaughtering the beasts. I would have to—*

The shadow of the helicopter raced across the open ground in front of the termite mound he was perched upon, blanketing him in a streaking moment of darkness as a volley of bullets ripped into the earth to his left. Leaping down from the three-meter structure, Teimbaka slung his rifle from his shoulder and ran. Flinging his body to the ground when the roar of the engine and the gusting wind from the helicopter blades seemed right on top of him. Then the flying machine shot past, whizzing over him, streaking thirty meters beyond before he pushed himself up from copper-hued dirt.

As the copter banked into an arcing left turn, Teimbaka quickly surveyed the area around him, deciding which direction offered the best chance of survival. West, a hundred meters farther past the turning helicopter, was a wide expanse of trees. Sprinting for the cover of the foliage, he loaded a bullet into the chamber of his gun. Ahead, he could see the copter leveling, the transparent nose of the craft pointed straight toward him. Just outside the rim of the cockpit, a long black barrel appeared, a man bending over it, taking aim. Teimbaka lifted the old Lee-Enfield single bolt-action rifle Selam had given him to his shoulder, halting just long enough to sight his target before squeezing the trigger. Gunshots erupted, a bullet missing Teimbaka high right as the pilot jerked the aircraft away. The copter veered hard upward and to the left, gaining altitude in response to Teimbaka's bullet striking the nose of the craft. Wasting no time, Teimbaka sprinted forward, ears attuned to the whir of the blades, hoping he could make the tree line before the black dragonfly returned. Then he stopped.

He could hear the trumpeting calls of elephants before he saw the first guardian male appear from the trees. It was like witnessing a small earthquake; he watched more of the herd lumber out of the woods, trees swaying one way and then the other as the massive beasts pushed between. Glancing up over his shoulder, he saw the small black chopper zooming toward the elephants.

"No!"

Extracting a bullet from the goatskin pouch tied about his waist, he loaded the breech and sprinted ahead. Taking aim at the black dragonfly, he fired the round at the copter's bubbled windshield. The bullet flashed against the metal frame just behind the pilot's seat. A blaring cry from the guardian male answered the resounding boom of the Lee-Enfield as Teimbaka took another bullet from the goatskin pouch and reloaded. Lifting the rifle to his shoulder, he hesitated. The elephants turned toward the tree line, the guardian male shepherding them back into cover. Relieved to see the elephants retreating, Teimbaka relaxed. But when he saw the black dragonfly dip low to cut off the guardian male's escape, his lips twisted into a snarl.

"No! By the Mother—no!" he screamed, leaping ahead.

He could tell the big bull was confused, the animal turning one way and then another, ears flapping, feet stomping, tusks scraping earth and throwing clouds of copper-hued dust into the air. Each time the elephant would start to run, the copter mirrored it, blocking the elephant from moving past, dipping lower, edging the beast farther into the open. Abruptly, as the bull elephant briefly stood immobile, the black dragonfly turned sideways. Teimbaka watched the man in the passenger seat shouldering his weapon to fire. Dropping to one knee, Teimbaka held his breath and took aim, squeezing the trigger an instant before the man in the helicopter did the same.

The bull elephant shuffled awkwardly backward, blood trickling down one side of its head. From behind the massive bull, the black dragonfly arose, swaying from side to side, the man with the rifle in his hands leaning precariously out of the cockpit, one hand clutching the metal frame of the cabin, the other holding on to the barrel of the weapon dangling below his knees. When the man fell from the helicopter, the bull elephant rushed past the man's body into the trees.

Rotors humming, the black dragonfly zoomed forward, blades tilted downward as the pilot steered the craft straight for Teimbaka. Fumbling for a bullet, Teimbaka backed away. The whirling blades edged nearer, rapidly closing the distance between them. With howling wind spraying dirt into his face, Teimbaka pinched a bullet from the pouch and slipped it into the firing chamber as quickly as he could slide the bolt back. He swung the rifle up to his shoulder and aimed.

Shards of rock and dirt shot into his eyes, forcing him to lower his weapon to cover his face. Debris sliced into the skin of his cheeks and arm. The roar of the whirling blades became a high-pitched shrieking, the strength of wind funneled by the blades forcing him to lean forward or risk losing his balance and tumbling backward. Hugging the rifle to his chest, Teimbaka dove sideways to the ground. Keeping his body rigid, he rolled right, spinning away. Momentarily clear of the blades' reach, he sprang up into a crouched run, heading for the cover of the termite hill.

Teimbaka flung his body forward, diving chest-first onto the ground. He scrambled lizard-like to the side, reaching the base of a termite steeple as the helicopter roared past. Pulling his legs beneath him, he sat up and swung the Lee-Enfield to his shoulder. Pressing his back against the base of the rock-hard earthen stalagmite, he rested the barrel of the rifle atop his propped-up knee. Left elbow raised outward, head bent over the stock, right eye sighting down the barrel at his target, he placed his finger on the trigger and waited. Just as the steel dragonfly drifted higher into a slow, banking turn, Teimbaka squeezed the trigger.

The helicopter swept smoothly in and out of its turn, hovering stationary for a moment before moving back toward him. As Teimbaka fumbled for another bullet, he saw the aircraft begin to waver, dipping right to left several times as if balancing a heavy weight atop the tips of the blades. Shading his eyes from the rays of the sun to the east, Teimbaka squinted, trying to focus on the pilot. But the man was just a dark shape contained within the silhouette of a dark bubble. Only when the dragonfly turned sideways could he discern the pilot talking into a handheld radio receiver. He could see little else. Then the helicopter banked away, soon becoming a dark speck in the hazy morning sky.

* * *

"Why are you here?"

Was it the old woman talking? Bin'ka winced with the thought, trying to channel the throbbing pain in the back of his head out through his ears.

No, that was your voice, someone told him, someone who sounded remarkably familiar. *Now get up. Get up!*

Bin'ka tried to do as the voice said, but something prevented him from moving, something heavy. The backs of his shoulders bore the weight of whatever object was keeping him pinned to the ground. *The ground?* Fingertips scraping soil, he began to wonder where he was—and how he got to be there. *Muhammad. He sent you into a building*, the familiar person told him. *Don't you remember? And then, an explosion. The building fell on top of you!*

"Why are you here?"

It is the old woman! Why does she keep asking me that?

"Muhammad," he grunted, hoping to infuse his body with the sudden rush of anger he was experiencing. "Muhammad!"

*

"Over here! Hurry! Please! I heard a voice!"

Under her breath, Talia cursed the slow reaction of the soldiers. *Inept imbeciles*, she thought. *No doubt the Afar will be running the country soon.*

"Please!" she shouted, trying her best to sound weak and needy. "It's my father! Over here! Please! I think he's still alive!"

When the reaction of the soldiers was nothing more than a passing glance her way, Talia ran to the nearest man, pressing her body to him.

"Please," she begged, pulling at the man's arm in such a way his elbow brushed against her breast. "Please help me," she repeated, falling limp to his chest.

Talia rubbed her face into the man's uniform and began to cry. Feeling his hands grasp her waist, she slid upwards, nuzzling her cheek against his neck.

"Will you help me?" she pleaded.

Looking into his dull brown eyes, she gripped his shoulders.

"It's my father," she tearfully explained. "Please, I'll do anything—anything. Just please help him."

"Where?" the soldier asked, winking as he slid his hand down over her buttocks.

"Over here," she told him, breaking free of his hold. Clasping the man's hand, she pulled on him so he would follow, saying, "Under those slabs of concrete."

As the soldier moved past her to study the area she was pointing to, Talia gave his hand an affectionate squeeze.

"Please hurry."

The soldier nodded, giving Talia another wink as he called several men over to help him. A half hour later, the soldiers helped Bin'ka to his feet.

"It is a miracle your father was not seriously injured, miss," the soldier she'd enlisted to help her said as he approached. "A crossbeam seems to have saved his life."

"How can I ever repay you?" she replied. Rewarding the man with a passionate embrace, she whispered, "Please visit us in the hospital."

With a seductive wink and a lingering touch of her fingers to the man's cheek, she hurried over to Bin'ka.

"Father!" she exclaimed, wrapping her hands around one of Bin'ka's massive arms. "Father!"

*

"How bad are you hurt?"

Bin'ka rubbed a hand across the back of his neck.

"Not badly enough to keep me from crushing Muhammad's neck next time I see him," he told her, wiping a blood-smeared hand on dust-covered trousers.

"You needn't worry about him." Talia pulled the driver's side door closed, slipping a key into the ignition of the Peugeot she'd driven out to Camp Lemonnier. "One of the Afar has robbed you of that joy."

"What do you mean?" Bin'ka groggily asked.

"Close your door," she told him, shifting into first. "I'll fill you in."

*

The night unfolded as Adiam had hoped it would, she began. But as soon as the phone call from the States had come in relaying the message the *Jameel* was safely docked and unloading, Akmir abruptly took his leave. Some excuse about needing rest, he said.

"A multi-million-dollar payday," Talia scoffed. "And you say you need to rest? Adiam knew something was up."

Bin'ka nodded at her comments, but said nothing as she continued.

The first explosion from Lemonnier occurred soon afterward, she went on, luring every facet of security and leaving the port pretty much undefended. That's when Akmir made his move. He had swept into Adiam's café, a dozen well-armed men wearing black keffiyehs behind him. A firefight ensued. The wait staff—Monica—most of the patrons, killed.

"But getting up the stairway to the third floor was a little more difficult than they had anticipated," she remarked at that point, smiling like an alley cat finding fresh fish on an unattended window ledge.

Adiam had taken a bullet in the shoulder. A surface wound, she assured Bin'ka when he looked over to her. Akmir—and the one traitor who survived the attempt at storming the stairway—fled. Adiam wasn't surprised by the move to kill him, she explained; it seemed he'd been expecting some sort of power play from Akmir for some time.

"But when we learned the Afar had blown up the munitions depot with some of the RPGs we'd supplied them," Talia said, "Adiam knew the attempt on his life was only a part of what Akmir had planned."

"What do you mean? What plan?"

"To take control of not only the Consortium, but the port as well."

"Madness," Bin'ka replied. "But—how did you—Adiam—how does he know this?"

"Adiam tried to get in touch with the other members of the Consortium and found most had been executed."

*

Crossing a dry riverbed, Talia slowed, looking into the rearview mirror for several moments before making a right-hand turn off the highway onto what barely qualified as a dirt road. The Peugeot bounced several times before Talia found the subtle grooves of tire tracks made by other vehicles taking the same route.

"That's when he realized you were probably in danger."

"So he *did* send Muhammad to get me."

"No, Muhammad was sent by Akmir. A ruse to get you to Lemonnier. You were to die in the confusion, we figure. And the plan almost succeeded."

"But how—?"

Talia went on to tell him she had been sent out to Lemonnier by Adiam to gather intelligence. Only by chance, she'd been taken hostage by one of the Afar. That's when she'd overheard a conversation describing how Bin'ka, the big man—the water buffalo—had been blown up in an old concrete storage house. He'd been sent in by his driver, who had pulled an RPG out of the trunk of the car and blasted the building with a round.

"Son of a bitch," Bin'ka cursed. "I will crush his skull when I find him."

"Too late. Like I said, one of the Afar beat you to it. Apparently he recognized him as being one of the slavers who took his sister a week or so ago. Slit his throat from ear to ear with one of those big curved knives they carry."

Bin'ka rubbed his temples.

"You okay? You look—"

"Just a ringing in my ears," he told her. "It'll go away."

"Good, because we're almost here."

"Almost where?"

"Adiam told me to give you this."

Bin'ka turned his head when he saw Talia slide her hand beneath the waist of her flowing, coral-colored pants.

"If I found you alive," she continued, holding up a small envelope between her fingers as she pulled her hand back out of her waistband.

"You see, we didn't really know where you were—or if you were to be trusted. But Adiam had a hunch you'd been set up." She gave him a passing glance, trying to read his reaction. "Because of the color of your skin," she explained when she saw Bin'ka's brow furrow. "Akmir's religious beliefs."

"I don't—"

"I am nothing," she told him, touching her chest. "As all women are nothing in the eyes of Akmir's religious teachings. And you—"

Bin'ka's expression was unreadable as he waited for her to go on.

"Because your skin is the color of night—you are a slave," she told him quite casually. "No matter how he might have otherwise acted toward you at times."

Bin'ka grunted and looked out the window.

"Read the note," she instructed. "I need to slow the car down to a crawl so we aren't blasted off the road." Talia gripped the steering wheel a little tighter. "If you can call it a road," she added with a nervous smile.

The terrain on either side of the Peugeot was desolate: nothing but sun-baked sand and rocks with a smattering of scrub bushes interspersed—so hot, dry, and remote there wasn't a reason in the world to be out in it unless one was a desert-dwelling insect or reptile. Even then, Talia thought, whatever type of creature might actually exist here, it would certainly flourish in hell too. Because that's what the area reminded her of: hell.

Easing the car to a stop, she slowly scanned the area around them, peering out the windshield as if she was half-expecting to find some sort of hidden message carved in the face of one of the larger stones dotting the landscape. Bin'ka, she saw, was studying the piece of paper he'd taken out of the envelope. By his expression, she could tell he was confused. His eyes squinted as he silently studied each word Adiam had written.

"The Legion of God?" he questioned, sounding puzzled. "What's that?"

"Not *what*. They're—"

"What—what is it?" he pressed when she abruptly stopped talking. "And why did you stop the car? We're in the middle of nowhere."

The figure capturing Talia's attention seemed to have appeared out of thin air. A ghost, she thought when it first emerged out of the ground outside the passenger side window some twenty paces from the car. But when she saw a weapon materialize from beneath the cover of a desert-colored camouflage poncho and recognized that the dark hollow pits she thought to be the creature's lifeless eyes were in reality dark-tinted goggles, she thought the manifestation more ghoul than ghost. Especially when she focused on the apparatus covering the rest of the figure's face: bulbous beehive-like protrusions on each side of where a mouth should be and a smooth-surfaced, hardshell, sand-colored hooded mask hiding features that might otherwise have given her a clue as to what the entity really was or what it looked like.

"Holy shit," Bin'ka said when another camouflaged figure emerged from the ground right in front of the car.

"Yeah—Adiam said it would be a shock. That was an understatement," she remarked. "How can they stand to wear all that gear?"

"A FAMAS," Bin'ka muttered, his eyes locked on the figure aiming an automatic weapon at the windshield as he approached the car. "These guys former Legionnaires?"

"FAMAS?" Talia whispered.

"The gun. It was standard issue—"

The tap of the barrel of the FAMAS against Talia's window ended Bin'ka's explanation.

Raising her palms to show the gas-masked figure peering into her side of the car she wasn't concealing anything, she slowly let her left hand drift down the inner frame of the door to roll down the window.

"Adiam sent us," she said. With a nod toward Bin'ka, she went on. "This is the man you're to—"

"Stay within the tracks."

Startled by the garbled, metallic-sounding voice, Talia flinched, her body jerking backward into her seat, her arms spasmodically lifting away from her sides.

"Down one!" the metallic voice screamed.

"I'm sorry! I'm sorry! I'm sorry!" Talia shouted, covering her ears against the high-pitched static. "I'm sorry," she quickly added, regaining what composure she could. Looking straight into the dark orbs looming an arm's length away, she said, "I wasn't expecting to hear someone talking through a tin can filled with buzzing water."

Waiting for the man—creature, ghoul, soldier, goblin; she wasn't quite sure what to call the thing standing next to her—to respond, she took a quick look around. She stifled her urge to gasp when she saw there were now several camouflaged figures surrounding the car, their weapons aimed at her and Bin'ka.

"Go," the buzzing metallic voice ordered. "Don't deviate from the tracks."

With a nod, Talia rolled up the window. Shifting into first, she eased the car forward.

"You'll break the steering wheel with that grip," she heard Bin'ka remark.

Looking at her hands, she saw the skin around her knuckles was nearly white.

"Don't remember ever seeing you scared."

"Aren't you?" she shot back. "Fanatics don't scare you?"

"It's not like we haven't dealt with their kind before. The Afar, warlords, soldiers of one government or another, rebels wanting to overthrow some government—seems like everyone's a fanatic." He shrugged. "It's what the world's come to," he threw in, turning his massive body sideways to look out the rear window. "They're gone."

Her eyes glued to the faint tire tracks she was following, Talia replied, "What?"

"They disappeared—the men who had us surrounded—I can't see a trace of any of them."

"Adiam said they're like nothing he's ever dealt with before."

"What do you mean?" Bin'ka asked.

"They—"

She glanced into the rearview mirror and ran her tongue across her lower lip.

"Don't *want* anything," she uncertainly explained.

"Everybody wants something," he replied with a dismissive grunt. "Everything has a price."

"Not them. Least not as far as Adiam could tell the few times he met with them."

She glanced over at him when he didn't respond.

"Ringing in your ears still?" she asked, seeing he was rubbing his temples again. "You look like you're in some pain."

"A voice," he mumbled. "Can't seem to—" He shook his head. "Go on."

Seeing the tracks ahead curving into a small stand of half-dead juniper trees, Talia slowed the Peugeot down to a crawl.

"They don't want the usual items: money, power, weapons, land." She gave a slight shrug.

"Cleansing of evil." She nervously laughed. "Whatever that means. That's about the extent of what Adiam could find out, anyway. You consider that wanting something?"

Bin'ka shifted his body as though suddenly uncomfortable with the way he was sitting, the car tilting from side to side.

"They're certainly well armed for not wanting anything," he observed. "Must be getting all that armament from somewhere—someone."

"I can't say yes or no to any of that," she told him, leaning forward against the steering wheel as the car entered the cover of the trees. "Adiam just told me to—"

"Damn."

The sleek bodied, steel-gray helicopter nestled beneath a layer of camouflage netting was massive. Four huge steel blades drooped from the main rotor, tail blades encased within a molded metal casing resembling a giant fan. Just as she wondered what purpose the large, barrel-shaped object mounted to the underside of the chassis served, Bin'ka spoke.

"Got her armed to the teeth. Cannon pods, missiles—even got her outfitted with what looks like anti-submarine torpedoes. Where'd they get all of it?"

Talia sensed him turning to look at her, but she wouldn't take her eyes off the barely visible tire tracks she was following.

"And where'd they get the money? A French Panther—that's at least five to seven million U.S. dollars on the black market."

Bin'ka threw his arms out in front of him, bracing himself against the dashboard when the car jolted to a stop.

"What the—?"

Another camouflaged, gas-mask-wearing figure stood right in front of the car. And, like the others, this one had a FAMAS cradled over an arm, the barrel pointed right at them.

Talia turned the car off and raised her hands. Bin'ka saw she had broken out into a sweat.

"Stick to the note."

"What?"

"What Adiam told you to say," she muttered between clenched teeth. "Remember to say it just as he wrote it."

Before she realized, the figure in front of the car had moved, Bin'ka's door suddenly pulled open.

"Who sent you?"

Again, the voice asking the question sounded metallic, as though the person speaking was talking through a long steel tube humming with an electrical current.

"Adiam," Bin'ka replied.

"Why have you come?"

Talia pressed her legs together as she waited for Bin'ka to reply. When she saw several more camouflaged figures appear—seemingly out of nowhere—their weapons trained on the Peugeot, she almost answered for him. But thankfully, Bin'ka said, "To retrieve a servant of the Lord."

"Down center!" the metallic voice shouted.

Talia caught the subtle adjustment of a gloved finger on the trigger of the weapon nearest her.

"Come," the metallic voice ordered, motioning with the barrel of the FAMAS for Bin'ka to exit the car.

"You going to be okay?"

Talia forced a smile.

"He said they wouldn't harm me. Don't worry."

The car tipped to the right as Bin'ka slid from the front seat. Talia reached a hand out to touch him.

"Remember the note," she hurriedly said.

But she wasn't certain Bin'ka had heard her because the door shut behind him as soon as he stepped out of the car. A tap on her window gave her a start.

"Back out," she heard a metallic voice order through the glass. "Keep to the tracks."

Talia turned her head to peer out the back window.

"That's impossible," she protested, turning back to face the figure.

But there was nobody there.

Taking a quick survey around the car, she didn't see anyone. As she reached for the key in the ignition, she heard the helicopter engine begin to whine. With a deep breath, she shifted into reverse.

* * *

"What will I look like when you see me?"

Claire wrung her hands.

"What will you look like? I—I don't understand."

"Will I be pleasing to you? Smooth of skin with flowing locks of honey-colored hair? Eyes as blue as the sky?"

Claire kept her eyes fixed to the trunk of the acacia tree, afraid to look to either side for fear the brilliant light emanating from behind it might blind her.

"Yes," she replied. "What you describe would be pleasing to me."

"And if I was disfigured? My face gouged by blowing sand, my body twisted and deformed, my eyes yellowed from sickness—what then? Would you see me?"

She remained silent for a time, for not only were the questions trouble-some, but the voice asking changed with every word. Man, woman, child; male, female; young, old. The voices came to her as wind-driven rain; water lapping against a shoreline; ice clinging to branches, melting beneath a warm sun.

"Would I see you?"

She pictured Lee's village: the house with walls, scores of refugees struggling to survive. Some nothing more than skeletons, too frail to move, clouds of flies swarming to decaying bodies, while others beseeched her for food or medicine, quivering fingers gnarled with pain. She had passed by many of the displaced that first day, carrying the dead girl in her arms. Watching them gather around her—yet not seeing who they were. Interlocking her fingers, she clasped her hands together and bowed her head.

"How will you know me—if you will not see me?"

"I— I've—" Trembling, fighting back tears, she replied, "My eyes were young then. They are no longer."

"Would you help me?"

Claire raised her head.

"Of course."

The brilliant light—white gold when she first looked upon it—dimmed to hollow darkness. The blood within Claire's veins turned cold at the changing, conjuring memories of the Serpent's room, twisting her muscles into knots as she felt the guilt of sin slip around her soul. Touching her face, her fingertips brushed away granules of ice from her cheeks. Behind the acacia, within a dense fathomless blackness, wisps of silver clouds appeared, edges sewn with shades of sunlight, fragments of rose-hued stars glittering just beyond. Ice became water. As it dripped from her face to her hands, her skin tingled where droplets touched, heat spreading through her veins.

"If I came to you as thousands—hungry and cold, bloodied by war— would you welcome me? Or would you bar your door and shout for me to go away? Pelt me with stones if I refused, leave my children to starve while bread went to mold inside your cupboard?"

"I would bring you to shelter and give what food I had," Claire answered without hesitation, her voice clear and strong, rising in volume as she spoke. "I would gather wood for fires, sew clothes from rags, tend your wounds till healed, cradle your children in my arms while praying dreams could still find their way to them while they slept."

To her dismay, Claire watched the rose-hued fragments scatter, rushing outward beyond the scope of sight, leaving gold-tinged threads of silver in their wake. These faded into what had been in place before they existed: a hollow darkness bereft of warmth. She shuddered, not understanding what she had done, the emptiness in her heart overwhelming, as though she had been placed inside a coffin and lowered into a grave.

"Angelique."

The name was whispered so softly, she wasn't sure she'd heard it. Rekindling the memory of kneeling in darkness in the field where Teimbaka buried the dead. The utter nothingness she experienced that night—when the beat of the kebero abruptly ceased—rushed back to her as though she was there. Saying words over a woman she barely knew. Praying to God. Coming to wonder if those prayers were ever heard.

Seeing what she thought to be the flaring of a match within the dark, she asked, "Teimbaka—is it you?"

The movement of the flame was so subtle Claire was unaware of it drifting toward her until a tail of translucent gold appeared, spreading outward, growing brighter as it lengthened. Smiling when the flame zoomed forward, she made the sign of the cross as it alighted behind the acacia tree, a radiating orb of icy fire too brilliant to look upon.

"And those who live with you—would they welcome me as you would?"

Claire placed her fingers to the base of her neck, touching her skin as if the memory of the child's voice she was hearing lay just beneath the surface of her flesh. So close to remembering who the child was, she reached out her hand, hoping he would take it. But she quickly withdrew it, clutching a handful of her skirt, when he asked, "Would they share their home?"

Claire turned her face to the side, not wanting to see the line of people materializing in front of her. She had seen them before—everywhere—streaming out of Eritrea, fleeing the Tigray, staggering across the border out of Sudan, beaten and bloodied from endless war. A great exodus of the forgotten—trudging to nowhere—neither welcomed nor offered aid. Left to fend for each other in another land beset by conflict, famine, and misery. Struggling with shame, she realized she had not done enough, could not do enough—would never be able to right the wrongs committed against the refugees. And those who could offer help—governments, both foreign and their own; warlords; people of neighboring countries—simply looked away. As she was doing now. Averting their eyes because the endless stream of the forgotten would become just that—forgotten—their passing meaning little, if anything at all, except to those who walked amongst them or followed their footsteps in hope of finding someone lost.

"What have we done?" she chokingly cried, her eyes filling with tears.

"And the animals?" the boy asked. "Those my Father blessed you with, those the Mother loves—will you keep them as intended? Protect and nurture them as expected?"

"No," she harshly whispered, her head shaking vehemently from side to side. "Please—" she pleaded. "Don't make me look."

"How will you know me—if you will not see me?"

A plain of butchered carcasses appeared—elephants, rhinos, tigers, lions, giraffes, and forms of creatures she could not recognize—strewn from one bleak gray horizon to the other. Tusks and horns cut from faces, hides peeled from flesh, bodies without heads, others without feet, hooves, or tails. Disfigured from wounds, mouths open in a perpetual gasp, as if each animal was aware the last breath of their life was being stolen. Their eyes were sunken and hollow—blackened by death—hordes of flies shifting from one orb to the next in a macabre ritual of rebirth.

"Which one am I?"

The question came as a cloudburst of rain. Claire left to wonder which drops had spoken, the decision becoming more maddening the more she tried to reason where to look. Frantic, she turned her head from side to side, scrutinizing each droplet where it fell, desperate to find the right ones before they were absorbed into the ground.

"I don't know!" she sobbed, burying her face in her hands. "I don't know! I don't!"

Trembling uncontrollably, she prostrated herself, her voice an agonized whimper.

"Forgive me. I— Forgive me."

Wind rustled the leaves of the acacia tree, swirling, gusting sideways then down, wedging beneath her body before rushing upward to the sky. Lifting her off the ground as it ascended, holding her stationary before setting her back to earth. Kneeling, head slightly bowed, hands clasped close to her heart in prayer, she fixed her eyes upon the bark of the acacia.

"Which one am I?"

The question came to her in voices she had heard before but never understood. The cry of a hawk, the trumpeting of an elephant, the roar of a lion, the howling of a wolf: these and a host of other voices asked her to decide. Afraid and uncertain, she began to weep. Venturing a look to the plain beyond the tree, she began to pray.

"I weep because I am not worthy to open the book or look into it," she recited in a murmur. "Forgive me, Father."

Claire gazed at the gruesome carnage laid out before her.

"I am not worthy to receive you."

Filled with despair, she covered her face with her hands.

"Only say the words."

Pressing her palms flat against her ears, she stared dazedly to the ground.

"And I shall be—"

Unable to finish, she staggered from her knees to stand, the radiant light dimming as she turned to go. Flames shot out from behind the acacia, winding streams of interlocking fire closing where she would walk, barring her from moving past. Like a jagged finger, a wisp of flame curled inward to her face, lapping at the edge of her chin.

"See me."

It was a boy's voice she heard, arising within the plain of dead animals. Although it was gentle and kind, Claire felt tormented by its sound. Slapping the fire away from her face, she sank to her knees, wailing. "I don't know which one you are!"

"Look upon me."

Prism-shaped rainbows glittered between falling snowflakes, each binding to the next. Rays of sunlight skewed in dizzying directions, casting a sparkling blanket of the purest gold upon the plain. Where golden light touched, rotted flesh healed, animals rising to stand in crystalline forms, brilliant hues of light-infused color refracting through their shapes upward to the sky.

"Look upon me."

The child's whisper came from within a swirling ball of incandescent snow, radiance cast outward from its center.

"I see you," she replied.

"Which am I?"

Snow became rain, prism rainbows erased by darkening clouds gathering in the sky. On the plain below, crystalline forms of animals crumbled back to earth, glass-like bodies whittled to granules of sand as Claire stared on in disbelief. The fire that had kept her from fleeing abruptly vanished.

"Which?"

A lone snowflake drifted into her vision, fluttering just beyond her lips, moving with the current of her breathing. Just as it began to melt, she opened her mouth, the snowflake turning to water as it came to rest upon the tip of her tongue. Looking up, she saw breaks in the storm clouds appear, glimpses of rose-hued stars visible beyond. As though witnessing a revelation, she whispered, "You are all."

Claire found herself as she had started, kneeling in front of the acacia tree, hands clasped before her in prayer, eyes averted from the brilliant light on the other side of the wood. Running her tongue across her lips, she felt the soothing moisture of the melted snow. Braving a look directly into the light, she asked, "Tell me how to help?"

"There will be pain," the child's voice replied. "And sacrifice."

"Tell me," Claire responded, undeterred.

"Take my hand."

A staff of fire appeared by her side, standing upright, ends pointing from earth to sky, blue-white along the surface, orange-red where flame met air. Claire immediately thrust out her hand to grasp it, but the staff drifted just out of reach.

"To help will mean to suffer," the child's voice warned.

"Then let it be so," she quickly replied.

As the staff of fire drifted back toward her, Claire reached out and took firm hold. Ignoring the pain shooting up her palm to her shoulder, she tightened her grip, enthralled with the prism rainbows hovering over her skin. As she gazed in wonder at the colors on her arm, a rough cuff to her shoulder caused her to fall sideways to the ground.

"What are you doing?" she heard a child's voice scream.

Stunned, blinking her eyes to try to focus, Claire looked up.

"Eden?" she confusedly asked.

"What are you doing?" Eden shouted again, the girl's face lined with the same recrimination Claire heard in her voice. "Haven't you heard me calling for you? Didn't you hear the gunshots?"

"N-n-n—no," Claire stammered. "What gunshots?"

"Look at you!" Eden snapped. "You're bleeding! Why have you thrust a thorn into your hand? And why are you kneeling in front of this dead tree?" she demanded, giving the charred trunk a dismissive glance. "Were you having a vision?"

The look of disapproval on Eden's face was harsh.

"*Keet ahn gohl!* Why would you have one now? Couldn't you wait?" Incredulous, she went on. "Why are you so stupid?"

"Eden—"

Claire suddenly tilted her face skyward, peering past the tops of the trees.

"What is that?" she asked, uncertain of the sound she was hearing.

Eden followed Claire's gaze, shifting uneasily on sandaled feet. An instant later, she was running for a cluster of trees, Claire reaching out a hand as if she meant to stop her.

"They're tracking him!" Eden yelled over her shoulder. "They're going to kill him!"

"Who?" Claire shouted, rising to her feet. "Eden! Eden! Eden!"

But Eden was gone.

Claire stared at the spot in the underbrush where the girl had run.

"Eden's gone," she murmured, touching her lips.

At the distant sound of gunfire, the confused look on Claire's face vanished. Crossing herself, she broke into a run.

21

J OHN TOO WAITED for the helicopter to streak past before motioning Eden and Claire to come out of hiding.

"Quickly," he instructed, waving for them to join him. "We must hurry if we are to catch up to Teimbaka before the soldiers do."

"You're sure it's him?" Claire asked, breathing heavily. "It's Teimbaka?"

"His," he told her, holding a longbow out toward her. "I found it with a few arrows near a termite hill a half kilometer back. Do you not recognize it?"

Claire stared at the bow, her eyes drawn to the faint hand impression near the center. Meeting John Too's unflinching gaze, she nodded.

"Follow me."

Before he could break into a run, Eden yelled, "Wait!"

"There is no time," he told her. "There are dozens of soldiers not far away. Maybe five hundred meters north of here."

"We must reach Teimbaka before they do, Eden," Claire added, motioning for John Too to go. "Otherwise—"

"What would happen?" Eden asked, defiantly folding her arms in front of her chest. "How will we what? *Save him?* The three of us? All we have are bows and arrows." Glancing at the weapons in John Too's possession, she gave the tabib and the abdar a stern look. "When they have guns and helicopters and missiles."

Claire glanced uncertainly at John Too before saying, "He'll be killed if we don't try."

"And what would happen then—if he died? What would change?"

"Eden!" Claire gasped.

"Oh, Tabib—please—there is death everywhere." Opening her arms to encompass all that was around them, Eden asked, "And what changes because someone dies?" Pausing, tilting her head to the side, she remarked, "Even when it is someone you love—when you do not wish for them to be gone."

"The wind blows where it wishes and you hear the sound of it," John Too quietly offered. "Yet you do not know where it comes from or where it is going."

"John 3:8," Claire murmured. "How did—?"

"Useless talk; is this not what Teimbaka would say?" he responded, stern-faced. 'What would change if he died?'" he scoffed, glaring at Eden. "How would we know? That is for the Mother to understand. And the Father," he added nodding to Claire. "The boy—"

"The boy," Eden mocked, rolling her eyes. "The one with the sparkling eyes?" she teased.

"When the last elephant is gone, we will be no more. He has told me. Believe or don't believe," John Too stated. "It makes little difference. But we have seen the spirit elephants," he went on, nodding to Claire. "Teimbaka is who they have chosen. He is Etiyopiya—he is of the Mother. I will not let him die because you do not understand."

"Abdar—"

A sudden, frightening explosion left them momentarily stunned. John Too grabbed Eden's wrist, pulling her after him as he started to run. But Eden slapped his hand away, wrenching her arm free.

"You would run where there are bombs?"

"He's there," John Too told her, reaching for her again.

"You're crazy," she countered.

Claire broke off running, muttering, "They will stagger and go mad because of the sword I've sent among them."

"They will all be there," John Too murmured as he watched Claire race toward the plume of smoke rising above the trees.

"They?"

"Spirit elephants," he replied. "And those who would see Teimbaka safe."

"Those who would see—" Eden paused, her expression questioning as she rubbed the side of her head. "Bouda?" she uttered, her eyes going wide.

"Have you not smelled him?" John Too said, laughing. "Even the burnt petrol fumes cannot block the stench of his hides. Hey! Wait!"

Adjusting the quiver of arrows strapped to his back, John Too sprinted after Eden, a longbow clenched in each hand.

* * *

"What are you doing?" Kamua yelled as the Land Rover jolted to a stop.

"You deaf?" Selam shouted back. "Or blind?"

Kamua stared at the back of Selam's head while the older man peered out the windshield.

"That was either a missile or a bomb," he muttered, giving Kamua the slightest of glances through the rearview mirror. "Either one means we're done."

"Done? But we haven't even—"

"Kamua," Tengene interrupted, positioning his upper body so he could turn and look at the young ranger. "We're not in Ethiopia anymore. We've got no jurisdiction here. This is a Sudanese problem."

Kamua heard Selam shift gears a split second after the sound of automatic weapon fire began. Craning his head out the side window, he could see a column of gray smoke rising above the trees.

"I'm turning back!" Selam yelled.

"Wait!" Kamua ordered, grabbing the carbine lying next to him on the back seat. "I'm getting out."

"This isn't our fight," Tengene countered, reaching over the back of his seat to try to grab hold of Kamua.

"Not our fight?" Kamua opened the side door and got out of the jeep, sliding his rifle and a field pack along with him. "How many butchered elephants have we run across?" he argued, slamming the door shut. "Twenty, thirty—forty? And what will all that ivory buy?"

"We don't have any authority in Sudan," Selam testily remarked. "Get back in the jeep."

Slapping the lower frame of the driver's side window as he moved toward the front of the vehicle, Kamua countered, "Guns, missiles, bombs, mortars, helicopters; and do you think George Henry's only going to use them within the borders of Sudan? Do you think he cares whether he's here, or in Ethiopia or Kenya? I've heard he's raided villages as far south as

Uganda," he assailed them, his voice filled with anger. "Not my fight," he scoffed, slapping the side of the Land Rover. "Old men," he derided, walking away. *Mbili nyani.*

"Did he just call us two baboons?" Tengene asked, a scornful expression on his face.

"Indeed he did," Selam replied, easing the old Land Rover into reverse. "Indeed he did."

* * *

Sarah awoke in a sweat, her body curled into a ball, shivering beneath the decaying hides John had given her. Seh-my sat next to her, the beast's brown-black eyes staring directly into hers.

"Water," she rasped.

Or she thought she had, for Seh-my gave no indication she had spoken, the animal's face impassive, not a flicker of movement to be seen. Only when she felt her body rising from the ground—lifted by some unseen force beneath her upper back—did the large dog-like creature's eyes blink.

"Sit up," she heard a voice softly command. "Drink."

The sensation of a hand to the back of her head coaxed her forward, her lips pressing against something round and hard. Liquid dribbled down her chin before she opened her mouth. When she did, a gush of fluid washed over her tongue. Though the water was warm and tasted of metal, she tilted her chin upward for more. Rewarded with another mouthful, she gulped so fast she nearly choked.

"Slow."

Closing her eyes, she tried to focus on the voice. She'd heard it before.

"John?" she asked, coughing.

"Yes."

She wanted to jerk her head away when something pliant pressed against her cheek, but found she was too weak and tired. Instead, she let her head fall back into the hand supporting it, welcoming the sensation of moisture spreading across her face.

"Where are we?"

"Boma," John replied.

"Boma?" Squinting against the glare of daylight, Sarah slowly opened her eyes. "Where's that?"

"Sudan—where the Mother is strong."

"The mother?"

"Look."

With John's help, Sarah sat up, crossing her legs beneath her. Dazedly, she began to take in her surroundings.

"My God!" she gasped, seeing how many dog-like creatures were massed around her. "There must be—"

"No, not *jib*," he said, smiling when she looked at him. "Not hyena," he explained. "Beyond."

"Hyenas," she muttered, awestruck. "Look at them all. How many are there? And why have they come?"

John's smile grew wide as the hyena he called Seh-my moved to sit beside him. It was then Sarah realized how big the animal was, for the top of the beast's head—when he sat—was equal in height to John's shoulder.

"*Säba*—or eighty—maybe more," he said. "But beyond. Look past. See the Mother."

Silently mouthing the words *see the mother* as though she was trying to comprehend their meaning, Sarah pulled the hyena pelts close about her shoulders as a shiver ran through her body.

Looking out over scores of hyenas, Sarah could see John had brought her to the top of a hill—a small mountain, as she saw it—terrain below seeming far away, even dreamlike, as if she were looking at a picture in a book. To the east, where the low-hanging sun burned as a fiery red ball behind a veil of curling black mist, was a vast expanse of savanna. She was captivated by occasional glints of yellow, white, and tawny gold reflecting up into her eyes. Thinking she was fainting, she placed a hand to the ground for support, fighting off dizziness as part of the plain began to move.

"Animals," she mumbled. "Dear Lord—look how many."

John knelt next to her, his face alight with joy.

"Antelope, wildebeest, zebra, gazelle. Moving with Her soul."

Briefly glancing at his face, she asked, "Her? I don't understand."

"The Mother—they," he told her, pointing to the vast groupings of different animals spread out over the plain. "She is them—they are Her. But look."

Pointing, he stood, gazing northward.

"There, She is forest," he explained.

Sarah turned her attention where John pointed, intrigued by the dense green foliage she could see in the distance. She imagined monkeys and gorillas there, along with an array of exotic birds, all chattering and yelping from vine-covered branches of emerald-leaved trees.

"And there, behind us, She is the lowlands and waterways that flood when rainy season comes."

As she struggled to turn her body, John slipped his hands beneath her arms, helping her to stand. Her gaze fell upon a cloud of pure white moving diagonally across a vast expanse of deep greens and fingers of blue, diamond light glittering here and there where sunlight touched the surface of water. When the white cloud abruptly changed direction, descending from the sky to alight near a broad swath of blue, Sarah sharply inhaled.

"The sacred birds," John said.

"Sacred?" Sarah probed, studying his face.

"The white ibis," he told her. "Come to share the morning with the Mother."

"The mother— I don't think I—"

"South, She is the mountains," he announced with pride. "And still She is more," he went on, his gaze drifting south to north. "Desert, lakes, valleys, streams—so much is She. But here—here She is strong. She is everywhere."

Sarah and John turned in unison at the sound of a distant explosion, each surveying the savanna east of them for the source.

"There," John said, pointing to a ball of billowing gray smoke. "Half a kilometer from here. Within that area of trees."

"I see it, but—"

"And there—look!"

Sarah flinched as John squeezed her arm.

"Flying above—"

"Helicopters—I see them," she said. "Two, circling. But why?"

Sarah saw John's expression harden. His hand released her arm.

"They hunt him," he said. "We must go."

"Go?" She reached out to grab hold of his hand. "Where there are bombs?" she asked, incredulous.

Stepping toward him, she stumbled, falling to one knee.

"You're weak with fever," he said, gripping her shoulder. "Stay. Seh-my will watch over you till I need you."

"You can't be serious," she weakly argued, sliding from her knee to her rump to sit on the ground.

The sudden cackling howls of the hyenas were maddening. Sarah bent her head to her chest, covering her ears with her hands. Beneath her backside, tremors awakened in the ground. Looking up, she saw the pack of hyenas charging down the eastern face of the small mountain, John running in their midst, the twisted horn raised in a clenched fist above his head. As she watched the hyenas move swiftly onto the level terrain of the savanna, she felt a warm puff of air blow against her cheek. Seh-my's snarl was deep and resonating, and Sarah cowered to the ground when the animal's large teeth appeared next to her face. Paralyzed with fear, she began to mumble the Lord's Prayer, the words turning into gibberish when the first drop of hot saliva from Seh-my's jaws fell upon her chin.

* * *

Dirk banged the back of his head against a metal crossbar, the jolt of the bump nearly throwing him off the bench where he was seated. The truck's suspension creaked and squealed from the strain of running over something large and unforgiving before resuming a steady hum as the tires reclaimed a smoother track. As he moaned from the blow he'd sustained, laughter erupted all around him.

"Do not fear, white skin," a man's voice taunted, a fist, Dirk guessed, striking him square in the chest. "You will soon be free of us."

The men—the soldiers—riding in the back of the truck with him laughed anew. At least he assumed all of them were laughing. But having been blindfolded—as well as having had his wrists and ankles bound with rope—he couldn't know for certain. And maybe he didn't want to know—part of him, anyway. After being punched, poked, kicked, stabbed, pissed on, mocked, and burned, he had no desire to be subjected to another display of ridicule by his captors. They'd tortured him to the point where he'd sworn to kill them the first chance he was afforded.

Fucking black bastards. I'll slice your balls off and shove 'em down your throats till you choke.

Problem was, he didn't think he was actually going to get the chance to kill them. George Henry had told him as much when the man—sorry, the god (Dirk silently smirked at the notion)—had tossed him to his underlings after he'd finished interrogating him. Death by fire, George Henry had decreed.

"You'll burn alongside the one who blew up my petrol," he told him. "Sometime in the late afternoon after we catch him. Yes, the burning will please me."

Late afternoon. Dirk focused on the hours he'd been the warlord's captive as the truck bounced over what he guessed was another large stone or cavernous pothole. *That gives me a few more hours.*

"Hey," a voice with foul-smelling breath said close to his ear. "Don't go dying on us, you hear?"

Dirk pictured the man speaking, certain it was the chimp-faced captain who'd placed the duct tape across his eyes.

"We want to roast elephant meat over your embers."

Dirk reflexively turned his face away from the putrid odor invading his nostrils.

"And pick our teeth with the bones of your fingers," the voice said, laughing.

As before, the entire truckload of soldiers laughed.

* * *

Squatting behind a clump of bushes, Teimbaka counted the bullets left in the goatskin pouch, grunting when he found he could place the remaining number in the palm of his hand. Even if he could get a clear shot at the pilots of the two black dragonflies circling above and bring the flying machines crashing down, he knew there would still be soldiers on the ground to deal with; seven bullets was not nearly enough to enable him to escape death. He was trapped, the ever-present thumping of helicopter blades reaffirming the notion his end was near. What more could he have done? he wondered. Stopping the slaughter of elephants for their ivory could not be done by one man—wasn't that what the spirit of his father had told him so many years ago? *No,* Teimbaka thought, *he said it would seem impossible at times.* He looked down at the bullets held within his palm. *But what is impossible?* he questioned. *And what only seems so?* Loading a bullet into the breech of his Lee-Enfield, he shook his head. *No time for useless talk,* he told himself. Sliding the breech bolt forward, he stood.

The first rock-like object he glimpsed falling to the ground out of the branches didn't immediately alarm him, but when two more fell in close succession—spaced eight to ten meters to either side of the first—Teimbaka leapt to the nearest thick-trunked tree, covering his head and compressing his body in an attempt to protect himself from the explosions. The maelstrom of shrapnel, dirt, and shards of rock sent hurling through the air decimated the bushes where he had stood but a moment before. Defiant, he aimed his rifle skyward, squeezing off a shot when he judged one of the metal dragonflies was right above him. Quickly reloading, he watched two more hand grenades fall through the canopy of leaves near the tree he was using as a shield. Crouching, he scurried to another tree a dozen paces away, breaking into a run once the weapons detonated.

Pushing through underbrush, sprinting around trees, Teimbaka tried to gain some distance between him and the sound of the helicopters. But when he reached the edge of a clearing, he stopped. After surveying the foliage around the glade, he turned his attention skyward. Fingering the bullets in the goatskin sack tied about his waist, he stepped out into the open and walked slowly to the center of the clearing, the Lee-Enfield held ready in both hands.

Listening, waiting, he realized the helicopters were moving away, the ensuing sound of two new explosions confusing. When he heard a woman's scream, his confusion turned to alarm.

* * *

"Abdar! Over here! Over here! Tabib's been killed!"

Eden's frantic cries barely pierced the haze blurring John Too's senses, her voice reaching him as a murmuring whisper in an ocean of pounding waves. Blinking furiously to regain his sight, he wondered if the explosions had left him blind as well as near deaf. Crawling along scarred earth, he searched for anything he might recognize by touch, concentrating on the sound of the girl's whisper to guide him in the right direction.

"Over here! Help her!"

"I—"

John Too coughed, his throat suddenly choking on putrid odors permeating the air, the stench suddenly overwhelming his sense of taste and smell. He began to gag on the bitter vapors rushing into his lungs. Ears ringing, head spinning, flesh beginning to tingle, stomach bunching in a wave of nausea, John Too fell to his side. As he felt his body begin to twitch, he thought he heard a girl's whispering scream. But he wasn't sure. The darkness of his blindness spread to every part of him, wrapping him in a cocoon no light or sound could penetrate.

* * *

"Abdar! Abdar!"

At the sight of John Too's convulsions, Eden pounded her fists into the ground, her face a picture of torment as she screamed into the sky. But the passing shadow of a helicopter silenced her, a troubled expression taking hold of her face as she sat back on her haunches.

"How can this be?" she asked, looking between John Too and Claire. "How can an abdar and a tabib both be gone?"

When her question became lost in the sight of blood covering one side of Claire's face, Eden looked away from the woman to John Too, hoping he would answer, hoping his spastic movements were merely a trick. At any moment he would sit up and giggle at her foolishness. But the boy's body was nearly motionless. His face frozen in a vacant stare, eyes wide and unfocused as though peering through murky water. Only a sporadic twitch of his hand and a quiver of his shoulder made her think he might still be alive. How was it she hadn't been harmed by the exploding rocks? she wondered. And what would become of her now?

"We missed one!"

Eden scrambled to the side, the toe of the soldier's boot grazing her upper arm as the man kicked out at her head. Outfitted in a camouflage uniform of various shades of green, brown, and cream, the man stepped clear of the underbrush, his weapon pointed at Eden's face. With what Eden perceived as an evil smile, he bent to grab hold of her arm.

"Been a while," he snickered. "Have you before—"

Eden thrust her hand up, her fingers spread wide, using them like tines of a pitchfork to gouge the soldier's eyes.

"Bitch!" he snarled, pulling away, placing his hands to his face.

When Eden saw the barrel of the man's weapon turn upward, she pushed out of her squat to stand, then turned to run. But another man was blocking her way, his black shamma tattered and frayed, so thin in places

Eden could see scars slashed across his chest. Then her eyes drifted to his rifle—his finger squeezing the trigger. The sound of the shot was deafening.

* * *

Teimbaka ejected the spent shell case from the breech of his Lee-Enfield, scouring the surrounding foliage for more soldiers as the one he'd shot fell lifelessly to the ground.

The drone of the two black dragonflies—hovering stationary, close above the area where he was standing—clamored for his attention, but he could only look at the woman lying on the ground, blood covering half her face.

"Claire."

Teimbaka rushed to Claire's side, placing his rifle on the ground as he knelt to her. Taking her wrist in one hand, he gently wiped the blood from her forehead, fingertips tracing the deep gash he found above her left eye.

"You know the tabib?"

Teimbaka jerked his shoulder forward, trying to free the fabric of his shamma from the girl pulling on it.

"She's dead," he heard the girl say.

Releasing Claire's wrist, Teimbaka placed two fingers against her neck under her lower jaw.

"Too bad," the girl continued. "We traveled far to get here. I helped save her."

Teimbaka bent close to Claire's cheek.

"Claire," he said. "It is not time. I'm here. Teimbaka. Claire."

"You? You are the one we've come so far to save?"

Again, Teimbaka jerked his shoulder forward when the girl pulled on his shamma.

"Now she's dead."

"See to John Too!" he snapped, eyeing her with disdain. "Take water from his canteen and splash his face."

"But they're coming," she argued, her eyes looking up past his head, where the sound of men's voices and underbrush being disturbed could be heard. "They'll kill us."

"It's the only way," he muttered.

"What are you saying? Are you mad? To die is the only way?"

Teimbaka reached out to grab the girl when she started backing away.

"They have medicine," he told her. Looking down at Claire, he said, "She is not dead."

He turned back to say more to the girl, but she was gone. She had run into the underbrush, he knew, to save herself. And who could blame her? His eyes drifting to John Too, he fleetingly wondered who the girl was. Then he saw John Too's eyes blink, a gurgling cough escaping from his throat.

"John Too," he called.

Behind where John Too lay, the bushes parted, the little girl backing out from the opening. Behind her stepped a grim-faced soldier.

"Watch out!" the girl shouted, her fear-stricken eyes focused on a spot above Teimbaka's head.

Teimbaka looked up in time to see the butt of a rifle thrust downward into his face.

* * *

John stared at the antelope horn, barely able to remember how he came to possess it. The Serpent's hold upon him had been strong then. Susenyo— and later, Akmir, after Susenyo had been killed—made sure that hold continued. He thought he'd put an end to it—the Serpent—when he'd run the horn through Gunstard's throat and watched the man bleed into the sand. He thought Claire would forgive him when she saw the Serpent vanquished. But nothing like that had occurred. Like the horn, he thought, gazing at its winding grooves. Paths twisted, melding into each other, having no end or beginning. One fluted cleft intertwined with the next—impossible to destroy one section without scarring the threshold to another. Why had nothing turned out the way he'd envisioned?

Forgiveness—he latched onto the word, knowing she—Sister Lady— never would forgive him. He knew that now. He'd defiled her, raped her— the woman he'd loved since a boy. And though John Too had told him over and over and over that it wasn't him—that it was the drug, the madness of the addiction that had driven him to such depravity, the look in her eyes— whenever she would dare meet his—reminded him of his filth, and of the bond they no longer shared. Still, he would sacrifice himself for her. He did not doubt this. But he wouldn't die for her unless she could be saved. And that was the dilemma now. She was in a tent surrounded by a small army of well-armed rebels: George Henry's men.

How they had found her he didn't know. Teimbaka, Eden, and John Too were captives as well, bound to a tree near the tent where Claire had been taken. Teimbaka and John Too seemed injured by the way they'd moved when the soldiers had unloaded them from the back of a truck. And Eden— he couldn't help it, he laughed—they had placed tape over her mouth. Even from where he was hiding—lying in chest-high grass some fifty meters away, hyenas spread out to either side of him—he could hear her yelling at the soldiers when they'd pulled her from the truck. She would learn, John thought. But then he realized she wouldn't—she wouldn't get the chance to learn. George Henry wasn't one to keep prisoners, he knew. The Nuer warriors he'd met since crossing the border from Ethiopia into Sudan had warned him of this. The warlord was crazed, they told him. Prisoners were either sold or killed.

Slavery or death; John mulled the terms—each difference, each similarity—finding them the same.

"Like the horn," he murmured, tracing his fingertip along the ridged grooves.

A moist nudge to his shoulder brought a smile to his face.

"*Kongo jib*," he said, chuckling. "How long have I been daydreaming?"

The large female spotted hyena placed her snout along John's cheek, gently pushing until he turned his face. Two soldiers—guards, he suspected— walked outward from the camp. Setting up a perimeter, he assumed. Thirty meters more and they would surely spot the hyenas gathered in the tall grass. The female hyena began to growl.

"*Kongo*," he said to her. "*En heed.*"

Knowing well the temperament of the animal, he could tell by her narrowing eyes and grunted breaths she didn't want to leave. It wasn't in her makeup to retreat from a fight.

"Beautiful one," he called her, scratching the back of her foreleg, "tell the others." Twisting his body to look behind him, he said, "Past those trees. Go."

With a haunting cry from the big female, the remainder of the pack rose from their hiding places, the two-hundred-meter stretch of chest-high, tawny grass where they'd been lying suddenly alive with yips, hoots, and laughing barks as the animals retreated. John watched, amused, as the two guards immediately froze. One raised the AK-47 he carried to a firing position while the other ran back toward the tent where Claire was being kept. When the soldier reached the flapped entrance of the khaki-green structure, John saw him salute and come to stand at attention. A moment later, a man emerged from the interior of the tent—bearded, heavyset, the dark black skin of his neck, face, and head shiny, as if some sort of oil had been applied.

"George Henry," John muttered.

And then George Henry did something John had never witnessed before. Strapping a pack of three cylindrical tanks to his back, he grabbed the rifle-like hose attached, a wide, unnerving smile breaking out on his face as the he strode toward the area the hyenas were vacating. John slid backward on his stomach as the warlord approached, but then stopped, curious to see what the man would do. When George Henry was fifteen meters from where John was lying, a stream of fire shot forward through the air, flames pouring out the end of the rifle-hose. The grass in front of John instantly ignited. Within several seconds, George Henry created a wall of flames as tall as a man, stretching fifty meters to either side of where he stood. The fire burned with the stench of petrol, the foul smell spread aloft in clouds of choking black smoke streaming upward to the sky. Unable to see past the flames, John pushed up from the ground to stand. The booming clap of a gunshot—a bullet flying so close to his ear he could hear it whizzing past— sent him diving for the safety of the ground.

"Dead boy! That's what you'll be!"

John listened to the angry bellow of the warlord as he backed away from the fire.

"You and the filthy breed you bring!"

A round of bullets strafed an area just to the right of him.

"You will not steal from me! Your time is done!"

A new stream of fire shot through the wall of flames. Earth, grass, underbrush—whatever the substance touched—was set instantly ablaze. John slithered farther back, scrambling to his hands and knees before turning to flee in a crouching run. Behind him, he could hear the sound of cheering rise above the crackling fire, volleys of gunfire erupting, as though the soldiers in the camp were celebrating. Glancing over his shoulder, he was reminded of another time when he had run from soldiers. There had been fire and gunshots on that occasion as well. But Claire had been draped over his shoulder. He had been carrying her to safety, he thought, the path taken unknowingly leading to the doorstep of Susenyo—and the Serpent. Their bond had been broken that night, their panicked escape both a beginning and an ending.

Like the horn, he thought, *like the horn.*

* * *

"Bouda!" Eden screamed.

But the tape covering her mouth turned her scream into a muffled cry, eliciting a mocking smirk from a passing guard. Ignoring the man, Eden focused on the spot where she had glimpsed John arising from the flames before the warlord and his men had fired their guns.

The bouda had come.

Not knowing if he had been shot or if he had transformed into a hyena to make his escape, Eden continued to stare at the spot where she'd seen him, hoping to be rewarded with another sighting of the mystical creature. She was certain it was he—John, Bouda—even though she had not been able to clearly see him from where she was sitting, bound to a tree some fifty meters away, her mouth taped over with thick, gray tape. But she'd heard the raucous cackling of hyenas—as had the entire camp. From the sound of the beasts' voices, the animals must number close to hundred or more, she guessed. Only a bouda—her bouda—could command such a gathering. What other explanation could there be for so many of the animals to be in one place? *Greatness lies within him,* she thought. *Even the scarred one's face had filled with hope when the hyenas had howled.*

The scarred one—Teimbaka, he who the abdar called Etiyopiya—was some sort of conduit between spirit animals and the living. She looked over at his thin, drooping frame, wondering what it was about him she could not see. For the man seemed near to his end: graying hair filthy and matted; face gaunt and scarred; lips split, oozing blood where George Henry's man had struck him with a rifle. His clothes—she glanced down at her own to compare—were tattered, worn, dirty. They barely covered the long pink scars slashed across his chest and those made by the whip that had crisscrossed his back, evident to all who looked upon them when George Henry ordered the man's shamma pulled to his waist. Why the warlord had become enraged at the sight of the scars, she didn't know. But she—as any who'd seen the number of lashes he'd suffered—wondered how this Etiyopiya could have survived such a beating. *He must have spent months in a hospital for his wounds to heal*, she thought. *But there are no hospitals where we've traveled*, she realized. *How did they heal?*

"Thank you."

Eden shifted her attention from the scars on Teimbaka's chest to his eyes, finding them kind and lively.

"For what?" she tried to say.

Her grunt drew a tired smile from the man, Eden noticing a slight wincing of his cheeks when his lips stretched with the effort.

"For Claire," he weakly said. "For saving her."

No, she wanted to tell him, it wasn't she who had saved the tabib. It was Abdar and Bouda who saved her. But the sudden eruption of cheers and a barrage of bullets fired into the air by the warlord's men froze her body rigid, her thoughts erased in a spasm of fear. Having witnessed celebrations of fanatical mercenaries before, Eden knew no good would come of this sudden showing of victory. Only bloodletting, rape, and torture were sure to follow. The millions of unmarked graves in Sudan and Ethiopia were filled with testaments of such depraved evil. Here and now, she feared, another such instance of savagery was about to occur. Why had she come? she asked herself. Why follow an abdar and a tabib on such a hopeless quest? This was going to end very badly, she told herself. Yes, the end would be very bad. And when George Henry suddenly appeared in front of her—the fire-spewing hose aimed directly at Teimbaka—she knew her end had arrived.

"Give the devil my greetings!" George Henry said, laughing.

Somewhere between horror and acceptance, Eden watched the finger of the warlord engage the trigger of the rifle-hose, a glob of liquid fire instantly spewing forth from the nozzle. Eden's scream was lost in a tirade of the warlord's curses as the ball of flame fell well short of Teimbaka. Once, twice, three more times in succession George Henry pulled the trigger of the weapon, becoming angrier and angrier at each effort as only a dribble of fire could be coaxed from the gun.

"Empty!" he raged, slinging the tanks from his back. "Fill them! Now!" he shouted, glaring at the men around him. "And bring me the white man!"

Eden let out a long sigh through her nose, glancing over to Teimbaka as the soldiers jumped to obey George Henry's orders. A moment later, when she saw two of the warlord's men throw a white-skinned man down from the back of a nearby truck, she wondered who the man was and how he'd come to be there. As the two soldiers dragged the man to the tent where George Henry had gone, Eden found some solace in the fact that she wasn't him. For while she knew her death would soon arrive—by fire it seemed— she had heard tales of what George Henry did to whites. Skinned them alive and staked them out for the vultures to eat, she had heard, while he and his men kept the bigger scavengers away. A slow torturous death by pecking was what the white-skinned man faced, she guessed. At least her death would be somewhat quick, she hoped. Still—as her eyes fell to the blackened soil where the liquid fire had burned—she did not much like the prospect of being burned alive. *It is as I foresaw,* she concluded. *This has turned out badly. Yes—very, very, badly.*

* * *

"Is this her? The nun?"

Dirk's head was jerked back by his hair, his face squeezed so tight the tip of his tongue poked out of his mouth as soon as the tape was ripped from his lips.

"Answer!" a voice hissed from behind him.

A slap to his face jolted his vision into focus.

"A white woman," he mumbled. *Sarah?* he thought.

"Is it she?" George Henry seethed. "The one who'll fetch money?"

Dirk studied the woman's features for a moment—gray-flecked hair cut short like a boy's, skin weathered by the sun, a deep cut over her left eyebrow, blood seeping from the wound, some smeared across her cheek and neck where it looked to have been hastily cleaned.

"Stake him!" George Henry barked.

"Yes, yes, yes—it's her!" Dirk croaked before breaking into a dry cough. "Her," he gasped, gulping in air. "Claire," he spit. "It's— She's— she's worth—"

Wheezing, bending forward, Dirk gagged trying to say more. Instantly, his head was yanked back until his face tilted upwards. Water was poured into his throat, Dirk gulping down what he could while trying to breathe.

Just as he began to sputter and hack, the water stopped, his head prodded level with a harsh slap to the back of his head.

"How much?"

"A—a million," Dirk struggled to say.

Dirk saw the look on George Henry's face as the warlord glanced over at the cot where Claire lay; greed was an expression he was all too familiar with.

"Enough to support your war effort for several months, enough to buy more missiles, RPGs, armored personnel carriers—a tank."

Dirk saw lines of doubt appear at the corners of the warlord's eyes.

"Hard to believe she—a nun—could fetch such a price. But her parents are wealthy and willing to pay—"

"Ransom," George Henry said with a smile. "Yes, she'll stay until the money is paid," he went on, nodding, gazing off into space. "Are there more of them—nuns?"

"What?" Dirk asked, confused. Shaking his head, he said, "And no—no, she can't stay here."

The instant silence in the close quarters of the tent was oppressive. Dirk sensed a deadly threat in the absence of sound, his assumption reinforced by the crazed, incensed look on George Henry's face as the warlord took a menacing step toward him.

"The Consortium can pay you now," he rushed to say. "You wouldn't need to wait. The money—"

The kick to his testicles was violent, his breath—his life, he felt—rushing out of his throat as the first wave of deep-rooted, oxygen-sucking pain spread upward from his balls. Unable to function—to think, breathe, or react—he tumbled listlessly to the canvas floor, his face etched in a silent scream.

"Dare you speak to me? Me—God of this earth? White filth! Self-righteous in your belief that *your race* is the ordained!"

A boot tip thrust beneath his chin rolled Dirk over onto his back. Teary-eyed, he stared up at a blurry dark form.

"Murderers, thieves, liars—sinners! I cast you to hell where you belong! Take him! Stake him—bring me my knives!"

"Money in a day," Dirk croaked, as hands lifted him by his armpits. "Weapons in a week! And more!" he cried. "I can get you more! More nuns, more hostages—I was traveling with one!" Stricken with panic when he saw the warlord's back turned toward him, he blurted out, "Sarah—her name's Sister Sarah. She was taken by a bouda!" he shouted, struggling to free himself from the grasp of the men taking him outside. "Stolen by a bouda!"

Dirk went limp when George Henry turned and held up a finger for the soldiers to wait.

"You've seen him—this *bouda*? Tell me of him. Tell me of this devil creature."

"I—I—didn't actually see him. But Alba's men said there were tracks," he rushed to get out. "Stole her from a tent—just like this one," he added, nodding at his surroundings. "Only tracks of hyenas where the tent had been sliced open. But the nun—Sarah's her name—she was gone. Wounded like this one," he hurried to say, glancing to Claire. "What does he do with them? Perhaps he knows the Consortium will pay good money for them."

George Henry remained silent, Dirk's stomach knotting tighter with each passing second.

"The Consortium," George Henry scoffed. "Alba," he grunted. "One, a filthy collection of thieves, the other a child, a disbeliever, followed by soulless mercenaries of a false god. They are nothing to me."

Dirk stared at the man, his mouth agape.

"I! I decide what takes place!"

Dirk shifted his gaze to the floor, hoping the unbalanced look in George Henry's eyes would disappear.

"A bouda come to steal from me? Me—God's incarnation on earth? Take from me? Deceive me? Sinners all! You shall feel my wrath!" George Henry bellowed. "Know the path to hell! Let those who oppose me perish by fire!"

2 2

B IN'KA TRIED TO get the pilot's attention, animatedly pointing at the smoke cloud rising some two kilometers ahead, port side of the cockpit. But as it had been throughout the trip thus far, the pilot gave no verbal or physical response; the gunship merely veered toward the area. Glancing over at the pilot, Bin'ka wondered what sort of man hid beneath a hooded helmet and gas mask. Was he black, white, Christian, Muslim, African, European? And who was he taking orders from—and why? What was the Legion of God? After having studied the pilot—and the four other similarly uniformed soldiers riding in the cargo bay—for the better part of a day, Bin'ka was no closer to knowing anything about them than when Talia and he had first set eyes on them. Even after they had lifted off from Bacha Alba's temporary campsite—where they'd obtained new information regarding George Henry's involvement with Dirk's whereabouts— the only reaction the pilot gave him was to repeat the same refrain Bin'ka had been listening to all day, as though the knowledge they were now dealing with George Henry—a ruthless, barbaric warlord—was of no consequence.

"Orders are to retrieve a servant of the Lord."

That was it, nothing added, no variation; the sentence a mantra. The metallic, buzzing sound of the man's voice made it that much more annoying each time it was repeated. Bin'ka felt he was talking to a machine.

Without warning, the gunship banked lower. Bin'ka was surprised when he felt a nudge to his shoulder and found the pilot motioning for him to look through the pair of binoculars he'd been given upon lift-off. The pilot spread two fingers and pointed to his eyes, then to the binoculars, then to the ground. Complying with the silent command, Bin'ka lifted the high-powered pair dangling around his neck to his face. Adjusting the zoom, he leaned forward and peered downward through the lenses. The ground below the Panther's glass-plated nose suddenly seemed a few arm-lengths away.

Orange flames flickered beneath gray curling smoke. A fire was spreading quickly, Bin'ka could see, feasting on the dry grass of the savanna. Rainy season was still a month away; he wondered if the fire might burn unencumbered until then. He grunted at the prospect before shifting the binoculars to another area. Vehicles—a dozen or more—popped into his field of vision. Trucks with covered beds, jeeps—these fitted with large-caliber machine guns—two armored personnel carriers, and what looked to be a Soviet rocket launcher were all parked to one side of a grove of trees. North of the vehicles, where the terrain gradually turned more arid, Bin'ka spied two black, light-framed helicopters; the open-air metal strut design of the tail assembly and the drooping rotor blades combined with the sectioned glass dome encasing the two-man cockpit gave them the appearance of dragonflies waiting to take flight.

"The tents," a metallic, electric voice buzzed in his ear.

Bin'ka changed his search area, his head jerking back when tents came into view.

"Not happy to see us," he muttered, seeing soldiers on the ground running to vehicles or grabbing weapons. "Don't think we'll be able to set down and talk, like we did with Alba."

"Is she there?" the metallic, electric voice shouted.

Startled by the display of emotion, Bin'ka looked over at the man.

"By the trees," the pilot's voice crackled. "Is that her?"

Bin'ka placed the binoculars to his eyes, shifting his field of vision in increments until he located the grove of trees.

"Prisoners!" he shouted. "Five!" Adjusting the magnification, he added, "Yes! A white male and—"

The gunship banked sharply away, bullets pinging off armored plating, a few ricocheting off the bulletproof glass of the cockpit.

"Return fire," the pilot's electrical voice calmly ordered.

Almost immediately, Bin'ka felt the pounding thump of heavy-caliber machine-gun fire spewing from the port-side cargo bay. Twisting his massive frame so he could see behind him, Bin'ka witnessed the bullets hitting their mark, half a dozen soldiers jerking violently to the ground before the rest standing in the target zone scattered for cover. Feeling the gunship leveling, hovering stationary, its nose facing northward, Bin'ka glimpsed a subtle hand movement by the pilot. An image of an armored personnel carrier materialized in the center display screen; one of the rockets attached to the strut wing launched a split second later. The trajectory of what Bin'ka guessed was a TRIGAT anti-tank missile was steady and true, the marked vehicle lifting several meters off the ground when the warhead made impact. A slight elevation of the gunship brought an outline of one of the lightweight helicopters to the screen. A second missile was fired a moment after the pilot locked on. A fireball erupted where the missile struck, the complete and instantaneous destruction of the craft bringing a smile to Bin'ka's face.

"Where can I get one of these?" he admiringly joked.

A jarring shudder ran through the frame of the gunship, shooting up through Bin'ka's groin out the top of his spine. Warning lights flashed on and off, the pilot fighting to keep the control lever steady as the Panther began to spin. Bin'ka clutched the straps of his seat harness, yelling, "What is it?"

"Tail rotor," came a static-filled reply.

"Can you—?"

"Prepare for hard landing," the pilot calmly announced.

* * *

Teimbaka gave scant notice to the explosions and gunfire raging around him, giving the spinning helicopter falling out of the sky scarcely a passing glance before Claire reclaimed his attention. Her pale, blood-stained face, the listlessness of her body, the bare nuance of her shallow breathing—all screamed for him to help her, pleaded for him to free his hands from the ropes binding him to the tree. Why wasn't he pulling her into his arms? her injuries cried out. When would he rest his forehead against hers and softly admit they should have never parted? Looking at her, remembering all she'd endured, he couldn't help but wonder what the Mother and Father wanted of them. What purpose did it serve for her to be made to suffer so? Staring at her bruised and battered body, he wished all of her pain transferred to him.

"Claire," he said.

"I think she's dead. It's why the warlord dumped her out here with us."

Teimbaka looked over at the white-skinned man, not understanding who he was or why he was there. He'd been severely beaten, Teimbaka could see, the red-black bruises blotting his swollen face a testament to the abuse he'd sustained.

"Not dead," Teimbaka somberly replied. "Not yet."

"Are you he?" the man asked.

"He?" Teimbaka dazedly asked, his eyes shifting with the sound of the gunship crashing to earth somewhere beyond the flames.

"The Lion—you know—of Djibouti?"

Teimbaka ignored the cheering shouts erupting from George Henry's soldiers, looking back at Claire as though the black coils of the Serpent were curling around her neck.

"Adiam said you'd be with her."

"Adiam." Teimbaka murmured the name, picturing Adiam as the youth he'd first met in the Kenyan forest: thoughtful, inquisitive, playing mournful tunes on his flute. How fitting this man should mention him now, Teimbaka thought, for he suddenly longed to hear the haunting wind-tones of the instrument. Would welcome its sound as he often imagined the dead he had buried in the field near the house of walls received the forlorn timbre of his drum when he laid them to rest.

Drum man, he had been called back then. Claire hadn't been afraid of that man the night she had sought him out—drum man. Alone—in a field full of graves—seeking answers from a man she knew nothing about as they buried the young nun she had been traveling with. Nor had he been afraid—or so he had told himself back then. He wondered if she was now—afraid. He knew he was. The years had made him so. Seeing her now—ghostly still, so near death—he was numb with the feeling.

"They're coming."

Teimbaka's eyes blurred with tears.

"Etiyopiya—do you not feel them?"

Lips trembling, Teimbaka reluctantly turned his face to look at John Too.

"The spirit elephants!" John Too joyfully announced. "Etiyopiya—they have come!"

* * *

"Detonate in thirty!"

Bin'ka didn't understand what the pilot meant when he said it. And before he could ask *what* was detonating in thirty, the four soldiers who'd been standing next to him turned and ran toward the flames, the pilot pulling him in another direction after shoving a FAMAS into his hands. Twenty-eight seconds later—Bin'ka had counted the time off in his head as he ran—a massive explosion occurred, shockwaves throwing him to the ground.

"Move!" the pilot's garbled, static-laced voice yelled.

Struggling to his knees, Bin'ka felt the strength of the pilot as the man jerked him to his feet. Glancing over his shoulder, Bin'ka saw a huge fireball and swirling pillars of black smoke where the gunship had rested.

"Keep moving!"

The sound of automatic weapons drew Bin'ka's attention to the line of flames. To his utter disbelief, he watched the four soldiers of the Legion of God run straight into the fire.

"Now!"

Bin'ka fought to keep his legs beneath him as the pilot pulled him forward. A moment later, he was running as fast as he could, trying to keep up with the pilot as they neared the line of George Henry's vehicles—the remaining black helicopter just beyond. Bin'ka came to an abrupt stop, dropping to one knee as five of the warlord's men appeared from the backside of the lead vehicle. Just ahead of him, he saw the pilot crouch low behind a clump of tall grass.

"*Kuna! Kuna! Kuna!*" he heard the soldiers yell.

Bin'ka raised his weapon to fire.

"*Tembo! Tembo!*" the soldiers shouted, waving their arms.

"Elephants," the pilot's electric voice hummed. The pilot grabbed the barrel of Bin'ka's FAMAS, tilting it toward the ground.

* * *

Kamua fired a shot into the air, muttering Swahili curse words under his breath.

"Stop, you stupid beasts!" he shouted, the effort sucking out what oxygen was left in his lungs. "*Tembo!* Turn!"

Frantic, exhausted, confused, he glanced ahead, not understanding the elephants' behavior. The gunfire he'd been hearing became louder, the smell of burning wood and grass more pungent, the flecks of ash falling from the smoke-choked sky denser. What were the animals doing? he wanted to scream. But he didn't have time. He had to keep sprinting, had to turn them. They were heading straight into a firefight. He could only imagine—after seeing the scores of butchered elephants he'd come across since parting ways with Tengene and Selam—George Henry and his army of followers were waiting up ahead. The elephants would be slaughtered, the spoils—the ivory—taken, regardless of what sort of fight between what two factions might be taking place. Reloading, Kamua veered closer to the swift-moving herd, loosing another round into the sky near the lead bull. But the massive beast kept moving. Kamua lowered his head and sighed. Slowing to a jog, he extracted another bullet from the ammunition strap slung across his upper body.

At the sight of three jeeps racing out toward the elephants from the direction of the gunfire and smoke, Kamua came to an abrupt halt. And then the first high-caliber bullets splayed across the chest of an elephant next to the lead male. The animal wailed in pain, head buckling beneath the weight of its body as it crashed into the soil. Kamua ran several paces ahead, aimed his rifle and fired.

"*Fala!*" he yelled when he realized his bullet missed.

As he angrily ejected the shell casing, another elephant tumbled to the earth.

"*Basha fala!*" he cursed, the death cry of the fallen beast blaring through his head. "Why won't you turn?" he screamed at the elephants, shoving another bullet into the chamber. "You'll die!"

When the familiar faded-green Land Rover appeared in front of the far side of the herd, Kamua thought he was hallucinating. But as the vehicle moved front and center of the elephants, he recognized the wiry, grey-haired man behind the wheel and the larger, heavyset body next to him in the passenger seat. Just as he was about to shout their names, he saw puffs of soil shoot upward in front of the Land Rover, the pulsing *thump thump thump thump thump* of heavy-caliber machine guns reaching his ears just as Selam turned the steering wheel sharply to the left. He could see Tengene clutching the frame of the open window while returning enemy fire with a volley of his own. Following the path of Tengene's bullets, Kamua saw one of the approaching jeeps come to a shuddering stop, the driver, as well as the soldier manning the mounted machine gun, toppling sideways to the ground. Raising his old Lee-Enfield above his head, he howled with joy. The next moment, he screamed, "No! No!" as Tengene slumped down in the passenger seat following a barrage of bullets ripping across the side of the Land Rover. Shifting his rifle to his shoulder, Kamua aimed it at the driver of one of the two jeeps moving toward him and fired. The soldier driving the nearest jeep fell face-first against the steering wheel.

Kamua cringed at the sound of a whooshing boom. An instant later, he watched the faded-green Land Rover explode into a ball of flames. The sight of his friends—his fellow rangers—instantly killed—incinerated—felled him to his knees. Numb, he let his eyes drift from the burning wreckage to the soldier shaking an RPG launcher above his head. Seething with rage, he stood, loaded his weapon and took aim. But shards of glittering light suddenly shot into his eyes, quaking earth causing him to fall. Kamua wrapped his arms tight around his body lest the pulsing ghost cries filling the air shatter his bones.

* * *

Eden wanted to scream, to untie her hands from their bindings, pull the tape from her mouth, and run from the cursed place where she found herself. What was happening? her thoughts shouted. What sort of monstrous, deformed creatures could appear from flames, firing bullets that pierced steel? Hell had surely sent these beasts, she concluded. What other explanation could there be? They were servants of the devil, conjured forth by the fire-spewing gun the warlord wielded, brought here to claim the souls of the soldiers they were sent to kill. Terrified *her* soul would be next—sucked from her body by the followers of zār through the strange protrusions sprouting from their mouths—she rejoiced when George Henry's men assaulted the freakishly masked beings with exploding rocks. She was relieved and awestruck when the entities vanished in flashes of blue light, feeling a sense of safety until the warlord turned his attention back to her and her fellow captives.

Grinning with an evil she felt must have been transferred from the devil beasts when they were killed, the warlord started toward her, shouting at his troops to gather, ranting they would witness more of his power, shouting, "I will strike down my enemies with flame!"

Why was she his enemy? she wanted to ask him. Why kill her? But with her mouth taped over, her questions were reduced to grunts, her screams, humming high-pitched whines. Even when she cried—as she was beginning to now—her weeping became a collection of congested snorts and sputters. Her fate sealed with her inability to speak, she closed her eyes as George Henry drew near.

"There," she heard Abdar say. "Look."

But she didn't open her eyes to look. The abdar was weak, she had come to realize, and babbled too much about things that made no sense: a boy with sparkling eyes, spirit elephants, a mother that was not hers, a father she did not know. *Abdar and Tabib have brought me to an early death,* she lamented with some bitterness. *What nonsense does he speak of now? I will not listen to it. Let him trick the others with his twisting words. Let him—*

Fearful shouts of "*Jinn!*" and "*Shaytan!*" erupted around her. Her eyes went wide with fright when she opened them to witness some invisible force breaking through the wall of flames. Sparks of fire shot up and outward scores of feet into the air, scattering in every direction, the earth trembling beneath her from what sounded like the beating of a thousand drums just below its surface. Panic-stricken, certain an incarnation of zār was about to materialize and swallow everything into a swirling black abyss, she tugged against the ropes binding her to the tree, hoping she could work her wrists free before her flesh rubbed through to bone.

"Shoot! Shoot! Shoot!" she heard George Henry command.

Mesmerized by the waves of streaking sunlight flowing from the opening in the wall of flames, Eden barely noticed the warlord running toward the otherworldly sight, or the pistol he was firing, or the scores of men trailing after him, their weapons blazing away at an entity she could not see. With a desperate tug, she felt the first trickles of what she knew was her own blood sliding into her palms. Undeterred, she tugged again. This time, her wrists came free.

"Wait," someone told her.

And then a massive hand clamped down on her shoulder.

* * *

"Bin'ka—how?"

Dirk reached up and squeezed Bin'ka's arm, desperate to know if the massive black man he was looking at was real.

"Is this the servant?"

The electrified metallic voice startling him, Dirk slid a few feet away, glancing uncertainly between Bin'ka and the oddly dressed soldier.

"Servant?" Teimbaka asked, rubbing his wrists, moving to Claire's side.

"Servant of the Lord," the electric voice crackled.

"That's her," Bin'ka told him, cutting the ropes from John Too's wrists.

"Bring her."

"Bring *her?*" Dirk interjected, rising to stand. "You mean *us*, don't you?"

"Orders are to retrieve a servant of the Lord," the gas-mask-wearing soldier stated, slapping a gloved hand against his weapon. "No others," he added, squaring his body to Dirk's.

"But I was sent to retrieve her," Dirk protested.

"She can't be moved."

Dirk recognized the concern on Teimbaka's face as he spoke, quickly pushing aside a memory of his own as he watched the Lion of Djibouti run his fingers lightly across Claire's forehead.

"She needs treatment—a doctor—a hospital, medicine."

"Bring her," the electric voice repeated.

Eden's scream was lost in a thunderclap, the resounding echo of the eruption shaking earth, bodies, and vehicles. Dirk turned in time to see a brilliant flash of diamond-gold shoot across the smoke-filled sky. A boy's voice murmured, "They've left," as an unnerving silence permeated the air.

"Now."

Dirk looked back to see Bin'ka lifting Claire off the ground, the soldier who'd helped set them free stepping toward the grove of trees.

"No!" Teimbaka snapped.

"I'm coming with you," Dirk rushed to say.

"The warlord's men!" Eden exclaimed. "They're returning!"

"Quickly!" the electric voice barked.

"But she—"

Dirk grabbed Teimbaka's arm, stopping him from taking hold of Bin'ka's.

"It's her family," Dirk hurriedly explained when Teimbaka angrily turned toward him. "Her father, he's—"

"Sick," Eden chimed in, pulling John Too to his feet. "He needs her to return home."

Dirk saw a moment of confusion pass across Teimbaka's face.

"And she wants to go," Dirk told him. "She sent a message to her order. That's why I'm here." With a quick glance at Bin'ka, he said, "To take her home."

Bullets ripped into the trees above and behind them, showering the area where they were standing with chunks of bark and wood. The rapid-fire burping of an automatic weapon paused momentarily before another round was fired, clods of dirt spewing into the air in front of them.

"Don't move!"

Dirk flinched at the sound of the warlord's voice.

"Go!"

The static-filled shout was accompanied by a burst from the soldier's powerful machine gun, George Henry's position sprayed with bullets while the soldier backed into the cover of the trees. Before George Henry and his men could return fire, Dirk followed the soldier into the trees, Bin'ka tossing Teimbaka his FAMAS as, he too—with Claire in his arms—raced into the woods. As Dirk worked his way through the underbrush and tree trunks, he glimpsed the soldier hurling something back toward the warlord's camp.

* * *

Teimbaka grasped the weapon Bin'ka tossed him moments before a deafening explosion unleashed a flash of piercing white light. Blinded, his ears filled with a high-pitched whine, he swung the automatic weapon out in front of him, firing indiscriminately, loosing round after round in the direction where he thought George Henry to be until the weapon's magazine emptied. Diving sideways, he rolled in the direction where he remembered seeing a line of vehicles parked, bullets zipping all around him, their impact reaching him as muffled thuds and pings. Careening into something hard, he placed a hand on the object, his fingertips probing deep, corrugated grooves. His eyesight slowly returning, Teimbaka slid his body behind the man-size rear tire tandem he'd run into, blinking his eyes into focus as he looked for John Too and the girl.

"Come out!" he heard the warlord shout.

It wasn't hard to locate John Too, the boy was sitting with his back against the same tree he'd been tied to, head slumped forward, shoulders drooping, blood spilling from a hole in the upper right side of his chest. Stunned, Teimbaka numbly searched for the girl. But she wasn't there.

* * *

Eden pushed through shoulder-high grass, weaving her way around tree trunks, yanking on the fabric of her dress whenever it caught the pointed end of a thorn or branch. *Abdar's dead!* her thoughts screamed. She couldn't believe it. Killed by a bullet from a faceless soldier. Who would have ever thought his life would end in such a way? Why didn't he run when she had tried to make him go? What was it he had said to her?

"The boy."

Couldn't he for once shut up about him? The boy, Eden dismissively smirked. *Where was the stupid boy when you needed him, Abdar? Where? And now you're dead.*

Clutching her shoulder when something grazed her, she tumbled forward, her thoughts turning to gunfire, how the one she had just heard sounded so much closer than those she was running from. Struggling to her feet, she stiffened. Something large was tramping through the brush behind her. One of George Henry's men sent to bring her back, she guessed. Frantic, she lurched forward, breaking into a hurried jog. A bullet splintered a tree she was running past; a voice shouted for her to stop. Another gunshot immediately followed, this one fired from in front of her, Eden coming to an abrupt stop when the bullet gouged the soil a meter ahead. Looking up, she saw one of the warlord's men standing some twenty paces away, the barrel of his weapon level with her chest, a wide grin on his face. As he motioned for her to turn around, Eden saw something large leap up and knock the man to the ground. A foul-smelling hand clamped over her mouth as two snarling hyenas came out from the cover of the trees.

* * *

Shielding his eyes from the flash bomb, Dirk crouched low to the ground. But he didn't stop running. The sight of the helicopter gave him hope, a chance of escape. Determined, he fought his way through the underbrush, struggling to keep pace with the strangely outfitted soldier.

Escape. He could get out of this godforsaken place. Deliver the woman. Get his passport and equipment back, have his debts wiped away. He could leave Africa for good. Could go far away. Maybe back to France, to Claudine—become Peter Benjamin again.

But then what? he bitterly asked. There was nowhere he could run where her face wouldn't haunt him, pull him back to Mogadishu, where her screams lingered, haunting the maze of narrow alleyways he'd led them into. As much as he didn't want it to happen, he pictured her face: all the good in the world contained in the softest brown eyes he'd ever known. Her name floated on the periphery of his thoughts, teasing and torturing, as if he dared say it, she'd come rushing back. And all the awful emptiness, the burning guilt, would come with her, grinding his face into the sadistic brutality he'd witnessed. Hell waited in the alleys of Mogadishu. And he had stupidly, arrogantly led them to it, thinking they'd be safe. Instead, a torturing inferno had swallowed them. But, in a twist of evil, it had spit him back out, allowing him to go free. Free. How was he free?

An earth-rattling eruption nearly knocking him off his feet, Dirk looked over his shoulder to see a truck on fire, flames spewing from its gas tank. The smell of burning petrol came with angry shouts from the warlord's camp. Bullets whizzed past his head. *Faster*, he told himself, *run faster. Don't let the soldier take off without you!*

When three of the warlord's men appeared from the cover of the tall grass twenty paces ahead, Dirk dove chest first to the ground. Glancing to the side, he saw Bin'ka standing motionless—an animal waiting to be slaughtered—the woman, Claire, limp in his arms. Was she already dead? he wondered. Had he come all this way to die for nothing?

The powerful sound of the gas-mask soldier's weapon shifted his attention forward. Dirk was able to see one of the men blocking their path to the copter fall sideways. Another lurched backward when a bullet struck below the man's waist. Pushing himself up, Dirk ran forward, stopping when he saw the gas-mask-wearing soldier collapse, blood spraying from his throat, weapon flying from his grasp. Looking ahead, Dirk saw the warlord's men turn their weapons upon him. Lunging for the discarded machine gun, Dirk rolled left as bullets ruptured the ground to his right. Coming out of the roll, he crouched to one knee and fired. A soldier jerked violently to the ground.

"Go!" he shouted at Bin'ka.

Dirk raced ahead, firing off another round. The soldier with the leg wound spun around as a bullet tore into his chest, the man's AK-47 pointing skyward, harmlessly releasing a final burst.

"You can fly this, right?" Dirk yelled as he and Bin'ka reached the helicopter.

Nodding, Bin'ka placed Claire in the passenger seat, buckling her into the harness before running round to the other side. Motioning for Dirk to check behind them, he engaged the engine. Dirk fired a volley at a group of soldiers running toward them before stepping onto the copter's runner. Slapping the metal frame of the cockpit, he yelled, "Go!" Then he fired the last of his bullets as the copter lifted off the ground.

* * *

Bin'ka eased the helicopter into the air, banking the craft away from George Henry's camp as soon as he'd gained sufficient altitude. Giving the fire-ravaged compound a final glance, he noticed a flash of blue light coming from the ground. Leveling the helicopter to hover, he tried to make out what it was. But an instant later, the blue flash disappeared. A burst of red-orange flames flared in its place. Staring at the pocket of flames, he couldn't help thinking it was burning in the exact spot where the soldier from the Legion of God had fallen. But that made no sense.

"What are you doing? Go!"

Grunting at Dirk's command, Bin'ka veered the craft northward, keeping the altitude of the copter low. Below them, the fleeting shadow of the helicopter added a surreal aura to the scene they were passing: three jeeps flattened like sheets of paper, a half dozen of the warlord's men strewn close by. Their bodies—like the jeeps—were crushed into the ground. Past these he saw the burning wreck of a car, a lone soldier of some unknown allegiance kneeling next to it, several dead elephants farther past. Just as he began maneuvering the copter into a slow, eastward arc, he noticed a big cat—a cheetah—standing alone, staring, it seemed, at the man kneeling next to the burning wreck.

"Let's get the hell out of here!" Dirk yelled, slapping the frame of the cockpit.

With a shrug of his shoulders, Bin'ka guided the helicopter east, trying not to think about whom he was leaving behind.

* * *

"Are you coming?"

Kamua stared into what was left of the smoldering Land Rover, not wanting to look, but unable to take his eyes off the two charred corpses inside.

"There's much to be done."

Why was he hearing voices? he wondered. He was losing his mind, he told himself. He had to be. There was no other explanation. What he'd just witnessed—no, what he *thought* he'd witnessed—couldn't possibly be real. Ghost elephants? A herd of wailing, stampeding behemoths formed of light? Squeezing the stock of his rifle between his hands, he shook his head.

"We mustn't let them get too far."

And now a voice—a woman's. Surely he was in a state of unconsciousness. A bullet must have grazed his skull, he supposed. Sending him to a place where he could still think, dream, and imagine—but not understand that what he was seeing, feeling, and hearing was an illusion. No, not an illusion, he thought, more a nightmare, because the pain felt all too real.

"Their remains will seep into the earth; they will return to where they began."

A wind—cold where it touched his skin—stirred him to move. Wiping the chill from the back of his neck, he rose from his knees.

"Ready?"

Startled, he turned to the voice, laughing when he realized he must still be unconscious. A green-eyed cheetah stood behind him, gazing at him—he was certain—as though the beast knew he was going insane.

"*Duma, karibu,*" he said, playing along with the illusion.

Chuckling, he closed his eyes and shook his head. When would he awaken? he wondered. Or was he dead?

"Hurry."

"Hurry? Everything is gone." Opening his eyes, he asked, "What is left?"

An old woman—was she old? he wondered—dressed in a flowing gray robe stood in the spot where the cheetah had been, locks of gold-white hair showing from the edges of the deep hood covering her head.

"What is left?" came her dismissive, ridiculing reply.

When the robed woman turned her back to him, Kamua did the same to her. His focus lured back to the charred remains of Selam and Tengene, their blackened corpses suddenly becoming those of his mother and sister, their bodies huddled in a corner of their burned-out hut in the village where he'd been raised, arms draped across each other's shoulders, fingers clenched in gnarled fists.

Gwok-gwonk-gwokwokwok!

Startled by the hooting call, Kamua spun round. Perched on the branch of a tree he had not noticed was an owl the size of an eagle, emerald-green eyes staring intently into his. Without warning the bird was airborne, swooping low, taloned feet extended. Thrusting his arms out for protection, Kamua felt the rifle jerked out of his hands. The bird circled once before flying east, the rifle held sideways beneath its body, evenly balanced between its feet. Before he realized he had moved, Kamua found himself running after the bird, thoughts of what was real and what was illusion lost within the hypnotic motion of flapping wings.

* * *

"Burn! Burn till your screams melt into fire!"

Teimbaka heard the rage in George Henry's voice, but not his words. Meaningless were they—words—as this moment had become. Claire was gone; John Too was dead; the spirit elephants had forsaken him. What did words mean now, especially those of a madman? Someone who would butcher his own people—how had the Mother's land become so troubled?

"Listen when I speak! Hear God!"

Teimbaka made no sound when his head was yanked back by his hair. Nor did he flinch when the blade of a smoldering knife was placed a breath's width from his eye.

"Gods," he mumbled with a sardonic laugh. "Too many—it is why the Mother cries," he said to no one.

The coarse fibers of rope looped around his wrists.

"No! Do not bind him," George Henry ordered. "I will see you slither across the ground as the flesh melts from your body," he hissed, stepping near Teimbaka so he could sneer down into his face. "Toss the boy into his lap. Let them burn together."

Knife removed from his face, head slapped level, Teimbaka watched the heavyset warlord walk several paces away. The fire weapon was slipped onto his back by two of his men. Looking past George Henry, Teimbaka saw scores of faces he did not know—worn, hardened, unforgiving. They gazed upon him without pity, the smoke-filled sky behind their heads as dark and ominous as the anger displayed in their eyes. Their anger the product of decades of having been treated as slaves, he supposed, hating just to hate—because there was no recourse for what they'd been subjected to. White men, black men, African, European—it mattered little who or which they killed. Wounds required ointment to heal—death the salve.

John Too's body was thrown against his chest as though the boy was a sack of refuse dumped into a ditch.

All arms and legs he was, Teimbaka mused, no bigger than when Teimbaka had first crossed paths with the boy on the fringes of the Danakil. Cradling him in his arms, Teimbaka ran his fingers across John Too's head, remembering with fondness when he—the boy—with such confident belligerence, had ordered him into the hills to find the words.

"The words," Teimbaka murmured, pausing to reflect. Gazing into John Too's lifeless face, he whispered, "Say them."

"Fire—burn the sin from this man's soul!"

Teimbaka looked up from John Too into the face of George Henry.

"Wash the filth from this land!" George Henry smiled, raising the firehose to his chest.

"Blessed are the children," Teimbaka muttered. Glancing down at John Too, he closed his eyes, saying, "For they are the will of God."

Preparing to be set afire, Teimbaka curled his body tightly around John Too's, his last thoughts turning to Claire as he waited for the flames. Upon hearing a click, he tensed. Then came another, and another, and another, and another—until Teimbaka realized the clicks were slaps: hand against skin. Mutterings of *evil, jinn, mabaya, bouda, shaytan,* and *shar* began to swell around him as alarm built to panic. Some small object flew against his face. Opening his eyes, he glimpsed a twinkle of green moving across his cheek. Brushing the object away, he saw an insect—a beetle—righting itself where he'd flicked it to the ground. Enraptured by the bright green color of its body, Teimbaka watched the beetle unfurl its wings before becoming a twinkling glimmer flying up onto John Too's shoulder.

Where the one green beetle landed, several more joined. Teimbaka swatted them off John Too's body as they set down. As cries of "A plague has come!" swirled through the warlord's camp, Teimbaka ceased his effort in trying to keep the bugs away, their numbers becoming more than he could combat.

"Burn!" he heard George Henry bellow.

Teimbaka laid John Too upon the ground, scrambling to the side when a cloud of shiny green bugs swarmed upon the boy. As he watched John Too disappear within the horde of insects, the smell of burning petrol suddenly flooded his senses. Teimbaka covered his mouth with his hand as flames and curling black smoke began to flare around him.

"Get them off me!" George Henry screamed.

The warlord's face was covered with beetles—thousands more hovering about his head. Teimbaka watched George Henry turn in frenzied circles, shooting arcs of flame through the air while a sea of green insects flowed across the ground beneath his feet. Cries of "Bouda!" suddenly erupted. Teimbaka looked past the crazed warlord to see his soldiers running away. Arms flailing, hands slapping at their bodies and heads, they fled northward past the line of vehicles, George Henry stumbling after them, spewing swaths of flames in his wake. Looking out across the burning landscape, Teimbaka glimpsed the figure of a woman behind the flames. She walked slowly toward him, a lone hyena by her side.

"Claire," he whispered, falling to his knees.

But it wasn't Claire. Although the woman's skin was white, her build was larger, her hair longer and darker, her face younger; Teimbaka left to wonder if what he was seeing was false, a mirage of his own making, mocking him for not having kept Claire safe. Around him, the sound of whirring wings howled to a rushing wind, the cackling calls of the hyenas lost in a maelstrom of flames, smoke, and roaring air.

* * *

Sarah stared at the pulsing green light, confused as to why it wasn't blue or red or a combination of the two. And why the man kneeling near the light was not wearing a uniform? His black robe was frightening, making her think he was saying a prayer before taking her to the morgue instead of the hospital she'd been promised. Perhaps he was a detective, she thought, there to probe her memory about her captor, kneeling to study the ground for tracks or clues. Or, worse, perhaps he was some sort of psychologist wanting her to recount every detail of her ordeal, asking her to relive every demeaning shattering thrust, salacious grope, brutal penetration her captor had inflicted upon her while she was bound and blindfolded.

"Don't ask me!" she screamed.

Or had she? For the black-robed man didn't move, didn't give any indication he'd heard her yelling.

"I don't want to remember!" she wailed.

The man in the black robe stared at her in stunned silence, as if he was seeing a ghost. Next to him, the pulsing green light quieted to a steady glow, then built in intensity, the glare making her avert her eyes. Again, the color of the ground—it was all wrong. Green where it should have been red. The blood still fresh, still flowing from the wound she'd opened in her captor's throat. How it had changed color to metallic green, she couldn't fathom. There was so much of it—a river of it, she saw, more than what she remembered. And she was in the center, the current leading her to the man in the black robe. Looking at him, squinting past the periphery of emerald brilliance shining on the ground next to him, she could see by the look on his face what he was thinking: *she* was to blame, *she'd* enticed her neighbor with some teasing provocative gesture. She'd aroused the man to such a state, he was driven to kidnap her, imprison her—abuse her in the basement closet of his home.

"He defiled me!" she raged, her body shaking uncontrollably as she fell to the ground.

The heat of fire on her skin threw her into a panic. Smoke stung her eyes, seeping up into her nose, leaving her struggling to breathe, clouding her mind so she couldn't think clearly.

"Who's there?" she cried when someone lifted her arm.

Recoiling when something wet touched her cheek, she thrust out a hand to push it away, gasping at the touch of bristly fur upon her palm.

"Go away!" she screamed.

"Sarah," a voice from above said. "I told you to wait."

They're placing me in the ambulance, she thought as her body lifted upward.

"Your fever is worse."

"The man in the black robe," she mumbled. "Who is he?"

* * *

John brought Sarah to his chest, propping her up against his body when her legs started to buckle. Through the smoke and flames, he saw Teimbaka kneeling in a tattered black shamma, a glowing green mound on the ground off to his side. Who was the man in the black robe? Sarah had asked. A beggar, a nomad, a madman, a false prophet, he wanted to say. But he knew he'd be lying if he did. Teimbaka was not any of those. And if he said he was, John knew he would be saying those words out of jealousy and hurt. And there was no longer a reason for those feelings to exist. Sister Lady was gone—taken away in a helicopter by Bin'ka and a white man. What must Teimbaka be feeling? he wondered. Claire meant so much.

Seh-my's sharp growl prodded him from his thoughts. John shifted his attention to the animal before focusing on what the hyena was looking at. Past the line of vehicles, out across the moving landscape of beetles, John could see soldiers working their way back toward them. They moved in halting steps, waiting for the sections of fire George Henry was spreading to burn out before hustling forward. Beyond the soldiers, John could see plumes of dust rising into the air. The sound of motors—powerful, laboring—grew stronger as the black outline of a truck came into view: reinforcements.

"Sarah—we must go."

* * *

It was just as Claire had described. How long ago that conversation seemed. Another lifetime. Yet, he could picture it clearly—as though she were sitting across from him at this very moment, her gaze lost in the flames of a fire, recalling the night Gunstard bombarded the orphan camp with mortars.

"The first explosion was terrifying," she'd told him, her eyes vacant, lines of pain haunting her face. "The flash, the shrapnel. I ran outside. John was close behind me."

And now here she was again—weaving through a line of flames, leaning on John, the first of several explosions bursting around them. He could see terror on her face, could feel the fear she must be experiencing, John pulling her along, almost carrying her as they made their way toward him.

Hyenas—several, he counted—yapped at their heels, waiting for them to fall, so they could attack while they lay on the ground—just as they had done to Tafari. Their lives would be over soon, he realized. Why else would scores of hyenas gather? Pacing, cackling, charging the flames, retreating— he saw them waiting on the far perimeter of the blaze. Uncanny how the beasts sensed death, he thought.

The eruption of a truck's gas tank sent a shower of flames across the sky, fireballs plummeting to earth like raindrops, shockwaves of the blast knocking Teimbaka to the ground.

"One bomb fell so close, the ground buckled beneath me. I—I fell," Claire had explained, her voice an apology. "Children screaming—every-where." Claire had paused for a long minute then, her body shuddering before she repeated, "I fell."

She had looked at him across the fire, her face a picture of tortured agony. Just as it was now, he saw. The past was still strong, still living within her, the flames flickering in her eyes just a reflection of the suffering smoldering inside her.

"Hurry, Etiyopiya! Get up! They're almost here!"

Teimbaka stared numbly at the man offering him his hand.

"John?"

The hyena heads perched atop the woman's shoulders seemed to nod when John replied, "Yes. Hurry. We must go."

Taking John's hand, Teimbaka rose to his feet.

"Where is John Too?" John asked, looking past Teimbaka to the grove of trees. "Did he escape?"

Head drooping toward the ground, Teimbaka ventured a hesitant look toward the woman leaning on John's shoulder. She was Claire, he saw—yet, she was not. Still, her expression of despair tore at his heart.

"I couldn't save him," he softly told her.

The rushing hiss of erupting flames came with the sound of gunfire, John drawing Sarah closer to him as a volley of bullets whizzed past their heads.

"This way!" John shouted, glancing back over his shoulder.

Both John and Teimbaka saw the warlord coming around the line of vehicles, unleashing streams of fire upon the ground.

"Take them!" they heard him bellow. "Throw them in the fire!"

"Run! Run!" John yelled.

Soldiers hurdled the flames at George Henry's command. John grabbed Teimbaka's arm, pulling him to move. With John leading the way, the woman stumbling by his side, Teimbaka began to run after them.

"Etiyopiya."

The word came to him as a whisper, sliding into his thoughts from a twisting knot deep inside the pit of his stomach. Turning, he glimpsed the ethereal form of a young spirit elephant melting away. Particles of golden moonlight drifted to the ground; glittering flecks of the spirit beast's remains flowed into the mound of beetles, the green aura of the insects ceasing as the last wisp of gold-white light disappeared beneath their bodies.

"Die now!" he heard George Henry rage.

It was the Serpent Teimbaka saw as he turned to face the man—coiled body standing erect, black scales shimmering with fire, eyes spitting flames.

"Etiyopiya!"

Scores of hyenas rushed past Teimbaka, the deafening onslaught of snarling, snapping jaws and men crying out in fear and pain lost in the moment Teimbaka took hold of John Too's outstretched hand.

2 3

"YOU'RE IN THE shit. But then you know that better than me, don't ya? Face bein' all over the TV and in the papers and such—didn't you see a camera? Everybody seen the news done seen you in the hall with the baby in your arms."

"If I thought the bitch was smart enough, I'd say she set my ass up."

Tugging the sides of his hood snug around his face, Chris flicked the deadbolt in place and stepped away from the door.

"But since I know she lives for the needle and can't think past where her next score's coming from, I know she isn't the one who made the clip and got it to the press."

Jim hung his shiny red Philadelphia 76ers jacket on one of the brass-colored hooks lining the white-tiled wall next to the walk-in refrigerator. Grabbing a clean apron from the stack sitting atop a tower of milk crates, he slipped his head inside the neck opening, asking "Who, then?" as he wrapped the long strings around his waist, tying them in a bow.

"Got my suspicions," Chris told him, peeking out through the pickup window to the little soul food restaurant facing the street front. "Somebody who has video equipment. Less you know, right?" he said, shrugging.

Jim dumped a bag of red-skinned potatoes into one of the large stainless steel sinks along the back wall and turned on the water.

"What am I supposed to say to the old lady? What folks gonna say when they see us with a baby—two old prunes that we be? Ain't natural."

"Tell your old lady: one, two, three, four, five," Chris evenly replied. "Five grand a month. Two years, tops. Tell her that's the deal."

Chris stepped away from the pickup window to study the contents inside the glass-fronted reach-in cooler standing along the wall.

"What story you all want to tell is up to you. Great-great-grandson, baby of a second cousin who died of an early heart attack—shit, I don't care. You got five thousand reasons to come up with somethin' people swallow. If I'm not back in two years—"

Chris slid the glass door of the cooler to the side. Pulling out a can of Mountain Dew, he said, "Do whatever you want."

Popping the aluminum ring top, he took a swig.

"Sell him, leave him on someone's doorstep, give him away, keep him, raise him as your own."

Walking back to the pickup window, he glanced out into the restaurant again.

"What if I just says no?" Jim remarked, pulling a double-handled stock-pot down from the stainless steel shelf over the sink. "Call the police and tell 'em you're here."

Chris took a long swig from his can of soda, eyeing Jim with skepticism.

"Kid goes to a state-run orphanage, then. And you'd be out five grand. Hundred twenty if you make it the two," he told him matter-of-factly. "Call 'em if you want. You think they're going be here any quicker than nor-mal? Come on, man, I'd be twenty miles from here before the boys in blue decided to roll up in this part of the city. And you'd be out all that dough."

Chris stepped over to the long stainless steel table in the middle of the kitchen and looked into the open duffel bag sitting atop it.

"And this little nigger be on his way to nowhere, not a soul givin' a rat's ass whether he live or die."

Jim swung the sink's long-neck spigot over the pot.

"How'd you get him out of the hospital without being caught?" he asked, turning on the water.

"Graveyard shift." With a slight shrug, he explained, "Just waited for the nurse to use the bathroom. Doubt she even knows he's missing."

Reaching a hand into his pants pocket, Chris pulled out a wad of bills, placing them on the table next to the duffel.

"Just another orphan in an over-crowded hospital that didn't want him anyway. A black boy at that; you know where I'm coming from?"

"Yeah, I hear ya," Jim said, studying the wad of bills.

Shutting off the water, Jim lifted the half-filled pot out of the sink. After moving it to one of the four burners atop the stove, he turned a knob, blue flames springing to life beneath the pot.

"Where you gonna be during all this? How I get the money every month?"

"You'll get it," Chris told him, moving back to the pickup window. "You don't," he shrugged, peering out into the restaurant again, "like I said—do whatever. But you'll get it. And as far as where I'll be? Let's just say I have some scores to settle." Turning, straightening to his full height, he added, "Here and there."

The soft squeak of a turning doorknob drew both men's eyes to the back door. Three sharp raps against the wood and the sound of a muffled female voice on the other side, angrily yelling "Open up!" got Jim moving. Unlocking the deadbolt, he stepped back as the door swung open.

"Why you got the door locked?" the heavyset woman stepping through demanded.

The woman's scornful look turned to one of surprise when she heard a baby begin to cry. Squaring her body to Jim's, hands placed against her broad hips, she barked, "What the hell is that?"

Stepping over to the table, Jim grabbed the wad of bills. Looking into the duffel, he said, "We best be gettin' some diapers and baby formula."

Slamming her purse onto the other end of the table, the woman looked like she was just about ready to unleash a tirade of curse words when the sound of the restaurant's front door opening and closing made her pause. Taking a step toward Jim, she asked, "Who was that?"

"Nobody," he replied, peeling a hundred-dollar bill out from the wad he was holding.

Dropping the bill into the duffel, Jim slid the bag across the tabletop until it was halfway between him and the heavyset woman.

"And please—for once, Rochelle—can you just do what I ask?"

* * *

Rue stepped into his office, flicking on the lights as he rushed over to pick up the phone ringing on his desk.

"Yeah?" he answered, checking the time on his gold Rolex. "Well, well, well—you been hiding in the desert somewhere? Staying clear of those—what you call them—Afar dudes with the big knives?" Laughing, Rue edged around the corner of his desk. "You certainly put yourself between a rock and a hard place, didn't you?"

Rue chuckled as he listened to the agitated voice on the other end of the line.

"What's that?" he asked, sitting down in his chair. "Mogadishu? Where the hell is that?"

Out of habit, he checked the bank of security monitors to his right, his face twisting to a scowl as he tapped the glass front of each.

"Yeah, yeah—I met him." Rue ran his hand under the side of the desk where the security monitors were situated. "Except he's a she," he said. "Lex is short for Alexis. And *she* loves ivory."

Placing the receiver down, he reached beneath the desk. He held a handful of cut cables in his fist when he straightened back up.

"Son of a bitch," he cursed under his breath. "Hold on!" he shouted, sneering at the phone.

Looking at the monitors again, he stared at the image of a hooded figure frozen on each of the screens.

"How'd he do that? Son of a bitch."

Picking up the phone, he said, "Akmir—Akmir! I'll have to call you back," before hanging up.

Pushing his chair away from the desk, he slipped his hand into the front pocket of his pants, extracting a ring of keys. Thumbing through them, he chose the smallest. Rolling his chair to the left, he inserted the key into a keyhole located in the left-side panel of the desk hidden just beneath the overhang. He turned the key to the right, using his thumb to push against a section of wood two inches to the left of the hole. When he took his thumb away, the edge of a hidden compartment popped out. Using both hands, he pulled the long, shallow drawer out of the slot and placed it on the desk.

"Son of a bitch," he muttered for the third time, staring dumbfounded at the small plastic figurine of a black cat lying flat atop a single one-dollar bill in the middle of the drawer. "You took it all."

* * *

"Yo, man, hit me up with another Crown and Coke. And shit—ain't you got no better tunes than this? And where be Super Freak? And you got fries or somethin' I can munch on while I'm waitin'? And don't this place ever get any snatch coming in? Shit—just be a bunch of old faggots here."

Griper stared at Goliath's broad, muscled back, in particular the red and green dragonhead tattoo peeking out from the collar of the man's black T-shirt. Tapping the handgun in his pants pocket, he took a quick look behind him.

"Nothin' but queers," he mumbled, surveying the motley collection of male patrons seated at the dozen or so tables scattered around the dingy, wood-paneled room. "A jerk-off fest."

Goliath placed a glass filled with ice and brown liquid on the bar when Griper turned back around.

"Drink," the massive man growled, nodding to the glass. "And fuck you."

"Uh-uh—don't play that shit with me, nigger," Griper countered with bravado, leaning back in his barstool, tapping the right-hand pocket of his pants. "Don't make me pull out the pig slayer and use it on you."

With a smug wink, Griper leaned forward, grabbed the drink from atop the bar, and took a sip.

"Find yourself face down in a pool of blood if I do," he boasted. "Just like that narc bitch cop they found down by the bay."

Griper leaned back, shoving his hand in his pocket as Goliath leaned over the bar.

"That was you?" the big man whispered.

"Right on, motherfucker," Griper glibly replied. "So you best be—" Clutching his drink, scowling as Goliath walked away, he mumbled, "Fuckin' big dumb gorilla—oughta be kissin' my ass for takin' the bitch out."

Griper swirled the ice cubes in the glass before taking another sip of Crown and Coke.

"Treat me like a nobody," he grunted. "Show some respect," he huffed. "A pig for a brother," he said a little louder, raising the glass in his hand as if he was making a toast. "Yeah—that's right—y'all should be— What the hell you lookin' at?"

Griper tilted his barstool forward to glare at the rangy, stubble-faced, white-skinned man standing at the near corner of the four-sided bar.

"Best be lookin' somewhere else, you know what good for you."

Griper reached for his gun when he saw the man slip a hand into the pocket of his tan coveralls. When Goliath leaned across the bar and gripped his arm, Griper tried to pull away. But Goliath's hold felt like a vice.

"Ready to see you now."

"'Bout time," Griper whined, slapping Goliath's hand off his arm. "Where he at?"

With a grunt, Goliath nodded toward the back of the room.

"I'll show you," he told him, releasing Griper's arm.

Goliath walked toward the corner of the rectangular bar, the scruffy-faced, white-skinned man hurrying to place a dollar bill and an empty beer mug in front of him as he approached.

"Pour your own," Goliath snarled, flipping up a hinged section of the bar just to the right of where the man was standing. "And don't leave no splatters."

* * *

Griper clutched the butt of the Cobra with his right hand, his eyes focused on the back of Goliath's head. Every now and then—every other step or two—he chanced a quick glance left or right, searching for any flicker of movement within the shadows of the storage room. But he found nothing lurking behind the stacked cases of beer and liquor, no hidden threats waiting to pounce on him from the shelves of dry goods packed floor to ceiling. When he heard what sounded like a ring of keys dangling, he breathed a sigh of relief. But as Goliath inserted a key into the door lock at the back of the room, he tensed again. Envisioning a trap, he pulled the Cobra from his pants pocket.

"Where you leading me to?"

"Said to bring you here."

Goliath removed the key from the lock, slid the deadbolt over, and opened the thick metal door. Stepping off to one side, he motioned Griper to step by him with a wave of his arm.

"Ain't stupid," Griper said, pointing the snub-nosed handgun at the doorway. "You first."

Goliath stared at him for a moment, then smiled. Without a word, the big man stepped through the doorframe. Cautiously, Griper followed.

"Where he at?"

Goliath looked down the east side of an alley, a nondescript single-lane stretch of uneven pavement running between two squat, square-roofed brick warehouses built around the turn of the century. What light filtered down into the manmade ravine came from the few businesses still operating behind double rows of glass block windows set twenty feet above ground. Except for the dim glow coming from the bar windows above and behind them, the alley was dark. Goliath nodded to a set of car headlights switching on just as Griper said, "What kind of shit you playin'?"

"You're to wait here," Goliath told him.

And then he was gone, Goliath stepping back into the storage room, shutting the door behind him. Griper heard the deadbolt slide into place. Turning, he squinted into the glare of the approaching headlights. The steady pulse of the car engine bouncing off the brick buildings reverberated through his body as the vehicle drew near.

"Shut your damn light off!" he yelled, shading his eyes with his free hand.

He clenched the butt of the Cobra as the car pulled aside him. The headlights stayed on.

"'Bout time you showed," he said in a loud voice, tapping the driver's window with the barrel of the gun.

Griper took a step back when he saw the rear passenger window slide down an inch. It was then he noticed the car wasn't the usual one Super Freak drove.

"Young man," came a female voice from the back of the car. "Might we have a word?"

Griper took a cautious step forward, leaning in and bending down to try to see through the opening in the window. The inside of the car was dark. Raising the Cobra up, he tapped the glass.

"You lost or somethin'? Best be on your way if you know what's good for ya."

"No need for such a crass display."

The soft illumination from the car's interior overhead light came on, revealing a figure in the far side of the back seat. Griper didn't know what to make of it at first—a bundle of some sparkly blue material wrapped in layers around some object that looked like a body. But then he noticed a set of eyes gazing at him from an opening in the fabric where he guessed he should be seeing somebody's face. Slowly, it began to dawn on him he was looking at a woman. The type he'd seen in some old black-and-white movies from way back when, where the foreign dudes in the film wore turbans—or whatever shit it was called wrapped around their heads—and the women covered their faces with veils.

"A harem girl? What the hell—?"

"I don't appreciate crude language."

"I don't give a shit what you appreciate, bitch. Where be Super Freak? And just who the hell are you?"

"I really must protest your vulgarity."

"My what? See this, lady?"

He stuck the barrel of the gun through the crack in the window.

"You ain't in no position to protest nothin'—you dig?"

"Is that it?" she asked. "Is that the gun you used?"

Griper tensed, pointing the gun at the woman when he saw her hand move.

"They tell me you killed a policewoman," she calmly said as she removed the folds of material from her head and face. "Is that true? Was it you?"

Griper studied her features: high cheekbones, small nose, rounded forehead, dark hair, delicate ears, almond-shaped eyes. Looking closer, he was drawn to one of her earrings: a crescent-shaped sliver of white, bottom capped in gold, dangling from a fine gold chain. The stone, or whatever substance the jewelry was made out of, seemed aglow in the car's light.

"Ivory," she said, displaying the earring with her fingertip. "Beautiful, isn't it?"

The window suddenly lowered another couple of inches. Griper stuck his face in the opening, placing his hands—and the gun—on the car's roof.

"Don't you think ivory is beautiful?"

She smiled then, quick and beguiling. Griper suddenly found himself saying, "Yeah—it's all right, I guess."

"It can be expensive," she told him, gently fingering the piece of jewelry. "Quality specimens can command a very high price. People all over the world love ivory."

"Ain't that the shit. Now why don't you—"

"That's why killing that policewoman was a mistake."

"What?"

"The activity of the law enforcement agencies down at the docks is now tenfold what it was before."

"What's that got to do with me?"

"We can't have a disruption of that sort taking place. It stymies business, you see."

"Just what the fuck you tryin' to say, bitch?"

"That the continued flow of business dictates a remedy, one that will satisfy the various law enforcement agencies involved in the investigation of the police officer's death."

"You best—"

"So is it?"

"Is it what?"

"The gun," she said, sounding somewhat put out. "Is the gun you're holding the same one you used to shoot the policewoman? Messy affair. Was shooting her in the eyes your own idea?"

"She done got what she deserved," he replied, twisting his lips into a snarl. "Pig for a brother. That's how it's gonna go down from here on out."

"That's very short-sighted thinking. And I'm afraid that's not how it will go down," she told him. "You understand that it's business."

Griper slid his hands from the roof of the car when he saw the woman lift a long, slender, yardstick-like object from the folds of her robes. Like her earring, the item was made of ivory. Near her hand, he caught the flash of a gold handle.

"Drive," she said, using the cane to lightly tap against the glass divider separating the front and back seats of the car.

The car moved before the side window fully closed, leaving Griper muttering curse words as he watched the long black limousine slowly roll toward the western end of the alley.

"Buenas noches, negro."

Before Griper could turn his head, a slashing pain ripped into his forearm. Glimpses of a thin-bladed knife, silver beads, a crucifix, and a wrist wrapped in a red, white, and blue piece of cloth flashed across his panic-stricken eyes as he watched his gun fall to the pavement. Hands grabbed his arms, spinning his body, pushing him to the wall. Cloth of some sort looped around his face, pulled taught into his mouth. His hands were bound together with what felt like strips of plastic. A bag of some sort—soft, light blocking—was shimmied down over his head. At the sound of a car's engine pulling close, he was pushed to the ground, a foot placed against his neck as someone bound his ankles together. Griper struggled against the sensation of his body being lifted, then a moment of falling through air before landing against something hard and unforgiving. He groaned when his head banged against something metal.

"No prints on the gun," a male voice—a spic, from what he could make of it—said.

Griper tried to move, but was pushed back.

"Relax, amigo," the same Spanish-accented voice told him. "Suicide is quick, si? We make it as painless as we can," he said, chuckling. "Normally, mi compadres and me, we would toast you for taking down el chancho. But alas—how you gringos say? There is a new boss in town? Yes? So it is just business. You understand. Vaya con Dios, my friend."

Then Griper heard the trunk close.

24

"WHO IS SHE?"

No one answered.

John gazed northward, a hyena—the largest Teimbaka had ever seen—pacing by his side. The animal was uneasy, moving in sudden starts and stops, ears erect, eyes focused on wisps of smoke rising into the sky from the direction they'd fled.

"They're better dried."

Teimbaka looked down at the girl dressed in purple.

"The leaves—I don't know what good they will do unless they're dried."

When she held up a handful of shiny green leaves, he waved his hand sideways, saying, "I'm not hungry."

With an audible sigh, the girl turned away. Numbly, he watched her place the leaves on the shoulder of the woman. The skin around the crude line of sutures was red and swollen; her wound was infected.

"Eden."

Teimbaka stared down at the hand John Too had taken hold of when they'd made their escape, slowly turning it from side to side.

"In case you wish to know *my* name."

He looked to John Too then. Saw him standing off on his own, facing southward. Was he looking for Claire? he wondered. Where had the water buffalo–man taken her? *How is it she's gone?*

"You are Teimbaka?"

Teimbaka let his eyes drift between John and John Too, each lost to the horizon he faced. The land—the Mother—something was changing within

Her. He could sense it, feel it in the emptiness inside him, see it in the slumped shoulders of the two boys. Claire was gone. How could that be?

"You don't look like much."

The girl's voice was annoying, amusing.

"Eden," he said.

"You talk," she quipped, flashing a bright smile. "I was beginning to think I would be the only one," she commented, nodding between John and John Too. "Why do you have so many scars? Tabib did not mention them when she spoke of you."

"Tabib?"

"Claire," she said, looking at John. "Sister Lady," she offered, turning her face to John Too.

"She said we had to find you, reach you."

He watched her eyes flit over his clothing, his feet, his hair; what was she seeing?

"I was expecting—"

Eden grabbed the canteen on the ground by her feet when the woman moaned. Carefully, she dribbled a few drops of water onto her lips. Shrugging, turning her face to him, she went on to say, "Something—you know—more."

A whimper—more a pained squeal—drew their attention to the large hyena. The animal yelped at the appearance of two more hyenas emerging from the scrub just north of the dry riverbed where they'd stopped. One limped—badly, Teimbaka saw—the other nudged it along, muzzle placed beneath the shoulder joint of the foreleg curled to its side. The smell of burnt fur and flesh suddenly awakened within his nostrils, the stench pungent. Taking stock of himself and those around him, he could see black streaks on their clothing. Their faces, legs, arms, and feet were smeared with lines of smoke residue, blemished in places with purple-red welts. Touching his beard and hair, his fingers came away grimy, caked with ash and the smell of petrol.

"I wonder if she knew."

Teimbaka furrowed his brow.

"That we had found you. We'd traveled so far. And for what?"

Eden glanced at the woman lying next to her and shook her head.

"It makes no sense," he heard her mutter. "She was so certain you needed to be saved."

Again, he watched the girl eyeing him, seemingly inspecting him from head to toe.

"What did Tabib see in you? What are you I can't see?"

"I—"

"Did you summon the bugs? Was that you?" she asked, tilting the canteen so a few drops of water fell upon the woman's forehead.

Teimbaka looked at his hand, then looked to John Too.

"No—not him I think," she said, following his gaze. "Although he is abdar. I thought him dead," she admitted, perplexed. "No matter," she shrugged. "No, only someone powerful could summon a swarm. I think it was she. Tabib," she explained, seeing the blank expression on his face.

Gently placing her fingers to the woman's wound, Eden lightly pressed down upon the leaves.

"Or you, I suppose" she offered, sliding her hand over to the woman's chest. "But I would say it wasn't," she went on, fingering the silver cross lying flat atop the woman's blouse.

As though remembering something forgotten, she touched where the bullet had grazed her shoulder before looking questioningly at John Too.

"I saw blood—a bullet hole in his chest. How did he heal?"

Teimbaka heard Eden talking, but not the words she was saying. Lost in the cross of silver glittering upon the woman's chest, he reached for the one he had worn about his neck—the one Lee had bequeathed to him—but found it no longer there. He had given it to Claire to replace the one taken from her—it too now gone. Yet, here was another. Brought to take the place of the ones lost? he wondered. He looked at the woman anew.

"Who is she?" he heard himself ask again.

"She is called Sarah." John was looking down at the woman as he spoke, the large hyena standing behind him. Several more of the animals gathered a few paces farther back.

"How did she—?"

"She was tracking Claire. Traveling with the white man. She said—"

Teimbaka saw what he thought to be anger in John's eyes before he heard the same emotion rise in his voice.

"She said she was here to take Claire away—home! Is this not her home?" he defiantly asked. "Did you know she would leave?"

John looked east toward the Ethiopian border, his hands clenched into fists. Teimbaka thought he could see tears in his eyes.

"All of it gone. Gone—because you didn't return."

With a low growl, the large hyena took a step closer to John.

"All of them—taken prisoner, sold—slaves. Why didn't you come back?"

"I—"

Teimbaka suddenly felt the chill wind atop Ras Dashen swirl around his body, saw the necklace of dried beetles come to life, the beetles' wings unfolding, the insects taking flight before bursting into flames. Sparks of their remains had fallen to earth, showering his brother's grave. Where was John's necklace of green beetles? he suddenly wondered. And Claire's bracelet? He couldn't remember seeing hers when she was lying at his feet.

"The elephants— I was—"

"Now Seh-my," John quietly lamented. "And many others." Grasping the fur on the back of the hyena's neck, he said, "Gone. For someone who's no longer here."

Teimbaka recognized the expression on John's face. Pain, mistrust, disillusionment, betrayal—all had crept into the boy's features the morning he'd returned from Welo.

"The baby died," Teimbaka remembered telling him that morning. "Sister Lady no longer needs what you bring."

John had lost his innocence in that moment, Teimbaka recalled. Now here he was again, standing before him having lost even more: belief, hope, purpose. What does a man become when these drift from his grasp? Wanting to take the pain from John's face, he tried to speak, but ended up saying nothing. Extending an open hand to him in the hope John would grasp it, that somehow the words lying in his heart would flow from his fingers into John's flesh.

"My place is no longer with you."

Teimbaka heard the shriek of the wraith as John spoke, saw the spark diminish, bleeding into a crack in the cave's stone floor. The cavern had turned pitch black; wings of dark angels had fluttered by his ears. He had not yet found the words John Too had sent him to find when the spark had disappeared. His body had gone numb—just as it was now.

"Bouda." Eden stood. "Don't go."

With snapping jaws, the large hyena moved in front of Eden, barring her from following as John began walking away.

"I would go with him," Eden said to the beast.

The hyena snarled, a jaw full of menacing teeth displayed beneath its curled lip.

"No!" Teimbaka shouted.

But Eden had already moved to stand next to the beast, rising on the tip of her toes, wrapping her arms around the animal's neck, burrowing her face into its chest.

"Let me," Teimbaka heard her whisper to the hyena.

And the beast was away, loping to catch up to John, Eden running after.

"Bouda!" she yelled.

Teimbaka waited for John to turn, but he didn't. Nor did he slow the pace of his walk. Accepting Eden's hand in stride when she caught up with him—as though he'd been expecting her to join him when she clasped her fingers around his palm.

"We must find shelter."

Teimbaka found John Too squatting next to Sarah, a hand placed against her leaf-covered wound.

"There is a storm coming."

* * *

Teimbaka woke with a start, blinking his surroundings into focus, trying to piece together where he was. The woman—Sarah—was sitting cross-legged across the embers of a fire, her back propped against the far wall of a shallow overhang, rays of sunlight coloring her hair auburn-gold. The smell of water—rain from the previous night—hung heavy in the air.

"Where is John Too?" Teimbaka asked.

"He left."

Teimbaka sat up.

"Left?"

"He said he had to meet someone," Sarah explained.

"Who?"

Sarah looked out the opening of the enclosure.

"A boy. He said you'd know who he meant."

Teimbaka looked into the embers of the fire, remembering the lightning and thunder of the previous night, John Too sitting in the firelight, Sarah's head nestled in the boy's lap, rain pelting the stone outcropping above them.

"He said you'd take me," Sarah said.

"Take you?"

"To find her—Sister Claire."

"Claire."

Hesitantly, he touched his lips, finding Claire's kiss still there. Lingering, tugging at an emotion pulled between sorrow and joy.

"He said you'd know where to go."

"I don't—" He shook his head.

"Dirk was with her, right?

"Dirk?"

"The man—the white man I was traveling with," she explained. "Adiam—you know him—he sent Dirk to help me find her."

"Adiam," he muttered.

"Djibouti, yes—you'll take me?"

"But—"

"I'm sure Dirk would have taken us all if there'd been room in the helicopter. He's probably arranging help to come back for us, don't you think?"

Djibouti, Adiam; maybe Claire's in the hospital, he thought. Was she waiting for him? Would she wait?

"Can we start soon? He said you've crossed the most desolate place on earth before. So this won't be hard, will it? Besides, we won't be walking long. I'm sure the search planes will spot us."

Teimbaka studied Sarah's face; she seemed happy. He glanced at her shoulder. The leaves were gone. As was the swelling and redness around the sutures.

"I know," she gushed, touching the area. "It's completely healed. I don't know how."

Teimbaka looked at the hand John Too had grasped. *Why didn't he wait for me to awaken?*

"How long ago did he leave?"

"Not long," Sarah told him, rising to her knees.

Teimbaka studied her as she stood and moved to the lip of the overhang. Her clothing brought back the image of Claire when he first saw her:

sky-blue shirt, ankle-length dark-blue skirt, silver cross dangling from a necklace shimmering with sunlight.

"Why are you here?"

"I was sent by the order. To find her," she told him in earnest. "Her father, you see, he—"

"Has taken ill," Teimbaka said when she paused.

"Ill? Who told you that?"

"Eden."

"Who?"

"And the white man. You call him Dirk?"

"Dirk? I—I don't know why he would have told you that," she offered. "Unless he was trying to lessen the pain."

"Pain?"

"Her father—Sister Claire's—he's passed on to heaven. Dead," she explained, seeing the perplexed look on his face. "He's dead."

Teimbaka slowly rose to his feet.

"And the order—well—there's quite a large sum of money her father— Sister Claire's—left her. Several million, actually. But she needs to sign some papers—back in America—for the funds to be released. Naturally, being a Sister of the Holy Cross, the order is expecting her to— Where are you going?"

Teimbaka stepped out of the shallow enclosure, his gaze focused due east.

"You said Adiam sent this man, Dirk, to help you find Claire?"

"Yes," she replied, taking a step toward him. "Why? He's been— Are we leaving?"

Teimbaka wanted to run, but knew there was no point in doing so. Djibouti was hundreds if not thousands of kilometers away. It would take him weeks to reach it, unless he could catch transport on a truck. Even then, navigating the territorial wars could prolong the crossing. So he walked briskly, with purpose.

"Will we be eating soon? I'm hungry."

Teimbaka glanced across his shoulder to find Sarah walking beside him.

"There's no need to hurry," she said, smiling. "I'm sure we won't be traveling on foot for very long," she went on, looking to the sky. "I didn't mean to upset you—about Claire's father. You seem worried. Is there something I don't know?"

Everything has a price.

He remembered when Adiam spoke the words—the proud expression on his face, the excitement in his voice. They had been in the labyrinth of the Serpent, Susenyo's warehouse of treasures. Claire had been one of those treasures: a possession sold on a daily basis.

"Everything's for sale," Adiam had proclaimed.

Now Claire was on her way back to Djibouti—to Adiam—a possession worth millions of dollars.

"The boy—John Too you called him—he said you are a great hunter. Is that how we'll get food?"

Teimbaka quickened his pace.

2 5

"MR. BENJAMIN."

Dirk opened his eyes.

"We'll be taking off soon."

Dirk smiled at the nurse peering down at him.

"Please, call me Peter." Leaning upward so he could prop an elbow behind his back, he said, "And I'm sorry—I seem to have forgotten your name."

"Mr. Benjamin—"

"Peter."

"After all you've been through."

Bending to him, the nurse touched the compress taped under his right eye, a tinge of red flush upon her cheeks.

"It's no wonder. Please. And it's Mary, Mary Turner."

"Ah, Mary," he sighed. "A beautiful name. Were you the wished-for child, or the rebellious?" Seeing confusion in her expression, he explained, "The Biblical meaning—Hebrew, actually."

"I'm afraid I wouldn't—"

"I apologize. I'm rambling," he said, groaning as he tried to sit up. "Still not thinking clearly, I suppose."

"Savages," she commented, fiddling with a large bandage wrapped around his upper torso. "I can only imagine the pain you're in."

Straightening, tucking a strand of honey-colored hair behind her ear, she asked, "You're certain you don't want anything—for the pain? I've got pills if you don't like needles."

"No, no—I'll wait. Maybe when we land in Paris. Or when I know my sister is better."

"Still stable," she told him, making a slight adjustment to the white cap emblazoned with a red cross atop her head. "We've kept her sedated. You were right."

"Right?"

"About her delirium. She's come to a couple of times. Seems totally out of sorts," she said, offering what he took to be a sympathetic smile. "Babbling on about—oh, never mind. I'm sure you don't need to hear this." Placing her hand on his shoulder, she offered, "She really does seem tormented. I can't imagine what she's gone through—what you both have."

"Could I see her?"

"We're about to take off."

"Just for a moment," he said, touching her hand. "I just want to—"

"Just for a moment, then."

* * *

She'd heard his voice—she was certain she had. Telling someone she needed a doctor, a hospital. It had been he, hadn't it? But that seemed a long while ago. Where was he? Why wasn't he here? Doctors and nurses had come by, gazing down at her, touching her, attaching tubes, sticking things in her mouth, under her tongue. Some had even spoken. But their voices, their words—they seemed to be talking through a glass of water. She could make out some of what they said—but not all, not enough to make sense of where she was, where Teimbaka was. Fuzzy. Everything was fuzzy. Maybe Teimbaka was sitting in a chair at the foot of her bed.

"Teimbaka," she muttered.

Her mouth dry, her tongue feeling the size of an inflated balloon, she tried to sit up, but something pressed against her shoulders, keeping her in place.

"There, there, Sister Claire—just rest quiet. You're safe. It's over."

Claire shuddered, tears forming in her eyes, blurring the features of the woman speaking to her, looming over her. *What did she say? Sister Claire? Dear God, someone knows my name, knows who I am.*

"It's over."

Over? Is that what she said? What's over?

"Teimbaka," she struggled to say. "Where's—Teimbaka?"

"Shhh—rest, Sister. I'll find the doctor. He'll give you something to sleep."

Sleep. Claire latched onto the word, wondering if she was asleep. The notion sparked hope she would awaken and find Teimbaka watching over her.

"Your brother's here. I'll be right back."

My brother?

"Hello, Sister Claire."

Startled by the whisper in her ear, an image of a face close to hers, Claire edged her head back and away.

"I'm taking you home."

Claire ran her tongue along the inside of her lower lip.

"Home?" she rasped.

"Here—tilt your head forward—water."

She felt a hand slide behind her neck, felt an object press against her lower lip. Drops of water—a few at first—dribbled into her mouth. Was she in the house with walls? she suddenly wondered. Had everything that had happened been a dream? Gulping down a mouthful of water, she focused on her surroundings.

"Teimbaka?"

"No, no, it's me. Your brother, Peter."

She stared at the man speaking: wavy black hair, unshaven white-skinned face. Beside him, just beyond each of his shoulders, stood two other people: a white man and a white woman dressed in white outfits—a doctor, a nurse?

"Teimbaka," she blurted out. "Is he here? You must tell me if he is."

"Stay calm, Sister Claire. Getting upset will only do you more harm."

Her eyes shot to the man moving in front of the dark-haired one. *What's he have in his hand?* Suddenly, she saw Susenyo holding a syringe in front of her.

"No!" she cried. "No!"

"Teimbaka is the name of the warlord who held her prisoner the last year or so."

Instantly drawn to the sound of Teimbaka's name, Claire shifted her attention to the dark-haired man. Shaking her head, staring at him wide-eyed, she yelled, "No! No! He's the one who—"

"Nurse!" the man in the white coat shouted.

Frightened by the flurry of bodies so close to her face, Claire struggled against the hands pinning her arms against her sides.

"No!" she screamed.

The prick of the needle puncturing her skin brought a wave of emotions, a flood of memories—all of them dark, disturbing. She began to cry.

"It should take effect immediately," she heard a male voice say.

Finding her arms freed, she placed her hands to her face and wiped her eyes. When she pulled them away, the dark-haired man was leaning down in front of her.

Kissing her on the forehead, the man said, "You'll be fine now. Rest easy. I'm taking you home. A quick stop in Paris, and then we'll be back in America, Philadelphia, our family."

Heart racing, Claire reached out and grasped the man's forearm.

"What have you done?" she sobbed.

She tried to press her fingertips deep into his flesh, wanting to pull him closer so she could scream into his face. But her fingers began to weaken, losing their grip. Her body, her head became immersed in a sensation of movement: swirling, tumbling, spinning—flowing without end.

"What have you done?" she whispered.

* * *

Talia took a deep drag off her cigarette, flicking the butt out the window when she heard Adiam hang up the phone.

"She's agreeable?" she asked.

Exhaling, she watched a stream of smoke gather against a background of sunrise pinks and reds before dispersing into wisps of gray floating upon a ribbon of yellow-tinged blue. Early risers, two gulls flew across the vista, Talia drawn to the shadowed gliding forms as she waited for Adiam to answer.

"The funds will be transferred by this time tomorrow."

"And if they're not?"

"Then Paris becomes a refueling stop for her return."

"At our expense."

Adiam's brief, mocking laugh made her turn from the window.

"I didn't know taking Akmir's place would turn you into him," he told her, an amused expression on his face. "He, too, never saw the benefit of goodwill."

"Enlighten me," she shot back, folding her arms in front of her. "How is giving the Red Cross chapter of France two hundred thousand francs, plus expenses, going to benefit us?"

Adiam pushed back from his desk, running a hand through his thinning hair.

"France still struggles from recession. It is only natural for charitable organizations such as the Red Cross to be suffering from lack of donations. Ours secured a plane and a medical staff without a lot of pointed inquiries. What favors it may bring to us in the future remains to be seen. But the foundation—a bond has been established. We become more global, more legitimate every day."

She watched him rise from his leather chair and place the pack of Camels lying atop his desk in his shirt pocket. She shook her head when he extracted the very same pack of cigarettes a moment later as he stepped across the room to join her at the window.

"Sunrise in Djibouti," he said, wincing as he pulled a lighter from his pants pocket, "is sunrise everywhere."

"Profound," she sarcastically replied, turning to look out across the Gulf of Aden.

"You are too young to remember," he countered, putting flame to tobacco. "Or, perhaps, too old to wish to."

A raised eyebrow, a slight shrug, a casual draw on his cigarette, a momentary touch to his wounded shoulder; Talia studied his movements, his inflections, weighing his reaction to the anger she was certain showed on her face.

"When we were both scavengers in the alleys and the sun was something to hide from."

Her eyes drifted back to the water, drawn to a ribbon of pink floating across a tranquil plane of turquoise.

"Best not forget where we began—how far we have come," he continued, exhaling a stream of smoke. "Simplicity, human nature," he said, taking another drag from his cigarette, "has brought us here. And will continue to guide us."

"Everything has a price," she said without thinking.

The first call of an eager muezzin—solitary, distant—elicited a tired, contemptuous chuckle. How much would the temples, the mosques, and the churches be charging today before granting the blessing of whatever god they were erected to worship? she wondered.

"Is it too early or too late, do you think?"

"For us to become religious?"

"No," he laughed. "For a drink. It's a day to celebrate, after all."

She responded with a questioning frown.

"The windfall from the *Jameel*, the bartered return of the nun, your place at the table. Come, let's go downstairs and have a bourbon. Sit on the sidewalk, smoke cigarettes—watch the port come alive."

Not waiting for a reply, he took her by the elbow and led her toward the stairs at the opposite side of the room.

"It still smells of bleach," she said, eyeing the alcove.

"A reminder to place your trust with care."

"Akmir," she hissed, taking the first step down.

"His day will come," Adiam said as he followed. "You gave Bin'ka the instructions?"

"When I gave him the passports for the nun and the journalist."

"Journalist?" he teased, laughing. "Is that how you remember your evening with Dirk?"

"Shut up," she retorted.

The stairwell echoed with their laughter.

* * *

The knock on the door was light, non-intrusive: three lightly placed raps upon polished mahogany, followed by silence. Objects blocking the light coming in from under the door—black wingtip dress shoes, size eleven, she knew—cast stunted shadows upon the fringe of darkness filling the room.

"Open." Then, "There," a woman's voice instructed when the door opened an inch or so.

"Will Madam require anything further this evening?"

A soft click preceded a pen-thin beacon of white light briefly illuminating the face of an ornate gold desktop timepiece before clicking off.

"I apologize, Mr. Lockett. I should have rung you earlier and told you to retire. Forgive me."

"It's quite all right, Madam. I was simply concerned by the hour. I wanted to make certain all was well."

"Late business, Mr. Lockett. Your concern is noted and appreciated. You may retire when it is your wish to do so."

"May I bring Madam anything before turning in?"

There was a long pause before the woman replied.

"Perhaps a cup of chamomile and a small snifter of brandy placed on my night table."

"Brandy, Madam?"

"Yes, Mr. Lockett. There are ghosts I need to visit," she mumbled.

"Sorry, Madam, I didn't hear the last part of what you said."

"We have an early day ahead," the woman said in a louder voice. "Have the car ready by eight. I will need to be at the bank when it opens."

"Yes, Madam."

"And, Mr. Lockett."

"Yes, Madam."

"Have Olivia air out Miss Claire's room."

"Miss Claire?"

"Mr. Lockett!" the woman barked when the door began to open wider.

"It's just—" The door edged back. "Miss Claire?"

"And have a guest room prepared as well."

"Yes, Madam."

"That is all."

"Yes, Madam."

When the door pulled softly closed and the stunted shadows moved out of the narrow bar of light filtering above its sill, the woman sitting in the dark room took a deep breath and sighed.

*　*　*

Feeling the warm, soft flesh nestled against his side disengage, Bin'ka halfheartedly reached out a hand.

"Where are you going?" he asked, though he didn't lift his head from the pillow or open his eyes to look.

The sensation of heat rising off to his right, the smell of lavender, brought a contented smile to his face.

"To fetch food and drink," a female voice giggled. "To replenish the energy you have spent."

"What if I'm not done with you?" he teased.

"We're hoping you're not." Giggling, the girl added, "Elaina has drawn your bath. Please, Master, indulge your senses while we prepare food and drink worthy of your power."

"And your name?" he inquired, opening his eyes, raising his head just enough to see a woman's naked body slip through an unseen opening in the many layers of semi-sheer curtains enclosing the room he'd been led to an hour before.

"Jasmine," came her reply.

"Jasmine," he sighed.

Rolling off a raised platform of red cushions onto a blue-white marble floor, Bin'ka gazed into a rectangular pool of clear, bubbling water. Wisps of steam—imbued with the scents of flowers, spice, and earth—rose from the surface, enticing him to enter. With delighted anticipation, he eased his girth down to the tiled lip of the bath before slowly sliding into the pleasingly warm, waist-deep water. Seeing a pillow placed within a shallow indentation opposite him, Bin'ka rolled onto his back, and with a slight push, propelled his body across the length of the small, rectangular pool.

"Master," he heard a woman's voice say as the back of his head nestled onto the pillow.

"Yes," he exhaled.

"An interesting name," the voice purred.

"Yes," he replied, inhaling a deep breath of fragrant steam.

"Is this what you would have them call you?"

"Who?" he asked, somewhat annoyed.

"Those you will see."

Reluctantly, tensing with an unwelcome surge of anger, he rose from his resting position to squat.

"See? Where?" he inquired, eyes alert, scanning the curtained enclosure for the woman's whereabouts.

"In chains. Where you travel."

"Mogadishu," he said, his attention focused on the slight swaying of a curtain on the far side of the cushioned platform. "How did you know I was going there?"

"They won't know how to feel."

He watched the curtain move as though someone walked behind it, but could see no defined shape causing the fabric to ebb and flow.

"When they see you are still enslaved."

"I'm free," he snapped.

"Master," the woman's voice taunted.

"Silence!"

Using a thick-muscled arm as a support, Bin'ka vaulted sideways out of the bath.

"Chains run equally—"

"Who are you?" he demanded, striding to the section of curtain in a near rage.

"Between master and slave."

"Why are you here?" he yelled, ripping the curtain aside.

A familiar-looking girl—naked, holding a wooden tray of fruits, nuts, breads, and portions of roast chicken—looked up into his face. Her face was a picture of frightened surprise as she let out a shrill scream and dropped the tray of food to the floor.

"Master," she meekly offered, trembling, bowing her head. "I didn't mean to—"

"Why do you talk to me of slavery?" he growled.

"No, Master, I haven't—"

"How long have you been standing here?"

"Just—just this very moment," she whimpered.

"Who was here when you arrived?"

"No one, Master. No one."

"You saw no one?" he demanded, scanning the sections of semi-sheer material hanging to either side of where they stood. "And stop calling me Master."

"Yes, Mas— No one.

"You lie!"

"No, Master!" she implored.

The girl cowered away when Bin'ka raised an arm.

"Just vermin. A—a cat—clawing at the bottom of the curtain! I shooed it away! I swear it, Master, I swear," she pleaded.

"Stop calling me Master!" he growled.

Shaking, she nodded. Wiping her eyes, she bent down and began picking up the spilled food. Breathing heavily, Bin'ka stared at the girl, struggling to decide if she was lying.

Tell me why you are here.

The words came to him as a rush of air, fabric billowing as if a door opened, ushering in an outside draft. The voice—the old woman's from the dock. He could hear her speaking to him as though she were standing next to him, watching the line of slaves herded onto the ship.

Are you free?

He watched the girl's hands—was her name Jasmine?—as they worked to pick up the spilled food. He could see no shackles on her wrists. Yet, she was a whore, working in a brothel. His eyes drifted to his own wrists, turning them from side to side.

Screaming—alarmed, frightened, panicked—snapped Bin'ka from his thoughts.

"Jasmine!" a woman's voice wailed.

Bin'ka bunched his hands into fists, raising them to a defensive position as a shape burst through the layers of curtain right in front of him.

"Jasmine! Master!"

A girl—naked, sobbing—threw herself against his torso before he could react.

"Protect us!" she wailed. "Protect us!"

"Elaina, what is it! What's wrong?" Jasmine asked, standing, wrapping her arms around the young woman. "You're shaking!"

"A lion!" Elaina cried. "Right outside!"

"A lion?"

Bin'ka tilted Elaina's chin upward to look at her face.

"You saw it?"

"No—no, Master. Others—others heard it roaring—saw its shadow."

Bin'ka looked away from the girl, his eyes scrutinizing each panel of hanging fabric.

"You must—"

"Silence," he hissed.

Heartbeats—subtle, rapid—beat against his skin, meshing with the heightened pounding of his own, the two women—Jasmine, Elaina—pressing their bodies close as he listened for sounds out of place. Quiet—nothing—the room caught in a moment of anticipation, as though holding its breath, the air still. Water rippled, wavelets lapped, building in intensity as he listened, an aura of emerald light softly aglow when he looked over to the bath.

Chains—

Her voice.

Clutching at his hands, Jasmine and Elaina wrapped their fingers around his wrists.

Run equally—

Pulling on his arms, they pressed their bodies against the soft flesh of his stomach.

Between master—

"Protect us, Master," the two women implored. "Protect us."

And slave.

Bin'ka's eyes widened as the two women wrapped their arms around his torso and squeezed.

Are you free?

EPILOGUE

FIVE—THEY TOLD HER she was five. Today was her birthday. Still, like most every other day she had ever known, Vera's parents had patted her on the head after she'd finished eating her breakfast roll, handed her a burlap sack, and sent her to the field to gather yams.

All day long they'd kept saying it was a special day. Why was it special? she wondered. She had not received presents. No pretty ribbon to place in her hair, or sticks of color to turn her lips red, like some of the girls she had seen in Kongolo the last time her father had allowed her to accompany him to market. Perhaps she and her family would need to move closer to town for her to receive those. Yes, she decided, her family would need to live closer to town for her to be given such items. They did not exist out here where there was only jungle, a dirt track leading east, and the fields she and her family worked. Too bad, she thought. A pretty ribbon would have been nice. Pink or yellow; those were her favorite colors.

"Five minutes, Vera! Yes?"

Turning slowly, her toes sinking into newly plowed soil, Vera cupped her hand around the candle she held, quickly waving to the dim figure of her mother before shielding the flame.

"And happy birthday!" she heard her mother yell.

Vera did another slow turn, giggling with the sensation of soil squishing between her toes. The edge of the jungle was another twenty paces ahead. She wondered what she looked like to the animals watching her approach. Did she look like a monkey in a dome of light, or more like a woodland fairy carrying a treasured yellow star? She hoped it was the second one. She'd love to be a fairy with wings flying through the jungle—animals, moths, and birds following to see where she would place the magical flame. Glancing quickly over her shoulder, she wondered how much time she had left. Her mother had said five minutes; how long was that?

*

"How would you like your special day to end?" her mother had asked.

Vera swallowed her last bite of roasted yams—she had to finish what was on her plate or her father would get angry—and thought. While her family waited for her reply, she let her eyes wander around the one-room hut, nothing piquing her interest until she came upon the red unlit candle lying sideways on the small wooden table her mother used for sewing.

"I would like to light the candle," she told them. "And take it to the edge of the jungle," she'd added before anyone could comment.

"The jungle!" her father exclaimed. "Nonsense, you'll do—"

"Shh! Lionel," her mother had cut in, frowning at her father when he looked like he might begin shouting in Portuguese.

Vera had wanted to giggle, but she knew better. The hut became very small when her father started to shout in Portuguese.

"Special day," her mother said to him with a nod. "Yes?"

So her mother had taken her outside after Father had given permission for them to leave the table. After lighting the candle, her mother sent her on her way.

"I'll be right here," she'd whispered, kissing Vera on the cheek. "Watching your every step."

*

Coming to a stop, Vera held the candle up as high as she could, peering under the halo of light at the jungle. In the growing darkness, she found the towering wall of foliage—broad-leafed plants, twisting vines, wide tree trunks surrounded by ferns—spooky.

It happened so quickly—the candle knocked from her grasp, a burst of air rushing over her outstretched arm, a blur of feathers swooping over her head—she didn't have time to react or be afraid. The large bird—it looked like an owl, she thought—hopped sideways as it landed on the ground. The candle rolled to a stop at an angle, butt end wedged into the soil, the flame still lit—a miracle, she thought. Frozen, not daring to move, Vera watched the owl-bird hop twice away from the candle before taking flight. Mesmerized by what had just taken place, she followed the flight of the owl into the depths of the jungle, losing sight of it when it banked sharply upward.

"Vera—are you all right?"

Her mother's voice seemed far away. Vera looked over her shoulder; she could barely see her mother or their hut in the dim light of dusk. She waved. Turning back to the fallen candle, she hesitated; the jungle, normally filled with sounds of animals—birds squawking, monkeys chattering, the buzzing of insects—was oddly quiet. Tentatively, she took a step a forward and then stopped. Something moving within the sphere of candlelight caught her eye, something shiny and green, shifting atop a dark mound of soil. Curious, she stepped closer, bending when she neared, the light revealing a small green bug—a beetle. Looking closer, she saw the beetle was having trouble walking, one of its legs missing, a black mark blemishing the shell where the appendage should be, thread-thin streaks of dark discoloration extending outward from the area, ending just below a faint circle of violet embedded in the upper portion of the beetle's torso.

"Poor bug," she whispered. "What happened to you?"

Placing an open hand into the dirt, she pressed down until her palm was level with the top layer of soil. Keeping still, she held her breath, breaking into a wide smile when the bug crawled in.

"I know you, don't I?" she asked, gazing at the beetle's metallic green body. "There were so many of you."

The beetle turned its face toward her as though it understood what she was saying. Vera giggled.

"Where are the others?"

Cupping the beetle in her hand, Vera picked up the fallen candle, holding it out away from her as she turned back to the open field. Peering downward, she searched the furrowed rows of earth, looking for more of the bugs. But she didn't see any.

"What should I do with you?" she asked, opening her hand.

With a slight movement of its pincers, the beetle raised its head and then collapsed, its body lying flat against her skin.

"No!" she softly exclaimed. "You mustn't die."

Glancing back toward her mother, she wondered if she should call for help. She turned back to the forest with a start when a gust of wind—warm, moist, her skin tingling where it touched—blew out the flame. Suddenly, the dirt between her toes felt cold, the silence of the jungle unnerving—the wall of darkness towering above her, terrifying.

"Mother!" passing silently from her lips, she stared into the depth of dense foliage, imagining an animal hiding a few paces away. A twinkle—like starlight glittering through a small break in the branches—appeared, tempting her forward. Head cocked to the side, she watched the star drift closer. Other illuminations—white, pink-centered, soft-looking—materialized on either side, floating downward through the canopy of leaves, each aglow, pulsing, ebb and flow synced to the rhythm of her breathing. Awestruck, Vera gazed at the lights, following their descent until one touched the tip of her nose.

"That tickles," she giggled, taking a step back.

A breath of warm wind eased the light forward.

"You're a flower," she cooed, reaching out her hand.

Vera ran a finger along the smooth-skinned vine she found attached to the flower, tracing its subtle curve, nearly pulling her finger away when the sensation of flowing water swirled over her hand. Enthralled, she slid her finger downward, following the vine to its axis. There, she offered the back of her hand, leveling it just below the petals. The blossom dipped, spreading warmth across her flesh where it touched. To Vera's utter delight, the flower opened, and then opened again. Five slender, ivory-colored, star-wing petals evolved into a collection, each layer glowing brighter than the last, revealing a brilliant emerald center flared with rays of orange and red.

Within her palm, the beetle stirred. Turning her hand, Vera uncurled her fingers. The aura of the flower strengthened, emitting a soft emerald beam, a subtle tint of orange and red appearing around the insect's torso. Vera saw one of the beetle's legs move. As she eased her hand farther upward, the emerald light took on a luminous quality, hues of reds and orange deepening, becoming more vibrant, radiating, flaring with bursts of incandescent energy. When Vera saw the beetle move a second leg, she shifted her hand until the tip of one petal rested inside her palm. Spellbound, she watched the beetle's wings open, a second pair unfurled. These wispy and delicate, the color of moonlight, tinged pink along the outer edges. Refolding both sets of wings, pincers slowly sweeping from side to side, the beetle crawled forward, the faint purple circle embedded within its metallic green body deepening with each footstep taken farther into the bloom.

"Vera!"

Vera turned at the sound of her mother's worried voice.

"Are you—all right?" her mother asked, catching her breath. "When I saw the candle go out," she huffed. "I ran as fast as I could."

Vera looked through the darkness into her mother's face. But it was hard to see into her eyes, to judge what her mother was feeling. Vera didn't know if she was in trouble.

"Are you all right?" her mother asked again, grasping her by the shoulders. "What were you doing?"

When her mother's hands slid from her shoulders, Vera looked back at the jungle. But an eruption of flame behind her—small, flaring, off to one side—distracted her. She felt the candle slip from her hand.

"Did you hear something?" her mother asked, putting the flickering match to the wick.

"Hear?" Vera repeated, confused, her eyes searching the jungle.

Her mother stepped next to her, the lit candle casting their bodies in shadowy radiance.

"You were standing like you were listening to something," her mother said, extending the candle outward so the light illuminated the fringe of the jungle. "What was it?"

"Glowing flowers," Vera replied. "And a bug," she went on, taking a step closer to the foliage. "But where are they?" she wanted to know, looking from side to side, extending a finger out toward the jungle.

Vera's mother reached forward, taking hold of Vera's hand.

"Glowing flowers?"

Clasping her daughter's fingers, she placed the inside of her wrist upon Vera's forehead.

"And a bug?"

"Green—bright green—a beetle—like the ones we saw before."

Again, Vera searched for the glowing flowers, not understanding where they had gone. Reluctantly, she looked up into her mother's face, candlelight sparkling in her eyes.

"The fairies must have taken them," she whispered.

"Oh, the fairies," her mother whispered back, nodding.

Vera smiled when her mother stroked her cheek.

"Special then, wasn't it? I told you it was a special day."

Vera nodded, pressing her face into her mother's thigh.

"Time to go in now, yes?"

Vera nodded.

Vera's mother turned the walk back to the hut into a skipping contest, Vera losing herself in laughter and the way the candlelight bounced and shimmied along the furrowed soil. As mother and daughter stood giggling and catching their breath at the entrance of their home, Vera took a last look over her shoulder, smiling when she saw seven orbs of light—moon droplets, she saw them as—softly pulsing against the backdrop of the jungle. Feeling the tug of her mother's hand, she turned to go inside, when the deep, rough-edged hooting of an owl made her stop—and wonder.